W9-AQP-384

THE
SANDCASTLE
EMPIRE

THE
SANDCASTLE
EMPIRE

KAYLA OLSON

An Imprint of HarperCollins*Publishers*

HarperTeen is an imprint of HarperCollins Publishers.

Library of Congress Control Number: 2016960399
ISBN 978-0-06-248487-1 (trade bdg.)
ISBN 978-0-06-269312-9 (special edition)

Typography by Sarah Nichole Kaufman
17 18 19 20 21   PC/LSCH   10 9 8 7 6 5 4 3 2 1
❖
First Edition

For those who will inherit the earth—especially James—and for Andrew, without whom this book would not exist.

ONE

I WON'T MISS these mornings.

I won't miss the sand, the sea, the salt air. The splintered wood of the old, worn boardwalk, burrowing beneath my skin. I won't miss the sun, bright and blinding, a spotlight on me as I watch and wait. I won't miss the silence.

No, I won't miss these mornings at all.

Day after day, I slip down to the boardwalk when it's still dark. I've worked hard to make it look like I'm simply a girl who loves sunrises, a girl who'd never shove back. One of those is true, at least. The Wolves who guard this beach hardly blink at me anymore, a rare show of indifference bought by my consistency, my patience. Two *years* of consistency and patience, every single morning since they plucked us from lives we loved and shoved us into gulags. I sit where the guards can see me—where *I* can see *them*—where I can see everything. I watch the water, I watch the waves. I watch more than water, more than waves. I look for cracks.

There've been no cracks. The guards' routine has forever been solid, impenetrable, the only reason I haven't yet made a break for it. I will, though. I am a bird, determined to fly despite clipped wings and splintered feet. This cage of an island won't hold me forever.

One day, when the war ends, I will eat ice cream again. I will run barefoot on the beach without fear of stepping on a mine. I will go into a bookstore, or a coffee shop, or any of the hundreds of places currently occupied by Wolves, and I will sit there for hours just because I can. I will do all of these things, and more. If I survive.

I am always ready for a way out, always looking to leave. I carry my past wherever it fits: tucked in at my back, hanging from my neck, buried deep in my pocket. A tattered yellow book. A heavy ring on its heavy chain. A vial of blood and teeth. My empty hands are my advantage—with nothing but my own skin to dig my nails into, with no one left to cling to, I'm free to take back this war-stained world. If everything goes as planned, that is.

It may not be obvious to anyone else, but things are changing. I see subtle signs of it everywhere, for better and worse all at once. Where there used to be only two guards at this beachfront station, now there are four. Where the guards once stepped casually around certain patches of sand—they've been loud and clear in warning us of the land mines buried there—they now step carefully, single file, if they even leave their station at all. Until last week, their post was equipped with a blood-red speedboat. Now they've traded sleek for simple, a no-frills green sailboat in its place meant to disadvantage anyone who tries to use it to escape. As if any of us could make it that far without being blown to pieces.

This quiet shifting of routine assures me the rumors are true.

Someone escaped last week, people say. Someone else plans to try. Today, tomorrow, next week, next month, I've heard it all. The rumors aren't about me—I'd never be allowed to sit here now, watching as always, if they were. This worked out exactly the way I hoped, that my being close to the beach triggers the assumption that I am up to nothing, nothing at all out of the ordinary. To change my routine would be suspicious.

Now I wait only for the guards to turn their backs on me, as they sometimes do, when they go for coffee refills inside their bare-bones old beach tower. They are far too comfortable with me looking comfortable. Too confident I'll stay put. They keep their eyes trained on the seawall, on those who've taken a sudden interest in the sunrise.

The boardwalk has been lonely for the better part of two years, but not now. Not yesterday, either, or the day before. Whether the others are plotting an escape or just hoping to glimpse one, who knows? This is undoubtedly the best spot for either, I figured that out my first week. From every other side of this island, the water leads straight back to mainland Texas. Better open ocean than that.

These fresh faces that peek out over the seawall and divert attention away from me—it's good, and it's not. Anyone could make a run for it at any time. The Wolves will redouble their security measures when that happens, no doubt, rain bullets and bombs over the entire camp. I can't be around when that happens. I need to make a run for the boat today, this morning, *now*, or I might never get the chance.

I have to be first.

Dawn breaks, a hundred thousand shades of it, so brilliant the sky can hardly contain it.

Two guards go inside their post, and the third turns—this is it this is it this is it—but then the air shifts. It starts with a seagull, warning on its wings as it flies straight for the ocean, like it wants to get far, far away. The two remaining guards meet eyes. I hear the rumble of footsteps, not from the beach but from beyond the seawall at my back, toward barracks and breakfast and the silk lab I've left behind.

A distant explosion shakes the entire island. Two more follow on its heels, five more after that. Gunfire, like a storm—so many blasted bullets I lose count—screaming, chaos. It's louder with every second. Louder and *closer*.

I freeze, every muscle in my body stiff. I'm too late, a split second too late—someone must have attempted escape from the wrong side of the island.

Looks like I'm not the only one who wanted to be first.

All four officers are out of the post now, running their tight zigzag pattern through the sand, toward the noise, careful not to blow themselves to pieces. They don't look my way as they pass.

I should have gone for it in the dead of night, shouldn't have waited for perfect timing—there is no perfect. These bullets and bombs are the consequences, I'm sure of it, security measures on steroids. I've missed my chance.

Or maybe not.

The green sailboat bobs idly at the end of their dock. No one has stayed behind to guard it.

I shift, about to make a break for it—but then that miserable seagull settles itself on the sand in the wrong place and sets off a mine. The earsplitting explosion is close enough to scare me still. Smoke and feathers obscure the guards' sandy footsteps, obliterating my only clue as to where the safe path is. Before last week, when they planted hundreds of fresh mines, I could have run it in my sleep. Not now.

People come spilling over the seawall, five and ten and fifteen, more with every second. If they're desperate enough to run this way, straight toward the sand and the mines, I don't want to know what they're running *from*. I scramble to the edge of the boardwalk. There's an opening below it, where wind has blown the sand away from the posts and planks. I will wait this out and try again, or I will die. It's a tight squeeze, just enough room for me but hardly enough room to breathe. My breaths are shallow anyway, shallow and quick. Sand sticks to the slick sweat on my neck and cheek, coating the entire right side of me. The grit is everywhere: inside my nose, between my teeth, behind my eyelids. But I breathe, never having felt so alive as I do in this moment, so close to death.

The noise is inescapable now, the sound of the desperate as

they run from death to destruction. Footsteps pound the boardwalk, shaking it. If it gives out, I will be splintered and crushed beneath it.

Sand scatters under the first pair of brave feet, not terribly far away from me. Two more pairs follow, and ten more after that. Then twenty.

The mines spray sand and skin high into the air. All over the beach, explosions burst like fireworks. Yet the feet keep coming, winding through pillars of smoke until—*pop!*—they are forced to stop.

It isn't pretty. It is a sickening, revolting mess.

Something heavy slams into the boardwalk, directly above me. The boards creak, sagging so low they press into my shoulder blades. Quickly, the pressure recedes—but then there are fingers, long and tan and delicate, curling over the plank's edge two inches from my face. A noise almost slips out of me; I bite it back.

Shots ring out, cracking wood, deafening and close. I don't feel anything—but would a bullet burn like fire, or would it be a blast of numb shock? The fingers grip tighter, knuckles white even in these shadows, and then they are gone. I shift, as much as I can in this tight space, and see three perfect circles of sunlight streaming through the wood just past my head.

Another shot rings out, and then, just like that, darkness overtakes the light—there is a *thud* above me, even heavier than the first, and a limp arm hanging over the boardwalk's edge. A limp arm clothed in crisp, tan fabric that would blend into the sand if not for the blood.

An officer. An officer is down, and they will find him, and if I stay where I am I will be covered in his blood as it drips through the cracks.

I could run now. I could follow the footsteps of the dead, step only in places where the sand has been tested. I could make it to the sailboat, if I am smart. If I am smart and quick. I could finally, finally sail to Sanctuary.

I inch out of my hiding place, careful to stay low. An enemy of an officer is a friend of mine, but that doesn't mean I'm safe—I still need to be as careful as possible, and quiet. A blast of salt-water breeze hits me, cool against damp sweat.

"Wait."

I freeze, though I've obviously already been seen.

"The guards are making rounds," the voice says. Soft, urgent. "They're not close, but they'll see me if you run."

I turn my head, just slightly, enough to look at her. She's petite, Asian—I don't recognize her. Her long, tan fingers ravage the fallen officer's pockets. Could this girl really have killed him, David against Goliath?

"Here," she says, tossing me a lanyard heavy with keys. Clever, an attempt to share the blame if someone sees, because why else would she hand over this freedom? Not that I'm complaining—I don't plan to be around long enough for blame. She stuffs his ID tags into her pockets and tucks his pistol into the back of her shorts. "I'm coming with you."

The pistol makes me nervous, but at least it isn't aimed at

me. "You don't even know where I'm going."

She tilts her head to the beach, to the sickening display of blood and bone before us. "I know you're not staying here," she says. "That's all I need to know."

"Is it clear yet?" Still crouched on the low side of the boardwalk, all I can see is the girl, and the officer at her feet. Even this much blood turns my stomach, but I keep it together. I have to.

"Clear enough that we'll have a head start. People are avoiding this beach now. . . ." Her eyes drift to the mess of death in the sand. The tide doesn't reach far enough to lick any of the blood away, and neither of us can look for more than a few seconds. "It's only a matter of time until they're all killed. The guards won't be distracted for long."

"Okay," I say. "Okay. We can do this."

"We *have* to do this. What else is there?"

She's right. And it isn't like I have anyone to go back for, not anymore. I take a deep breath. "Follow—"

"Crap, they're on the seawall—they see us. They see us! Go!"

I spring to standing and take off. The smoke has cleared, not completely, but enough. I don't look behind me to see if she's there. I don't look at what remains of all the people I might have eaten breakfast with later this morning. I only look ahead, at the ravaged sand, darting left and right like the officers did when they first noticed the air shifting.

Bullets burrow into the sand, into bodies already dead, into a wake of people who trail behind us. So many bullets from only—I risk a glance—two guards. I dodge their shots, keep running until the sand is smooth ahead of me, untested. I stop short, not sure exactly how to proceed, and the girl from the boardwalk barrels into me. It's everything I can do to keep from losing my balance, from taking one wrong step that could end everything.

But of those who've fallen in with us, only two stop. The others push past us, sights set on the sailboat. Between their footsteps and the spray of bullets that follows them, the sand is broken—and they are dead—in a matter of seconds.

I suck in a breath, choke on sand and smoke, but force myself to keep going. The boardwalk girl follows, along with the two girls who stopped with us. I recognize both their faces from the seawall, peeking over, today and yesterday and the day before.

I lead the way, fast as I can. The guards' boat isn't far now. If we press on we might actually make it. More shots ring out, but this time they're fired by the boardwalk girl, directed at the officer who usually guards the boat—bullet and blood, he collapses before he can make it back to the dock—then at the other guards who chase us, their pistols dead. This girl is an impressive shot, unsettlingly so. She keeps pulling the trigger long after she runs out of bullets.

No one shoots at us anymore.

No one follows us at all.

But I keep running. I can't stop. We're past the minefield

now, into guards' quarters—where the guards would be if they weren't dead or hunting—and down the endless dock where their boat is tied up.

I climb up and over the boat's side, collapse just long enough to catch my breath. I'm vaguely aware of the three other girls as they join me, one of them a blonde who works to untie the knotted rope, our only anchor to the dock. The sky starts to sway as the tide pulls us out to sea. It hurts to breathe, it hurts to think. Everything hurts.

It is worth it.

TWO

I CAN'T TELL my own tears from the sweat.

I could easily spend hours lying limp on this deck, looking like death, but after only a few breaths, I peel myself up. Break over.

"Either of you know how to sail?" the boardwalk girl says to the two girls who followed us here.

"I know how," I say, before either of them has the chance to take over. My dreams of this moment never included anyone's agenda but my own.

"Do it, then."

The boardwalk girl turns her back on us and stalks to the far end of the boat, which isn't all that far, but is probably enough distance for us to whisper about her without her hearing.

We don't. Yet.

One of the girls, the blonde, raises her eyebrows at me. "Would you like some help? I used to sail with my family, before . . ."

So many sentences end that way in our post-peace world. Before, ellipsis. No one ever needs to say anything else. We fill in the blanks with our own unspeakable memories.

"Yes." The boom is familiar in my hand, as if I never stopped sailing. "Yes, please." She moves to help me, and the other girl—beach-wave hair the color of a penny, a splash of dark freckles across her cheeks and nose, silver-gray eyes—looks on in earnest.

Before, ellipsis: sunny summer days we all assumed would go on forever, filled with smiles that came easily. I sailed every day that summer, sometimes with Dad, and sometimes with Emma, but mostly with Birch. Birch was salt and sand and starlight kisses, refreshing like spring rain: easily my favorite part of every day.

How drastically things have changed.

"I'm Hope, by the way," the blonde girl says. Her friendliness catches me off guard. It isn't something you see every day. Really, it isn't something you see anymore at all.

I glance down at her left hand out of habit, and there it is, tattooed on her pinky in thin, wide letters: H-O-P-E. Red ink, unlike mine, which is green. Our barracks are on opposite ends of the New Port Isabel gulag, then—I'm not surprised. Not one of these girls looks familiar, save for the past few days at the seawall.

"And yours?" she prods, when I say nothing.

"Eden." *As in, the Garden of,* I silently add, like I always used to say. It's been so long since anyone's asked my name, or even bothered to use it, I'd almost forgotten what it felt like on my tongue.

It feels like freedom.

"You're steering us in the wrong direction."

I look over my shoulder. The boardwalk girl stands beside copper-hair-freckle-splash, her arms crossed. A-L-E-X-A, the letters on her pinky read. They are violet: I've never seen anyone with violet letters before. I didn't know violet was even an option.

"Seems like any direction away from barracks is the right direction," I say, making no move to adjust the sail.

"They'll come after us," Alexa says, not missing a beat. "We need a faster boat."

"And how are we going to get a faster boat?" It's copper-hair-freckle-splash speaking now. I'd started to wonder if she'd gone mute from shock, but mute she is not. "Sail straight into HQ and ask them for one?"

Alexa's glare is sharp. "Yes. This *is* one of their own boats, so I think we could pull it off."

"And then what?" the girl continues. F-I-N-N-L-E-Y. Red letters like Hope's. "Dodge their bullets when they realize we're not in uniform? Even if we manage to steal one of their speedboats, what are we going to do, try to outrun them? What do you plan to do when we burn off all the boat's fuel? I guess we could swim until our arms give out, but—"

"I get it," Alexa snaps. "You know better than the rest of us. You have a better idea, I'm sure."

Finnley's jaw twitches. She meets Alexa's glare, a challenge. "Matamoros."

I bite back a laugh. Even if the Wolfpack hasn't spilled over into Mexico, which I highly doubt, people say it's been a cartel kingdom for as long as I've been alive.

"What?" Finnley says, turning her steely eyes on me. "It would work. I know exactly which route—"

"It would *never* work," Alexa spits back. "You're delusional if you think it would."

"Eden?" Hope's voice is quiet, but cuts through with as much force as Alexa's. "Matamoros?"

Her thoughts are written all over her face: she and I are the only ones who know how to sail. We could override Alexa, if we want. If *I* want.

I try, really try, to look like I'm giving it actual consideration. "We'd make it to shore," I say. "They'd shoot us with heroin needles, not guns, dress us up then strip us down, and we'd be caught in a living nightmare until they're done with us. That's what I think."

Hope knows it's true, I can tell, and so does Finnley. Thick hopes, thin plans.

"I was thinking," I say, bracing myself for Matamoros-level disbelief, "we could sail out to Sanctuary."

Their stares burn hotter than the sun, Alexa's in particular. She puts a hand on her hip and cocks her head. "You *are* aware Sanctuary is just a myth, right?"

Everyone knows the rumors. I know the truth.

"You have no way of knowing that," I say. I adjust the sail, mainly to avoid looking at her.

"And you do?" Alexa fires back.

"Even if Sanctuary is a myth, where else are we going to go?" Finnley says. "Not Matamoros, apparently, and for sure not back to barracks. I think Eden has a point. We shouldn't rule out the possibility of the amnesty island—why else would they go to the trouble of planting so many mines on the beach if they weren't trying to keep people from escaping to it?"

"Because they're sadistic?" Alexa says. "Because who the hell puts anything worth anything on an island anymore?"

"It's not a myth," I say. But I'm not about to spill the details of how I know this.

I don't mention how Dad pulled me aside in secret, just before the Wolfpack took him. How he told me he'd been called in for questioning by the head of our gulag, interrogated for hours about his engineering and sailing background. That happened often, Before, as he was the lead innovator for the project that set the Envirotech scandal in motion—the project that set the *world war* in motion. He'd suffered more interrogations than I could count. This one was not like the others.

I don't mention how his eyes glittered when he said he'd rather die than help the Wolfpack with anything, not even the hopeful-sounding proposal they'd made him: they wanted him to develop a neutral island territory, a secluded spot where war-ending negotiations would take place. It would be a venue to display proof that the Wolves weren't violating our basic human rights—that they were capable of offering kindness, even amnesty, to at least a few of their imprisoned. A sugar-coated show for the rest of the world, in other words. One I hope to be part of.

And I certainly don't mention the way Dad never came home—how two officers showed up at my barracks door with his wedding ring, his pocket survival guide, and a vial of his blood and teeth.

Spilling those particular details would be a surefire path to Matamoros, because who'd trust me if they knew the truth? That my father's work led straight to this war, to all we've suffered at the Wolves' hands? That Sanctuary could very possibly mean our death, not a better life?

I certainly wouldn't trust me.

Alexa moves to where I can't avoid her. "Even if the island itself exists, and the ocean hasn't swallowed it whole, do you really believe freedom does?"

The ring I wear on a chain at my throat, and the vial of death in my pocket: these say no.

But the information I found inside the survival guide, written in his perfect and distinctive handwriting, says otherwise: I am convinced Dad changed his mind, convinced he believed lasting freedom could indeed be found on the island—that he gave his life to establish it. That he was trying to lead me there, if only I could find a way out of camp.

And I have.

"I have to believe in something." I dare to meet her eyes.

"And I think you do, too. No one runs with that much conviction unless they know what they're running toward."

"You're wrong," she says, holding my stare. "I was only running away."

THREE

PAGE FORTY-SEVEN OF *Survival: A Pocket Field Guide* is covered from edge to edge in pencil markings, narrow cursive stretched thin, letters leaning heavily to the right with no regard whatsoever for the original printed text. No blank pages or margins remain in the book—he used every bit of space and then some. I've read Dad's notes so many times I've practically memorized them, but it's a comfort to hold the actual pages his hands touched, run my fingers over the spots tinged brown by dirt and sweat.

Sanctuary Island, it says at the very top, with a double underline. The rest of the page is a single unbroken paragraph, but my eyes land immediately on the passages that have always fascinated me.

Neutral territory. Weapons-free zone.

Temples hiding among ferns, structures formed of stones and secrets.

Monks who grant refugees immunity from both sides of the war by inducting them into their monastery. Hologram tattoos given to all who approach peacefully, without any hint of hostility. All of these things wait for us, according to Dad's notes.

But no one knows for sure.

I adjust the sails according to the hand-drawn map at the back of the field guide, using the setting sun for directional reference. I feel the other girls' eyes on me, but no one objects, so I take that as permission to choose the direction I want.

"Alexa?" I ask. "Was there a compass in that bench?"

Earlier, we pried open every inch of the sailboat—the fallen officer's keys helped with only half of what we were able to get into—and found a respectable supply of emergency bars, along with a single Havenwater bottle. The cartridge is nearly dead, but it should be good for at least a few more days' worth of sterile, desalinated water if we ration things right. Alexa also discovered a pile of navigational equipment—mostly charts and instruction manuals and two bright orange life vests tucked away in one of the benches.

She pulls a compass from one of her pants pockets and tosses it to me. "Knock yourself out."

"You could help, you know."

"Yes," she says. "I could."

But she doesn't. She retreats to the far end of the boat, as she has for all but half an hour of our first day at sea. I hear her tear into the wrapper of an emergency bar.

"It's probably for the best," Hope says. Her voice is so soft and sweet, she doesn't even have to lower it. "She makes me uncomfortable."

"Because of her gun?" I ask. "It's out of bullets, if that's it."

"Not the gun so much as how she shot it," Hope says. "Just . . . everything. How she *is*."

Hope's too kind to throw out specifics, but I'm not blind. The way Alexa acknowledges us only when it's absolutely necessary—how she can't be bothered unless her own comfort is directly threatened. "I get it," I say. "Makes me uneasy, too."

I reach for Dad's field guide on the bench where I left it a while ago, but it's not there. I go from zero to panic fast, ready to turn the boat on its sails if that's what it takes to find it. I scan the wooden deck, and the benches, and finally spot it: its mustard-yellow cover winks at me, bright between Finnley's hands. Something inside me snaps at the sight of her holding it. It's not like she's Alexa—Finnley's prickly and stubborn, yes, but Hope knew her before they ran for this boat. Hope trusts her. The problem isn't Finnley, it's that the field guide is private.

It's only a book, I remind myself. It's only a book about bugs, and plants, and making shelter, and starting fires, and purifying water, with Dad's own personal notes written in along the way. And then there are his entries about Sanctuary Island, his charts and his maps, and a few sketches that remind me of the year he won an award at work for his architectural blueprints. He took me out for three-hundred-dollar steaks with the bonus they gave him.

The map to the island became public knowledge as soon as I pulled the book from my pocket, but the questions they'll inevitably ask about the other things . . . I'm not quite ready to answer.

"What?" Finnley says, glancing up over the top of the field guide. "Do you want it back?"

I want to say, *You don't just take other people's things without asking.* I want to say, *That's all I have left of him.* But what comes out is, "No, it's fine."

I don't have to let it bother me. She didn't mean anything by it.

"Where'd you get this thing, anyway?" Finnley's eyes narrow as she flips from page to page. "Must have taken a lot of work to keep the Wolves from noticing it."

She has no idea.

That it landed in my hands at all had to have been a mistake. They would never have given it to me if they'd bothered to crack it open. Surely they read it—why wouldn't they?

But they gave it to me that day and never looked back. I've been more than careful ever since.

"I, um—" Heat rises in my cheeks. The field guide is so closely tied to my father that I struggle to think of something, anything, to say about it. Any answer I give will only lead to more questions.

"Seriously, though, where?" she presses, folding a fresh crease into one of the field guide's pages. I wince, even though I've creased so many corners the book could be deconstructed origami.

"Come on, Finn, that's personal." Hope takes the book from her, closes it. "Eden obviously doesn't want to talk about it. Sorry," she says, handing the book over to me. "People take so much. We should all be allowed to hold on to at least one private thing."

Finnley doesn't say another word about it, though I'm certain she wants to. Perhaps there are some things of her own she'd like to keep only for herself—we all have our secrets, I guess. I send a thousand silent thank-yous to Hope.

"So, you guys"—I gesture to the tattoo on Finnley's pinky, desperate for a subject change—"you're both red. Where did they bring you in from?" Ink color varies based on where each of us were first processed, whatever the Wolves had on hand. Most of Texas ended up with green.

"Santa Monica," Hope says.

Matamoros suddenly makes a lot more sense. She and Finnley had hoped to cut through Mexico, I'd bet, climb up into California—they were trying to run *back*.

If only. If only there were home or family to run back to. If only the Wolves hadn't shaken the world so thoroughly, if only things weren't so splintered or broken. There is no going back.

"Where did they put you for work?" I ask.

"Metalworks," Hope and Finnley say, blandly, in unison.

None of us were originally stationed at chorehouses, not in the beginning—they preferred to pretend we didn't exist at all. Cockroaches. Only when the Allied Forces intervened, and the Wolves stepped up their war efforts, were we driven into chorehouses. They turned us into ants, made us carry five thousand times our body weight.

Finnley starts in about how blisteringly hot the crucibles were in their foundries. She holds up her hands. "See all the scars where I've been burned?" Raised, wrinkled lines crisscross her palms and forearms. A thick, gnarled scar mars the pad of her left pointer finger.

"Those weren't even bad burns, compared to some we've seen," Hope chimes in. "Like the guy who dumped his crucible out just to make a point."

She doesn't elaborate. It's probably for the best.

"We've learned to be careful," Finnley says. "Also, the Wolves threatened to dump melted lead on our feet when too many people were out with injuries. It was motivating," she deadpans.

My station at the silkworm house sounds like an absolute oasis in comparison. I tended larvae, fed them mulberry leaves three times daily as if they were my own pets, and then I harvested their cocoons to be shipped off to the silk labs. It was a stifling, sweat-soaked job, but it was no metal factory. Still, I've suffered my share of burns. It was my job to boil the cocoons at the end of every cycle, live moths still inside them. I hated it. It was like killing myself every time I dipped them into the vat, these flightless creatures kept alive only to serve and then die. Silk technology is amazing, has done incredible things for the world, but it is born directly out of so much death.

"You think the scars are bad," Finnley says, and only now do I realize I'm staring. "The reason we have them is even worse."

I look up. "Yeah?"

"We worked in a bullet factory."

I don't know what's more atrocious: the fact that these girls were scarred while making weapons for the very people who enslaved them, or the fact that the Wolfpack needs a bullet factory at all. They seized every shelf in every store—and every factory—and every abandoned basement—and every military base, even, thanks to thousands of well-placed Wolves and an abundance of strategy and luck. To think, they've exhausted their supply of all those bullets. Or, if they haven't yet exhausted their supply, they plan to.

I believe it. I wish I didn't.

"So," I say, mainly to direct the conversation toward something less horrific, "you guys obviously knew each other before today."

Hope and Finnley are quiet for a long moment.

"We've known each other since Zero," Finnley finally says.

So much for less horrific.

Zero: the day the Wolves took over—the day they took everything. I'd been in the cafeteria line during my first week of sophomore year at Veritas. I'd chosen the salad bar over pizza and fries, mainly so my already-tight purple skirt wouldn't turn unflattering-tight during biology lab, and I'd just popped a cherry tomato between my teeth when the doors burst open. They spilled in: ten, twenty, fifty officers. For a high school cafeteria.

"Like, since lineup?" I ask. "Or barracks?"

"A little bit before," Hope chimes in. "I'd seen her around school, but we'd never met. We ended up in the same group as they herded us away."

"One of the officers hit her," Finnley says. "He hit her so hard she fell down in the parking lot and tore her knees up on the gravel. I stayed behind to help her up."

"He hit *you*?" Looking at Hope, I just can't imagine it. I can't imagine why anyone, not even an officer, would raise a voice at her, let alone strike her hard enough to knock her down. "Why?"

Tears sparkle in her eyes. "I said no. No, you can't take me."

With that one little word, everything makes sense. No one says no. I watched Birch take his last two steps over saying no.

"How did you . . ."

"Make it out alive?"

She leans her back against the mast and stares out at the endless horizon. "The officer was my older brother."

FOUR

THE ENEMY WORE sheep's clothes for many years before it bared its fangs and went for blood.

Fathers. Brothers. The barista who made your daily latte, the guy behind the fish counter at the grocery store, the girl in Sephora who taught you how to line your eyes. All seemingly unconnected, until one day they were a force.

After Zero, it all made sense: the neon fliers stapled to telephone poles, the #wolfpack hashtag everyone assumed was a fandom of some sort, the pendants people wrote off as a passing trend. The signs were all around us, but we were too wrapped up in our own lives to really question them.

Which, I guess, was their point. It was a good point, at its heart, albeit a bitter one—that too many people were out of touch with reality, floating on the hard work of others who were killing themselves just to survive. That too many of us were too entitled, too ungrateful. Too used to all we touched turning to gold.

They weren't altogether wrong.

These issues are as old as humanity itself, people who have and people who want—but then came the floods. *We want a better life* became *We want life, period.*

Society imploded.

It started with the Kiribati islands. Rising seawater swallowed seventeen of the original thirty-three islands gradually, over previous decades, but then—all at once, it seemed—every last island went under. First, there was the typhoon. Next, the tsunami. It's terrifying to think about, really, that the chain of events that sparked a world war began with the world itself—the ocean, more specifically—ravaging a people who were minding their own business out in the middle of the Pacific. Anything can happen to anyone, whether they deserve it or not.

But, as things go, no one here cared until it was our shores starting to go under. Our disasters piling up on top of one another, San Francisco and the Carolina coast and New York City. Our tourists dying in cliff-side resort collapses, our Girl Scout troops on the Kure Beach Fishing Pier when the posts gave out.

The floods weren't major, weren't national news–worthy, but they continually overstepped their bounds—up to thirty times during 2049 alone, in some places. Over and over, damage and ruin and death swept in with the tide. Still-healing wounds were repeatedly ripped raw.

Emergency response teams were unable to keep up. Contaminated drinking water, sewage flowing down every street, disease spreading among die-hards who refused to leave. FEMA distributed Havenwater bottles, one cartridge to be shared among every thousand who couldn't afford them, one cartridge to every rich family who could. Once the mandatory evacuations kicked in, once the economy fractured and the dollar lost its wings—

That's when people panicked.

They wanted a safe world. A forever world. One that wouldn't get swept away, one where they wouldn't have to fear their children going hungry, their children soaked up to their necks in contaminated salt water but never able to drink it.

The upheaval started with Kiribati, and was sealed with a promise: Envirotech will save you. Envirotech, pioneer of Havenwater bottles and silk technology and all manner of other eco-savior solutions. That's when my father began to lose sleep, when the wallpaper Mom picked out before she died became plastered with blueprints, research about artificial limestone reefs and biosynthetic cities grown from protocells. That year, Envirotech presented him the award that bought us that most amazing steak dinner and a brand-new car.

It also bought us a war.

Envirotech planned to develop the Atlas Project—a cutting-edge, ocean-based habitat my father was entrusted to direct—but then the news broke that the residences on board would be extremely limited in number, and sold to the highest bidders. Come one, come some, come live: if you're rich. That part wasn't supposed to be public knowledge, not yet, but it took only one bitter insider—a coworker Dad knew, not well, from Envirotech's financial department—to spill a flood of secrets.

Fear mixed with bitterness never ends well, and fear mixed

with power? Ends worlds.

What began seed-small picked up speed, picked up strength, until it became a wrecking ball waiting for the perfect moment to drop. That moment came when the Supreme Court upheld Envirotech's right to set their own prices, in the name of commerce and capitalism and centuries-old dreams. No doubt the honorable justices wanted to grow old with their grandchildren, like everyone else. Difference was, they could afford it.

The Wolfpack's wrecking ball proved swift and colossally destructive, with enough momentum and manpower to smash the entire country to pieces. To this day, I still hear them chanting when I have nightmares of Zero Day: *Prison for privilege! End Envirotech! Our time is now!* Our time is now, our time is now: tattooed on their faces and forearms, on their backs like angel wings, on my memory forever.

In the beginning, during those first few weeks of camp, after we'd been sorted and stamped, a few of the officers—Wolves, we called them, though they were undeniably human to the core—would greet us, and they didn't raise their voices. These, who were made more of fear than bitterness, would be almost apologetic over the fact that they weren't allowed to let us inside the nice areas they'd claimed as Wolf territory. One even threw away his half-eaten ice-cream cone right in front of me and said there was no rule against us eating trash. It sounds cruel, but he meant it as a kindness, and I took it that way.

But not all factions were created equal. Some were more militant, with officers who went straight-up psychopath on us. And not only us—the rest of the world, too, when they tried to intervene in the Wolves' efforts to flip the status quo on its head. All attempts at contact from the Global Alliance of Territories and Dominions were met with radio silence, then hostility, according to word around camp. The Wolfpack had already seized the lives they'd longed for—they'd broken into all the bankers' systems, shoved the formerly privileged into barracks with naked wooden boards for beds. And later, into factories and foundries and fields. All of this, so they could eat, drink, live, love, sleep, *be* as we'd been, Before. I doubt a world war was ever part of anyone's motivational propaganda, but, well. People defend what they love. The rest of the world loved justice—human rights.

The Wolves *think* they love justice, think they've created equality by inverting the scales.

I think the Wolves love only themselves.

It's been nearly two years since I've eaten ice cream from the trash, and almost as long since my father's vial of blood and teeth made its home in my pocket.

Two years can eclipse an entire lifetime, it turns out.

FIVE

A MULTITUDE OF stars dot the black sky, like snow clinging to the walls of a glass globe. It's cold for this time of year,
the sort of sandpaper cold that rubs you the wrong way no matter how you turn against it. I wish I had more than the yellow
cardigan I wore to the boardwalk this morning. I wish I had
Birch.

Finnley and Hope are huddled together on the port side,
while I am stretched out on the starboard bench. They've spent
most of today talking in hushed voices with only each other.
Finnley's spent today talking, anyway—Hope mostly listens,
more patiently than anyone I've ever seen. I'd worry they were
plotting a takeover, a course shift toward Matamoros despite it
being the worst of bad ideas, but Hope isn't as strong with the
sails as I am. Whatever's going on with them, that isn't it.

Meanwhile, Alexa keeps to herself, hasn't said a word in
hours. I suspect she's as sleepless as the rest of us.

The ocean shushes and rocks us, a lullaby. But she is not a
mother to be trusted. Tomorrow, she could shake us until we
break. She could toss us and flood us and devour us.

Soft footsteps brush against the wooden deck. Alexa.

"They say the sharks come out at night," she says, taking a seat in the middle of everything. If she decides to stretch out and sleep there, Hope and I will both have to step over her when it's time to adjust the sails. "They're thirsty for blood, and they have an endless supply of teeth that are sharp as razors."

Her words slither and coil. We are still and quiet, as if we can keep them from biting us if we pretend they're not there.

"We're more likely to drown than get eaten by sharks." Finnley's words. The waves shush them almost as soon as they're spoken.

Hope shifts. "What do you think it will be like?" Her voice is quiet.

"The drowning?" Alexa says, in too light a tone. "Or the sharks?"

"The island. Sanctuary."

Will the temple's stones be gritty and gray, crisp and pristine, or will it be covered in moss and crumbling from age? What will the monks be like? I imagine them in red, draping robes, with shaved heads that gleam in sunlight, chanting in monotones loud enough to summon whales and fend off ghosts.

"If it even exists, which I doubt, I think it will be a jungle," Alexa says. "With boa constrictors that will strangle us while we're sleeping, and a thousand different kinds of bugs just waiting to chew their way to our hearts."

I force the image of boa constrictors from my mind—sharks I can handle, but not snakes. Snakes filled my earliest nightmares long before so many other painful atrocities crept in to join them.

The boat creaks and sways, waves licking its sides. One deep dip and we could be swallowed whole.

It's not until Hope speaks that I realize we've been silent for several minutes. "I think we'll eat a lot of fish," she says. "And I think it will be peaceful. Sand and water and seagulls and shells. Sunsets where the sky is so pink-orange you can't even remember what it's like when it's blue."

For so long, I've thought I was the only one who romanticized sunsets anymore. Most people don't go out of their way to watch them: it's too depressing, they say, the reminder of things we lost that we'll never get back. Things that were stolen from us.

Maybe it's common in Hope's corner of New Port Isabel for people to be so—well—hopeful. But then Finnley says, "I've been thinking about this. You guys have seen the footage, right? How the Wolfpack's been razing port towns for the past few months, even as far as Hong Kong? Seems like they're being pretty hostile in their takeover. Guards and guns, that's what I think we'll find."

And then I have my answer. Finnley is the pragmatism to Hope's idealism.

The footage is something I try to forget about. Every night, after dinner and before bed, it is inescapable: massive screens where billboards for beach rentals used to be, war propaganda projected on walls around every turn in our barracks, audio-only announcements that echo from cracked, overgrown parking lots. This nightly news is meant for the Wolves, not for us. Even so, it's everywhere.

Some people live for it, people who should be disgusted by it like I am. It is their escape, this sick form of reality TV. Never mind that we were allowed to roam New Port Isabel when we weren't on duty at our stations—we were every bit as imprisoned as the people we heard reports about. It's just that we're still alive to hear about their towns being burned, the gassings, the counterattacks. People forget we're still alive only because they simply haven't killed us yet.

The fact that people would choose to watch the footage rather than a sunset—and consider a sunset more depressing— is, perhaps, the most tragic thing to come out of this war.

Alexa's sitting up now. "What do you think? You're too quiet over there."

It's never quiet in my head, so I don't always realize I don't speak much. "I . . ." What *do* I think? "I think it will be beautiful." That much, I believe. "And there are a lot of islands in the world. I still believe it's possible that one of them is a refuge." If it isn't, Dad gave everything for nothing.

For once, Alexa doesn't say anything. Her eyes are full of starlight, flickering with every dip of the boat. She watches me.

It is an unsettling way to fall asleep.

SIX

I WAKE UP choking on my own vomit, lose everything I've ever eaten over the edge of our boat. The waves mince it away, sharp as knives and just as gray.

"I'm sorry!" The wind blasts Hope's apology toward me, then dumps it out to sea. "I'm trying—I—"

Our sail is as choppy as the waves, loud as a helicopter. Hope struggles against the boom while Finnley expels bucketfuls of ocean from the deck. Even Alexa is doing her part.

"Why didn't you wake me?" I tie my hair in a knot and take over for Hope at the boom.

"We figured you needed to rest up for the next shift," she says.

A wave jumps in over the starboard lip, undoing all of Finnley's work.

"There may not *be* a next shift," I snap.

The boom is stubborn. I push all my weight against it, digging in with my heels, until it submits to me. The sail calms from a boil to a simmer. With one more push, it stops hyperventilating and takes a deep breath of salty air. Though the waves are still rough, they're no longer bucking-bull wild.

Alexa slumps against the mast and slides down to sit, as if all the work I've done has really taken it out of her. For the first time, I see an aberration in her prickly demeanor, a softness that wasn't there before. Or, at least, was hidden. It's like she's only just discovered she's not invincible, that this life could be over in one too-deep dip of a boat.

How could anyone live through the war and not be intimately familiar with this truth?

I let out a long breath. "How long were we out of control?"

Hope's cheeks are flushed red from effort, and probably a good dose of embarrassment. "Not long. You woke up on the first dip."

"Were we still on course before that?"

She glances over at Finnley, who nods. "It was pretty smooth all night until one strong gust caught us off guard."

I study Hope, try to read her eyes for honesty. "You *swear* we are still on course? For Sanctuary—not Matamoros?"

"Unless I read the compass wrong," Hope stammers, surprise lighting her face. "I'm not a good enough navigator to find Matamoros from all the way out here, even if I wanted to."

It isn't as reassuring as it should be, since the boat's been in her control all night, but I am mostly certain she's not lying. From the looks of it, it never even crossed her mind to change course.

"Matamoros was a stupid idea," Finnley says, from up near the bow of the boat. "We're over it."

Her tone makes me uneasy, rose petals spiked with thorns.

I decide to take her at her word rather than take the bait—the last thing we need is a fight.

"Thanks for working on that," I say instead. "Looks a lot better." She's done a remarkable job of getting the water out. Only a thin layer remains on the deck, too shallow to do anything about and not deep enough to be a problem.

A flash of yellow catches my eye at the front of our boat, close to Finnley's feet.

No.

"I tried to hold on to it," I hear Hope say as I rush toward it. "It fell when I was trying to fix the sail."

Dad's field guide floats, facedown, on what little bit of water is left. I kneel to inspect it. While it's not bloated or drowning, the tattered cover wilts under my touch. *It will be fine*, I tell myself. *It will be crispy and dry by noon, as long as the sun comes out.*

"I'm sorry," Hope says. "Eden? I'm sorry, I'm so—"

"It's fine," I snap. She was trying to help, she was only trying to help.

It isn't something I'm used to anymore, help.

Water swirls around my knees, between my toes. I peel the book open and am grateful to see it was crafted, well, to survive. Its pages are heavy; though saturated, they hardly curl at all. And while water drips from the limbs of every *t* and *k*, and pools in every curve, the printed text is no more melted than a girl climbing from sea to sand.

Dad's inky words are fuzzy, as if they've sprouted mold, but are still legible in most places. Only along the outside edges of the pages do they blur together. The map is still intact—for now, that's all we need. Hopefully the hopeless bits were non-essential.

I make my way back to the other girls and find them looking like death. Hope is pale with exhaustion, her cheeks no longer pink. Finnley's hair is at once limp and wild, some unruly strands trying to fly away and others weary from the trying; her face is haunted with shadows.

"You two should get some sleep," I say, even though it means putting myself on duty with Alexa, who is still curled into herself at the base of the mast. I'm strong enough to sail without her help, but none of us is strong enough to stay awake and alert indefinitely.

Finnley shoots a sharp glance at Alexa, who stares blankly at the side of the boat. "Are you sure? I could make it another hour or two, I think."

"You've already been up all night. We've got this." If Alexa feels our eyes on her, she doesn't show it. "Give Alexa the compass. It'll be fine."

Finnley pulls the compass from her pocket and holds it out. "You do know how to read a compass, don't you, Alexa?"

Alexa twists, not enough to make eye contact. "Of course I know how to read a compass. I'm not an idiot." She extends her hand and waits, like a spoiled child asking for candy.

To Finnley's credit, the look on her face doesn't find its way into speech. She plunks the compass into Alexa's hand and retreats to the port side, where Hope has already curled up to sleep, using one of the bright orange life vests as a pillow.

"Wake us if you need us," Finnley says, resting her head on her arms. They're both out in less than a minute.

The sailing is smooth for a good long while. Alexa and I stay quiet, mostly, hide in our own heads. I think of Birch, of Dad. How I'd much rather be confined to this boat with people I love, people I trust. How I'd give anything for them to be here to help me navigate—the water and everything else.

A couple of hours in, Alexa shifts toward me on our bench. "Um," she says, "is the arrow supposed to be jumping around like this?" The compass rests, open, in her palm.

I bend over to take a look. The compass needle is frenetic, oscillating from NW to NE, with an occasional detour to S.

"That's . . . not normal," I say. The needle jumps from due west to due east in the time it takes my gaze to catch on the purple ink on her pinky. The purple ink, which, just yesterday, clearly read A-L-E-X-A.

Today, half the *X* is missing and the *E* is completely gone.

SEVEN

ALEXA TILTS THE compass, watches the arrow. "What does it mean?"

I want to ask her the same question.

I can't stop looking over at her finger, triple-checking to make sure it wasn't a trick of light—it wasn't—but I decide to curb my curiosity until after we deal with the more pressing issue of our faulty compass. We are trapped on a boat together, after all, until we reach Sanctuary. There will be time.

"Something's interfering with it. You're not wearing anything magnetic, are you?"

She rolls her eyes. "I've been on the boat the whole time. Wouldn't I have thrown it off earlier if the problem was me?"

She makes a good point.

"In that case, your guess is as good as mine." Not entirely the truth, but I'm not sure enough of my thoughts to present them as a viable answer. "Could be a geomagnetic anomaly, maybe?" I leave it at that.

But by *could be*, I am fairly certain I mean *it is*.

"Huh," she says, turning the compass around and around in her hands.

From what I remember, Dad's notes in the field guide never mention the Triangle by name. But on his hand-drawn map, Sanctuary Island is inside an enormous scalene, three uneven sides made of blue-ink dots and dashes. His notes aren't so much explicit about the odd experiences he had as they are permeated with evidence of them.

Gingerly, I peel the already-drying pages away from one another and find the one that keeps coming to mind. In bold text, at the top left of the page, the heading reads HOW TO NAVIGATE WITHOUT A COMPASS.

It is the most deeply dog-eared page in the entire book. In the margin, Dad made a column of times, with a second column of notes to its right. One paragraph of printed text has a neat blue asterisk beside it. I skim it and find it rich with information we can use.

The fact that this page is covered in information we can use brings at once both reassurance and dread. Reassurance, that we will likely not be lost at sea—at least, not because of a failed compass. Reassurance, that some of Dad's team crossed the westernmost side of the Triangle and returned to shore in one piece, well enough to deliver his remains.

His remains: that is where the dread comes in.

I've never lingered on what might have reduced Dad to a vial of blood and teeth, and the officers who delivered him to me in that form didn't volunteer the information. This is not to say I've never slipped into that cesspool of tragic thought at all—only that I've always pulled myself out before I drowned.

I don't have much to go on, not really, but I believe he's dead. It isn't so much the vial that's convinced me, as chilling as it is—it's the ring. If there's anything he loved more than me, any-*one*, it was Mom. I am one thousand percent certain he wouldn't have parted with his wedding band unless someone pried it from his cold, dead hand.

So I make theories.

Maybe he fell overboard during a storm on his way back home, maybe he was swallowed up by the hungry sea like Kiribati, maybe the others who were with him dragged his bloated body back in with a net. Or perhaps he simply starved on Sanctuary Island and his corpse was too much dead weight to bring all the way home. What would I want with a corpse, anyway?

I cling to these theories when I'm feeling logical. Hopeful.

But then there are days when, after being steered back to barracks by a too-tight grip on my upper arm, I think with my gut instead of my head.

It's then that I spiral toward the strange, toward the severe.

Maybe he was taken by something mysterious, for example. Something unexpected his team encountered on their mission to subdue the island, something that made him sweat soul and blood.

Or maybe his disappearance wasn't a mystery at all. Maybe he simply outlived his usefulness to the Wolfpack, and they—*poof*—distilled him into blood and bone. After what was, surely, a grim and cruelly enforced death. Maybe he said yes and yes and yes, until one day he said no, and was shot, swiftly and finally, just like Birch on Zero Day.

And then, like always, I come back around to the only thing I know, for sure, to be true: my father was not a liar. His disappearance doesn't change that.

Whatever awaits us on the island, if there is even the slightest chance we'll find the freedom my father wrote about, it has to be better than the cages and clipped wings we've left behind.

Following the instructions in the field guide, Alexa and I craft a makeshift compass out of ballpoint pens and rope, using sunlight and shadows and the hands on her watch to guide us. These are actually two different techniques combined, in part rather than in full, since we don't have everything we need to fully complete one of them as outlined in the book.

When we are back on course and sailing smoothly, I pull our Havenwater bottle and an emergency bar from one of the benches we pried open. It takes effort to ease the bar out without making noise; Alexa isn't quite so careful. The crinkle of plastic nearly wakes Hope, all the way on the far end of the boat, but she simply stirs and turns over. We devour our bars like heaven-sent milk and honey.

Alexa stares out to sea. She sits on the bench, hunched over with her elbows on her knees, turning the Havenwater bottle around and around in her hands. The salt air tugs at her black hair. She lets it fly, in no rush to tame it.

I work my hair into a long, messy fishtail braid. There are at least twenty different shades of sand in my braid, from bright and sun-bleached to the color of the beach when the tide pulls away to sleep. I loop a thin strand of hair around the tail of the braid to tie it off.

Now would be the perfect time to ask about the missing letters on Alexa's hand. But the longer we sit in silence, the more difficult it is to imagine breaking it, especially with a question so confrontational.

"Why didn't you run?" she asks, turning her eyes from the ocean to me. They are black coffee, dark chocolate—bitter but rich. "On the beach back there. You were hiding. Why not run?"

It seems obvious to me, but then again, I was not the one standing over a dead officer when we met. It's not like I had access to a gun like she did. "Did you kill that officer?"

So much for not being confrontational.

To her credit, she is steady under such a direct question. Steadily simmering, through narrowed eyes, but steady nonetheless.

I am the first to break. "I hid because I thought I could wait it out before I ran for the boat," I say. "And because I'd been to that boardwalk enough times to know the sand was explosive."

"Wait it out," she repeats. Not a question, just a statement. A judgment, maybe.

"I . . ." I bite my lip. "It seemed wise to learn from other people's mistakes."

"Let them step on the mines first, you mean."

It's obvious that's exactly what I mean. When she puts it that way, it sounds much worse than I intended. Something black stirs in me, a cloud of octopus ink obscuring my moral compass. It's not my fault the mines were there, and it's not like stepping on one would have saved anyone else. Even if I'd stood up and boldly warned the stampede not to step onto the sand, I would have been trampled or shot.

But still. People died, and I am here on this boat, very much alive, because I stepped carefully around their broken, lifeless limbs.

"Then we took the same approach," she says. "Essentially."

I don't follow, and my face must clearly say I don't follow, because she smirks as if pleased to have made an inside joke with herself. She pours what's left of the half-full water bottle into her mouth and drinks, drinks, drinks until it's empty.

"We both used them to set off the mines so we wouldn't have to," she says, finally. "So we could escape. Right?"

This is not new information. I nod as if to say, *Obviously.*

"The difference between us is that you made your plan after it was too late to save anyone," she says, "while I was the one who set the factory explosions that flushed them out in the first place."

EIGHT

ONCE UPON A time, the world was full of dreams, despite its heartache, and love, despite its brokenness.

Once upon a time, the world was full of color: the egg-yolk yellow of highway stripes framed by pitch-black tar and a blurred rainbow of wildflowers.

Now the world is being swallowed by the sea—and what's left is choked in green, weeds of envy and power. And, sometimes, a love for justice taken to painful extremes.

It's become difficult to tell the weeds from the flowers.

NINE

ALEXA IS A dandelion. She hides her secrets well, as if they are petals on the verge of dissolving into wisps. Even her confession—this huge, glaring, so-honest-it-hurts confession—only raises more questions.

I try to form words. I fail.

"Don't tell the others," she says. "It will make things weird."

Hope and Finnley have a right to know. But then again, things *are* weird, now that she's shared her secret. "Why did you tell me?"

She's watched me for the past few minutes, but something about the way she watches has changed. Her eyes are still sharp, so sharp they cut me, but it's like looking at a chef's knife and realizing it's meant to cut through tomatoes, not human hearts. The sharpness isn't aimed at me—not anymore.

"Because you know I killed that officer, and you're not afraid of me."

I want to tell her she's wrong. I *am* afraid: I am terrified, not of her past, but of her ability to talk about it so plainly. Of what other secrets she's folded and tucked, neatly, out of sight and mind. Of what inspired her to commit these acts.

Perhaps it's this she sees—how I want to dig beneath her skin, to search her secrets until I understand them. Perhaps empathy outshines my fear.

I should get my questions out now, take advantage while I have her ear. I'll have to build up to confronting her on her ink, though. Break her walls down first.

"Do you regret it?" I ask.

"Regret what?" She bites absently at her thumbnail. "Killing him, or telling you?"

I wait her out, because I shouldn't have to specify.

She doesn't answer. I guess that *is* my answer.

"I was going to run," I say. "I could have done it, too. I really think I could have made it."

Without the explosions.

Without the death.

"I'd've been dead in a heartbeat," she says. Her eyes flicker toward mine, just for an instant, before looking back out to sea. "We all do what we have to, right?"

That's when I see it: Alexa is every bit as alone as I am. She had no one at camp—she couldn't have, not if she set off all those explosions. There would be five people on this boat, not four, if she'd wanted anyone to make it out alive.

If Finnley and Hope were trying to go back home to Santa Monica, maybe Alexa was trying to get to someone, too. "Who is he?" I ask. "Who is it that you miss?"

Just like that, her walls go up again.

"Doesn't matter," she says. "He's gone."

She puts ten thousand volts into the word *gone*, and I'm not about to touch it.

I extend an olive branch instead. "I know exactly how you fee—"

Alexa holds up an abrupt hand, startling me silent. Her eyes cut over my shoulder to the other girls.

I glance behind me. Both Finnley and Hope are awake now, staring at something out to sea. Neither seems to have heard my conversation with Alexa. What caught their attention? I scan the ocean, but only see sunlight glinting on the water. Endless, in all directions.

"Eden?" Finnley says. "Is that it?"

Alexa and I exchange a look. At least I'm not alone in my confusion.

"Is . . . what . . . what?" It's possible my perfect vision isn't as perfect as I assume it is—that it's taken a turn toward old-lady-blind since my last visit to the optometrist, half a year before Zero Day—but every line I see is crisp, every color vivid. There just isn't anything other than water and sky to see.

"The drawing in your book, of the island," Finnley says. "It looks a lot like it, don't you think?"

There's only one book she could mean, and only one drawing that looks like an island. I flip open to the pages, which once—from what I can tell—held a wealth of knowledge about how to catch fish. But Dad completely obscured all the printed text with an ink-blue drawing, lines of varying widths shaded with cross-hatching and tiny dots. A beach stretches from edge to edge: behind it looms a tight thicket of trees, and before it are curling, frothing waves. And then, at the left, there is an intricate sketch of a tall, unmistakable totem pole that juts skyward where sand meets trees. The ink at the pages' rims bleeds together from the swim the book took across the soaked deck this morning, but even so, it is a clear picture of what we're looking for.

Which would be helpful if there were anything but water to see.

"Can I take a look at it again?" Finnley stretches her hand toward me, but her gaze is undeniably fixed on something. "The drawing, I mean?"

I cross to their end of the boat, field guide in hand.

But the book falls to the deck before I can pass it to Finnley. I nearly fall right along with it. After only three steps, and no squinting whatsoever, the horizon has a new shape.

"Alexa," I say, "you're going to want to see this."

TEN

MY FATHER WAS a meticulous man. His grammar was impeccable, his face was always baby-smooth and smelled of mint, and he couldn't stand dirt under his fingernails. His eye for specificity, for perfection, stretched across every facet of his life. I see it in every dot, every line, and every curve of the drawing—they match every dot, line, and curve of the island before us.

Which is why it makes no sense that we've arrived early, according to his meticulously outlined instructions on how to find it.

Not to mention the way he neglected to write a single word about this baffling trick of nature. How is it possible for an entire island to be seen from one half of a boat while, at the same time, remaining hidden from the other?

But it is, unquestionably, Sanctuary Island. I am a vane in the wind, oscillating from joy to fear and back again at everything this means—all it proves. Sanctuary Island exists! Whether we will find sanctuary there is another mystery altogether. Now, at least, I know it is *possible*.

Hope and I work together to adjust the sails, turning our

boat until we can see the island from every angle on deck. When it's clear we've passed whatever barrier made it elusive to us, we sail toward it.

At first, it seems close, like it will take us less than an hour to reach its shore. And it looks small: an hour's run around the perimeter. Too small to be a haven for refugees.

But though we slice easily through the water at a respectable pace, it takes the rest of the afternoon to reach sand. When we do, it's obvious the island is much vaster than it first appeared.

As we pull into the shallow water, which is sparkling and crystal blue, we are dwarfed by our surroundings. Trees stretch four times the height of our sail, an intimidating force behind the naked beach. Farther down the strip of sand, nine enormous blocks of stone form the totem pole, its many sides chiseled with shadowed, exaggerated faces. The only thing that looks small here is the sky, a thin stretch of blue mostly obscured by the swaying green leaves of the treetops. The breeze allows shards of sunlight to pierce the otherwise impenetrably thick canopy of foliage.

I hoist myself up and over the side of the boat as Hope lowers the sails. The water is inviting, calm and cool as it tugs at my calves. Finnley joins me in the water, and together, we guide the boat up onto the sand.

Our progress slows as we meet resistance; without the ocean to help us carry the boat, it is a heavy beast. Alexa and Hope climb out into the ankle-deep tide. With one firm push, we're moving again, inch by inch until the boat is just out of water's reach.

Alexa is the first to abandon us. Her feet make neat prints in the smooth, wet sand, the only sign of life on this island other than the stone tower. "It's good enough," she calls over her shoulder. "Shouldn't wash away from there."

I'm not entirely sure I agree, and in fact I'm pretty sure I *dis*agree, but dragging it even this far has made my entire body ache. I feel eyes on me, Hope's and Finnley's, their hands still on the boat as if they're ready to push for another hour if I say we should. Hope's face is flushed, and her limbs are so thin I'm surprised they haven't snapped. Finnley is a little sturdier, but not much.

"Even if it washes away," Finnley says, "it's not like we have anywhere else to go."

She's right, not that it's much comfort. "Let's come back to it," I say. "It'll be fine for now. Grab the Havenwater bottle and as many emergency bars as you can, just in case."

Relief flashes in Hope's eyes, but she makes no comment. We load our arms with supplies and follow Alexa's footsteps until the sand turns powdery and sticks to our feet. Her footsteps veer toward the stone totem; we veer with them. Alexa studies the tower, dwarfed by its height, by the backdrop of jungle behind it. We join her in the shadows.

"This . . . isn't the temple, is it?" Hope asks.

"It doesn't match the description in the field guide, no," I say.

I run my fingers in the carved grooves and curved contours of one of its faces. "The field guide seems to indicate that the temple itself is somewhere deep in there." I tilt my head toward the jungle.

We stare at the totem. It stares back.

"Ooooookay," Alexa says. "Have fun staring at rocks—I'm over it." She flips her hair over her shoulder and walks back toward the surf.

A breeze rustles the leaves; waves lick at the beach. It's peaceful, serene. Nothing like the place we came from, sand laced with explosives and blood. No officers standing guard, no bullets and no blades.

And yet, the idea of being trapped here—*even if it washes away, it's not like we have anywhere else to go*—sends an unseasonable chill through my bones, one that branches from my spine to my ribs and lingers longer than is comfortable.

No one ever prepared me for hope to be so tangled with fear.

ELEVEN

"YOU'D THINK THERE'D be a welcoming committee," Alexa says as Finnley and I trudge past with the last of the supplies from our boat. Alexa turns over and flops an arm over her eyes. Her torso is coated in sand.

Hope arranges our stash of emergency bars in a neat pyramid beside the tree we've chosen as our temporary home, close enough to see the totem, but not so close it's staring directly at us. There's a clearing here, just outside the jungle, large enough for the four of us to stretch out side by side. Alexa has been horizontal since the moment we discovered it.

"I'm not surprised it's like this," Finnley says, despite the fact that she was so vocal about expecting a greeting of guns and guards. It must not come easily to her to admit when she's wrong. "It makes sense that the temple would be as far from the shore as possible, and that people seeking sanctuary would have to work for it." She drops an armful of random items into a hole I just finished digging.

For once, I agree with Alexa. "But wouldn't people who seek sanctuary be tired—or *dying*, even? It doesn't seem fair to make the exhausted work for peace."

"If someone wants peace desperately enough, having to work for it won't stop them from searching."

The three of us turn to look at Hope. She doesn't speak much, but when she does, people listen. Has she always been like this? How much of her is a product of the war's chiseling and how much is due to sun-kissed genes, good parenting?

"I do wonder," Hope continues, "about security. Why *isn't* anyone standing guard?"

"Maybe they are. Maybe we just can't see them."

Whatever made Hope must have skipped over Alexa.

I glance over my shoulder, suddenly convinced she's right. Maybe Finnley's original theory wasn't so far off after all. I see only trees, an ominous force of them, all shades of green until shadows stain them black. And then there are the hard, dead eyes of the totem carvings.

"Let them watch." Finnley rummages around in our hole of random items. "Yes," she breathes, pulling a Leatherman knife from the pile, along with a small box. "We would have been screwed without a blade. And, oh! Waterproof matches, excellent."

Finnley and I take the lead on setting up camp, mostly because Hope is an enthusiastic follower and Alexa is more interested in sunbathing. Our plan is to first establish a home base, then set off in search of the temple. The island is large and the jungle looks dense. Depending on how well the temple is hidden, it could take an afternoon to find it, or it could take a week. Or longer. Especially with no welcoming committee to guide us.

I flip through Dad's field guide. "Shelter, fire, food, and water," I say. "Those seem like the most important things to focus on. How's the Havenwater doing?"

Hope glances at the display embedded in its side. "Should be good for about four more refills."

"Okay, so, we should focus on fire before food or water," I say, "since we'll need to cook or boil whatever we plan to consume."

Finnley agrees, which is affirming. She sees the world in black and white, I'm noticing, through a grid of logic. Leaps of faith: not her strong suit. One foot in front of the other, though, and she's an asset. It's empowering that she thinks my thoughts are solid ones.

"Eden, you and Alexa should gather some of those long, thin leaves and start weaving mats," Finnley says. "You said last night that you worked in a silk factory, right?"

That isn't exactly what I said, but I don't correct her. The cocoons I tended were used for tech, not textiles—the only similarity there is that they both come from silkworm saliva. Still, I know the basic principles of weaving. I once knew a girl at the silk house who stole a cocoon and tucked it in her pocket when only I was looking. She'd unravel it in the dead of night, then tediously weave the delicate thread into soft, slippery fabric. It was only as big as a bookmark when they caught her behind the silk house, dyeing it mulberry red—so many sins all at once.

That was the last time I saw her. I was told to burn it, this beautiful symbol of rebellion, the only thing that got her through each day.

I tucked it into the field guide instead.

Finnley shakes the box of matches, tosses it to Hope. "We'll collect sticks for the fire."

"And for weapons," Hope adds. The word sounds wrong coming out of her mouth. "We can whittle them into spears and use them to kill fish. Or small animals." She pauses. "Or . . . large animals."

"Or humans." Alexa finally looks interested in the conversation, propped up on one elbow. "What?" She shrugs. "We might need to defend ourselves."

Her confession from the boat—*I was the one who set the factory explosions that flushed them out in the first place*—has lingered at the edge of my mind ever since. I don't know whether to be horrified or impressed by her, terrified or in awe.

Mat-making doesn't sound so unpleasant compared with the far more complicated task I have ahead of me: extracting answers from Alexa.

The only thing that convinces Alexa to move from her place of comfort is the promise of *more* comfort.

"Do you really want sand . . . um . . . everywhere?" Hope's question—in the context of a discussion about how we'll have to wash our clothes sometimes, underwear included, and how we'll want mats to sit on while they're drying—is all it takes.

"Fine. *Fine.*" Alexa stands, dusts herself off. "Let's go."

Though we can't quite see the sun from here, a hundred variations of pink and orange blaze in the sky. "Meet back before dark?" I ask.

Finnley nods and sets off with Hope into the trees. I'm secretly glad our task doesn't require going fully into the jungle just yet. Alexa and I should be able to find everything we need just by walking its outer edge.

Narrow-leafed plants, perfect for weaving, wave in the breeze like fans for cooling summer-steamed kings. We pluck as many leaves as we can and tie them into a bundle with the sleeves of my yellow cardigan. I won't be wearing it again anytime soon in this heat.

"Out with it," Alexa says, with a firm yank on a handful of leaves. "You're acting weird."

I try to summon the directness she's somehow perfected over her lifetime. The trouble is, I don't know which question to start with. I settle, finally, on this: "Tell me how you did it." I sever a thick bunch of leaves with the knife, and the bare stalk springs away.

"Do we have enough leaves to start weaving?" she asks.

We do, but I don't say so. I shift my weight and hope silence will draw the truth out of her.

She tears five leaves from a ravaged plant, one at a time, and stuffs them into my cardigan bundle. When I still don't speak, she rolls her eyes. "How did I do what, exactly? How did I make the bombs? Or how did I keep them a secret from the Wolfpack officers?" Her words are a wild flood rising between us, and my ability to talk back is swept out to sea.

"Or," she continues, teeth tight and words terse, "how did I do it alone? Or how can I live with myself with so much blood on my hands?"

Her eyes are glassy with tears that don't slip out. I'm tempted to feel guilty for pressing her too hard until I remember she was the one to spill her secrets in the first place. And that secrets aren't the only thing she's spilled.

"Put the knife away," she says.

I follow her gaze to my hand, where my knuckles have gone white around the Leatherman's handle. I hadn't even realized I was gripping it so tightly. I hadn't realized I was still gripping it at all.

Carefully, I fold the knife and tuck it into my pants pocket, where it settles snugly beside the vial of my father.

"I told you before, when we first met, I wasn't running *to* something—I was only running away. And that was the truth."

In one smooth motion, she slips the prong of her watch's clasp out of the leather band. Unlike most people, she wears it backward, with the face to the inside. She lets it fall to the sand without a second look, and holds her hand up as if to wave.

Her wrist is porcelain pale except for a small tattoo, just below her palm: a wolf's face.

The wolf's face.

TWELVE

"YOU WERE *ONE* *of them*?"

Her face, all sun and shadows, shifts with the breeze. The sharpness in it puts me immediately on guard—I can't look at her without seeing everyone the Wolfpack has taken from me.

"Don't look at me like that." She rips another handful of leaves from the nearest plant.

I look away, out to sea. Everything I want to say, to ask, is tangled in a knot at the pit of my stomach.

She thrusts the leaves into my cardigan, so forceful and sudden the entire bundle falls to the sand. "This was a mistake," she mutters, and stalks back to the clearing that will be our home.

I don't protest.

I bend to gather the fallen leaves and see the clasp of her watch glinting in the sunlight. She shouldn't have been so careless—does she not realize she'll be forced to spill her secrets without it? I could call after her, but I don't. The others have a right to know. I'm not about to tell them, not about to make things that easy for her—she deserves to look them in the eye when they find out. See their rage. Their pain.

I go out to the beach, plant myself where the tide pulls at my toes. It's been years since I've had the freedom to sit this close to the water, thanks to the Wolves—thanks to *Alexa*. Bittersweet memories pull at me with every wave: my tiny family, just Dad and me for so many years, at the pier. Moonlit campfires with Birch, marshmallows burned to blisters and blackness. Seashells, starfish, sandcastles. The flock of gulls that stole our picnic bread.

All the things I took for granted.

A crisp breeze blows in, raising every hair on my arm. I turn out the leaves from my cardigan and slip into its well-loved sleeves. It will do well enough for now, while the sun is still out. I hope the foliage in our clearing will provide a better barrier when it's time to sleep.

I work the leaves into a mat, weaving them over and under in a pattern that puts my mind at ease. By the time I've woven three petite mats, the sky is the sunless gray of dusk and my fingertips are raw. My pile of leaves has drastically diminished—there won't be enough for a fourth mat.

A pair of bare feet appears beside me: Hope's. "Mind if I sit?"

"Good luck," I say, brushing away what remains of my leaf pile. "The beach gets pretty crowded this time of year."

"*Tourists.*" She sinks to the sand and stretches out her long sun-kissed legs. She shakes her head. "Did you ever think you'd miss tourists, of all things?"

"I never thought I'd miss a lot of things."

I never expected to *lose* so many things.

"My older sister always complained that tourists were the

worst," she says. "She waited tables at a seafood restaurant out at the Santa Monica Pier."

"Did your sister come to Texas with you?" After Zero, people were shipped to gulags all over the country, mostly along vulnerable coastlines, to break up as many long-standing relationships as possible. I was one of the few who stayed put. One grandparent on each side, a couple of stray uncles—other than Dad, I have no idea where the rest of my family ended up. If they're even alive.

When she doesn't answer, I turn my eyes from the ocean for the first time since she sat down. She curls her knees into herself, wraps her arms around them. Rests her chin. "I didn't even get to say goodbye."

I don't recall ever meeting anyone who *did* get to say goodbye. "I didn't, either," I say. "Not to my mom, and not to my grandparents." Mom's been gone a lot longer than the war, though.

"No siblings?"

"Only child." Birch was practically family, and if we'd made it to our twenties together, he probably would've become my *actual* family.

"Sometimes I think it must be better that way," she says. "Easier, I mean. Not necessarily better."

Though I haven't lost siblings, I know exactly what she means. I've thought it myself, hundreds of times: when pieces of your heart are ripped away, it's easy to wish you'd never known what a whole heart felt like in the first place. But no one can deny a whole heart beats better than a broken one.

Hope burrows her toes into the sand. "It's so dark out," she says. "That happened fast."

If not for the sliver of moon that hangs over the horizon, we'd both be obscured by the night. We should probably head back to the clearing soon—the wind has picked up, and the chill in it chafes. A campfire will help.

"I wish we could spend the night out here near the water," I say. No part of me wants to be around Alexa right now. Even if she did run from her life in the Wolfpack, she's part of the reason our world is so toxically fractured. It's not that I don't respect her boldness in leaving—I do.

It's just that wolves are predators, and they've conditioned us to fear them.

A conflict in the clearing rips this still moment to shreds: raised voices, harsh tones. Finnley first, then Alexa. Panic. A fire flickers near the base of the big tree—it's hard to tell if it's burning within its boundaries, or if the wind has blown the flames out of control.

Hope is already on her feet, halfway back to the clearing. I almost don't want to help. In all the sleepless nights I spent staring at the ceiling, wishing for Sanctuary, I never factored a former Wolf into the equation. But this is my home now, too—*our* home. Like it or not, this is all the family I may ever have again.

So I gather my three woven mats and run.

"She's a *Wolf*!" Finnley explodes when I arrive. The fire

burns neatly within a ring of smooth white stones. "When were you going to tell us, Alexa? Or were you just going to kill us tonight in our sleep? Did you think we'd ignore the gun tucked into your shorts forever?"

Alexa is right up in Finnley's face, her eyes jagged as black crystals. "If I'd wanted to kill you, you wouldn't have made it on the boat."

As much as I'm inclined to hate her for her history, this much is true: she protected me at the boardwalk, when I first emerged. Warned me not to move. She could have fired that pistol, put me out of her misery.

"Maybe you were just using us to get to the island," Finnley says, not backing down. "Maybe you'd been spying on Eden for months, maybe you believed in Sanctuary all along and needed her to find it."

Alexa's jaw tightens. "If you can remember all the way back to yesterday," she says, through gritted teeth, "I was against the idea of coming here."

"So if you weren't running here," I say, "where, exactly, did you expect to go?"

She turns on me then, and I'm surprised to see tears in her eyes. "How many times do I have to tell you? I was only running away."

In the same way I knew the truth in her words about not killing us, there's something in the way her voice catches, and in the way she holds herself, like she's swallowing a breakdown. It may not be a lie, but I'm pretty sure it isn't entirely true.

"Wait, what do you *mean*, 'How many times do I have to tell you?'" Finnley looks between us, eyes like steel blades. "You knew about this, Eden? And you didn't say anything?"

"I only just found out—"

"And, what, you thought we'd be okay with you sitting on a secret like that?"

"No, I—"

"Maybe you're one of them, too," she says. She rips the mats I've woven right out of my arms, twists my wrist up for inspection.

I yank it away. Grit my teeth so only steam comes out, glare hard even as my eyes fill with tears. Traitors. "Do I look like someone," I say, as evenly as I can manage, jaw still tight, "who would give up her entire life just to stomp the flames out of everyone else's?"

Hope steps between us. "I don't think she meant—"

"You don't think I meant *what*?" Finnley's words snap Hope's mouth shut. "Looks aren't everything, Eden. Just because you look like you used to be a privileged girl from a five-million-dollar mansion, it doesn't mean you actually were one."

I'm stunned that my Before clings to me well enough for her to notice, even after all the Wolves have done to scrub it away. Then again, maybe it shouldn't surprise me. Ten times out of ten, we oppressed share a history of privilege. Still, not everyone's privilege was as extreme as mine—much of the middle class landed in barracks along with the rest of us.

"I'm right, aren't I? Well, aren't you *lucky*," Finnley says. The fire falls out of her voice, finally. Withers like embers as they fade to ash. "At least you had memories of sweet dreams to carry you through your incredibly rough days of feeding silkworms."

Alexa makes a face behind her back. I bite my tongue.

"Finnley." Hope's voice is quiet. No one shuts her down this time. "No one here wants a fight. We're . . . kind of all we have right now."

Finnley throws a handful of sticks into the fire; the flames swallow them up in a fit of sparks. "You have no idea," she says, barely over a whisper, "what it's like to be forgotten." Her tears sizzle as they fall, fast and fierce, onto the blisteringly hot rocks. "What it's like to be overlooked and left behind when all your friends join the Wolfpack and you haven't even been invited. What it's like to wish you were one of them, because you *deserve* to be, because you were never privileged, never rich." She swallows. "And then to hate yourself for ever having the thought. To hate yourself for ever being friends with the sort of people who had such a taste for other people's blood."

Whatever I expected, it wasn't this. I glance at Alexa, brace myself for an aftershock in response to Finnley's last comment, but it looks as though her thoughts are a thousand miles away.

"I know what it's like," Hope says, staring into the fire. "To hate them, but to love one. To question whether you ever truly knew them, how you could have missed all the broken things when you live one room away."

Her brother, no doubt.

The fire pops, hisses. War is like this: consuming, ravenous, feeding and feeding until there's nothing left to take and all that's left is ash.

"I never had a taste for blood." Alexa. Still a thousand miles away. "I was just doing what I thought I needed to do in order to survive."

THIRTEEN

SURVIVAL:

It isn't as easy as air in, air out.

It isn't as easy as bite, chew, swallow.

It isn't easy.

Not all Wolves began with a taste for blood; I believe that to be true. Not all Wolves wanted life at the expense of life. Wolves wanted life—but not at the expense of their *own* lives.

So bloodthirst won. Tooth and claw, the desire to survive at any cost. The softer ones allowed it to happen, lest they get caught up in the dying.

Bite. Chew. Swallow.

Survival is born as much from fear as it is from bravery.

FOURTEEN

WE STEP CAREFULLY around one another. No one has triggered any more emotional land mines, but then, we've hardly spoken in two hours.

"I'm taking these." Finnley grabs both life vests from the storage pile and doesn't look back.

"Who says you get the pillows?" Alexa snaps.

"Take mine," Hope says. "It's fine." She swipes one of the vests from Finnley and drops it on Alexa's spot near the fire. Alexa planted herself there an hour ago, as close as she could get without singeing her mat or her hair.

Hope and Finnley settle themselves just inside the jungle. A thick barrier of foliage and several body lengths separate their mats from our clearing.

My spot is under a big tree, not too close, but not far. The sand is cold and gritty, despite the fire, and my cardigan makes a poor pillow. I opted to go without a mat—better that than someone resenting me for not weaving another one. It's going to be a long night: not too comfortable, too many bugs.

"I'm not dealing with the fire all night, just so you know," Alexa says, after another stretch of silence.

No one volunteers. No one says a single word.

With Finnley keeping her distance from Alexa—and Hope keeping Finnley from boiling over—the job falls to me, I guess. "I'll take care of it," I say. I don't really mind. It isn't like I'll be able to sleep anytime soon.

I don't think I'm alone in that, either—the stillness is rigid, not restful. Alexa pretends to sleep, but her muscles look too tense in the firelight. And every now and then, I think I hear Finnley or Hope shift beyond the brush, but the brittle crunch of leaves is too careful, too controlled.

For the past two hours, I've been trying to piece together how Finnley ended up on the wrong side of the Wolves' line. How many others are there, just like her, who I never knew about? I think about the lines that divide us, how we could draw them endlessly, forever, until everyone ends up alone inside their own jagged piece. How some lines are easier to cross than others.

Lines drawn in sand are notoriously fragile. All it takes to erase them is one swift wave, one strong pull of tide. Lines drawn by Wolves, though, are drawn in blood, brutal and based on instinct and assumptions. If we appeared wealthy, if the silk tech implants in our fingerpads weren't knotted or gnarled—a seamless procedure cost thousands, and it was easy to tell who hadn't been able to afford one—we were targets. If we went to this private school or lived in that zip code or drove these luxury cars or had our own personal Havenwater cartridges—if *any* of these, we were put to the wrong side of the line. It was a science of emotion, not of exactness. It was surprisingly accurate.

Finnley's left fingerpad is a mess of scars. Most implant scars are on the right, since people use their dominant hand to pay for things. Her seamless, smooth right pointer must have given the Wolves the wrong impression. She wasn't wealthy, only left-handed.

Silk technology has had a way of drawing its own lines.

Like the invisible lines that crisscross the globe: third-world borders shifting to first-world powers, first-world powers falling from grace.

Humanitarian efforts to the third world made a drastic impact on health and welfare. First there were the Havenwater bottles, six thousand flung to the far side of the world. And then, when Envirotech discovered they could mold silk proteins into as many uses as engineers could dream, came the edible, unrefrigerated medication in the form of plastic cards. New families, new *cities*, began to thrive. Landlocked Africa and Asia look nothing like they did even thirty years ago. Silkworms have stirred the landscape of world powers into something no one predicted.

Silk tech has been good, for them. Here, it's mostly caused problems, further stratified people who are only trying to survive. No handouts here—it wasn't bad enough for that until we'd already been overgenerous with our aid, until other parts of the world were on the rise and we'd slipped slightly into decline. There were only those with money, and those without. Those with clean water, with the best medicine, and those without.

Those with seamless skin, and those with scars.

We've all been sliced into, every single one of us.

It's just that some of our scars are less obvious than others.

My eyes fly open at the snap of a twig. The sliver of moon is directly above our clearing, and the fire has dwindled to embers: I must have fallen asleep, and for a while. Waves crash against the shore, louder than before, at high tide.

I toss a few fresh branches into the fire, making sure the last lingering flame catches at least one of them. Our supply hole is within reach; I fumble around until I find the flashlight I put inside earlier.

Another twig snaps. At least, I think it's a twig, and not just shifting supplies.

"Hello?" I whisper.

Nothing.

"Alexa?" I shine the light in the direction of her mat, hoping she's simply gotten up to relieve herself. No such luck: she's curled up like a child, serene in her sleep. She doesn't so much as shift when I whisper her name.

Something crawls across the back of my neck. I shake it off, but it sets me even more on edge than before. "Hope?" I step carefully toward the brush that separates us. "Finnley?" The flashlight's beam is strong, but not strong enough to shine as far as their mats. A few steps later, I see they're fast asleep, too.

The fire cracks and pops, devouring its fresh fuel. I sweep the flashlight's beam over the sand, in all directions. Still nothing, no one. We haven't seen another soul on this island yet, but that doesn't mean we're alone here. Based on Dad's notes in the field guide, we never *expected* to be alone—but we also never expected our first encounter with whoever lives here to be in the dead of night.

I creep back toward the tree where I slept, listening for any other sign that things aren't as they should be.

Leaves rustle, deep in the jungle. A monkey, I tell myself—a strong breeze.

A few more twigs snap, not as loudly as before. I sit at the base of the tree, lean my head back. Stay as still as possible, in case whatever is there turns out to be less than friendly. I listen for what feels like hours, but nothing ever shows itself. Eventually, the noises begin to stumble on top of one another, often enough that I'm convinced it's just the living, breathing jungle and nothing else.

The last thing I see before succumbing to sleep is the pink-purple sky, dawn unbroken.

The first thing I see, when I'm shaken awake, is Hope.

"It's Finnley," she says, her usual serenity stripped from her face. "She's gone."

FIFTEEN

"DID SHE MENTION any plans to go exploring?" I ask.

Alexa feigns disinterest as she unwraps one of the few emergency bars we have left—we'll have to learn to fish with spears soon, I note—but her eyes cut toward us when she thinks we're not looking.

Could Alexa have done something to make Finnley disappear? As neat an explanation as that would be, it feels off. Alexa slept straight through the night, never flinched once when I added tinder to our fire. And Finnley was the one who insisted on keeping her distance—not the other way around.

Hope paces in the clearing. She's been pacing so long the sand has begun to pack under her feet. "She told me she wanted to go look for the temple, but I assumed that would be after we were all awake, not at the crack of dawn."

"We never did make concrete plans, I guess," I say. "I thought we were all on the same page, that we'd go together. In broad daylight."

That's all it is, I tell myself. She woke up early, she slept through all the noises that set my skin on edge, she wanted to go off on her own without Alexa, without me. I certainly wouldn't want to explore the jungle alone, in near darkness, but Finnley was clearly upset with us last night. With Alexa and me, anyway. I haven't mentioned the noises to the others—I can't change it that I didn't speak up as soon as the twig snapped last night. How would they look at me if they knew I could have prevented . . . whatever happened?

Nothing happened. Nothing, nothing.

But the noises that set me on edge: I can't quite put them out of my mind.

I've seen things since the war began, heard too many things I wish I could forget, enough to know when something isn't as it should be.

The girl from the communal bathroom, for example. I saw her every morning, every night. We never spoke, just brushed our teeth with wiry, paste-less brushes—until one morning, she stopped showing up. I asked after her, but no one gave any answers. It was as if she'd vanished from camp altogether.

And the elderly server from the daily oatmeal line: he faithfully dipped his ladle into the steaming black cauldron despite his hands, red and raw and peeling and blistered. They seared him with cattle-prodding irons whenever his line moved too slowly. He didn't last six months.

Then there was the pastor who wouldn't divert from his message, whose underground congregation showed up one Sunday morning to find him pierced in the same way his savior had been.

I hoped we'd escaped those who creep in the night, who love

to steal, kill, and destroy.

Now I'm not so sure.

We agree to stay at the clearing only as long as it takes for me to whittle three thick sticks into sharp-tipped spears. Even Alexa seems eager to look for Finnley, which surprises me— she doesn't strike me as the type to care so much—but I decide not to comment. She searches up and down the beach, never going so far that we can't see her, but eventually returns to our clearing. Alone.

Hope flips through the field guide as I whittle. If Finnley *did* go off in search of the temple, we reason, she would have based her plan on the information inside my book. She certainly spent enough time studying it on the boat, enough time to memorize the details Dad included. As long as she didn't ask questions, I'd told her, she could thumb through to sharpen up her survival skills. Now I wish I'd kept it closer to my chest like I'd originally planned.

"I don't see anything in here other than what we already know," Hope says. "'Temples hiding among ferns, structures formed of stones and secrets'—it would have been nice if whoever made this had drawn a map."

Perhaps Dad hadn't lived long enough to be so thorough. The thought digs its fingernails into my brain, and I do my best to pry it away. I already told Hope there weren't any other telling details, but she wanted to scour it anyway. See if she could find any hidden clues for the determined to decipher.

"Finnley thinks there might be a code," she says, which snaps me straight to attention—I nearly slice my hand with the knife.

"What? What sort of code?" If anyone should have figured out a code, it's me. I've devoted years to learning that book. To learning Dad.

Hope bites her lip. "I tried so hard to pay attention, but I kept falling asleep while she was talking last night—and, really, she was whispering, so that didn't help. I remember her saying something about the markings?" She sighs. "Sorry, I know that's not helpful. Everything written in here could be called a marking, technically."

The markings. The markings?

I reach for the book, and she hands it over without a word. The only markings that come to mind are where Dad kept a tally of how many fish they'd eaten. But maybe that was symbolic? I flip there, and yes, there are definitely two lists—fish caught, fish eaten. Thirty-two marks in each column. Any symbolism I try to impose upon it just feels ridiculous. Sometimes a fish is just a fish.

"I was wondering if maybe these"—Hope holds her hand out for the book, and I pass it back; she flips to Dad's drawing of the island—"might be Morse code?" She points to the ocean, its rolling waves shaded with lines and dots that cover half the page.

Oh. *Oh*. I can't unsee it, now that she's pointed it out. How have I never noticed so obvious a thing hiding in plain sight?

It's all over the book, too, everywhere his sketches appear.

Alexa hovers behind us, studying the page. "Either of you know how to decipher it?"

"The only bit of it I know is SOS," I say. "And there's a whole lot more written here than just that."

"I don't even know *that* much," Hope says.

Alexa gives a little half laugh. "If there's one thing a survival guide should have, you'd think it'd be a Morse code cheat sheet."

My heart sinks. If it were a message meant for me, surely he would have made certain I was equipped to read it. Right? Maybe I'm missing something. And if Finnley knew how to read it, she might know things about Dad that even I don't know.

She might know things about Dad I don't *want* her to know.

Alexa moves around to our supply hole, digs halfheartedly until she finds what she's looking for. It's a tiny black memo pad, no bigger than her palm, no thicker than a matchbook.

"Where'd that come from?" I ask.

She shrugs. "Found it on the boat. Maybe there's something helpful in here?"

If I'd been the one to find it, I would have shown everyone immediately. Also, I would already have it memorized. Alexa and I are not so similar.

When she opens it, it becomes clear it's not a memo pad at all, but a calendar-at-a-glance. "Thought it was worth a shot," she says. "Anyone want a souvenir to remember the year 2055 by?"

The summer of '55, maybe. September: not so much. I'm surprised the calendar didn't start over after Zero Day. That the numbers continue on in bold black, not Birch-blood red, as if the world kept turning as usual.

In reality, it feels more like the world imploded.

SIXTEEN

OUR PLAN IS this: we agree to search for the temple, since it's the most logical place she would have gone, as far as we can think. Along the way, we'll keep our eyes open for footprints, broken branches, and trails where she might have been dragged away against her will.

My motives aren't as pure as simply finding Finnley, if I'm honest. If she was able to decipher the Morse code, I want to know. I *need* to know—more about my father, more about the island. Maybe she read something about the temple location; maybe she knows something we don't. Maybe she went on her own for a *reason*.

Or maybe her blood is being used to ink a new calendar.

I push the thought away.

"Only two refills left on the Havenwater, just so you know," Alexa says.

"Great," I say. "Let's add fresh water to the list of things we're searching for. Can you pack the canteens in my cardigan?" We found two in the sailboat, full of water and lock-sealed, but we've been saving them as a last resort in case of emergency— the Havenwater filter having only two refills left definitely qualifies as a near-emergency. We could probably stretch it to four refills, depending on how brave we feel, but that's risky.

For the first time since I met her, Alexa doesn't push back, or—worse—ignore me completely. I pass out the spears I whittled, one for each of us.

Hope turns hers over in her hands. "Anything else before we go?"

"Something to mark our path?" I suggest. "Something to cut up, to tie around tree branches?"

"Could we use the life vests?" Alexa offers.

"Too bright," I say. "We need something that won't stand out quite as much. If someone *took* Finnley, it doesn't seem like the best idea to leave a trail of bread crumbs for them."

"But wouldn't they have taken us already, if they were going to?" Hope says. "And who says there's a *they* anyway? We haven't seen another soul on the island."

"Just because they haven't taken us yet," Alexa says, "doesn't mean they *won't*. Maybe it's a head game—maybe we're lab rats in some sadistic social experiment; maybe they're waiting to see how long it takes for us to turn on each other. Take each other out, save them some work."

Alexa's words catch me off guard. It isn't that they're illogical words—it's a frighteningly plausible theory. It's just that her theory is so far from anything I expected this island to be, based on Dad's notes in the field guide. So far from everything I still *hope* it will be.

It's the most passion I've seen out of Alexa yet, though, so I don't extinguish it. "Maybe so," I say, "but I think it's far more likely that Finnley simply set off without us." That's what I'm choosing to believe, anyway. It's the most logical theory, especially in light of how things blew up between us all last night, and in light of the possibility that she cracked the Morse code. "At any rate, we're losing time. I'd rather use nothing to mark our path than use the super-obvious life vests. Just in case."

"We can cut my pants off," Hope says. But she has less meat on her bones than I do, and I wouldn't feel right taking her up on it, especially because of how the temperature plunges at night. I look to Alexa, but she has nothing to spare—her shorts hardly cover the essentials as it is.

"Let's use mine instead. I was thinking about making them into cutoffs anyway," I lie. I'll just have to weave a blanket to go with our sleeping mats.

"Are you sure?" Hope says. "I really don't mind."

"No, it's fine," I find myself saying, though I'm not completely sure it is. But I've already spoken up, and Hope looks relieved, so I slice my pants to shreds.

We set off for the temple, blind leading blind, marking trees along the way. It's lush and green and sprawling with life, leaves so thick we only know the sandy ground is there because we haven't fallen straight through to the center of the earth.

The branches scrape and tickle my bare legs. It's an odd sensation, comforting and unsettling at the same time. So many days, back at barracks, I longed for a place exactly like this: a place untouched, a place where life grew up without any inter-ference. A place totally unlike what our world has become, all cracked concrete and wild overgrowth at war with each other.

Now that I'm here, it's not like I pictured it. I imagined free-dom would bring with it a sense of peace. Stillness. Silence, and rest.

It hasn't.

When it's silent, I wonder *why*.

Thousand-year-old jungle vines twist around one another, clinging to tree trunks thicker than the three of us combined. I imagine boa constrictors twined with them, ready to strike, like they did in so many of my childhood nightmares. The far-ther we go, the thicker the undergrowth is. Paranoia creeps in: I can't stop thinking about what might be hiding just under the green that obscures the sand. Even the illusion of snake is enough to make me want to run back and hide on the beach. But what then? I haven't come all this way just to hide.

I chop at the undergrowth with my whittled stake, test the path as I step in it. There are no snakes, not even the occasional lizard. No tracks or trails or broken things, no makeshift signs to mark a path—nothing at all that hints at where Finnley might have gone. Nothing but sand.

Perhaps she doesn't *want* us to find her. Perhaps she doesn't plan to return.

Then again, there have to be a hundred variations of paths she could have taken. At this point, it seems most promising to focus on the temple—the final destination, no matter the direction taken to find it.

After at least an hour, maybe two, our only measure of progress is that we've trekked deep into the jungle and have had to start rationing our path-marking fabric. We've seen no sign of Finnley, no sign of anything remotely temple-like. It bothers me that Dad's instructions were so clear on how to find the island, but that he left next to nothing for us to go on as far as finding the temple itself.

It bothers me quite a lot.

We come to a small clearing, where the branches at our feet finally begin to thin out. Large, mossy stones recline like weary explorers who've given up and succumbed to the petrification process. In three directions splitting off from the clearing, the tree canopy arcs high overhead like a series of naturally formed tunnels. Like everything else on this island, they are sprawling and overgrown.

"We really should be making a map," Hope says. Tentatively, she runs her fingers over one of the mossy stones. "Seems like it would be easy to get lost out here." *Seems like it would be easy for* Finnley *to get lost out here*, I hear, tucked into the folds of the words she actually says.

Alexa rolls her eyes and sprawls out on one of the larger stones, which is long and flat and bedlike. "We're marking our path," she says. "It'll be fine."

I have a dull pencil—another of Alexa's surprise storage compartment finds—but there's no space for me to write in the field guide. The pages are completely covered in Dad's neat blue ink. "We'll run out of fabric soon," I say, flipping through to make doubly sure there are no empty corners. "It's a good idea." Instead, I rip September from the pocket calendar Alexa found on the boat. I could fit a tiny map on the back, and maybe even a few notes.

Hope, who's been carrying my cardigan full of our supplies, twists the Havenwater lid open and pours a small trickle down her throat. She paces the clearing from one end to the other.

I take a seat, begin jotting descriptions of the landmarks we've passed so far. "Want to sit, Hope? I can move over."

She considers the moss and makes a face. "I'm good. Thanks, though."

The moss is slick under my thighs, slimy and cool. I don't know how Alexa can relax like she is, stretched out with so much of her skin in direct contact with it. I write as quickly as possible, just so I can stand up again, even though my muscles are enjoying the rest. We've been walking on a subtle incline all morning.

From the corner of my eye, I see Hope pinch the bridge of her nose, squeeze her eyes shut. She looks a little pale. The sip of water she takes is so tiny I'd be surprised if she felt it go down at all.

"You sure you're okay?" I ask. "You don't look so great."

"I was a little dizzy for a second, but the water's helping." She takes another tiny sip. "I've been trying not to drink more than my share, but . . . I think I'm getting a little dehydrated, maybe?"

I have a vague memory of this happening to my mother, once, when I was very young—we'd spent all day in the sun, sailing, and she'd spent all her energy tending to me instead of herself. We ended up staying the night in the emergency room, waiting as a mess of tubes replenished what she'd lost.

"Drink what you need," I say. "We'll just have to find more."

But this is a problem. Do we keep prioritizing Finnley? Or do we turn our focus fully to a water search for now, so that we're *able* to keep looking for Finnley?

I know which way I'm leaning.

I lay out our options. "I vote water," Alexa's quick to say. Not a surprise, really.

"Hope?" I ask.

She's quiet for a minute, but finally, she meets my eyes. Hers are heavy. "I vote water, too," she says. "I don't *want* to, but that's my vote." She knows what Alexa and I do: we could wander around the jungle for the rest of the day and still never find Finnley.

"We're not abandoning her, okay?" I say. "We're just . . . making ourselves stronger so we can search *harder.*"

Hope swallows, nods. "Yeah," she says. "Yeah, okay." She looks a lot better already, now that she's had a bit more to drink and has torn into an emergency bar. She reaches a hand out to help Alexa up from her bed of stone. "Ready?"

Alexa gives an exaggerated sigh and waves Hope's hand away. "Go on without me," she says. "Come back and let me know when you find water."

I bite down on my cheek, hard, before anything I regret saying fights its way out. Too late, I see a shift in Hope's eyes, a fierceness none of us has seen in her before.

"You are not a *princess*, Alexa. And we are not your slaves."

Alexa bolts upright, stunned. And Hope isn't finished yet.

"Eden and I have been nothing but patient with you, ever since we were so unlucky as to end up on that boat together. And you? You've been nothing but ungrateful, nothing but unhelpful." Hope's eyes are bright; her cheeks are flushed. "I *defended* you to Finnley last night, did you know that? I have a high tolerance for people I don't understand—there's always more going on than I know, so I try to give the benefit of the doubt. But I have just about *had* it with the way you sit around letting us do all the work. You are every bit as stranded here as the rest of us, and you are going to pull your weight from now on, because I am *done*."

The rustle of leaves in the trees becomes as still as these old stones, for one eternal second.

And then the silence is broken by Hope's footsteps, by her deep, shaky breaths. She makes her way slowly into one of the canopy tunnels, walks far down the path without a single glance back.

I give Alexa a pointed look before turning to follow, let it linger. Her eyes are empty, unreadable, but it isn't long before her footsteps fall in with mine.

SEVENTEEN

WHEN ALEXA AND I have caught up to Hope, I pull the field guide out and flip to page fourteen. "'How to find water,'" I read. I skim the page, trying to pick the printed text out from my dad's notes. "There are a lot of clues we can watch out for, according to the book—animal tracks, swarming insects, bird flight paths. Things like that."

I wonder if my father used this exact section of the book when he was here: if he, too, wandered for hours with his team, looking for a water source. If they ever found one.

A thought occurs to me. "You know, searching for water might actually *help* us find Finnley," I say. "Wherever the temple is, they probably built it next to a water source, right? So if we can find water—*when* we find it," I amend, "we can stick close to the banks, follow it around while we look for the temple."

Hope straightens, everything about her a little brighter. She hasn't said as much, but I'm positive she feels guilty for being dehydrated—like if only her body could keep up, we wouldn't have had to shift our focus from Finnley.

"If we find any mud, there might be some groundwater

available." Alexa looks almost embarrassed to have spoken. "It's a trick my grandmother taught me during the floods, when all the public water was contaminated and we didn't have access to a Havenwater—if there's mud, you can dig a hole about a foot deep to see if any water fills it up. You can strain the mud out with cloth."

"Alexa, that's . . . really brilliant," I say. "Thank you."

"Still good to use the Havenwater," she says flatly. "Never know if what you dig up will make you sick."

The way she says it makes it sound like she has personal experience with this, more than she'd like. I think back to camp, how she was every bit as alone as I was. "Is that what happened to your grandmother?"

When Alexa doesn't answer, I glance over. She doesn't meet my eyes, just absently stirs a patch of leaves around with her stake, looking for animal tracks that aren't there. "The Wolfpack promised her the whole world, told her they'd have a place waiting for her after the takeover if she wanted to move inland," she says. "She didn't make it that long, though. Infection took her out quick."

"Why didn't *you* move inland?" All of us in barracks had questions about this—why some Wolves chose active guard duty over moving into our freshly abandoned mansions, with our sparkling pools and our pristinely manicured lawns. It was obvious, with most of the guards at camp, guards whose definition of *a better life* translated to *more power*, a sadistic desire to watch us suffer firsthand.

Alexa wasn't one of those.

Just like on the boat, when I asked her who she missed, her walls go up. She misses her grandmother, I'm sure, but if her grandmother already passed—and she had a chance to move inland, but didn't—this thorn in her side has to do with something else. Some*one* else.

"I thought I could help" is all she gives us.

After that, we're quiet for a good long while, all of us lost in our own heads. I pause to make notes whenever we pass anything unusual—a tree with a knothole black as tar, a section of sand with sparse foliage cover, some bright blue flowers unlike anything else we've seen. At one point, I mistake a particularly serpentine growth of vines for vipers, and Hope has to coax me back from near heart failure.

I should know better by now, though. There've been no snakes. No tracks, no swarms, no flocks. There hasn't been *anything* promising—we've seen absolutely zero sign of life. We're doing everything right, everything the field guide tells us to do, but it hasn't yielded a single glimmer of hope.

"Doing okay, Eden?" Hope asks, and I blink. Look up. Lighten the death grip I've put on the field guide.

Where *are* we? Where are we, that a girl can disappear in the night without a trace? That we can walk through the jungle for hours and find nothing at all as it should be—nothing that hints at the life, the freedom, my father wrote about? Where we haven't seen so much as a bird? So much as a *bug*?

This . . . is not good.

"Yeah," I say, for my sake and theirs. What good does it do us, all the way out here, if we let frustration get the best of us? "Let's keep going."

We press on, all of us dragging a bit after such a long day, pausing occasionally to eat and rehydrate and sharpen the dull tip of the pencil with our knife. I've just started making a fresh batch of notes on the back of tiny, torn-out November '55 when Hope lightly grasps my elbow.

"Do you guys hear that?" Her voice is quiet, like she's afraid to scare off whatever it is she heard.

I tuck my notes inside the field guide, snap it shut. Close my eyes. Listen. No longer is the soundscape simply full of rustling leaves, tree limbs creaking in the breeze: after all this searching—finally—we hear it.

"Water?"

She grins. "And not just ocean waves," she says. "Sounds close, too."

I could cry, I'm so relieved. It's exactly the lift we needed after such a dispiriting day. *Water sounds (northeast)*, I note, beside my most recent landmark entry.

Alexa pulls our last full canteen out from the cardigan supply pack and breaks the seal. She guzzles a quarter of it down, more than any of us have dared to drink at once.

"What?" she says, when she notices Hope and I are staring. "We'll find more soon, right?"

"That isn't an excuse to be careless," I say, and *wow*, is it an unexpected blow to my gut: I sound exactly like my father.

Alexa tightens the lid, but instead of settling it back into the cardigan where it belongs, she holds it out to me. "Want some? Come on, you know you're thirsty."

I am—it still feels wrong not to ration properly, though. After a moment's hesitation, I accept, drink slightly more than I otherwise would have. It's an act of faith, a determined commitment: we *will* find water, and we need to find it soon.

"Let's do this," I say. We set off with renewed enthusiasm and energy, the sound of water closer with every step. Until we hit a particularly dense bit of foliage, that is, and the noise becomes so muffled we have to strain to hear it.

Hope breaks away from us, rushes ahead on the path. "You guys!" she says, bending down. "Look!" With delicate fingers, she holds up the corner of an emergency-bar wrapper. "Maybe Finnley came this way?"

Adrenaline rushes through me, and I'm hopeful for two glorious seconds—until I see a familiar patch of vines, the very same viper-like vines that nearly gave me a heart attack earlier. I remember, clearly, eating an emergency bar at the time. I'd almost choked on it.

"Guys," I say, completely deflating, "we've passed this spot before."

EIGHTEEN

THE SEARCH FOR water is like trekking toward a desert mirage, or like trying to find a rainbow's roots, or like stretching up on tiptoes in hopes of plucking the moon out of the sky: the constant bubbling of a brook is always within earshot, yet when we retrace the path where it's loudest, we see nothing but more jungle. We walk until the afternoon light becomes thin without seeing so much as a drop.

We've gone through most of our water, too. So certain we'd find more, we haven't been as careful as we were this morning. At least we aren't thirsty.

I swat at a mosquito, and a little bead of blood rises up on my sweat-sticky arm. A mosquito! We haven't seen any other insects—maybe this, finally, is a sign that water really is close by and we simply haven't found it yet. The itching sets in right away, and the redness. But then there's a stinging, something I've never felt from a mosquito bite before, and I realize—it isn't the bite that's stinging. It's my right palm; it's the backs of both thighs. It's like eating fresh serranos, the way they bite, then burn, then set your insides on fire.

"Aghhhhhh!" Alexa's shriek pierces the air.

Hope and I whirl around just in time to see Alexa double over, her hair falling out of its knot and into her face. When she straightens—if you could call it straightening—we get a better look: every inch of her arms and legs appears to have been dipped into a vat of molten sunlight. There are no blisters, just smooth lobster skin instead of her usual cappuccino tan.

"What is it? What happened?" Hope is at Alexa's side before I can take two steps.

Alexa cuts a glare through the hair that hangs over her eyes. "How should *I* know? You've been in this jungle for exactly as long as I have, so it's not like I'm the expert."

Hope rolls her eyes, lets her head loll in a way that says her patience has worn as threadbare as Alexa's filter. Mine isn't doing much better.

"I think what Hope means," I say, taking care to keep sharp edges out of my tone, "is, like, did you step in anything, or touch anything?" My thighs are still on fire, but I can't think of anything other than the mosquito that might have caused it. It's not like I've been lying on the beach like Alexa, inviting ultraviolet rays to ravish me.

"Are you kidding? You guys would have killed me if I'd slowed your precious pace," Alexa says, practically spitting her words. "I've *literally* been stepping in everything you've been stepping in. I haven't sat down in hours, not since those rocks."

"Would you calm down?" Hope says, on the verge of needing to take her own advice. "We're not accusing you of anything."

I contort, painfully, trying to get a good look at the backs of my legs. "Hope, you never sat down on the rocks, did you? Did you touch them at all?" Her skin looks every bit as pale as before, except for a slight flush in her cheeks.

"Only enough to know I didn't want to sit down. I don't do moss."

Even as she's speaking, I know that has to be it: she holds both hands up, and her right fingertips are tinted pink. I also see, on her forearm, three mosquito bites.

"Guys, I think it was the moss—the longer we were in contact with it, the worse it affects us, maybe? Maybe it's some kind of poison ivy?"

"Great," Alexa says. "How do you fix *that*?"

"Soap and water? For poison ivy, anyway," I say. "No clue if that would work for us."

"Do we have soap?" Hope asks.

"Well . . . no. Maybe water will be enough?"

Alexa snorts. "So we went through everything only to arrive at a deserted island where girls just vanish in the night without a trace—and we hear water but can't see it—and now it has poisonous moss. *Excellent*." She walks past us and winces when a long, thin leaf barely brushes against her calf. "Congratulations," she says, not bothering to look back. "I am now officially motivated to find water." As if a nearly dry Havenwater bottle wasn't motivation enough.

This time, it's Hope who is slow to follow.

"What?" I ask, trying desperately to ignore the burn on the backs of my legs. For once, Alexa is eager—and I am eager for the same reasons—but Hope doesn't budge.

"It's weird, right?" Hope's voice has such presence for being so quiet. "She would have turned back to look for us, I think."

Finnley.

She is an invisible force among us, the reason we ventured into the jungle in the first place. And yet, she is a viper in the trees, a black widow in the leaves: a truth we are reluctant to face.

I don't know how to respond.

Hope already knows there's a lot more to the island than what we've seen. She knows Finnley could have taken any number of routes, for any number of reasons. That even if she'd turned back to look for us, the point was, it was unlikely we'd find one another before nightfall.

And I think she knows, on some level—because she knows Finnley better than the rest of us—that Finnley wouldn't have gone off by herself in the first place.

That's just something we've all been pretending to believe to make one another feel better.

I slap another mosquito, flick it to the jungle floor, and try not to think about how quickly life can end when someone with more size and strength simply wants to be a little more comfortable.

"Yeah," I admit, to myself as much as anyone. Nothing in the field guide prepared me for this. "It's weird."

NINETEEN

I'M NOT SURE there's a living soul left on the earth who'd be able to pick the real me out of a lineup of look-alikes. Whatever has become of Finnley, at least she has that: someone who knows her. Someone who knows her well.

The day before Zero was full of all the things I never knew I'd miss.

Live-tweeting the Kiera Holloway movie marathon with Emma, who'd been my best friend since kindergarten—how frustrated we were that our apps kept freezing from service outages. We'd stuffed our faces with the s'mores Dad made, with the too-hot marshmallows that oozed like lava when we bit into them.

And then, after the marathon ended, I met up with Birch to watch the surfers ride their waves. It was unseasonably cold out for a Sunday in September, especially after the sun fell below the horizon at our backs. He'd stripped down a layer so I could warm up. If I try, I can still remember how soft his flannel shirtsleeves felt against my skin, how the fabric was warm like him, how it smelled like spearmint shower gel and the coffee we'd picked up on the way.

It's the little things I miss, really.

Like with Emma: even before I saw her at school the next morning, I knew she'd have her hair braided like Kiera's in the movie, a deliberately messy fishtail with shimmery gold thread woven in.

And Dad: when he brought us hot cocoa to go with our s'mores, he'd stuffed each of our favorite mugs with marshmallows, and even remembered to sprinkle cinnamon and cayenne pepper and sea salt on top of Emma's. She'd preferred it that way since we were six.

I miss everything about Birch. But when I try to remember him, it's not his face I see, or the ten shades of blue in his eyes, or the calluses he had on his hands from playing his beat-up guitar. Instead, I see the frayed edges of his flip-flops, loose threads and broken stitches. I see the pineapple air freshener that hung from his rearview mirror, smell its faux-fruit sweetness mixed with dust from his air-conditioning vents. I remember that flannel shirt, the one blue button he sewed on when he lost the original red one, the way he always rolled up his sleeves, no matter the season. How he had more than enough money to buy new things, but loved the comfort and predictability of spending his life with the things he knew. Perhaps that's why he spent so much time with me.

Those are the irreplaceable things.

Even if we get our movies back, and our shimmery gold threads, and our starlets and screenplays and glossy magazine covers—even if we get our marshmallows, our chocolate, our mugs with rainbow handles and clouds on them—even if we get our surfboards, our sandcastles, our soft summer nights—

It isn't the same as knowing someone as well as you know yourself.

It isn't the same as being known.

TWENTY

ON OUR THIRD pass through this stretch of trees, we skirt the edges of the main path, even venture into the wild overgrowth—we are relatively certain now that no fangs or forked tongues await us. Still, we're careful to push leaves aside with our stakes, mostly to avoid contact with the plants. The fiery stinging of the poisonous moss hasn't let up at all; we're not eager to meet more.

"You guys!" Alexa calls, from a shadowy area on the far side of the path. "I think I found something!" She bends down, disappears behind a fern. When she stands again, she holds up her stake: the end of it is slick with mud. "There's a ton of it over here—and it gets soupier this way—"

Alexa cuts herself off, glances at us only briefly before taking off. She darts deep into the jungle, far from the path. Hope and I run after her, careful to avoid the mud so we don't get stuck in it.

But all at once, without warning, she vanishes.

A scream pierces the air, clearly Alexa's. I look high into the tree canopy—maybe she's been caught up in some sort of trap? I remember one from Emma's favorite Kiera Holloway movie, a net that scooped its unsuspecting prisoners into a precarious, dangling bundle. There's nothing like that here, though. Nothing but treetops as far as I can see.

Hope cautiously steps toward the spot where Alexa disappeared. I follow, stopping suddenly when we hear Alexa again, calling out for us.

"Look *down*," she cries.

Hope and I exchange a glance. Look down? There's nothing but mud and foliage at our feet.

"Try not to fall, though," Alexa says.

Gingerly, I inch forward, lean in toward her voice—and then I understand. It's an illusion, like how we could see the island only from certain places on our sailboat. I understand the *what* of this, anyway, but not the how. Not the why.

I pull Hope up so she can see it, too. "Whoa," she breathes.

The land drops off a mere few feet in front of us. Across the chasm, which is narrow and quite deep, the jungle looks every bit as dense as it has for hours. It would have been very, very easy to step straight off the cliff's edge without meaning to, especially if we'd been running as fast as Alexa.

I peer over the edge, finally see her. She's standing on a wide, smooth ledge about twelve feet down—the cliff wall is a jagged mess of rock ledges, better than a sheer drop, but only slightly. Way down at the bottom, a stream trips on itself for as far as I can see in both directions. No wonder we've been hearing water all this time. A troubling notion strikes me: what if there are more of these illusions? What if Finnley is still back near the beach somewhere and we just couldn't see her?

I keep this thought to myself for now. I can only imagine how *perhaps this terrible day has been for nothing* would take the wind out of everyone's sails.

"Are you all right?" Hope calls down. "Did you break anything?"

I don't see any blood on the ledge, and she's okay enough to stand. Those seem like promising signs.

"Landed a little hard, might have sprained my ankle a bit? Hopefully not?" she says. "Nothing feels *too* excruciating. I can stand—and walk—ungh. Legs are still burning like crazy, though. It's going to be hell getting down to the water."

I can relate. It's as if needles and pins cover every inch of flesh, sharp and shifting with each slight movement. My nerves are on fire. Clambering down the side of a cliff wall would be tough enough on a normal day, thanks to my rather severe distaste for heights—add in the burning on the back of my thighs, and I'd almost rather jump and pray for wings on the free fall.

Otherwise, it looks like the hardest part will be getting down to the first ledge, where Alexa is—from there, the rocky shelves are closer together. Not all of them are this wide, and some look more prone to crumbling, but for the most part we should be able to use them like stairs.

We come up with a plan: I'm taller than Hope, so the jump to that first ledge won't be as drastic for me. She and I clasp wrists while she lowers herself down to Alexa, who spots her. We'll do something similar on the way back up, we decide, pile on top of one another until we reach the highest ledge. If necessary, whoever's at the top can make a rope out of vines to help the others climb back up.

Hope makes it down just fine, and I land without too much trouble. My ankles sting from the impact, but everything else is on fire, so the pain blends right in. We take careful steps down the cliff's rocky face, cling for our lives. Our shoes scrape loose pebbles and send them flying. It's a long, steep downward climb.

I spend most of our descent looking straight up—at the clouds, at the trees, at everything towering high above us that makes me feel closer to the ground than I actually am—so I won't be staring at how far we'll plummet if the ledges give out.

But the ledges don't give out, and neither do we, and just as the sky turns to dusk we dip ourselves into the stream. It's cold and clear, deeper than it looks. The others stay close to the bank, but I'm tall enough to go to its deepest point, where it comes all the way up to my shoulders. The water dulls the pain in my legs almost immediately. After this long and discouraging day, I'm savoring our hard-won victory.

"This"—Alexa dips her head under, and when she resurfaces, her black hair falls like freshly ironed silk around her face— "was worth it."

"Feeling better, then?" Hope is the only one of us actively trying to get clean: she sits on the pebbly bank, scrubbing and scratching at the layers of dirt that cake her feet.

"You have no idea," Alexa says.

The breeze in the leaves, the cool water—it is almost *peaceful*.

"Um . . . guys?" Hope examines the crook of her elbow, rubs vigorously at it. "Does this look weird to you?"

I swim closer to where she sits on the bank, and she slips into the water to meet me. "Looks like all of your other mosquito bites," I say, when I've seen it up close. "Does it itch? Don't scratch them, they'll get infected more easily."

She shrugs, twisting her arm to compare the spot with the constellation of bites on the other side. "It almost looks like . . . a needle mark?"

"I think you would have noticed someone stabbing you in the arm with a sharp object," Alexa says. She dips under the water again, shakes out her hair.

"It really does look like all your other bites," I say. "Or maybe you were stung by something else?"

Hope digs her fingertips into her temples, shakes her head. "Ugh! I am *so freaking paranoid*!" Her broken voice echoes from the walls of the ravine. "I was sleeping *two feet away* from her." A pair of tears make twin ripples in her reflection.

"What happened with Finnley is not your fault, Hope."

I am the preacher, I am the choir.

Hope is not the one who heard things in the night.

We stay in the water until stars fill the thin strip of sky directly above us. It's like stepping into a freezer when we finally emerge—the ravine could be a certifiable wind tunnel, and on top of that, we have nothing to dry off with. And we don't have a fire. Or our box of matches, or blankets, or clean socks. Or anything that might pass as warmth.

All we have is one another.

So, like it or not, we huddle up, as close to the ravine wall as we can get. We should probably be afraid of everything we don't know—and everything we *do* know—and the risk of sleeping in a riverbed that could be so easily flooded if a storm were to pop up in the night—but we're too cold, too exhausted.

"I miss blankets." Hope's voice is quiet, barely more than a whisper. "I miss my cat."

"I had a cat, too," Alexa says after a moment. "He hated me. Still miss him, though." She's quiet for a beat, then adds, "I miss my grandmother's piano. How she used to give lessons."

I miss so much, too much. More than I'm ready to say out loud. "I miss chocolate," I say. It's a surface-level truth, a plant with deep roots. Really, I miss Dad making hot chocolate. I miss sharing it with Emma. With Birch.

Hope shifts, shivers. I peel my cardigan off, offer it to her. She stretches it out, wide enough so we both fit underneath. Alexa moves in closer, too.

"I hope Finnley's okay," Hope says.

Our whispers turn to silence under the infinite sea of stars. I'm the last to fall asleep, I think.

It's the deepest I've slept in as long as I can remember.

TWENTY-ONE

IT'S THE FORGETTING that's the hardest: those quiet, still moments just after waking, the blissful peace of a girl who never lost everything she ever loved.

It's the forgetting that's the hardest, because how could I forget?

The heavy weight that slams, faithfully, into me every morning—well, most mornings; some mornings I never feel peace at all—has become more peaceful than peace. Like it means I *remember*. Like I'm not the world's worst daughter, or girlfriend, for feeling whole when I should be broken, calm when I should be frayed, warm when I should feel the cold air of their absence.

Should.

It's the forgetting that's the hardest. And the remembering, too.

TWENTY-TWO

BEFORE, I HARDLY ever woke up with the sun unless it was a Saturday to be spent on the water. In order to sail out to our favorite island for a lunchtime picnic, we'd have to head out by eight. We'd get up early, sometimes so early the thumbnail sliver of a crescent moon was still bright white, to put fruit and Goldfish crackers and peanut-butter-and-honey sandwiches into Ziploc bags. Dad always prepped his fancy coffeemaker the night before with enough beans for each of us to fill our travel mugs to their brims.

The girl I was Before would not recognize the girl I've become.

The grasshoppers, for example. I've eaten six this morning—for a protein boost, according to the field guide—and I think they may still be alive inside me. Otherwise, the tickles and jabs in my stomach aren't from wings, or antennae, or the spindly legs that felt like fish bones as they slid down my throat. And this is no Saturday morning picnic: we are on a mission. Our plan is to search for the temple until midday. Whether we find it or not, we'll head back to our beach clearing after that. Hopefully Finnley will be waiting for us in one of those places.

We've been trekking since dawn, following along the stream in hopes of finding the temple. The ravine itself is too narrow for any sort of structure, but perhaps there's at least an entrance, some easy way for its residents to access water. Sticking close to the stream helps with our water issues, too—when we've drained what's left in our Havenwater bottle, we'll be able to fill it one last time before the cartridge dies. We'll boil and sterilize our freshly replenished canteen water as soon as we return to camp.

Alexa's stomach growls so loudly it echoes from the cliff wall. She tries to reach into the yellow cardigan for an emergency bar, but Hope swats her hand away—we're trying to eat grasshoppers while they're in rich supply, since we won't be in the ravine forever. Our stash of emergency bars isn't endless.

Hope carries my yellow cardigan, knotted at the sleeves and corners, like we all used to carry Coach and Kate Spade purses. She slings it around and digs deeply into one of its pockets. "Grasshopper?" she offers, holding one out to Alexa.

None of our designer bags, on the inside, ever looked like: wallet, iPhone, lip gloss, sunglasses, pockets full of thoraxes.

Alexa wrinkles her nose. Again. This is the fourth time Hope's tried to get her to eat, and the fourth time she's refused.

"I'm just saying, you'll feel a lot better if you eat one," Hope says, popping one of the particularly lime-colored grasshoppers into her mouth. A hundred muscles in her face fight one another as she tries to make the experience look pleasant.

"Yeah. *Right.* I think I'm good."

I take one for myself—because I *should*, not because I want to—and choke it down.

The ravine is mind-numbingly monotonous. Steep, pebbled cliffs stretch high above our heads, and the tree canopy stretches endlessly higher. The stream runs away from us, affirming my feeling that we're heading toward the middle of the island and not the coast. Branches, shoots, and roots poke out from the cliff walls like the outstretched limbs of the thirsty and neglected. In an emergency, they'll be our closest shot at an escape plan—the rock ledges aren't consistently solid or close together. It isn't exactly comforting.

"How much farther until we can turn back for the beach?" Alexa asks. She's been mostly tolerable ever since Hope lashed out at her near the poison-moss rocks, but the day is wearing on her already. Her ankle's tender, she says, but not so bad she can't put weight on it. Personally, I'm impressed with how well she's keeping up. All things considered, she could be complaining a lot more.

"Another hour or so," I say, but that is no more true or untrue than if I'd just announced we would certainly find the temple before we turn back. I have no idea what time it is—Alexa's watch was purely for show, and the sun is mostly obscured by trees. I'm basing pretty much everything on my somewhat unreliable internal clock. And the truth is, anyone can say anything, really.

We walk and walk, straight forever and then around a bend. Like yesterday, I can't help but feel frustrated by how silent Dad was about the specifics of this place—for all his meticulous detail, he sure left out some important bits of information.

Unless he, too, was caught off guard by the strange things here. Maybe he never got the chance to write about them.

Maybe he discovered the cliff, and the ravine, exactly like Alexa did.

Maybe he wasn't as lucky when he fell.

I shove the thought away. Focus on life, not death. On survival.

Four grasshopper snacks later, something bright and narrow stands out amid all the brown. I squint. "Is that . . . a bridge?" It's still a long way off, and partially obscured by another bend in the ravine.

Hope and I pick up our pace. Alexa matches it, quick on her feet despite any lingering ankle strain. The closer we get, the more apparent it is that we have indeed come upon a bridge—but not just *one* bridge. It's a whole system of them, angled like escalators, a way of getting out of the ravine. They look a bit rickety, all frayed ropes and jagged planks, with gaping holes where the worn wooden boards have fallen out like beggars' teeth.

But they're the only way up. And we can't go any farther, because the ravine dead-ends with a stony wall covered in moss. If there's any sort of entrance here, it's extremely well-hidden. Still, the presence of a bridge is enough to spark my hope— bridges don't build themselves.

We drink what's left of our clean water, not that there's

much, then fill the Havenwater bottle to its brim. Our stream ducks under the wall's gaps, twists through its cracks. We won't see water again for a while, I'd bet.

"Coming?" Hope says, stepping precariously up the first inclined bridge. She's tougher than she looks, much tougher than I initially gave her credit for. "We should probably try to space ourselves out, cross one at a time—it doesn't feel super sturdy."

Alexa waits for Hope to cross the first bridge, then begins the climb. I'm last. The boards are narrow and far apart, tied to the ropes with only one knot on each end. They creak and bend—one bends so much it starts to splinter. Quickly, I shift to the next board, and the next. The bridges jolt and sway despite our efforts to stay steady.

If we'd studied the bridges before we began to climb—*really* studied them, instead of just glass-half-full assuming they'd all be functional enough—we would've noticed the next bridge in front of Hope has no planks on it. As in zero boards to step on. As in ropes only.

Six body lengths below, three body lengths above: it's high enough to break us if we fall. If we can just make it past this bridge, the last two look relatively secure. Turning back would leave us right where we started, wandering the base of a ravine with only grasshoppers for food, and no fire to purify our water.

"So," I say. "Who's going first?"

"I'll do it," Alexa says, which surprises me. It's only when she volunteers that I realize I've spoken just for the sake of acknowledging the challenge before us—I assumed Hope would continue on in the lead. Or that I would, if she was tired of going first.

But Alexa is serious. "Toss the supplies up to me when I'm on the other side—it's best if we go one at a time." Gingerly, she makes her way up to the bridge where Hope stands. She shimmies out onto the solitary rope, grinning. "We did ropes courses at camp every summer when I was a kid."

I make careful note of how she holds herself, how she moves, so I can do the same. Facedown on the rope, she stretches her arms out in front while keeping her stronger leg bent, hooked around the fraying line. She makes it look easy, the way she pulls herself across. Hope and I toss the cardigan, Havenwater bottle, and canteens to Alexa when she's firmly on the other side; only our grasshoppers don't make it, drifting hopelessly from pocket to ravine pit. We pass our spears up with more success.

Hope eases out next. Her movements aren't as fluid as Alexa's, and she isn't as fast, but she makes it to the next bridge in one unbroken piece.

Single-rope bridges aren't my strong suit, it turns out. Positioning myself is awkward, and the rope feels like it could slice through me. Its frayed pieces poke at my bare legs, burn as I struggle to pull myself across. This is all arms, all balance. And a mind game, as I have nowhere to look but down. My mouth goes dry; my palms start to sweat.

"Flip upside down if you need to!" Alexa calls out, the

unlikely cheerleader. "Cross your ankles over the rope and hang like a monkey—then you can use your legs more."

I'm hesitant, when my arm muscles are already screaming, and when my palms are this slick, to flip upside down and hang. Especially when I haven't had the benefit of seeing someone else do it first. Then, though, at least I could look at the sky, instead of how far up I am. And maybe it'd be over sooner.

"Okay," I say. "I'm going for it."

I bolt my ankles together, let myself flip. My father's ring slips from where I've tucked it behind my shirt, tugging the chain around my throat, heavy and choking. Gravity wants nothing more than to suck me down into a jagged, hard embrace. I grit my teeth and give everything I have—otherwise I'll *lose* everything I have. The rope shakes and sways, my arms tremble violently, my hands are slippery with sweat. But soon, Alexa and Hope are there, helping me up to the next bridge.

The final bridges are like a dream compared with the nightmare of everything before them. We practically float to the top.

Hope leads the way. "You guys . . ." Her voice trails off, but it doesn't matter. Alexa and I see the view for ourselves soon enough.

We've found it.

The temple.

TWENTY-THREE

THE TEMPLE IS a sprawling mass of stone and moss, rough and unrefined, yet delicate. Intricate carvings cover the walls, the arches and geometric patterns and runelike symbols all cut directly into the stone. Some of the carvings are incredibly complex, like the entire wall full of three-dimensional jungle creature statues.

It looks ancient, like whoever lived here before must have died out long ago. Parts of the temple seem strong enough to withstand whatever nature might throw at it, while other parts are more . . . weathered. Like the entire section off to the right; its walls lie in crumbled heaps amid the jungle's hungry tentacles.

The temple itself might just be the most amazing thing I've ever seen—tree roots that have grown right up over the walls, holding them in place like the hands of God, repeating patterns so perfect it's hard to imagine a person carving them without the help of a machine—but it is disconcerting and eerie to see it so wounded and abandoned. Alexa, Hope, and I trek around its perimeter, looking for any sign of the monks who supposedly live here.

"Hello?" I call out. "Anyone?"

"Finnley?" Hope's voice ricochets from the stone walls. "Are you in there? Hello?"

No one comes to greet us, but it could be worse. No one comes to kill us, either.

My father was not a liar, my father was not a liar. *Temples hiding among ferns, structures formed of stones and secrets.* The temple is here, so are the ferns and the stones.

The secrets: if only they were so plainly seen.

We come to a series of moss-covered arches held in place by thick stone pillars. I take a deep breath, swallow down the fear that's started a slow climb up my throat. "This must be where we go inside."

But honestly, I'm hesitant about going inside. If we were welcome here, we would have been greeted already. Right?

Neither of the others makes a move. Hope looks wary, like me, but Alexa is a live wire. "Are you kidding me?" she says, kicking a pillar so hard dust flies out of it. "You still honestly believe this place is going to be a refuge for us? You are out of your mind, Eden. Look around. Whoever lived here before couldn't even keep themselves alive. We haven't seen a single animal bigger than a bug since we got here. Not one fish. Don't you think that's weird?"

"I—yes," I say, after a beat. "I admit that it's weird." Why does nothing about this island make sense?

"I mean," she goes on, "how are we going to eat? I'm already starved out of my mind—"

Hope plucks a grasshopper from a nearby rock, dangles it in front of her face. "Hungry?"

Alexa scowls. "*Not* the point." She kicks another pillar. "This entire mission has been one giant fail. I think it's pretty obvious Finnley only wanted to get away from us, not hide out in some old ruined temple."

"You didn't have to come with us, Alexa," I say. It takes effort to keep my exasperation from full-on steaming out of me. I don't think she honestly believes a word she just said, and I challenge her on it: "If you didn't believe we would find her out here, why didn't you just stay at the beach?"

"Right, like *that* would have gone over well."

Hope walks toward the arches, doesn't wait for us to follow. "We're already here," she says. "Might as well look around." Her ponytail is lower, dirtier than on the day we met, and she's cuffed her grimy pants just below her knees. I suspect she may be tougher on the inside, too.

"Finnl—*aghhhh!*" Hope screams, recoiling.

Alexa and I rush up to meet her, under the first arch. A thin line of blood slices horizontally across her shin, but there's nothing overtly dangerous anywhere near her.

I dig in my back pocket, hand her one of our last remaining pieces of path-marking fabric. "Here," I say. "To blot the blood. Best to let it air-dry for now—we'll clean it back at camp after the water's sterile." I keep to myself the details about how quickly wounds can get infected out here. How could I have neglected to bring our box of matches?

"Where exactly did this happen?" I ask, and Hope shows us.

After a quick search of the jungle floor, I find some long leaves like the ones I used to weave our mats. Carefully, at the same height as the blood on Hope's leg, I wave one of the leaves around. With a sizzle, something invisible slices the leaf clean in half.

"Um," I say. "So, that's not good."

"Neither is this," Alexa says. She's over by the wall, pointing at one of its smaller intricate carvings. I take a closer look, and my stomach drops.

The wolf's face would have been easy to overlook amid the other carvings. Someone took great care to carve it in the same style as the others, to place it on one of the heavily decorated walls where it wouldn't stick out. It is too much like the one on Alexa's wrist, too much like the ones plastered on so much propaganda back home. This is no coincidence.

"This is supposed to be neutral territory," I say. And it still could be, I suppose. But I never imagined sanctuary, and amnesty, and peace, and neutrality, to look so derelict. I hoped this place would be further removed from the people who stole our peace. I hoped it would be thriving. I hoped my father's words would lead us to freedom.

I hoped.

Alexa shakes her head. "This is classic Wolfpack," she says, running her thumb over the carving. "Hiding in plain sight."

She depresses the wolf's face, and a web of electric-blue laser-like beams crisscrosses through the entire length of the arched path. The first crosses in the exact place where Hope sliced her leg. This quantity of highly advanced technology—the hostility of it—it is *not* good. Alexa's face is paler than I've ever seen it, and for the first time, I see fear on it. Her eyes are bright and glassy, the deepest brown with laser blue reflected in them.

I guess she wasn't lying, after all, about only wanting to run away.

TWENTY-FOUR

I WORK THROUGH all I see, measure it against all I know.

"We don't *know* they're Wolfpack," I say, as much for Alexa as for myself. "If the Wolfpack helped set things up here for Sanctuary in the first place, it makes sense that there'd be some overlap in their security systems." I tread carefully, leave Dad out of it—that it took his life, possibly his *death*, for me to know what I know. "Doesn't necessarily mean the people inside are hostile, right? Maybe it just means they want to control who goes in and out."

Even though I don't admit it, I'm not entirely convinced we'll find anyone inside at all. If our voices weren't enough to alert them to our presence, surely Hope tripping the laser system would've done the trick. Then again, why go to the trouble of having a merciless laser system at all if there isn't something inside to protect?

"I vote we quit while we're ahead," Alexa says. "Finnley definitely wouldn't have made it inside—she'd be, like, in pieces from all the lasers."

"That's terrible, Alexa," Hope says.

But it's the truth. It doesn't seem possible to outsmart the laser system. The beams are too low to the ground, too close together—too everything—and we'd end up a lacerated, bleeding mess before we even reached the second arch.

"Maybe . . . ," I say, not sure if I should tell them what I'm thinking. Because if what I'm thinking turns out to be true, it would mean Finnley was deliberately stolen from our camp. There's no way she would have made it through these lasers without help—and help didn't make itself known when we asked for it, so why should it be any different for her?

I come out and say it, because if those things are true, she might need us to find her. "Finnley could be trapped in there." If I'm honest, though, Finnley isn't the only reason I want to get inside. I can't stand the thought of turning back after all we've been through when we're this close—I have to know if there's anything inside. If *any* part of what Dad wrote is true.

"Well, I don't really care about Finnley," Alexa says, and Hope makes a face. "What? It's not like I know the girl, and she pretty much accused me of being a *kingpin* the other night. Can you blame me?"

The kingpins are our generation's tyrants, the ones who led an insurgent movement inside the Wolfpack once they'd already established power. Each rules over one of the five enormous—formerly fifty not-so-enormous—United States. They're the ones who planted and pruned their connections inside the Pentagon, the CIA, the White House, Hollywood, the Ivy Leagues, even the Red Cross. They're also the ones who took down Envirotech, where my father worked. My father is most likely rotting somewhere, while his traitorous coworker, Anton Zhornov—the reason they were able to take down Envirotech at all—was named fifth kingpin in the pentumvirate.

They live like royals, how they *think* royals should live. They live like power isn't proven until you've well and truly crushed someone—and no one calls them on their hypocrisy, because the underdog-to-alpha story is just rags-to-riches, glorified. They're so lauded by their own for breaking the cycle of privilege in power, people don't realize they've simply traded one broken thing for another.

Power tastes like blood to the Wolves, and one drop isn't enough.

"Why are you so afraid of your own people, Alexa?" Hope's eyes are hard. "What did you do?"

I forget that Hope doesn't know what I know, that Alexa set off the explosions that flushed us out; I haven't told her because I didn't want to jeopardize what little trust we've built. If anyone back at barracks put the pieces together, and if the people inside this temple are indeed Wolves, and if they maintain regular communication with people back on the shore—I can understand why Alexa doesn't want to push her luck.

But Alexa would rather push her luck than spill her secrets to Hope, apparently. "I'm not afraid," she says. And the look on her face, all coldness and sharp corners, as stony as the walls that surround us, betrays nothing of the fear I most definitely saw before. "In fact, I'll lead the way."

* * *

Despite every warning siren going off in my head, I suggest we attempt to enter somewhere else: the crumbled-to-pieces section we saw when we first arrived.

Hope shifts her weight off her injured leg. The bleeding has already dried into a dark, crusty line. "So breaking in through the unsecured part is going to win their favor?" She shakes her head. "I don't know, you guys."

But in the end, that is exactly what we do.

We test every step with leaves, waving them in front of us as we climb to make sure there's nothing waiting to slice us in half. So far—halfway up the rubble—so good. No bleeding legs or spliced leaves, no thick covering of poisoned moss.

I hear Alexa groan. "I'm going to sleep for a full day when we get back to the beach."

"Same," Hope says. "I'm going to sleep *forever.*"

For once, we are on the same page. My muscles ache from all the walking we've done, and from the rope bridge. A day spent with sun, sand, and the constant crash of ocean waves sounds incredibly therapeutic right now. Perhaps we should have just accepted the Sanctuary we'd already found and been happy with that.

Once we're at the top of the heap, I feel a surge of pride. "I think I see an opening!" From this angle, it's obvious the rubble used to be a wall, and that we're standing in the middle of an open courtyard. Most of the courtyard's inner walls are still intact, but there's a thin vertical strip of black toward the back corner. Carefully, we make our way over to it. It is indeed a way in.

"We've come this far," I say. "Let's go."

We encounter no lasers, no security measures of any kind. We're cautious, quiet. We listen for sounds of life, sounds of struggle. Other than the soft brush of our footsteps against stone, the temple is completely silent.

It's also dark most of the way, except for occasional small patches of light that come in through cracks in the walls. Finally, the tunnel dumps us out into an open space like a rotunda, with carved-window ceilings that let light in whenever the leaves shift in the breeze. The air is cool but stale, with a strong ripeness to it. I don't want to know what might be hiding in the shadows. If only some of the breeze would find its way inside.

"You guys."

There's something unsettling about the way Hope says this—she sounds like someone who's noticed the first crack in the snow as it becomes an avalanche, like if she keeps her voice calm enough it will stop the town below from being buried. She stands facing the far wall, muscles stiff and rigid. In this meager light, I can't quite see what she's found.

"The shadows," she says, in that same careful tone. "I think they're alive."

I hear them before I see them: the scuttle of thousands of tiny limbs, the *click-clack* of shells as they scurry haphazardly down the wall. It's like a waterfall, this mass of beetles, this thick and heavy and determined swarm that pours toward the floor over every inch of the stone walls. More and more spill out through the cracks, thick bodies materializing through the thinnest gaps. The floor is a black, shimmery carpet now. It's hard to move without the crunch of life underfoot.

"I think maybe it's time to get out of here." My attempt at replicating Hope's careful voice comes down like my heels on the beetles' heads—sudden, blunt, final.

"They're *on* me!" Hope shrieks, shaking her leg. Several fall off, but more climb up in their place. "I think they're trying to eat me!"

Beetles don't eat people, is all I can think. I've scoured Dad's field guide more times than I can count, and beetles are not listed in the dangerous insects section.

Yet, for the most part, they swarm past Alexa's ankles, and they swarm past mine. They climb up Hope, on her right leg only, and not even all the way up to her knee.

They stop at the thin line of dried blood on her shin.

Hope brushes more beetles away, and a fresh trickle of red drips down her leg. She wipes that away, too, staining the heel of her hand. More beetles scurry up, frenzied.

They live for blood, I realize.

And not only that: they look well fed.

TWENTY-FIVE

"CLIMB ON MY back," I say. "It'll be harder for them to get to you."

Hope's thin frame isn't as light as it looks. Then again, she looks like dandelion wisps that could be blown away by a child, so I shouldn't be surprised that her bones and flesh and spirit pack more weight than is visible.

The beetles are already onto our attempt to outsmart them: they scurry up my legs, each tiny step like a freshly sterilized needle on my skin.

"Alexa"—I'm breathless from kicking them off, stomping on more, trying not to lose my balance—"grab the last two strips of fabric from my pocket. Use one to wipe the blood from Hope's leg, and tie the other around it to keep them off!" Kick, kick, stomp, *stomp*. "Toss the bloody one on the ground—maybe it'll throw them off enough to give us a head start."

Alexa throws the rag several feet from where we're standing, and it works, at least for a few glorious seconds.

"Run!" I say, trampling over the horde of beetles as they swarm in the opposite direction, toward the rag.

A few stragglers—the smart ones—keep trying to climb up

my legs, but I kick them off. Alexa and I run, back into the dark and winding tunnel, as fast as I can manage with Hope on my back. I try not to think about the blackness, about the *click-clack* scuttle that follows us, about the silent things that could be even more dangerous, or even deadly. I try not to think about how very, very far off the temple is from everything I so desperately wanted it to be.

I force myself to think other thoughts, better thoughts. My panicked mind lands on, of all things, how my mother used to smell like spring-rain fabric softener. I imagine her being there to greet me, on the other side of darkness, ready to stuff my sweaty clothes into our front-loader washing machine. I imagine the bubbles piling up against its window, watching them like I did when I was maybe four or five years old. I imagine taking a shower, the smooth lather of soap and the fresh scent of clean, fluffy towels. I imagine falling asleep in soft sheets, then waking to a day of sunshine and buttered toast and *Good morning, Eden!*

But once we reach the end of the tunnel, I have to face reality in the broad light of day. I never had some of those things, and I never will.

Hope scrambles off me when we're close to the edge of the courtyard, even though many of the beetles still hunt us. The bandage Alexa tied around Hope's leg seems to be doing its job well enough—it's like they can still smell her blood, so they follow, but the makeshift bandage masks the exact source of it. We climb up over the rubble, not at all tentative like we were when we first arrived.

It's odd, the way the beetles struggle in an attempt to follow us beyond the temple's ruined wall: they climb over one another, burrow under one another, until they are a mass of flailing appendages piled up against some invisible barrier.

Not one is able to break through.

I bend, hands on knees, catch my breath. That was intense, and baffling, and a thousand other words that wouldn't be strong enough.

Hope shifts, examining the innumerable pinprick red dots covering her leg. They cover mine, too, in all the places where the beetles stepped.

"So," she says, breathless, "was that 'classic Wolfpack,' too?"

Alexa gathers our pile of supplies, the sharp-tipped spears and cardigan-wrapped bundle of supplies we had to leave outside in order to climb the rubble in the first place. She throws a sharp glance toward the beetles, who are still scrambling over one another, trying to get at us and failing. "I don't know what the hell that was."

TWENTY-SIX

MY FIRST AND only bee sting happened on my eleventh birthday, right after I'd blown out the candles. It was the most perfect day in May—pre-sting—not only because of the deep blue sky and the scratch-made chocolate cake my father had toiled over past midnight the night before, but also because of Birch.

Emma's parents had just been through the most harrowing divorce over the holidays, introducing our entire class to terms like *prenuptial agreement* and *homewrecker* and *life in prison*. Emma herself had been hopelessly scarred over what her father had done to her mother's lover—the thing that earned him life in prison, and eventually death there, too. But it wasn't like she had to tell anyone what had happened for them to find out. Everyone just seemed to *know*, thanks to the segments they ran on the nightly news for more than a month. And for some reason, everyone avoided Emma as if her parents' sins were something she had inherited from them. As if they were contagious, able to be caught by simply making eye contact.

So when Emma arrived at the park for my party, in the spotless white sundress her mother had pinched pennies to buy, there was an eternal second where *this was a mistake* hung in the air. Not because I didn't want her there—I very much did—but because I didn't want her there if it was going to be the same as school, where kids were cruel and the days ended with Emma shrinking into herself, hiding behind her stick-straight brown hair.

But Birch.

Birch—who was just another kid in my class at the time, who I mainly knew because he was exceptional at spelling and always won our Friday-afternoon bees—gave her the biggest grin.

"Got a seat over here, E," he said. No one called her E, but apparently Birch could, and from then on, Birch did. And because he was popular with the guys, and crushed-upon among the girls, they all parted like the Red Sea there at the picnic table, making an E-sized space just for her.

The bee sting came just after I'd wished for Birch. Suddenly, he wasn't merely the cute, popular boy who could perfectly spell things like *phlegmatic* and *onomatopoeia* on the first try—he was the boy who'd single-handedly stopped my best friend's trajectory toward social implosion.

There've been a lot of things like that over the years, bee-sting-on-a-perfect-birthday things that aren't as they should be.

Like how Emma, a girl with a heart-shaped face and sugar-spice soul, could turn into a social disease just because of her parents' drama that she had nothing to do with.

Like how Birch was able to reverse months of wrongness

with one simple phrase. Even though it was a good thing, it was odd, how easily and permanently things changed.

Like how I wished for Birch, and then got him, only to lose him in the end. Like how I somehow, foolishly, thought that a wish came with forever attached to it.

And now, after everything, if there's one thing that should just be *right*, it should be Sanctuary. We made it out of the gulag alive, managed not to get blown to pieces on the beach. We sailed, survived the open ocean, made it to the island. We found the temple, even. The fact that there's a temple here at all validates so much of what we set out to find.

But it isn't peace we've found, after all.

It was our last hope in this broken, chaotic world. Where is there to go from here?

TWENTY-SEVEN

OUR TREK BACK to the clearing is a strained, uneasy endeavor.

At least it won't take as long as the first: rather than following the ravine back to the earlier paths we took, we marked out a more direct route to the beach using the map and notes I made. We should be back to our clearing within a couple of hours, according to our estimations.

Those hours cannot pass quickly enough.

Alexa was right; this mission really has been one giant fail. At least we found water—at least we'll be able to keep ourselves alive out here for a few more days. But for what? There is no Sanctuary, only strange upon strange. Did my father really give up everything for *this*?

Not that he had much left—but we did have each other.

In the first days after Zero, in barracks, you couldn't walk two feet without seeing someone who'd been destroyed by what had gone down. Half the girls in my division quarters had been torn from their home regions; most had seen loved ones killed or abused. We were the orphaned and heartbroken, the stray and confused.

All things considered, I was one of the lucky ones.

Dad and I had been close for as long as I could remember. I loved my mother, too, of course. But when all her love started bleeding out after the accident, Dad and I salvaged as much as we could and poured it all back into each other. In those first days at barracks especially, I never felt the freedom to grieve—not when Dad was in the men's quarters, the next division over, and the other girls had lost everything.

We saw each other so often back then, despite his being stationed with all the other over-thirties, doing hard manual labor at the seawall and the artificial reefs. It was weird, though. I'd known Dad so well, for so long, but never knew how hollow his face could look just under his cheekbones. And I'd never considered that his beard would become speckled with gray, especially since he'd always kept himself clean-shaven before. He'd been something of a health nut, too—organic this, grass-fed, free-range that—so it was odd to see him shoveling plain porridge into his mouth, or picking the mold off whatever cheese or bread they piled up for us.

In some ways, that was worse than losing Mom. I never had to see her become someone unrecognizable. I never had to see her at her most miserable.

But then, when Dad was collected by the Wolfpack to help with their mission on Sanctuary Island—and when they brought him back to me in a vial, even more unrecognizable than before—I saw all I'd taken for granted.

I never realized how much of home I'd had with me all that

time. How, even with everything we'd both lost, even with everything we'd been forced to give up, even in the misery of living shadow lives of what we'd had before—we still had each other.

And I never realized just how alone I'd feel when he was gone.

We're just past halfway when the sky breaks open as if it's been smashed with a hammer. Rain falls heavy and hard, with enough force to pierce straight through the tree canopy. Whatever lies beneath the green carpet of leaves—sand or dirt, I'm not sure—turns to thick sludge, sucking on our feet with every step. It feels like the rain has also activated some substance on the green carpet itself—the long, thin leaves cling to my ankles like tentacles.

"How are you here?" Alexa says, behind us.

Hope and I whip around. The tentacle leaves have wrapped themselves completely around both of her ankles, rooting her in place, and she is still.

"Alexa?" I say, but she doesn't seem to hear me, or see me.

"I thought I'd never see you again, Cass," she says, reaching her arms up as if to touch someone. There's an honesty on her face, a soft vulnerability I hadn't imagined possible. It's a different sort of honesty than when I saw her fear—her eyes are wide open, sparkling even, and her cheekbones have lost their edges.

Hope pries herself away from the tentacles that curl around her, steps tentatively toward Alexa. She stands right in front of her face, where it's impossible to ignore her.

And yet, nothing.

This place is not normal, is all I can think. This place is—is—

I blink.

"Birch?" I squint. Tilt my head.

I don't remember him being with me before, but then again, I can't remember who *was* with me, so maybe I'm wrong? And I'm all wet, for some reason, drenched and dripping even though it's perfectly sunny out, and even though Birch is perfectly dry.

"I asked them to put some cinnamon on the whipped cream, just like you like it," he says. I hadn't even noticed the coffee before, but now I can't think of anything else. I reach out to take it from him and it is hot, warming me all the way to my heart, all the way to places that have been frozen for so long. But I can't remember why they were frozen in the first place.

"You're shivering," he says. "Are you cold?"

His flannel shirt smells like campfire smoke, and I have the oddest sensation that there should be a fire burning, that we should be sitting down and not standing. But he wraps the shirt around my bare shoulders, helps me into the sleeves, and buttons the mismatched buttons all the way down, staring with his deep blue eyes into mine the entire time.

And if I thought I was warm again before, with just the coffee, I was wrong, a million times wrong. Because when his lips find mine, I ignite. I could live in this fire forever.

But then he pulls away, and I get the strangest sensation that he meant his kiss as a goodbye, not a hello. And Emma is here now, like a radiant angel, her tan the perfect shade of bronze and her hair in the long mermaid waves she'd never quite been able to attain. She was always beautiful, but never like this. Birch takes her hand in his and they both smile at me, sincere and brilliant.

Their smiles are like knives, carving my heart out. Through the knife slits comes a blast of cold air that pushes out all the warmth I'd finally felt again.

Birch pulls Emma in close. I turn my eyes away, but there they are again. And when I look in the opposite direction, they are there, too. Their lips touch, and even when I shut my eyes as tight as they'll go, when I bury my face in my arms, I can't unsee them. My face is wet, and I get the vague sensation that I'm crying, but then again it might just be the rain that isn't falling on this sunny day.

A knife scrapes at my ankles, at whatever is holding me in place, digging in tighter and tighter until all at once the pressure dissolves and I am standing in a veritable monsoon. No Birch. No Emma.

"Eden, can you hear me?"

I look down, and there's Hope, slicing the tentacle leaves away from my legs with our knife. Alexa is with her, staving off the leaves before they have a chance to take hold again. She and Hope shift from foot to foot, presumably to keep themselves from getting trapped.

"I can—" I start, then clear my throat so my words are actually audible. "I can hear you."

And before I know it, they are on both sides of me, and my feet are moving again. "What," I say, still struggling to catch my breath, "was *that?*"

No one answers. Probably because there are no answers.

Together, we make a lot of progress, and eventually there's no trace of rain, not even a hint of mud, and the leaves are just leaves again, tickling our ankles without latching on.

But while the scenery changes, and the weather changes, my mind is still stuck trying to make sense of Birch, of Emma. Of Birch *with* Emma. Of the extremes I went through in a matter of minutes: love, security, fear, envy.

The worst part is, it stings like truth, like the only truth I've ever known. Perhaps it's because the truth is woven so neatly with the lies. Even though I can tell them apart, logically—even though I know Birch would *never,* and Emma wouldn't either—it's like someone dug fingernails into my soul, scraped out all my insecurities, and molded a neat little picture to carry around with me for the rest of my life.

I'd love to leave the picture behind, but that's not quite how fear and insecurity work, I guess. They cling, they dig, they find a way to resurface, even—maybe especially—when you're sure you've fought them off for good.

Birch loved me until the day he died. I know that, in my head.

I can only hope these lies will dissolve and I'll be able to *feel* it again.

TWENTY-EIGHT

FIRE AND ICE: my first night in barracks was the coldest of my life, and one of the most painful, seared into my memory.

My finger, hot and sore from the tattoo they'd carved into me. I'd never been so glad to have a four-letter name.

Triple-decker bunk beds, twelve to a room, made of unfinished boards and too-long nails that threatened to impale me if I rolled over too far on the plank of wood I was supposed to pretend was a mattress. Really, we were like unwanted objects on storage shelves.

The other girls, some silent and some loud, some puffy-eyed from all the tears and some like steel, all of them—all of us—forced to learn how to deal *without.*

The chill left behind where our comforts had been ripped away, the burning anger that replaced it. The numbness that set in when those extremes became too much to deal with.

So I counted the knots in the wood above my head as I lay flat on my back and tried not to think of the pillowcase I'd had for as long as I could remember, with its faded, threadbare hearts, or the gentle hands that made it for me. I pressed the fleshy part of my thumb into one of the sharp, shiny nails until it broke through the skin and a little bead of blood popped out, just to see if I'd wake up from the nightmare. And when I finally slept, the actual nightmares were even worse, with Birch and his last two steps on an infinite loop.

Time hasn't softened the nightmares: it's simply given them more variety.

TWENTY-NINE

OCEAN WAVES CRASH against the shore under the dusky blue sky. I never thought I'd be this happy to see our little clearing, with its woven-mat beds and ashy campfire remains, but it is like running through a sprinkler on a hot summer day: the epitome of relief.

We've barely set foot out of the jungle when Hope stands up a little straighter. Everything about her is on alert. I follow her gaze, out to where we docked our boat.

"Am I hallucinating," she says, her tone flat and muted, "or is our boat, like, a pile of broken boards floating out to sea?"

"I don't think you're hallucinating," I say. But then again, maybe she is. Maybe we all are.

Regardless, I can absolutely affirm that what I see is no longer our beautiful green sailboat, lazily perched on the sand in one solid piece, but a wreck of debris littering the ocean.

My chest tightens, and tears prick at my eyes. It isn't like I've been actively thinking *We still have a way off this island, if it doesn't turn out like it should*, but that is exactly the disappointment that surfaces. Because let's face it, this island isn't turning out like it should.

And perhaps a way off it would be nice.

I keep these thoughts to myself. It's my fault we came here in the first place, after all. Sure, they agreed to the plan, but only because I did everything I could to convince them it would be worth it. I convinced *myself* it would be worth it. And what have I brought on us? We've lost Finnley. We've been plagued by poisonous moss, bloodthirsty beetles, and nightmare-inducing tentacle plants.

Either we will look back on all we've endured and say, in the end, *This was worth it*—or we will be scarred, in all senses of the word, and worse off than before. Perhaps we won't even be alive to realize what a grand failure this was.

Alexa kicks at the sand. Her fists are shoved as far as they'll go into her tight shorts pockets, and her face says war. "I'm going to rebuild our fire." She turns on her heel, doesn't look back. "You're welcome to join me."

Hope runs in the opposite direction, toward the tide and the various pieces of our boat. Soon, she is waist-deep, wrestling with one of our massive white sails, trying to sever it from the boom and keep it from floating farther away.

And I stand, paralyzed, torn over whether I should try to save pieces of our past, or if I should run full speed toward the way things are now.

I've never been very good at letting go.

THIRTY

WHEN THE FIRE is blazing again, when it sparks and crackles and sends smoke swirling up to the stars, we huddle around it, all of us seated on the sail I helped Hope pull back to shore. We eat the last of our grasshoppers, a pair of stragglers Alexa found hidden deep in my cardigan pocket, their spindly legs tangled in loose threads; we boil ravine water in a metal cup salvaged from the boat on our first day here. Our shoes are tattered and caked with mud, lined up in a neat row to dry by the fire. Our toes are wrinkled from today's rain, none of which—oddly—left our sand even the slightest bit damp.

Idly, I use a long stick to draw lines in the sand, thinking about how much better things would feel if only we had some marshmallows to roast. I pretend we are Girl Scouts, that we're simply camping out overnight on the beach. That our fathers are a phone call away, that everything we've been through will earn us an entire rainbow of merit badges.

Somehow, I doubt a merit badge ever existed for surviving ancient temples equipped with highly advanced laser systems. Or for surviving the island itself.

I can't take it anymore. I have to say something. If they're going to blame me, they're going to blame me. Nothing I can do about it, so I might as well get it over with.

"Things here"—I'm not exactly sure how to continue, because everything I could possibly say seems like the biggest understatement ever made—"are not exactly *normal*. Are they?"

I speak to the fire as if it's my only audience. Scrape E-D-E-N into the sand with my stick.

"Today was the worst day I've had in a long time." Alexa's voice is a rare sort of quiet, like stardust and embers, full of energy that could flicker out in a heartbeat. "Maybe ever."

I bite my tongue. Today was pretty terrible, but the worst ever? No one handed me a vial full of my father's blood today. I didn't have to watch Birch die.

"What did you see in the jungle?" Hope asks. "I heard you saying you were sorry, over and over."

My head snaps up. I must have missed that part, somewhere between Birch's hello/goodbye kiss and my heart breaking.

"Zero Day," Alexa says, then immediately continues, "I know you probably think I have no right to painful memories from Zero, since I'm Wolfpack. *Was* Wolfpack." She talks to the fire, too. Like if she directs her confession straight into the flames, her words will burn up and maybe so will her guilt. "But that day was hard for me. And I didn't think anything could be harder than living it, but then today—reliving it—seeing Cass—"

Her voice cuts off, like the pain of the memory has congealed into something so thick it can't get out of her throat. We wait for it to dissolve.

"I thought if I was in a position of power, I would be able to save him, find some untouched place in the world where we could just be together," she says, still talking to the fire. "But part of earning that power meant I had to tie a rope around his neck, tight, and drag him to barracks. He cooperated—he *trusted* me. I promised I'd find a way to get us out. This"—her voice gets even smaller; her lips barely move—"the explosions, everything, it was supposed to be our escape plan."

Hope stiffens, presumably adding up the details of all things Alexa for the first time. But instead of demanding an explanation, or another place to sleep, she says, "What went wrong?"

Alexa wraps her arms around her knees, looks up to the stars. "Kind of hard to escape with someone when they've been relocated without warning, and when no one will give an explanation."

"So that's what you saw today?" I ask. "Your—boyfriend? And how you had to pull him with a rope?"

She rests her chin on her knees, lowers her eyes. "Yes and no. I saw my very favorite memory with him, and then suddenly, things morphed and he had the rope around his neck, with the end of it in my hand. Except it wasn't the same, exactly. The rope was thicker, with splinters that dug into his skin and made him bleed. He was sweaty, and dirty, and his eyes—it was his eyes that were the worst." She shakes her head. "So accusing, and bloodshot, but also so . . . empty? And he just kept saying, 'You promised! You promised! You promised!'"

Her tears shine in the firelight. "I thought I could save us both," she says. "But it looks like I can't even save myself."

"He's the reason you ran away, then?" I ask. "Cass?"

She nods. "He was the only reason I ever joined," she says, "but it turned out to be hell on us. I wanted out a long, long time before he went missing."

"Well," Hope says, "you're sitting here now. And we're not dead yet—that has to count for something, right?"

It's good that Hope is taking the reins on working through this with Alexa. It isn't that I don't care, or that I don't feel, because I very much do. I feel so much, in fact, that if I let it all out—the fullness of sorrow and fear and guilt that have grown together inside me—it's likely my bones would collapse, into the void where those things have lived for so long.

So instead, I focus on the more concrete things: bits and pieces of information we know, things that might make a picture if we can fit them together. A picture that might provide answers, answers that could lead to freedom.

From more than just the Wolfpack.

"It's fascinating to me," I say, when there's a lull, "that our hallucinations were so similar . . . similarly structured." I tell them about Birch, about Emma. I tell them the facts of what happened with as little emotion as possible, peel open my wounds only as much as I have to. "Plants don't *do* that, right? They don't latch on to you, and they don't have the ability to make you see your very best memories and your very worst fears—right?"

But no one speaks up. Because apparently, here, that is

exactly what plants do.

"And the moss," I continue. "And the beetles. And the laser security system, and the monsoon that didn't leave so much as a puddle out here, and the way our boat is in pieces."

"And Finnley," Hope says, quiet.

"And Finnley," I agree. "But her disappearing seems like it's in another category from all the weird island things, because none of us ended up in obvious pain because of it. Or maybe it's just me who sees it that way?"

Alexa tosses more sticks into the fire, and sparks fly. "It's almost like the jungle doesn't want us anywhere near the temple. But that doesn't make sense, because jungles aren't sentient."

"Also because the temple is deserted," I add. "What's left to protect?"

My voice dies out as Hope's finger goes to her lips. She holds herself perfectly still. "The water," she whispers, careful enough to blend with the crackling of the fire.

But her eyes aren't on our boiling ravine water, which one of them set aside to cool when I wasn't paying attention. I follow her eyes out to the ocean, where black waves crash on the moonlit beach.

And farther out: a shadow on the horizon, a blackness that blots out all the stars behind it.

A ship. A rather *large* and intricately designed ship, from what I can tell—booms and masts and rolled-up sails and a web of lines holding the whole thing together. Like a pirate ship, if I had to name it.

"Looks like we've got company," Hope says, still in a whisper.

In studying the ship's outline against the night sky, I completely failed to notice the shadow of the smaller rowboat headed for our shore, the glint of moonlight on its oars. Now that it's docked, though, and now that they've lit a torch, I can't look away.

Especially because of who's inside it: three boys—all of whom look slightly older, and a good bit more muscular, than we are—and one girl.

One Finnley.

THIRTY-ONE

HER HAIR IS different.

That's the first peculiar thing: torchlight shining on her copper hair, which is short and sleek and angular and altogether un-Finnley-like. Not that I knew her for long before she disappeared. But when I met her, her beach-wave hair looked like it hadn't touched scissors or a comb since before the war, unruly grown-out layers tied in a low ponytail. I'm sure it's her, though. Clean clothes and fresh hair can't hide the distinctive splash of freckles across her nose, or the way she carries herself, with a sort of curious confidence.

The second peculiar thing: she is in no hurry to return to us. Surely her group sees our camp, with its blazing fire, but they don't acknowledge us if they do.

Finnley strides alongside the three guys as if she's one of them, toward the tower of stones farther out on the beach. If not for her haircut—which makes me inexplicably uncomfortable—I'd be inclined to trust them, seeing someone I know so at ease in their company. Trust by association. But I'm suspicious of this new hair of hers and, really, the entire situation. So suspicion by association it is.

Confrontation is inevitable—may as well get it over with. I get to my feet, grab one of our whittled spears just in case. Alexa and Hope follow my lead.

Our footsteps are quiet in the sand. We slip closer, study them as they examine the stone totem pole. The guys have at least a full foot of height on Finnley, who's barely over five feet. They're solid but not bulky, muscles clearly shaped by working enormous sails over rough seas. With their V-neck shirts, tight-cut pants, and boots—heather gray to charcoal gray and every gray in between—they look nothing like the pirates from the movies Emma and I used to watch. Only one of them has long-ish hair, wavy and especially red in the torchlight, while the others wear theirs—one dark, one ashy blond—much shorter. They appear to have thrown their communal razor overboard within the past day or two.

The dark-haired one bends down, runs his fingers over a section of the lowest part of the tower. A thin blue light, as vibrant as the temple lasers, snakes over one smooth face of the stone.

"Excellent," the blond says, when the image is fully drawn. Obviously pleased, but not surprised. His lean, muscular arms are covered in tattoos, a bright jungle of Hawaiian flowers and ferns.

"Is that a map of the island?" Hope whispers.

Tattoo Sleeves looks our way, and the others with him straighten. It isn't exactly an unfriendly look, but something about it unnerves me. Maybe it's his eyes, intensely deep and sparkling under intimidating brows. Suddenly it feels like the worst idea in the world to rush a confrontation.

Alexa takes a sharp inhale. Before I can stop her, she's stepped out of our patch of shadows and into the moonlit sand.

"Shut it down," Tattoo Sleeves says. "We've got friends."

I pay close attention to where the dark-haired one places his fingers so that when we're alone again, I can reproduce whatever it is they are so eager to keep from us. He presses, not swipes, at the lowest spot in the left corner. The blue light disappears.

"Sky Cassowary?" Alexa walks tentatively toward the blond. The flower tattoos ripple as his muscles tighten. "Is that you, or am I hallucinating again?"

The sharpness in his eyes softens, but not enough for me to loosen my grip on the spear.

"Alexa Pierce," he says, not making even a slight move toward her. The challenging tilt of his head, the torchlight flickering in his hard, glassy eyes, the tight curl of his lips—all of it says he's not exactly relieved to see her. "Is that you, or am I back in the nightmare I left on the mainland?"

Alexa rasps a low laugh. "Nice to see you, too." She tosses her hair over her shoulder, an attempt to look calm and collected, not at all rattled by his harsh coolness. And it probably works, for the others. But I see the tension in her fists, balled at her sides. Her worst fears are coming true.

"This your Wolf, Cass?" The dark-haired one approaches Alexa, appraising her. As if moonlight, firelight, and starlight are enough to illuminate her entire character in this single dark moment.

I drive my spear into the sand, draw a line between our two groups. "You've come close enough."

He's a little forward for my taste.

To his credit, he holds his hands up in surrender. Doesn't even test the boundary I've set. "Fine with me," he says. "We don't mix well with Wolves."

I'm about to tell him we're not *all* Wolves, but reconsider. If our being Wolves keeps him on his side of the line, Wolves we'll be.

Funny, though. He's the first person I've met who doesn't seem afraid in the slightest of what a Wolf might do.

"They're harmless, boys," the redhead says. He hitches a satchel over his shoulder and sets off in the opposite direction. "But that doesn't mean you shouldn't be careful."

Finnley, as silent-but-present as the strange totem of stones, turns to follow him.

"I'm sorry," Hope says, "but can someone explain what exactly is going on here?"

The dark-haired guy flicks his gaze toward Hope. Waves crash on the sand once, twice, three times. "No," he says, finally. Simply.

And walks away.

THIRTY-TWO

"FINNLEY! WAIT!"

Hope is over the line before any of us can stop her. Cass, Alexa's Cass, puts himself in Hope's path before she can get any closer. He doesn't touch her—he doesn't have to. His eyes alone are a force field.

"You don't know who you're dealing with," Cass says. "I can't let you near her."

Alexa is fire, a tempest, as she joins Hope's side. "I don't recall Hope asking your permission."

"Well, Alexa, you are a Wolf, aren't you?" Cass gives a mock bow. "Didn't know asking permission was in your vocabulary."

"Arrow to the heart," Alexa says, as if saying the words lightheartedly could repair the damage.

"Cass." The dark-haired guy puts a hand on Cass's elbow. An entire conversation happens in a language I am not fluent in, a silent language made up of varying degrees of narrowed, hard-as-iron eyes. "Enough," he finally says. And then, to me—me, at the back of the group, still standing behind our line in the sand—he says, "Have a minute with her. But if anything happens, don't say we didn't warn you."

His eyes linger long enough for the message to sink in. They're serious—they seriously believe there's something dangerous about Finnley. Finnley! Who helped us sail here, who built our fire, who has been close with Hope, one of the most gentle people I've ever come across, for years.

Then again, Finnley didn't fill Hope in on her plan before she mysteriously disappeared. Maybe I didn't read her right. Maybe none of us did. Maybe I should have given more weight to my instincts, to her whispers and her thorns.

The redhead passes his torch to Finnley. She holds it with her inked hand, the F-I-N-N-L-E-Y on her pinky reasonably confirming she's the same girl we came here with—not a twin, not a clone.

And yet.

Something is off about her, and not just the hair. I can't put my finger on it, not even when I join Hope and Alexa just a few feet away from her.

"Where did you *go?*" Hope's voice is like a rainbow, seven separate yet inseparable shades of emotion. "We looked everywhere—we spent two entire days in the jungle! I ate *grasshoppers*, Finn, and you know how much I loathe insects. Why didn't you tell us you were leaving?"

Finnley shakes her head, her sleek new hair. "I . . ." Her empty eyes sparkle in the torchlight. "I wish I could tell you." She glances at the guys, who linger a bit down the beach, close to the edge of the jungle.

"They didn't—those guys didn't *hurt* you, did they?" I start toward them, because *hell no* they will not hurt one of us and get away with it, but Finnley's free hand closes around my wrist like an iron vise. It lasts for only a microsecond before loosening up, so quick and drastic a change I wonder if I've imagined it.

"No! No, no." Finally, Finnley is there, behind her eyes—I wonder now if she's been here the whole time, if maybe I'm seeing things. Again. "The guys have been nothing but honorable with me, Cass especially. Food, water, privacy, respect, all that good stuff."

"All that good stuff," Alexa repeats. "Seriously? What sort of 'good stuff' did Cass give you, exactly?"

Finnley looks confused at first, but something subtle shifts on her face. "Look, I'm not sure what you're implying, *exactly*, but I'm pretty sure the answer is *nothing like that happened.* And"—she looks at me, and this look, it is not friendly—"I think I'd know if I had been hurt, all right? Alexa's people certainly taught me enough about pain—not all of us had the chance to become privileged little Wolves, as we all know too well."

"Okay, okay, okay!" I step between them before things take a turn for the even-worse. "I think, Finnley, what we're all trying to say is that we were worried about you. And *yes*, that includes Alexa. And we're just confused about the details of why you wouldn't tell us, why you wouldn't even tell Hope, where you were going. Even now, we're only trying to understand."

Her eyes are empty again, and yet there's so much force in them, trained steadily on mine. "I'm a bit fuzzy on the details."

Her voice is as heavy as a sack of gravel, a threadbare one that could spill open at any minute. "I woke up in the night, covered head to toe with ants, and then the next thing I know I'm sitting in a pile of my own vomit, chained to the bottom deck of a ship. Those guys over there busted me out, and they don't bombard me with questions, and they aren't the ones who suggested we sail to this island in the first place—so if you'll excuse me, we're done here."

She stalks away from us, joins the guys where they've stood all this time, pretending they haven't heard every single word.

"Well," Alexa says, "that was delightful."

I didn't think it was possible to be more confused than before, but if there's one thing I'm learning, it's that possibility won't be confined to a cage. It will bend bars, break locks, and fly away when you're not looking.

THIRTY-THREE

OUR BEACH, LIKE every other beautiful and peaceful thing in this world, is not endless.

The boys—and Finnley—set up camp so close our fires practically hiss and spit at each other. I cross my own line in the sand, approach the dark-haired one: he seems to be their leader. He acts like he is, anyway, all attitude and swagger. Hope and Alexa follow me, spears in hand.

"Could you not find anywhere else to settle down?" I say. "You had to plant yourselves this close?"

"Didn't *have* to." He settles more kindling into their fire, keeps his back to me.

"It's a big beach. Thought you wanted to keep your distance from Wolves."

He glances over his shoulder. "Never said that. Said we don't *mix well* with Wolves." His gaze flickers to my wrist, where my wolf tattoo would be, if I had one. I pull my arms down to my side, hope I've been quick enough to hide my pale, inkless skin.

"Well, you're pretty much in our camp," I say. "Isn't that the definition of mixing?"

One of the other guys, the redhead, comes over to back him

up. Together, they are a tall, intimidating force. Alexa and Hope shift forward subtly, so they're beside me instead of behind. It's our three to their two—Finnley and Cass keep their distance on the far side of the fire, paying us no attention.

I'm convinced now that the dark-haired guy is their leader. "Way I see it, *you're* in *our* camp," he says. "And I seem to remember someone drawing a line in the sand, so, no—technically, you're trespassing."

I stand a little taller, set my jaw. "We were here first."

"No one's telling you you can't stay."

His unwavering calm infuriates me. "You show up with Finnley, who's been missing for two days, and you just—just—expect us to be okay with you sleeping twenty feet away from us? You expect us to feel safe?"

He studies me, sparks and embers flickering in his clear blue eyes. "I don't expect *anyone* to feel safe." His tone chills me.

Because he isn't afraid. Despite what he just said, he doesn't seem afraid at all.

What does he know that I don't?

I match his stare, dare him to say another word. He's not one to lose a challenge, I see—I'm the first to break. I want to ask: *Why are you here?* I want to ask: *How did you find this place? What do you know?*

But in the end, I say nothing. Questions are worthless if you're not prepared to offer up answers of your own—and I'm not.

"Let's go," I say under my breath to Alexa and Hope.

We turn our backs on the guys, and it feels like defeat, like surrender. We cross the line in the sand. We keep our heads high.

We need a breath, and some time to regroup, but this? This is not over.

Hope and Alexa and I set off to find a place that's better suited for us. Namely, anywhere else. Anywhere but the jungle.

At first, we make a valiant attempt toward optimism: *We'll hardly notice these jagged rocks beneath us if we weave extra mats!* and *Maybe only the deep-in-the-forest moss is poisonous!* and *Sure, it's freezing out on the sand, but look at all those stars!*

But our exclamation points leap over the sheer edge of the cliff we come upon and are carried into the jungle by a swarm of dragonflies. On our walk back to our clearing, we veer wide away from the moss, and the rocks that really are quite jagged, wishing we had more layers to wrap ourselves in on this salty-breeze night. It's so cold the stars start to look like shards of ice that have chipped from the iceberg moon.

Our fire has dwindled to a pile of glowing embers by the time we return. Meanwhile, twenty feet away, the boys have ignited a veritable bonfire.

"Do they have to be so obnoxious?" Alexa says. For someone who, not two hours ago, was upset over one of the so-called obnoxious, she isn't very eager to go work things out with him. Then again, if my sweet dream ever called me a nightmare, I'd probably react the same.

But he won't. And even if he was alive, he wouldn't.

"At least they're quiet," Hope says, stoking the embers with some fresh kindling.

I glance at their camp. One shadowy silhouette sits off by himself, and another is horizontal, leaning on one elbow, near the others. Their backs are to us, but it doesn't make me feel any less *observed*.

"Too quiet," I say, lowering my voice to a whisper. "We can hardly talk about how we can hardly talk."

There's something unsettling about their commanding—yet undemanding—confidence, even though they seem more than content to keep their distance from us. They're determined, and determined to keep their secrets. Their camp may be quiet, but the energy coming off it—off *them*—is like an electric fence: unapproachable and, in this case, unavoidable. One wrong move and *zap!* No more wrong moves.

But I'm like a moth who can't turn its eyes away from the light.

And I'm not the only one.

"I just don't understand the whole . . . Finnley . . . thing." Hope curls her knees to her chest and rests her chin on them. I get the sense she wants to say more, but she just sighs, leaving it to us to fill in the *hows* and *whats* and *whys*.

"And, Alexa"—Alexa stiffens at the sound of her name, and I can already predict what Hope will say next—"that was Cass, right? *The* Cass? From your hallucination?"

Alexa's jaw twitches, tightens, makes no move toward

opening up to spill all her deepest secrets. Which, I conclude, means yes.

"This island is the worst," she says instead, loud enough the beetles may have heard her all the way back at the temple. The boys shift at the sound of her voice, but otherwise don't acknowledge her.

Wrong response, apparently.

Alexa is on her feet now, stripping nearly every scrap of fabric from her body.

"What are you *doing*?" I whisper, as harshly as I can manage. I'm not harsh enough to stop her.

The boys are looking now, no doubt about that. Alexa tosses a scowl their way and runs full speed into the breaking surf. With one strong wave, she goes under.

Tears prick my eyes. I don't know what madness this is, but it's so much more than a midnight swim.

"Alexa!" I shout, running toward the water, with Hope quick on my heels. But Alexa doesn't come up.

No one can stay under forever. I just hope, when she resurfaces, she's still *there*. Images of the Kiribati disasters flood my mind, a thousand thousand lifeless shells. Days ago, I would have wished a watery death on any—all—of the Wolves. Any sort of death.

Not now.

Hope and I are soon shoulder-deep in salt water. It's hard enough to keep our own heads above the waves when they crash, let alone look for Alexa's in this darkness. The current pulls us farther and farther out of our depth. Alexa gasps somewhere behind me, close but not close enough, and my hope is floating on every one of her breaths because I'm so afraid they'll be drowned out, that all I'll hear is silence. I remember learning, a long time ago, when everyone I knew had a pool and a pool house to go with it, that drowning is more silent than splashy. But not even that is a comfort.

A light touch wraps around my wrist, and tingles course through me—please, no—I hate jellyfish—but there is a distinct lack of sting. The light touch becomes a firm grasp, and then another hand steadies me in this most unsteady tide. It's too strong, too bold, to be Hope's.

Dark hair, light eyes: the most intimidating of the three boys. His glare is fierce, intense. Nothing at all like the gentle way he holds on to me.

"Alexa!" I shout, as we brace for another wave. We're far enough out now that it doesn't crash over our heads, but it's powerful enough that we're on quite the ride. His grip stays firm. "Save Alexa," I repeat, and take in a mouthful of seawater. I spit it out. "I'm a strong swimmer."

He doesn't let go of me, and honestly—not that I'd admit it to him—I'm glad. It's been years since I've swum in ocean waves, in *dark* ocean waves. Not once did I ever swim alone.

"Cass is already on it," he says. "And the other one's safe on the sand." His voice matches his face more than his gentle hands, like he'd much rather be swigging rum with the boys around their giant bonfire.

"No one asked for you to come out after us, you know," I say, very much aware of how ungrateful I sound. This isn't ideal, especially on the heels of conceding a territorial dispute—I don't want them thinking we're helpless, because we're not. We ride the momentum of another wave, let it carry us closer to the sand.

"Oh, no?" Finally, the hint of a smile is on his lips. "Maybe *you* didn't."

He doesn't elaborate, but I'm pretty sure I understand. Alexa was begging for their attention before she ever set foot in the water. She sits now, huddled and shivering, on the beach with Hope. Cass cared enough to save her, apparently, but not enough to stay with her. I wonder if this was enough to pass her test.

When it's shallow and we are able to walk, he finally lets go of me. He's a little faster than I am and doesn't wait up. His bare back and legs are slick with water that catches moonlight as it drips down his skin.

"You can warm up by our fire," he calls over his shoulder. "All of you."

The more I'm out of the water and exposed to the beach breeze, the more impossible it becomes to decline—we could get a sunburn from their fire, it's so much more powerful than ours.

The sand coats my feet, all the way up to my ankles, gritty and grating between my toes. I'm not in a hurry to catch up with him: the fire will take care of the chill in the air, but I anticipate a deeper sort of coldness once the seven of us are gathered together in a single group for the night.

I'm not wrong.

THIRTY-FOUR

I PLANT MYSELF far from the fire, far from the others, closer to the ocean than the jungle. Alone. It isn't like I'm missing anything, though: before I turned my back on them all, Hope had managed to fall asleep, and Alexa was simmering beside her, glaring daggers into Cass and the others. They ignored her.

Together, the fire and moon glow bright enough that I'm able to study the field guide. This island, my father—what we've found here doesn't make any sense. I scan every sketch for traces of code, every page for something I might have missed, to see if I can make out any patterns. It's useless. Deciphering it is impossible without a key to clue me in. I flip back to the beginning, start over with the actual words on the page.

For those who travel straight and narrow, the inscription on the title page reads, *for those who go steady and slow, for those who do good and do well.* My father lived by those fundamental tenets, lived with more focus and patience and integrity than anyone I've ever known. I've adopted this credo as my own over the years.

Straight and narrow.

Steady and slow.

Do good. Do well.

I try to do him proud.

A pair of folded black pants falls to the sand at my side. I snap the book closed, look up, and see Dark Hair Light Eyes Water Savior. He's put on a fresh black T-shirt and some tight gray pants since I last saw him. The pants in the sand appear to be sewn in the exact same style.

"Put them on or you'll freeze." He's not exactly friendly, but not exactly *not*. It's the first interaction I've had with anyone in an hour.

"You should give them to Alexa," I say. Boy pants are always too straight where I have curves. "Thanks, though."

He picks up the pants, sits down in their place. "You say that as if I care if she's warm."

"And you care if *I'm* warm?" I hold my limbs tightly in place so I don't graze any part of him. At least he's giving off body heat.

"Care is too strong a word."

"What are you doing here, then?"

In the firelight, the blue of his eyes sparkles like clear, shallow water on a sunny day. The skin on his face is smooth and flawless, and up close, his days-old stubble is more clean-cut than I originally gave him credit for. I've learned you can't implicitly trust a nice appearance, though. Not even that of someone who passes up the opportunity to drown you in the waves.

Admittedly, that does win him a little of my favor.

"Here-on-this-island here?" He cocks his head, smirking.

"Or here beside you?"

I give him a pointed look. "We both know you aren't going to spill any secrets. You're too smart for that." And he is. I know it as soon as it's out of my mouth: just as it's wise for me to be wary of him, he's wary of me. Nothing personal—it's the way things have to be. It's sad, really, that the world has turned to this.

"I'm here because of the look on your face when she ran out into the water," he says. "You clearly hate the Wolves, so logically, it made the most sense to let the water have its way. But then another part of you took over, and you went out after her anyway."

I have never felt more naked in my life.

Or more understood. Birch and I worked our way up to that level of reading each other, but it didn't happen overnight—and it certainly didn't happen in the span of one glance.

"I'm right, aren't I?" he presses.

I don't deny it.

He looks long and hard into me, like he can see every secret thing I've tucked away, even from myself. "I suspect we have a lot in common," he says, standing. He wipes the sand from his palms, and extends the pants out to me like an offering. "Keep them—they look like they'd fit you, but if you're uncomfortable in them, at least use them as a blanket."

Out of instinct, I scan his hands and wrists for the markings everyone has: a wolf on the wrist, or a name on the finger.

He has neither.

"Name's Lonan, by the way," he says.

I take the pants. How does he not have any markings?

"Eden," I say, still searching him for any telling tattoos, anything at all to help me piece together a picture of what his life has been. A name is nothing, it turns out, when it comes to learning someone.

"Eden," he repeats. "Try to get some sleep."

THIRTY-FIVE

DAWN COMES EARLY, with a patchwork sky of heavy clouds, their silver linings dulled to gray. Bits of blue peek through where the clouds are stretched thin.

There are more pleasant ways of being woken from a night of restless half sleep than hearing Alexa talking at Cass. Not *to* Cass—there is a difference. She follows him around like a mosquito, one he has yet to swat away or even acknowledge, as he stuffs various items into a tattered gray duffel bag.

When I take a look around camp—*really* take a look around—I'm surprised to see they're the only ones making noise. Her unrequited pleading and his commotion create quite the scene.

Hope, wondrously, sleeps through all of this.

At first, I think the redhead is asleep. He's flat on his back, barefoot, knees bent and pointing toward the sky, arms flung over his face as if to shield him from the sun. But he must hear me, or maybe my silence creates a force that somehow presses back against Alexa and Cass, because he's the one who speaks first: "Make it *stop*."

There are so many ways to reply to this on the spectrum of sarcasm to sincerity, but ultimately, he must know the only way to make Alexa stop is for Cass to warm up to her.

"Where are the others?" I ask, meaning Lonan and Finnley.

"Supplies," he says, letting one arm drop to the sand, pointing in the general direction of the ocean. "Rowboat."

Not a morning person, I gather.

I don't see the rowboat, not at first, but I'm more alarmed by the other thing I don't see. "What happened to your pirate ship?"

One corner of his mouth turns up. "*Pirate* ship? Are we that savage?"

"Savage? No," I say. "Pirate-like, though? I think you are, maybe."

Finally, he uncovers his eyes, squints at me. Waits to hear me out.

He isn't as guarded as Lonan, especially since he's still half asleep. This could work in my favor. Clearly, they know something about this place; it's not like they accidentally washed up on the beach—they came here for a reason. It's possible they're seeking Sanctuary, just like we were. They knew about the totem map, though, and we didn't. What else do they know that we don't?

I need to be careful. Get answers without looking like I'm *trying* to get answers.

"Your ship—it looked like a ghost ship, all dark and haunted. I'm thinking you make people walk the plank and dive blindly to their deep, watery deaths." I say all of this very dramatically, to let him know I don't *really* believe these things. And

I don't. Then again, I didn't believe in bloodthirsty beetles or tentacle plants that dredge up a person's worst fears. "Also," I go on, "when we met you, you were looking at a map, so I can only conclude that you're searching for some buried treasure you want to keep hidden from the rest of us." That part I'm serious about. I only hope I'm playing this well enough to get something real out of him.

The other corner of his mouth quirks up to match the first, but it isn't exactly a smile. "All good pirates have their secrets," he says. "Except we're not pirates. We're Deliverers."

"Deliverers, as in *people who cut out other people's livers*?" I ask in mock horror. This brings out a true smile in him—step one in getting him to reveal all the secrets he's tucked away. In all seriousness, though, Deliverers? What is *that* about?

"We can't tell you everything," he says. "But I think it's safe to affirm that your liver is in no explicit danger." His smile is like the sunshine missing from this bleary day, radiant and warm.

"That's a relief," I say. "My liver thanks you."

He laughs again, so I decide to press my luck. "So, this *everything* you can't tell us—"

"Sorry." He cuts me off. "I should have said I can't tell you *any*thing."

"Not now, or not ever?"

He hesitates, and just like that, I know one of them will spill sooner or later. "Not yet."

"I just want to know one thing," I say, because he hasn't built a wall or shoved an iron gate in my face. "Why don't any of you have the markings?" I twist my wrist, hold up my E-D-E-N pinky.

His nose crinkles when he smiles. "Told you that much already. We're Deliverers."

"That is *not* an answer."

"Then ask me something I *can* answer."

I sigh. Best to go back a few steps. "Your ship—ghost ship, or no?"

"It'll come back around in a week or so. Ship's mission doesn't stop just because its commanders are on special assignment," he says. "Also, the ship wasn't safe here. Didn't want it to end up like yours."

In splinters, he doesn't have to say. Useless.

"Phoenix! Cass! A little help?"

The redhead—Phoenix, it seems—turns at the sound of Lonan's voice, farther down the beach and deeper toward the trees than I'd initially been looking. Finnley is with him.

Hope stirs as Cass and Alexa blur past her. "What's going on?"

Phoenix rolls to his feet in a fluid motion that is at once relaxed and controlled. He leaves nothing behind, no unspooling secrets for me to collect, not even a *nice talking to you* or so much as a glance.

"No one will say," I tell Hope. I rise to my feet, dust the sand from where it collected in the folds of my cutoffs. "But that doesn't mean we can't find out."

* * *

"Ridiculous," Lonan says, when I declare we're coming with them wherever they're headed. He runs a hand through his hair, shakes it out.

"Things aren't straightforward in there," I say, motioning to the jungle. *In there.* I really, really do not want to go back in—but my desire to know what they're up to wins out. They've willingly stranded themselves here for a week, for a mission so secret they've practically sutured their lips shut. That we've sought the same island cannot be coincidence. "You need us to help you avoid the traps we've already discovered."

"And besides," Alexa says, "we'll follow you anyway, whether you agree to it or not."

Cass, who knows this better than anyone by now, gives Lonan a piercing look from his deep, shadowy eyes. "*If* we allow you to come along," he says, speaking to Alexa but still focusing his attention on Lonan, "you will have to be quiet."

"But—" Alexa protests, and is promptly cut off by Lonan.

"Fail. Already. *You* stay behind." His eyes scan mine, and Hope's. "You, too," he says to Hope, but in a much nicer tone. "You're better off out here, where it's dry—that slice on your shin needs a chance to close up before it gets infected." He rummages around in a nearby supply pack, tosses her a small flask. "Use this to clean the sand out of it—just make sure you leave a little for me to drink at the end of the day."

As he bends over to zip the pack back up, a sliver of silver glints in the sun: a dagger, sheathed at his hip. He adjusts his shirt to cover it, but it's too late, I've seen it.

"I'm not so sure it's a great idea to split up," I blurt out. From any angle, it seems unwise. Me, alone with them in a vicious and unpredictable jungle? Not ideal, especially now that I know Lonan has a dagger. As for leaving Hope and Alexa on the beach, all I can think of is how Finnley disappeared before, how she came back . . . changed. I want, desperately, to ask her what she thought she'd discovered in the field guide—if she can read the Morse code. But she's glued herself to the guys, and I don't trust them enough to bring up my father's book in front of them. Especially when I have no idea what the Morse code says.

"Last chance to come with us starts now," Lonan says. "Take it or leave it. I won't extend an invitation again."

Finnley will go, for sure. If I stay behind, my chances of getting her alone go from unlikely to zero. And I certainly won't be able to extract answers from the guys. How worth it is this? I don't think I'll be able to live with myself if I let this opportunity slip away—if I play it safe, let fear get the better of me. It'll eat me alive, all the wondering.

An irresistible curiosity pushes me over the edge: What if they know what happened to my father?

I meet Lonan's eyes, as boldly as I can. "Give me the dagger you're trying to hide. Let me carry it," I say. "Consider it a peace offering."

To my surprise, he removes it, sheath and all, and holds it

out in his open palm. But when I reach for it, he pulls it back. "Let me wear the ring at your neck," he counters. "Consider it my way of saying *I don't trust you, either.*"

My father's wedding ring, heavy on its thin chain. It isn't dangerous; it isn't a weapon. Again, it's like Lonan sees straight through to the core of me, like he knows the ring is something I'll never be able to part with. That it's one of the only things in this world that makes me feel safe.

I want answers, desperately, but not at this price.

"I—I can't."

He holds my eyes for a second too long. My fingers instinctively clutch the ring, so tightly, but Lonan is gentle as he peels my hand away. He settles the dagger in my palm, closes my hand over it.

"Don't kill me," he says, intensity levels off the charts, "or the boys will rip the chain and throw your ring into the middle of the ocean."

I blink, at a loss for words.

"My leg *is* pretty sore," Hope offers, always the peacekeeper. "You should go, Eden." I appreciate the vote of confidence, that she thinks I'll be able to hold my own.

Alexa, the reason we so often *need* a peacekeeper, says nothing. I get the sense she is simply waiting to have the last word, that she is an alligator about to snap. But she remains silent, and puts on a face that says she is content to sit around and play nurse to Hope. I don't buy it, but I'm not about to question it.

Going with them is a risk, for sure. I'll just have to make sure it pays off.

"I'm in," I say.

And it's into the living nightmare we go.

THIRTY-SIX

IT NEVER CEASES to amaze me, all the things I took for granted.

Before: when smiles appeared without asterisks attached, when tears were for more than just sorrow, when truth was black and white and gray and not permanently tinged with blood.

Before: when the space between two people was charged more with *ally* than *enemy*, when dreams were made of clouds and not lead, when freedom seemed more like inevitability than miracle.

I'd look at the night sky from the pool chair in my backyard—in springtime, when the air was light and cool, before it congealed to its thick summer soup of humidity and mosquitoes—and imagine the stars were literal diamonds, like in the lullaby. That the immense blackness was the true ground, with solid earth their sky, and that we were all hanging precariously by our toes.

When Zero hit, I realized there was more than one way to turn a world upside down. That things weren't as reliable as they'd seemed, and at the same time, not as impossible, either.

And that the diamonds would always be too far out of reach, no matter what lies the world-turners deluded themselves with.

Out of reach or not, though, two things were clear: one, people live for the chase.

And two, never stand in their way.

THIRTY-SEVEN

NOT FIVE STEPS into the jungle, all signs of sea, sand, and sky evanesce, giving way to a thousand different shades of green.

Cass, Finnley, and Phoenix lead the way under the tree canopy, single file, with Lonan beside me at the rear. It's hard to tell whether Finnley's intentionally keeping her distance from me, or if it's the guys who are trying to keep us separated.

I'm not familiar with this part of the jungle: we veered far down the beach this time, before venturing inside to an area I haven't yet explored. They have a Plan-with-a-capital-P, it seems, one I'm not privy to. I try not to let it bother me, focus instead on trying to figure them out.

Besides, I have a plan of my own, and it hinges on me looking like I'm just along for the ride—ask too many questions, I'll never get answers. For now, it's sharp ears, sharp eyes. Watch. Observe. Just like I did back at the boardwalk, every morning for two years.

"You sure you don't want to go back and consult the map before we get in too deep?" Lonan's voice is startling, loud.

Cass points at his head, doesn't look back. "I've got it all up here, man. We're good."

This is the second time Lonan's brought up the stone-pillar map, and the second time Cass has insisted he doesn't need another look at it. Even though Lonan's the one pressing the issue, he seems almost relieved when Cass gives him resistance. *No way in hell we can study it with* her *around,* his look said, earlier. As if my eyes are sharp for treasure map details, yet blind toward not-so-subtle unspoken messages.

But perhaps I am blinder than I think, because other than the obvious things, their mixed messages are extremely difficult to read. It's clear enough that the three guys are a simmering force, all secrecy and drive fueled by passion and self-preservation. And there's evidence of integrity there, the tough but flexible ligaments that hold them together.

The muddy side to all this, though, is that even with their dagger sheathed at my hip, I can't—I *shouldn't*—let my guard down. Passion and integrity can be a volatile combination when you're the perceived threat. What was it he said, when he asked for my ring? *Consider it my way of saying* I don't trust you, either?

Problem is, I can't prove I'm not a threat until they prove *they're* not a threat, so.

"I see the pants fit," Lonan says as we make our way deeper into the jungle.

They'd zipped up easily, and though they were snug, the fit was comfortable, not restrictive. Before the war, that would have been cause for celebration, but now it's slightly worrying. "Remind me to eat more today," I say, as if I haven't already been eating everything available back at camp. If there's anything I learned from my junior high health classes, it's that starving a body can backfire in all sorts of ways, and that physical exertion requires calories. Comfortable pants are nothing more than a convenient illusion, one I need to be wary of—jungle trekking plus a diminishing supply of food means I'll have to pay close attention to how much fuel I give my body.

"Phoenix has food in his pack, and a few fully charged Havenwaters, too," he says, pushing aside a curtain of vines so we can pass. "Make sure you get some when you need it."

A *few* Havenwater bottles! And fully charged? It's a relief, and it isn't. Who *are* these guys?

Past the vines, the jungle floor becomes a visibly steep incline. Cass unzips one of the small pockets at his hip and pulls out something that looks like a petite syringe. He plunges the tip into a nearby vine, but it's hard to tell whether he's injecting it with something or extracting something from it. Either way: very odd.

"This way," he calls back to us, with a look that says we are exactly on track, an answer to all Lonan's doubts about his map-keeping abilities.

A rocky path carves up the incline like a waterless riverbed made of smooth black stones. Thick vines snake up both sides of it for as far as I can see, intertwining and overgrown—but there are no actual snakes, as far as I can tell. Cass heads up first, climbing the rocks as if they were a steep staircase. He uses his pincushion vine as a railing.

"So, I'm assuming you've been here before?" I ask.

Lonan shakes his head. "Negative. But we know enough to know what we're looking for."

I can't resist. It's like he's handed me an opening on a silver platter. "And that is . . . what, exactly?"

"Whatever path doesn't try to kill us—that's the one we want," he says, his mouth quirking up. It's hard to tell how many more layers there are to this baseline truth.

Cass continues the climb, followed by Finnley, then Phoenix. "After you," Lonan says. *Just in case you fall*, he doesn't have to add. I'm not sure if I'm flattered or insulted: I know the old etiquette rules, the ones that tell guys to put themselves between girls and danger. I go with flattered, because it reminds me of Dad. Sidewalks, escalators, you name it—nothing would get to me without going through him.

In a way, that hasn't changed. His vial is at my front hip, and his field guide is tucked in at my lower back. Protected on both sides.

We climb up and up and up. It isn't completely vertical, but it is steep, like we're climbing a piece of earth that decided it would rather live with the clouds than under the tree canopy. I can't tell from here if it actually pierces the canopy—the foliage thickens along our path about three-quarters of the way up the trees—but either way, we have a lot more climbing to do.

I risk a glance behind and below—*not* the best idea I've ever had. The height is dizzying, and there's so much green everywhere; pulpy vine collects underneath my fingernails as

I dig them in. I nearly choke on my own saliva—it's hard to swallow—why can't I *swallow?*—and my heartbeat pulses hard in my chest and in my head as I force my dry mouth to work the way I want it to.

"Phoenix, water!" Lonan shouts. His hand closes just above the back of my knee, steadying me. Even through the sweaty fabric of my pants, his unfamiliar touch is scorching. "Eden, look here—no, stop looking at the ground, look at *me.*"

I tear my eyes away from the infinitesimally small leaves on the jungle floor below us, focus instead on his clear blue eyes. They are like the shower I so desperately need, like the pool in my old backyard where I'll never swim again. Like the water Phoenix tosses down to Lonan so I can flush away my anxiety.

A few sips are all it takes for the world to stop spinning.

"Better?" Lonan asks, taking the bottle from me and tossing it back up to Phoenix.

"Better," I say. Heat rises in my cheeks. "Thank you."

He nods. "Hate to be the one to tell you this, but we have to keep going. Think you can manage?"

He's right—we are too far up to turn back now, so much higher than anything I've ever climbed. "Can't afford *not* to manage," I say. When I'm steady and sure again, I wipe my palms on my pants. The vine is slick enough with sweat from Cass, Finnley, and Phoenix without mine thrown into the mix. "Let's do this."

I concentrate on one step at a time, imagine there's a giant pit of feathers to catch me if I fall. It's me against the world—and if I can't control the world, I can at least try my best to control myself.

"Careful coming through," Cass says, reeling me back into this present moment, everything but his voice obscured by a thick wall of foliage. "The stones are pretty jagged at the transition, and it's impossible for me to inoculate every plant, so try not to touch anything but the same vines we've been using." Finnley disappears through the leaves, with Phoenix close behind her. It's my turn next.

"Inoculate?" I ask, but either no one hears or no one wants to answer. My best guess is that it has to do with the way he violated the vines with his syringe earlier.

This makes my mind reel: they say they've never been here, yet Cass knows exactly what kind of antivenin will work on the plants, exactly which plants to use it on. Where did they get so much intel? Whoever gave it to them has definitely been here. But judging by how much they hate the Wolfpack, it makes me wonder who else might be so familiar with the island.

A shiver spreads through my entire body. The abandoned temple, the Wolfpack lasers—what if they were wiped out by someone even *worse*?

"You okay?" Lonan steadies me, his hand at my lower back. I've stopped moving, I realize.

I try to hide my panic, but my hand instinctively flies to the dagger at my hip.

"Hoooooooly hell, you're terrified right now, aren't you?" He looks me in the eye, puts his hand on mine where it hovers over the dagger. Our fingers only lightly touch.

"Do you blame me?" My fingers tighten around the hilt. "Tell me why you're here. I can handle it."

I hope I look more convincing than I feel.

His lips part, enough for me to see *answers*, just waiting for their chance to escape. But he shakes his head. "You have no reason to trust me, I know that. But I can't, not until I'm sure."

His non-answers are infuriating. "Sure of *what*?"

"I could knock you down from here, right this minute—you know that, don't you?"

"Not. Helping."

"I'm not going to, Eden. And I'm not leading you somewhere else just so you can die later." He closes his hand around mine, tightens my grip on the dagger. Pulls it up to his own throat. My hand shakes so badly I nick him: a little trickle of blood slides down with his sweat.

"It is not a safe road ahead of us," he says. Swallows. "But *I* am not the danger." He nods at the dagger. "Do it. Kill me, if it'll make you feel better."

He's willing to hold a dagger at his throat, but not willing to tell me what I want to know: it is checkmate, and he is well aware of it. There are no moves for me that won't end badly. If I kill him, then what? Cass and Phoenix will be the end of me. And what reason do I have to go that far? I've lost track of how many times he could have taken my life by now.

He hasn't. He's only given me fire and water and warmth.

I pull the dagger away. Sheathe it before I do something I'll regret, my hands still trembling.

"Let's go," I say.

He's shaking, too. Deep breaths, Eden. One in, one out.

I keep my head down so nothing but my hair touches the foliage wall, maneuvering carefully to avoid plunging to my death, slicing myself on the jagged rocks, or risking poisonous-moss-like burning by touching the other plants.

Instead of finding ourselves under the bare blue sky, we are even more closed in than before. Two stone walls, overgrown with moss, line a narrow path. Bits of sunlight pierce a canopy of leaves overhead, while underfoot, the black rocks give way to a stone staircase. Compared with the climb we just made, this ranks a zero on the difficulty scale. The others have waited for us.

At the top of the staircase, the leaves thin out above us, and we are truly on top of the world. But it's short-lived—the tunnel dead-ends at the gaping mouth of a cave.

Phoenix pushes past Finnley and Cass, slings his backpack from his shoulders, and rolls out his muscles. "Lunch if you want it," he calls, not bothering to look behind him as he disappears under the stony arch and into darkness.

"This is the right place? You're sure?" Lonan and Cass share a too-long look.

"Would I have dragged you all the way up here if it wasn't?"

Lonan concedes, biting back whatever words are on the verge of slipping out. "I trust you, Cass—you know I do," he says, like someone trying to convince himself. "It's *them* I don't trust."

Them. "Them?"

All eyes shift to me, and just like that, it's end of discussion. Nothing in Lonan's *them* seemed to be referring to me—in fact, it's almost like they forgot I was standing there at all. Even now, with their eyes boring into me, I can feel it isn't me they're talking about. So *who*, then?

Whether the cave is the right place or not, it's where we end up, in the shady-cool space that's practically black-lit and glowing with phosphorescent material. Phoenix sits directly on the floor, unpacking a feast from his bag.

The water, the bread, the cheese, the grapes: they are everything I've been missing for way too long, like bite-sized bits of life and memories and happiness that take me back to Before.

That is, until Cass reaches to tear off a hunk of bread, and I see it on his wrist: a phosphorescent wolf. Not a tattoo, but otherwise exactly like Alexa's in size and shape and placement. The longer I stare at it, the more I see it's a hologram, not simply a glowing image.

Finnley has one, too.

Lonan and Phoenix do not.

THIRTY-EIGHT

SURELY THEY KNOW, I think, as I chew, chew, chew a too-big bite of stale bread dipped in vinegar. I chew so long, so hard, that my jaw gets tired and I have to wash the bread down with water. Surely there's something I'm missing—some reason we're sitting here feasting together like we're at the Last Supper instead of splitting off from those among us with *wolf holograms* on their wrists.

But we eat our grapes in peace.

Until.

Phoenix turns his back on Finnley to reach for another water bottle. *Ziiiiiip* goes the big pocket of his pack—and the little pocket at Finnley's hip. She pulls out a syringe, exactly like the one Cass used on the vine, and plunges it into the meatiest part of Phoenix's shoulder. It happens fast, so fast, except for Phoenix as he slumps—that part is painfully slow, and in that second, the cave springs to life.

Lonan pounces, swats the syringe from Finnley's hands. "Go get it, Eden!" he shouts as it clatters against a far wall. "Sedate her!"

I freeze, torn—I wouldn't say I definitively trust Lonan *or*

Finnley—but then Cass turns on Lonan. Cass's eyes are even more serious and intense than usual, with a dash of rabid ferocity thrown in for good measure. Lonan launches all his weight at Cass, who thrashes wildly, syringe in hand. Lonan expertly avoids it, though it comes dangerously close to piercing his neck.

I head for the far wall, for Finnley's syringe, but she beats me to it. She comes at me with eyes the same breed of wild as Cass's. Is this really the same girl who escaped with me from the boardwalk, the same girl who helped navigate our boat across the ocean? What *happened* to her when she went missing?

I barrel into her. We collide, we fly, we slam into the cave floor. She struggles to get out from underneath me, to contort her arm around enough to jab the needle under my skin, but I have her pinned well enough to avoid that. It's both of my hands against one of hers. Finally, I pry the syringe from her iron grip.

In her shoulder? In her neck, in her thigh?

"It isn't going to kill her—do it *now*," Lonan says. "Anywhere'll work."

I aim for her shoulder, like she did with Phoenix; but she hasn't given up the fight, and it isn't her shoulder I pierce. A bead of blood surfaces when I pull the needle out, just below her collarbone.

Now the fight is over.

Sweat drips from pieces of my hair that fell from where I tied them this morning. Our ragged breaths—mine and Lonan's—are the only sound that fill the cave. Cass is slumped and still where Lonan took him down.

"What"—I manage, between deep breaths—"was *that*?"

He paces, runs both hands through his hair and then through his stubble. I can't tell how many facets there are to his fury, or how much I've contributed to it. His fists are balled at his side—it's obvious he wants to hit something, or throw something—but he controls himself. Barely.

"Seriously, Lonan," I press, "what just happened? Clearly, you know more than you're saying, because you knew how to sedate them. She could have killed me—I could have *died*."

"You wouldn't have died," he says, but he is shaking. Shaken.

"Maybe not from the syringe—"

"Fine." He holds his hands up in surrender. "You're right—you're right." He paces, paces. Runs a hand through his hair. "The sedative is good for two hours. It doesn't kill—it merely neutralizes. But no, you're right, the needle wasn't our only threat. You're right."

My breaths are difficult, like I'm breathing a year's worth of air with each one, simply because I can. Breathing is so easy until it's not.

"Well," I say, when things even out again, when I can form words. "Looks like you have just under two hours to tell me everything you know."

I've won, and he knows it.

"Bring the cheese," he mutters. "The bread, too." He heads for the mouth of the cave, a black silhouette against the tunnel's bright green leaves. "Let's get some air."

THIRTY-NINE

"I WOULDN'T TOUCH the moss, if I were you," I say. Lonan is most of the way up the tunnel wall, climbing toward the flat rocks that form the roof of our cave.

"I'll take my chances," he says, though the way he subtly adjusts his grip so he's completely clear of the moss isn't lost on me. "Coming?"

"Why can't we just talk down here?"

"Cave seems to be a trigger spot," he says. Whatever that means. "Can't afford for them to overhear us."

Again with the *them*. "Them, as in Finnley and Cass?"

"No." He pushes himself solidly up onto the cave roof and holds out his hand. "Come on. I'll take the food while you climb, and then we'll talk."

I toss the bread and cheese up to him and trace his path. Fortunately, it's not too steep a climb, or impossibly high. At the top, the difference in scenery is incredible: blue skies in every direction, with such a thick spread of green it's almost as if we're having a picnic in a sunny field. Beyond that, sunlight glitters on the endless, empty ocean.

I have the sudden, uncontrollable urge to laugh, even though nothing about this is particularly funny.

"What?"

"I mean, *look* at us," I say. Him, in his modern-day pirate attire, when in another life maybe he would have been, I don't know, a soccer star? Prom king, most definitely, especially if the people voting had a thing for mysterious bad-boy types. And me, a girl who's had to learn the hard way what she's capable of. All those years of prosperity, burned away by the fire of this harsh new world and the pressure of simply *having* to be strong in order to survive. I never considered myself particularly strong, Before, but, well—I'm still here, aren't I?

"Look at us," I say again. "When you were a little kid, did you ever imagine you'd end up hiking on an island like this and stabbing your friends in self-defense?"

It's the closest he's come to a smile since I've known him. "No," he said. "I never did imagine this."

He's quiet for a long time, staring out over the ocean. And while I hate to interrupt the sentimental moment that seems to be playing out in his memory, time doesn't just stop for sentimental moments.

"So."

I don't have to elaborate. He knows what I want to know.

"It's complicated." He runs a hand through his hair, something he's done enough times now that I've picked up on its meaning: he's uncomfortable and doesn't know how, exactly, to untangle himself. "Tell me about the war from your perspective, and I'll fill in the cracks." He points to my finger, where my name has been forever branded as property of the Wolves. "I'm guessing there's a lot you don't know, given your history."

All the time in the world—all the *words* in the world—wouldn't be enough to express the hundreds of days that have passed since Zero. I keep it to the basics: the Kiribati disasters, the devolution of our own shores, Envirotech stepping in as saviors, how it would have been easier to move into a colony on the moon than land a spot on the ocean-based habitats they were developing.

How the Wolfpack movement started with the underpaid and overworked, the thirsty and the sick.

How their sudden surge of power was unusually stealthy and organized and effective, an unprecedented feat among underground movements.

How the wealthy were moved to gulags along the coasts, because we are most vulnerable there, because the reefs and seawalls weren't going to build themselves.

How there was a distinct turning point—when the kingpins emerged from their anonymity and revealed themselves as the Wolves' alphas—where things got dramatically worse. How the Global Alliance tried to intervene. How the war spread to the world stage.

I leave Birch out. Dad, too.

I simply say, *People have lost so many loved ones,* a sentence with roots so deep they'd poke out the far side of the planet.

I talk about heavy, life-altering things as if I'm reading

from a history book—as if I live in the far-distant future where schoolkids know nothing of the fear we've faced, nothing of our oppressors.

If only.

"Here." He shakes the crumbs from the dish towel that protected Phoenix's loaf of bread before we devoured it, hands it to me.

For the tears I must be crying.

"Your account is more accurate than I expected," he says, and I wonder why his account would be any different from mine. How he managed to escape the things that have, quite literally, scarred an entire population. An entire *world*. "From your perspective, it's all shadows—but things aren't quite as black and white as you think."

I tear off a hunk of blue, veiny cheese and put it in my mouth before I say something I regret.

"There's a resistance at work," he continues. "You may not remember much from that morning, just before Zero went down, but if you try, I bet you can think of how odd it was that a good portion of the school didn't show up for class that day." Quickly, he adds, "Not just your school—*all* schools. Businesses."

I've always assumed the people who were missing were the Wolves: that the only people who weren't caught off guard by Zero were the people *enforcing* it.

"People knew," I say, knowing even as the words come out that it must be the truth. How could it not be the truth? There had to be cracks in the movement. Nothing involving humanity is perfect, or seamless. "Why didn't they do anything about it *before*?"

"Some did," he says. "Spreading the word in places where they couldn't be traced—word of mouth, mainly, whispers. But not enough, and many were killed over it. It quickly became clear that our best strategy would be to let Zero happen and work instead as a secret force in their midst. Better a few lives lost and many saved in the future."

"A *few*?!" Tears spring up in my eyes, but I'm less sad than angry. Surely I must have heard him wrong.

"Yes, in comparison to how many we could—"

"Were you there when they burst through the doors? Did you see their faces—their guns, their masks?" I can't stop. Maybe I should, but I can't. "No. No, you didn't, because you *knew* about it. And you don't have to live with the horror of those memories seared into your brain, of seeing the person you love crumple to the ground, seeing his life just, just *evaporate* through the hole they shot in him." I breathe deep gulps of air, close my eyes so I don't have to look at Lonan. But when I close my eyes all I see is Birch. *Dying* Birch.

I'm shaking, shaking so hard, and to his credit Lonan doesn't say a word. He gives me enough space, enough silence. Enough to remember. And when he wraps his arms around me, I'm surprised to find I don't have much desire to push him off. No one's held me like this in two years. He's strong, steady enough to hold my broken pieces together even though I am on the verge of completely falling apart. Gentle, even.

"No, I didn't see what happened at Zero," he says, his voice low and cracking and intense. "I was at home, in my kitchen, scrubbing my parents' blood out of the grout in our tiles, because I didn't know what else to do. And you're wrong," he says. "I do have to live with the horror of that memory. When I close my eyes, all I see are the bloody wolves' faces carved into their arms, their palms, the soles of their feet."

Now I'm the one who's speechless. Speechless and still, eyes dry and staring out into our picture perfect top-of-the-world meadow.

"I'm sorry," I say, my voice barely above a whisper. His arms haven't let up at all around me, and I haven't tried to move from them. Perhaps he isn't so much trying to keep me together as he is trying to keep himself from falling apart.

"They were the founding members of the Resistance," he finally says. "And I would have been with them—there to save them, or to die with them—if they hadn't insisted I spend the night camping in the woods behind Phoenix's house."

We sit there for what feels like forever. It seems almost wrong to change the subject after both of us let our hearts spill out like that. When the air around us has lost its heavy emotional charge, I ask, "What does all of this have to do with what happened with Cass and Finnley?"

His chest expands, and I move with it. "The Wolves found out the Resistance is still thriving," he says. "And they've found a way to infiltrate."

FORTY

INFILTRATE.

I'm clear on the meaning of the word—just not exactly clear on what it means in this context. "So they're, like, planting their own people to spy on the Resistance?" *Spying* doesn't seem like a strong enough word for the way Finnley and Cass attacked us in the cave. "Or what?"

"Yes, essentially—but they're not using their own people as the spies."

Of course that makes sense, given what I've seen. Finnley, Cass: they're using people who wouldn't necessarily be suspected.

"We've kept the Wolves from locating the island we use as Resistance headquarters," he continues, "but they know we've got contacts spread out all over the place, in all the mainland sectors. They hide the compromised among us and use them to tear us down, one by one."

This world is an even more tangled mess of weeds and flowers than I ever imagined.

"That's what those holograms mean, then—that they've been compromised?" I ask. "And the Wolfpack put the holograms on, not the Resistance?" We sit farther apart, now that we're all business again and both trying to distance ourselves from the things we see when we close our eyes.

He nods. "That's why I couldn't be sure I could trust you," he says. "Not until I knew you didn't have the mark."

"But you trust Cass," I say. "And Finnley, too, even though you just met her."

"Wrong," he says. "I keep Finnley close to keep an eye on her." He tears off the tiniest crumble of cheese, pops it in his mouth. "But I've been working with Cass for a while now, so I trust him well enough, when I'm sure it's actually him in there."

I have questions, so many questions. "Alexa said Cass was one of her prisoners, and they were planning to escape together before he was mysteriously relocated—but you said you've been working with him. How?" Before he can answer, I cram in another question: "And how did Finnley get on your ship?" And another: "Phoenix said you guys are called 'Deliverers'—is that some Resistance thing? What's that all about?"

"Exactly what it sounds like," he says. "We get people out and deliver them to a place, our island base, where they'll be safe. And yes, it's the core mission of the Resistance, though we've had to shift focus since the war began. Pulling out those who've been compromised has had to take priority over pulling out innocents."

Sanctuary, or at least something like it—it exists!

But it looks like we aren't on it. What is *this* island, then? My first thought is that maybe we've all landed on a decoy island, but no, it can't be that. The guys are too intent on being here, too on-a-mission.

My head hurts.

"As for Cass, he was one of our undercover mainland contacts—he knew a guy who knew Phoenix. A number of those mainland contacts have been disappearing, then resurfacing in entirely different sectors," he continues. "*Changed.*" He picks off another cheese crumble, eats it. "Some are changed more than others; some are just a shade off from normal. There's a theory going around that the Wolves are planting something in their brains that allows them to spy on us through them, control them. From what we can tell, the theory's spot on."

This is all so much to take in. I assumed they'd convinced Finnley and Cass to *agree* to spy, somehow. But this, this is worse. This is *wrong.* "So . . . wow," I say, still processing. "They force them—they make them into human security cameras, almost?"

"If security cameras came programmed with instincts to take down their enemies, yes." He sighs. "You can see what a problem this has the potential to become. We've been intercepting their ships for months now, and we've been marginally successful at preventing people from being replanted in the sectors."

"And you think that's what happened to Cass and Finnley?"

"We *know* it is. Cass was pulled out of his sector last week, not by the Resistance, and he's definitely been compromised," Lonan says.

Last week, last week: the timing is too perfect. *Cass* is the prisoner who went missing from New Port Isabel, the reason so many rumors went flying. And people say he escaped on his own—Alexa thinks he ran without her on *purpose*. No wonder she was so desperate to leave her entire life behind. There wasn't much left to save.

"Fortunately," he goes on, "two nights ago, we intercepted the Wolves' ship before they could plant him back on the mainland. Finnley was with him on that ship."

Two nights ago—Finnley disappeared from our camp three nights ago, if my count is correct. An entire day seems like enough time for someone to perform a procedure and put her on a ship. The unsettling implication of Lonan's words, of what he hasn't explicitly said yet, slams into me all at once. "But that would mean the other ship came from . . . here."

He nods. "Finnley's holo-ink was fresh when we found her— we've installed a black light to test for the tattoos, back on the ship. The fact that she was here on the island with you, just before, proves this is the place where we'll find answers."

"But no one's *here*. Everything's so deserted—we haven't even seen a single animal since we arrived." I almost bring up the temple, but decide against it. If someone had performed a procedure on Finnley the day before, surely we would've found a lot more than death traps and ruins.

Or they would've found us.

"It seems to be an unusual island," he says, in the understatement of the century. "We've sailed past it for months, but it never showed up on the radar, and it was invisible to the naked eye. I suspect some brilliant someone made it that way on purpose."

"How did you find it, then?"

He averts his eyes. "Knives at throats have an uncanny knack for producing information."

The crew of the other ship. Nothing comes without the price of blood these days, it seems. How many other ships' crews have they bled for island intel?

But for all they've learned, they still have questions. "You said you came here to find answers," I say. I want answers, too. The words *hologram tattoo* are carved into my mind: according to my father's notes, they were the marks of peace. According to the syringes Finnley and Cass nearly plunged into our necks, peace lives on an entirely different planet. "So. What's your plan?"

"We've intercepted and recovered a good number of the HoloWolves"—I make note of the term, assume it's used to describe those who've been compromised—"but it's gotten to the point where we have to do more than just detain them in makeshift holding cells on the Resistance island." He exhales, deeply. "According to this last ship's crew, there's a lab, somewhere on *this* island—and we've been told there's a cure. The beach totem's map was marked with various symbols, but we're not sure we're translating them correctly, so it's possible we'll have to backtrack before finding the lab."

The churning in my stomach says he's right, despite the fact that this place is completely uninhabitable and void of all the usual signs of life. That there are answers here, even if they aren't obvious. Precisely *because* they aren't obvious.

Whoever is here doesn't seem to want to be found. Yet they have no problem finding us.

I'm getting a bad, bad feeling about all this. "How do you know they were telling the truth? About the cure, I mean."

His eyes see something I can't. The memory of blood as it drips down the throats of his informants, perhaps. "So far, every bit of intel the Wolves' crew gave us has checked out. We hadn't been able to find the island, but with their information, we were finally able to. We already knew how the sedative syringes worked on the HoloWolves, but what the crew said matched up with that, too. And the totem map has yet to check out, but there was a map there, like they told us, and we were able to access it with the instructions they gave us." He shrugs. "Their intel hasn't failed us yet."

"Assuming the map *does* lead you to the lab—what then? You just plan to walk in there and ask for the cure?"

He smiles, but it's not a bright one. "Yes," he says. "That's exactly what I plan to do."

I smile back, sure he must not be serious. But he just leaves it at that, and the bottom drops out of my stomach. "That sounds like a suicide mission, Lonan. Seriously? That's your plan?"

"They'll want me alive." His words are confident, final. Unnerving. "Or, at the very least, they'll drag out my death. Which means maybe I'll at least have a shot at finding the cure, or I can be a diversion while Phoenix goes in to find it."

It should be comforting that he's so certain they'll want to keep him alive—or, at least, not kill him immediately—but, no. Alive means he has information they need, or he's useful to them somehow. Slow death means he's done something terrible.

Nothing about any of this is comforting.

"Why would you *do* that?" The words, the panic: it all spills out of me. "Risk everything, when your plan is so terrible?"

Again, his eyes go somewhere far, far away. "My parents died for the Resistance," he says. Shakes his head. "They were much better people than me. Also, I believe in what they were hoping to accomplish."

It hits so very, very close to my heart, a razor-tipped bullet flying on wasp-poison wings. My father lost his life to this war, too. I thought he'd lost it to establish peace on this island. Not anymore.

Lonan isn't the only one who wants answers. Lonan isn't the only one who wants to carry out the mission that cost his family their blood.

"The other reason is," he goes on, "we have cause to believe they're using the HoloWolves as more than just spies." He runs both hands through his hair, keeps his forehead buried in his palms. "The Resistance is pretty sure the Wolves are building an army. The sooner we find the cure, the better chance we have at taking down the entire war."

Of course the Wolves wouldn't want to fight their own war, now that it's escalated to the world stage, not when they finally seized the lives of luxury they'd always wanted. It's terrifying, really, that anyone, anywhere, could be listening in on private conversations on behalf of the Wolves—that the Wolves did this to innocent people without their consent. That the Wolves who turned them into spies—into weapons!—are *here*, on the island with us. Somewhere.

And then something else occurs to me: "You've been totally open with your plans around Cass and Finnley, right? What, did you think you'd just sneak up on the Wolves and find the cure for this without being found out—with spies in your midst?"

He cracks a smile, and it sends a chill straight down to my bones. "Best way to find what you're looking for is to draw out the enemy and force them to lead you straight to it."

FORTY-ONE

THERE'S A RUSTLE in the leaves below us.

Not an animal—deliberate movement, a parting of the curtain of foliage at the foot of our stony staircase.

I'm so still, so rigid, I could be a pillar of marble, an intricately carved statue with the likeness of *oh, crap* on my face. Out of the corner of my eye, I see Lonan. As confident as he sounded, with all his talk of drawing out the enemy, it's clear he pictured himself having the upper hand whenever they actually arrived—*not* on top of a cave, with nowhere to go but into the fray. Assuming there will be a fray, of course. Which seems likely.

A head of shiny black hair pops through the green, and the fear that froze us evaporates. *"Alexa?"* It comes out like a sigh of relief.

Lonan isn't as relieved. In fact, he looks livid. "I told you not to follow us!"

"You told me I had to be quiet if I did." She tosses her hair, leans down to look back through the foliage. "And it looks like I succeeded." *I win*, her I'm-superior smile says.

A few seconds later, a weary-looking Hope hoists her torso

up and onto the stones at the base of the staircase. She's wearing my yellow cardigan, huge on her tiny frame, its sleeves pulled all the way to her knuckles despite this steamy heat. Alexa hooks in under her arms and helps to pull her the rest of the way up.

"Surprise," Hope deadpans. In this moment—well, in many moments—she and Alexa are stark opposites. It's like Alexa has leeched all of Hope's energy, and Hope had no choice but to trail along behind her in a futile attempt to reclaim it.

"Everyone else in there?" Alexa starts toward the cave.

"Proceed at your own risk," Lonan says. "We'll be down in a few minutes." But of course Alexa proceeds as Alexa typically proceeds: heedlessly. Hope follows her inside.

Lonan shifts beside me. I wonder if he's feeling as jolted as I am, having to put on armor again so quickly after peeling down to our raw, tender layers. Some of what he said rubbed roughly against me—*better a few lives lost*—a *few*, I still can't get over that—yet I find myself connecting with him, our lives both marred by a common enemy. Our top-of-the-world silence was one of the few true moments I've shared with anyone in a long, long time.

I lower my voice, just in case Alexa and Hope are still within earshot. "Are Cass and Finnley going to—you know—"

"Remember?"

"I was going to say *switch into lunatic mode again*," I say. "But yeah, that, too."

He runs a hand through his hair. "As far as I've observed,

whatever made them this way keeps them sane-seeming almost all of the time," he says. "They'd be less effective spies if they were constantly attacking people. But certain things trigger the attacks, and I'm not sure if there's someone actively controlling them or if they've been brainwashed to react that way in response to, oh, who the hell knows."

He folds the dish towel that's likely still wet with my tears, tucks it in at his hip. "And," he continues, "the holograms only show up in trigger spots and under black lights. I don't think they're aware that something's wrong with them. Generally speaking, that is—Cass knows, but only because Phoenix told him."

"And Finnley?" I'd assumed he'd been open about his plans with both Finnley and Cass, but maybe I was wrong. It sounds like he's been more careful than he let on. "What did you tell her you were looking for out here?"

Lonan grins. "Buried treasure," he says. "So we can buy our way into the Wolfpack's good graces."

I think of all I know about Finnley: not well-off, Before, and then left behind to burn her skin raw in the bullet factory. If anyone has reason to crave good graces, it's Finnley.

"It isn't technically a lie," he says, mistaking my silence as a judgment. "I simply didn't get specific about exactly what sort of treasure we hope to find."

"Or that thing about the Wolfpack's good graces," I add.

"Right. That thing is also not entirely true."

"At all."

"At all," he agrees. "Anything else? Ask your questions now; we only have a little time left before the sedatives wear off."

The entire reason I came into the jungle today was to ask questions—but now that I have my chance, I'm not sure where to begin.

Or how.

How do I open up to Lonan about my father—my father, whose ideas set off the chain reaction that left Lonan's parents dead and bleeding on his kitchen floor? How do I fish for answers about his work on the island without laying everything out in the open?

Just like in barracks, I feel like I'm almost not allowed to grieve. Not allowed to wonder.

I've come all this way, though, and what if he knows something? What if the only thing holding me back from the truth is my fear of breaking the fragile connection that's started to form between us?

Trust is always a risk. I have to ask.

I take a deep breath, pull the field guide out from where I tucked it into my pants. "You sail all the time—any idea how to interpret Morse code?" Of all my questions, I settle on this one because it could be the key to unlocking all I don't understand about this place. Details, secrets. I flip open to Dad's island drawing, point out the dots and lines that shade the entire ocean.

"Where did you *get* this? How?"

I can only imagine what he's thinking—that I have a drawing of the very island he's spent so many months trying to find.

How much of the truth should I tell him? What if the Morse code says something horrible or incriminating? "It was given to me a long time ago," I say. True enough, safe enough.

"And this is how *you* sailed here?" he asks, and I nod. "May I?"

It isn't easy to let go of the book, but I hand it over. He takes a closer look, scans and studies, eyes darting back and forth. He flips forward a few pages, landing on one of Dad's blueprint sketches, flips back. There's something he wants to say, I can tell—but then he snaps the book shut, and my entire lunch threatens to come up.

"What? What does it say? It's something terrible, isn't it, it's—"

"No, no, nothing like that," he says. "I wish I could tell you what it says, Eden. It's definitely Morse, and I'm decent at it—but only the standard international version. That message, though, it's written in American Morse code, which is basically obsolete. Whoever wrote it either wrote it to someone with very specific knowledge, or wrote it only for himself."

My hopes sink. It does makes sense that Dad might have written the message just for the sake of getting it out, that he might have created a record of some secret, deep part of himself to live on even after his death. He was that way, always a journal-keeper, often private.

It's just that knowing most of him isn't enough. I want to know all of him.

"Can I—um." I gesture to the field guide. "It's special."

"Oh! Sorry," he says, handing it over. "Of course." He doesn't press me, doesn't ask why it's so special.

Maybe one day I'll work up the nerve to tell him. Maybe he'd understand.

"Thanks for trying," I say. I tuck my disappointment away with the book, try to clear my head of it and focus on this present moment.

"We should probably get moving," he says.

"Yeah. You're right." I take a deep breath, steel myself for whatever we'll face when the sedative wears off. "What's next?" No one ever *really* knows what will happen next, but still, it's a comforting thing to ask. A hopeful thing that assumes the day will proceed predictably.

"We continue our treasure hunt"—he shifts to the edge of the roof and curls his fingers into the crevices of the rock wall like he was born climbing—"unless we are found first."

FORTY-TWO

THE FIRST TIME I cracked open Dad's field guide, after it became my inheritance, I scoured every page for traces of him: fallen eyelashes, pencil marks on paper scraps–turned-makeshift-bookmarks, mustard stains from when he actually used the guide on recreational camping trips.

Funny, I couldn't help but think, how the little yellow book that helped him survive in the wilderness ended up being the one thing that outlived him.

I read the pages for comfort, memorized them, especially on days when I should have been eating turkey and cranberry sauce; on peppermint mocha days when I should have been tossing crumpled wrapping paper into piles at my feet; on so very many days when candles should have been plucked from cakes, dripping with wax and freshly wished-upon.

On all the other days, too.

Some pages were harder to memorize than others, like the ones about protocells and biosynthetics, with all their formulas and multisyllabic science words that basically boiled down to *this is the future of the world, how we stopped Venice from sinking— our country should embrace the self-healing organisms that protect so much of the rest of the planet.* Those were the entries I read purely for Dad's markings, for the comfort in their familiarity. He wrote most of his notes with blue ink, but also had a thing for colored pencils. *Neon's like poison for my eyes,* he always said. Anywhere a normal person would've used a highlighter, he used the pencils, tracing light outlines around the letters until they practically glowed.

I also coveted his sketches—like the one that pointed us toward this very island—and the notes he'd made that were completely at odds with the survival subjects printed on the page. Like with that biosynthetics entry, for example, he'd written his notes on top of a section about respiratory physiology, along with a detailed account of one of his early dates with Mom, before they were married: she'd had the worst week. Her cat had just had two toes amputated, and spent the afternoon bumping into everything because he couldn't see around his giant cone. Mom called to cancel their date—she felt bad for the cat, who was terrified—but then Dad showed up on her doorstep an hour later with grocery bags full of top-notch steaks, Mom's favorite cabernet, and a bouquet of peonies. Nothing at all to do with respiratory physiology, this entry, except maybe for the way he always said she took his breath away whenever he saw her.

You shouldn't have, she said.

Why do people so often say the exact opposite of what they mean?

I'd do anything for you, he told her.

Dad was good at pretty much everything he tried. And of all the things he was good at, he was best at keeping promises.

I'm not sure why the field guide—Dad preserved in the field guide, rather, and bits of Mom, too—brings me such comfort. For a long time, I thought I found comfort in it because it was proof that this world was capable of producing great people, when so little evidence of greatness existed. So little evidence of *good*ness.

But how can that be comforting when this world is what it is?

Maybe it's because I know, deeply, that they may have taken everything from Dad—his home, his freedom, his me—his *life*—but that his goodness was the one thing they couldn't take.

Maybe that's it.

Maybe it's knowing they can't take *everything* that has always given me comfort.

But if what Lonan says is true—that the Wolfpack alters people into spies, into weapons; that they can take control of a person's will—there is no comfort in that. There is only horror, and the cold hope that Dad died before they'd perfected the process.

FORTY-THREE

"WHY ARE THEY asleep?" Alexa asks as soon as Lonan and I are back inside the cave. Finnley, Phoenix, and Cass are still exactly where we left them, slumped and unconscious on the cold cave floor.

"I think the real question," Lonan says, "is why aren't *you* taking advantage of the rest time, too?" He passes Alexa without so much as a glance, goes straight over to the far wall where Hope is sitting, on the darker side of the room. "How's the leg?"

"Clean," she says. "Thanks. But sorry, I . . . um. I forgot to bring your flask?"

"I'd drink it all today, and that'd be problematic, so it's for the best. Unless we have any more injuries, of course." Lonan gives me a look, as if we have secrets. Which I guess we do.

"Sorry," she says in a small voice. "I'll try not to hurt myself again."

I'm certain it isn't Hope that Lonan's concerned about—she isn't the one who turned on us, who attacked us. But Lonan doesn't correct her. I guess we are holding our secrets in locked cages, for now.

"Aren't you hot in my sweater?" I say this purely because the silence had started to gape, because it is something to say. My mind is still running circles around everything I talked about with Lonan. "Why would you wear that on a day like today?"

Alexa snorts. "That's what I've been saying for hours now."

Hope's pupils are wide and dark, crazy dilated in these shadows. "I—I don't know? I am a little hot, actually. It was cooler back on the beach." She pushes the sleeves up to her elbows.

The slick sheen of sweat covers her neck, her chest. Dirt is caked to it where the back sides of her legs have touched the ground. "Maybe you should take it off?"

She shrugs. "I don't know. After the moss yesterday, the leaves and everything kind of freak me out. I think I'd rather keep my arms covered."

"At least have some water; you must be dying!" I say. "Alexa? Could you grab her a bottle? And maybe some grapes, too? They're right there, next to Phoenix's backpack."

"Eden?" Lonan's voice echoes from around the corner. It is so dark that way that I can't even see his silhouette. "Can you come look at this?"

If he honestly thinks Alexa won't follow me—Hope, too—he isn't thinking at all. But he strikes me as the type who *over*-thinks, two, three, even four moves ahead. So what is he up to?

I roll my eyes for Hope and Alexa, like Lonan is this enormous hassle. "Be right back," I say, then call out, "Coming!"

I hurry, knowing I'll have only a slight head start before their footsteps follow. I pray Alexa will at least get the water for Hope before coming after me.

It is still so dark, I know I've found Lonan only when he wraps his fingers lightly around my forearm. "Distract your friends," he whispers. "The others will wake soon. Phoenix will be the first up, but we won't have much time to move Cass and Finnley out of the trigger area of the cave—I'm almost entirely convinced it's the phosphorescent material that activates the triggers. They were fine until we all sat in that area to eat. I don't want you anywhere near, if things go wrong."

"If what things go wrong?" Alexa is quicker, quieter than I give her credit for.

"If we don't find a way out of here," Lonan says, as if that's what we've been talking about all along. "Can I count on you and Hope to help Eden find the other opening? Our intel says there should be one on the far back side."

I don't want to leave Lonan alone with Cass and Finnley, not after how wildly they attacked us earlier. Phoenix will be with him at least, and he likely has more strength than Hope and Alexa combined. It actually does sound wise to get Hope away from whatever might go down—she seems a bit weak right now, and definitely underhydrated, thanks to sweating buckets through my cardigan all day. She'll have to take her grapes and water to go.

"I didn't come all this way to sit in a dark cave forever, so fine, I'll help," Alexa says, an edge to her voice. "Just so you're aware, you don't have to lie to me. You can trust me, you know."

In this total darkness, she could be talking to Lonan *or* me. Or both.

But it is Lonan who absorbs it for the both of us. "No," he says, "I don't know that I can trust you, actually."

"You trust *Eden*—"

"Prove yourself like Eden, and I'll trust you, too." He has such even control over his spiny words, like he's offering her an arsenal of swords instead of brandishing them against her. "I'll let Hope know you're waiting for her."

I want to call out *Be careful!* as he leaves us, but then I'd have to explain the things Lonan doesn't want Alexa to know. I trust Alexa enough, but she'd never be able to keep her mouth shut—Lonan would know immediately that I'd spilled all his secrets, and then where would his trust for me be? In pieces, I'd bet. And then we'd all be stuck not trusting one another in this trigger-happy cave, together with Cass and Finnley, live-wire HoloWolves who could—and likely *would*—turn on us. Lonan's sedative supply can't be infinite.

I keep my mouth shut.

Hope joins us. "I hear we're looking for another way out?"

"He could have at least given us a flashlight," Alexa mutters. "Or a torch, whatever."

If I listen hard enough, I can just make out the sounds of whispers from the phosphorescent cave, the scrape of bodies against the cold, hard floor. We'll know soon enough if Lonan's theory is a raging failure. "He has other things on his mind."

"Says the only one of us who knows what those things are."

"Listen, Alexa"—I turn on her, though it is pitch-black darkness—"do you want to get out of here alive or not?" *Or not,*

not, not: the words bounce from wall to wall like the lasers at the temple, every bit as electric. "I don't want to keep his secrets any more than you want me to keep them." The words are a hiss through my teeth. "But he has more secrets, I'd bet, secrets that could lead to real freedom, and I want them. If I tell you a single word, that's it—we *will* be cut off from their information. We need them, and we need them to trust us." On the other side of this, I could possibly convince Lonan to take us back to the Resistance island—freedom is freedom, even if it doesn't look like the temple we initially set out to find. Freedom, plus the secrets about *this* island I hope to discover along the way? Clearly, sticking with the guys is our best option. "You're going to have to trust me on this. Do you think you can manage that?"

Voices rise above mine, Lonan's and Phoenix's and—I strain to pick them apart—there's Cass's, too. Finnley should wake next. I don't hear the sounds of hostility yet, but things could flip in an instant. And, according to what Lonan said about the Wolfpack using them as spies, they are likely monitoring our every move, even if they're not actively attacking us, even if they're not aware of it.

Such complications.

"Yeah." The word barely comes out, and Alexa clears her throat. It almost sounds like . . . is she *crying*? Alexa does not strike me as someone who cries easily, or even at all. I would not be surprised to learn she's never cried a single tear in her entire life. "Yeah," she says again, this time more solidly. "Fine. We're good."

Torchlight floods our dark tunnel, and yes: her dark eyes are bright, bright. She looks at me just long enough to make sure I get the message—that she means what she said—and then her walls go right back up again.

"What is *she* doing here?" Finnley follows Lonan, Cass, and the torch, with Phoenix at the back of the pack. "I thought we didn't trust Wolves?"

Lonan was right. Finnley has zero clue what's been done to her—what she did to us. She has no clue that *she* is one we are guarding against, that she, too, is a form of Wolf. That, or she is a brilliant liar. From the short amount of time I spent with her before she disappeared, she struck me as blunt—maybe a touch passive-aggressive—but not necessarily a liar. I conclude she is either being ruled by someone's will other than her own, or the people controlling her have ensured their subjects black out during attacks. Maybe both.

"We don't," Lonan says.

We file through the tunnel together, ex-Wolf and HoloWolves and syringe-carrying sheep, one after the other, in a single, straight line. It would almost look as if we were a unified contingent, if viewed from precisely the right angle.

From where I stand, all I see are cracks.

FORTY-FOUR

THE PITCH BLACKNESS doesn't last forever. Sunbeams stream in through the top of the cave after we've taken a few sharp turns, and soon we see a strip of intensely blue sky.

It isn't the exit we hoped for.

Instead, we've found a path so narrow we have to walk single file. We're walled in on both sides, by moss-covered stones that stretch straight up toward the sun. It's difficult to avoid the moss, but so far, we've managed. Hope is still wearing my cardigan—I get it now. I want to ask for it back, but can't bring myself to do it. When it comes to these unpleasant bits of nature, her tolerance is much lower than mine. I'll just have to be careful.

It's strange, the way paranoia works: the farther we walk in peace, the more I wonder what's waiting for us up ahead.

If there will be another trigger.

If there will be another attack—what could happen here, between these narrow walls, with no easy escape route.

If, if, if.

This is life now. Watching, wondering, waiting.

Even in the calm, there is no rest.
I take a breath. Take a step.
One foot in front of the other.

FORTY-FIVE

WE FIND THE opening we're looking for on the far back end of the cave, as we hoped, but it is anything but ideal: there's nothing on the other side of it but a dizzying fifty-foot drop. The outer wall of the cave continues, sheer rock in three directions—left, right, and straight down. I focus on the sky, try not to lose it like I did on our earlier climb.

"Is that a bridge over there?" Phoenix asks.

I don't see anything, not at first, but it turns out I'm being overly optimistic. "Like . . . *way* over there?" If I squint, I can just make it out. "Yes, I think that is a bridge."

"It's not *that* far," Phoenix says.

Alexa shifts beside me. "If it isn't, we could always swing from the ropes, right?"

"You and ropes," Cass says, under his breath. I'd almost forgotten they had such a history with each other, but this comment brings back in screaming color everything Alexa told us yesterday, about Zero, how she dragged him to barracks by the neck. I expect her to bite back, but she's unusually quiet.

"There's a ledge jutting out of the cliff side," Hope says,

moving to the front of the pack. "See? It goes all the way to the bridge." She places one narrow foot on the ledge—a ledge so insubstantial it blends in completely with the rest of the cliff wall. I don't know how she noticed it.

"Wait!" Lonan says, before Hope takes another step and accidentally kills herself. "We'll need something to hold on to. Phoenix, you've still got fishing line in your pack from the ship?"

"You know it." Phoenix unzips the front pocket of his pack and produces a half-empty roll. "This enough?"

"Better be." Lonan unsheathes his dagger and begins to wrap the line around the hilt, around and around and around. He ties it off with his teeth. "Eden, hold the roll, will you?"

He plunks the small plastic disk in my hand before I can refuse, begins letting out the entire length of the line. I see where he's going with this and hope mightily that it's long enough to stretch all the way to the bridge. Also, that he's a sure shot when throwing a dagger.

Turns out we're lucky on both accounts. Either that, or Lonan doesn't take risks unless he knows he can come out on top. It really isn't as far to the bridge as I'd first assumed—the empty disk has *48ft* printed on it, and it wasn't full to begin with.

Lonan tugs on the line, hard. It holds.

"How are you going to secure this end?" I ask. There are no branches around that look strong enough to support our weight as we cross.

"You're looking at it," he says, biceps flexing. And then, before any of us can protest: "Cass and Hope, cross first. Finnley and Alexa, get ready—when Cass is across, you'll go with Phoenix."

"And me?" I ask.

"Help me anchor while they cross," he says. "Not sure I have it in me to hold it steady for six individual trips—two team trips are manageable, but only if they're not all on me. That way I'll still have strength left to hold it when it's your turn."

"What will *you* hold on to, though?" Hope asks.

"I'll free-scale it," he says. "I used to free-climb all the time, Before."

"Both of us did," Phoenix adds. "We'll be good. You good?" He glances around, meets everyone's eyes. None of us look particularly *good*, but none of us has a better suggestion. "All right. Cass, you're up. Hope—ready?"

"I've got you," Cass tells Hope. It's the first time I've seen something other than his bitter-with-Alexa facet. While he's still unapologetically intense, this softness with Hope makes me wonder if he had younger siblings—and, if so, what happened to them in this war.

Determination flashes in Hope's eyes. "Ready," she says. "Let's go."

Lonan gives me a look, tells me everything I never knew I needed to hear without saying a word: You are strong. You can do this.

"All I need is some counterforce," he says. He faces the cave wall, pulls the line until it's tight over his shoulder and starting to dig in. "Just lean as hard as you can against me; like, *drive* me into the rock wall."

Oh. *Oh.*

Well. Looks like we'll be getting to know each other *very* well. I press into him, all of my front against all of his back, like we're . . . like we are much more intimate than we are. He's respectful about it, which helps. It isn't as awkward as I expect, and while it's definitely too much too soon, it isn't unpleasant. At least, not until Alexa and Finnley pile on behind me and pin us even harder to the wall.

But it works: Cass and Hope make it across with little trouble. And with all the weight on Lonan, he isn't burned out when it comes time for us to support the other three on our own.

"Listen," he says, when it's just us holding the line with everything we have. "There's something I need to tell you." I wish I could see his face. "I wasn't entirely honest before—about why we're here—and it's eating at me. The drawings in your book, they threw me off guard. Not even the *guys* know about them."

"I mean," I say, slightly confused, "why *would* the guys know about them? It was only you who saw them."

He pauses. Great, now we're both confused. "You said the book was special," he says. "You said someone gave it to you—with all of these sketches already inside? Or did you make them?"

I laugh, I can't help it, and the line slips the tiniest bit. Immediately, I readjust, wrap my arms even tighter around Lonan's waist. "No, I didn't make them. I don't even know exactly what they *are*." Lonan isn't the only one with half-truths. I guess that makes us even.

"You don't know what they are."

It isn't a question—he doesn't believe me.

"And you do?" I counter.

His silence gives him away. He knows—*how* does he know? Blueprints for the Atlas Project habitat were never made public, not even when Zhornov leaked all of Envirotech's secrets that sent the world spinning.

"The Allied Forces approached the Resistance, and the Resistance gave me a mission," he says, and it is the absolute last thing I expected him to say. "The other guys, I haven't even told them, that's how secret it is—they think the only reason we're here is to find the cure, the HoloWolf cure."

"And you're not?"

"No, we are. That's just not all *I'm* supposed to find."

"And the Alliance sent you," I say. "Like, *the* Allied Forces—the entire-rest-of-the-world-aligned-to-take-down-the-Wolfpack Allied Forces? They sent you. You? To find *what*?"

"Same thing you're here to find, looks like," he says.

What? "I'm not looking for the habitat," I say, the word *habitat* out of my mouth before I can stop it. "I'm looking for Sanctuary—the amnesty island? Refuge from the war, immunity?"

He deflates, tightens up his grip on the line. I risk a quick glance behind me, see Finnley and Alexa and Phoenix making slow, careful progress toward the bridge. They're over halfway across now.

"The amnesty island was just a cover," he says. "It doesn't exist, never did."

"But—" I cut myself off. My father's words, my father's *life*: I can't let them go. Not here, not when they could so easily slip right off the edge of this precipice.

"No, Eden. There's a refuge, that's for sure, but not from the war. From the *water*." He takes a moment to let that sink in. "They're still building it, the Wolves—they never stopped, not really."

And with that, everything clicks into place.

My father's special assignment wasn't Sanctuary: he knew *everything* about the Atlas Project. He dreamed it up, he designed it. He believed in its potential, so much that he continued to work on it even when he learned of Envirotech's motives to profit from it so extremely. The Wolves must have known who to pull to resurrect the project, must have known through their inside connection with the traitor turned kingpin.

Working for the Wolves must have been Dad's breaking point. He would never have lied to me—maybe they lied to him, told him he'd be working on a refuge island just to get him to say yes. Yes and yes and yes, until finally, one day, he must have said no. Just like I've feared since the day I learned he was never coming home.

"It's . . . it's *here*? The habitat, the Atlas Project?" They must have extracted all his knowledge, probably tortured it out of him.

"That's what I'm supposed to find out. The Alliance is fairly certain the *science* is here, a lab at the very least, given the extremes they've taken to hide the island. Maybe the habitat, too. But the science is all they're concerned about, really—getting it out of Wolfpack hands and into their own."

This, too, makes sense. If Envirotech wanted to profit from it, the Wolves simply want it for themselves. "What does the Alliance want with it?"

"They want to replicate Atlas, build hundreds of habitats—they've got contractors and investors lined up for miles."

I work it out on my own: more habitats mean more residences, which means more of the world will survive if future disasters pile up on themselves, if not even the planet's best-prepared can thrive. If the war doesn't drive humanity into extinction first, that is.

Something isn't adding up. "The Allied Forces—they're in this purely for the humanitarianism?" That seems too thin a reason. "Why go to such trouble? And why send *you*?"

"Deliverers and Resistance know the seas better than the Alliance does, and we already have a presence here," he says. "And, no—saving the world from water isn't all they're hoping for. But they believe it could tear the Wolfpack apart from the inside if they were to secure the science, build their own refuge habitats. *Think* about it."

I hear Alexa let out a whoop in the distance. "They're across," I tell Lonan, after a brief glance. The fishing line dips as Phoenix, at the bridge, adjusts Lonan's dagger in the tree—the weight of three people at once must have loosened it a bit. With one forceful drive, the line pulls taut again. "How's your arm?"

"Still attached," he says. "It'll hold up when it's your turn, don't worry."

"It's my turn now."

He twists around to face me. "If I don't make it across"—his face lights up in panic when he sees mine, and he backtracks—"no, don't worry, I'll totally make it. It'll be fine. But *just in case*, promise me you'll track down whatever information you can about Atlas, and find a way to get in touch with the Alliance. Promise?"

I think I understand what he means, how it could cause the Wolves to implode: so much of their empire is built on fear, the desire to survive, to *thrive*, taken to unholy extremes. In possession of the Atlas Project habitat, who knows what promises they've made—how many Wolves stay loyal just because they honestly believe the kingpins will follow through.

But I know those blueprints. However many promises they've made, 98 percent of them will be broken. There simply isn't space for everyone.

So if the Allied Forces can follow through where the Wolves can't, it's possible that 98 percent of their loyal might defect. It's not a bad strategy at all, especially combined with their plan to cut the HoloWolf army off at the knees. If we can find the habitat science on top of that—get it away from the Wolves and into Alliance hands—we might actually make a difference in ending this war. I could help *create* the freedom I've craved for so, so long. Do what Dad never got the chance to.

"Yeah," I say. "I promise." I intend to keep it, and I don't intend to need to. "Do me a favor and stay alive, though."

He grins. "You got it."

His eyes meet mine, and they're stunning, but I can't take it—there's something there that reminds me too much of Birch. I break. "Better go."

I take a deep breath.

FORTY-SIX

I AM NOT afraid of falling.

I am not afraid of Lonan's arms giving out.

The stony cliff walls do not dig or scrape against my back, my toes do not go numb, my hair doesn't stick to my face or neck, the fishing line does not nearly slice my fingers clean off from all the pressure, my inching across isn't slow or painful, the ledge does not crumble into dust and pebbles with my every move.

Except I am. And it does. And they do.

And I'm only halfway across when I admit these to myself: halfway across when the dagger slips from the tree.

It's not Lonan whose arms give out, after all.

I press myself into the wall at once, squeeze my eyes as tight as they'll go. Make myself still as death. There's shouting among the boys, Lonan calling to Phoenix, Cass cursing the dagger. It isn't hopeless—the line is slack in my hands. It definitely isn't strong enough to support me, but it didn't fall completely out.

And I haven't fallen. Yet.

Some of the shouting is directed at me: *Eden, stay strong! Eden, don't move. Eden, Eden, Eden.* I don't move, but it isn't so much strength that holds me there as it is complete paralyzation. Closing my eyes only makes it worse, makes me dizzy, so I pick a leaf on a distant tree and focus on it until it blurs. Soon—or not soon, I'm not really sure—the line straightens out, is strong again. They've all piled onto Cass like we did with Lonan, with Alexa at the back.

"Slow and steady," Lonan calls, his voice muffled by the wall he's still pressing himself into. It's been a while now—I only hope he isn't too burned out to cross on his own when I'm finished.

It's this that motivates me to move. The longer I'm frozen here, the longer he has to hold the line. He will not drain himself of strength on my account, not if I can help it. I swallow my fear, take another sideways step. Dust and pebbles crumble from the ledge, but it is stronger than it looks. Stronger than it *feels*. Like me.

When I'm close, Alexa breaks away from the pile and reaches for me. We grab wrists as I step firmly onto the rock platform where the bridge is attached, my palm locked directly on top of her wolf tattoo. *It feels like skin*, is my surprising first thought, and of course it does. It feels like normal skin and not like something that's been charred, scarred beyond recognition. I always imagined it as a burn that never dies.

Lonan scales the wall like he was born doing it. He makes it across in little more than a minute, with no hint of fear or pain anywhere on him.

We've all learned to hide these things well, I guess.

And we're all as strong as we have to be, when it comes down to it.

FORTY-SEVEN

SMOKE AND FLAME and embers and ashes: these are not always so obvious, not always welcomed with the fanfare of piercing alarm bells. Fire slips in when you least expect it, in my experience. It slips in with silence.

The worst fires take root and never leave.

Smoke: The futile longing for a place I'll never see again. Dusty hardwood floors. Blades of backyard grass poking up between my toes. Our aquarium full of fish.

Flame: What if I'd stepped in front of Birch? What if I'd pushed him out of the way—would it have mattered? Changed anything? Would he be here now, wondering the same thing about me? Maybe we'd be here together.

Embers: The ring. The book. The vial. The cracks in my closure, where hope and fear grow up like tangled weeds. Hope, that maybe I'm wrong and my father is alive—*fear*, that maybe I'm wrong and he's alive. Everything that would mean.

Ashes: My ability to trust, and everyone I ever trusted.

Survival is more than merely getting out in time.

Survival is fighting, every single day, to climb out of the

ruins and into the unknown, come what may.

We're all as strong as we have to be.

FORTY-EIGHT

WE STAND ON the rock platform that juts out from the cliff wall. "You'll be fine," Lonan says. I'm still a bit shaky from crossing the ledge. "There are five people in front of you, and I'll be right behind."

The bridge stretches out from our platform, a net of cocoon-white fibers so high in the trees it'd be a butterfly's Mount Kilimanjaro. It's obviously man-made, woven and wide and just sturdy enough, an entire network of pathways connecting tree to tree. No ropes here after all.

Phoenix, Cass, and Finnley are practically to the far side already, where the bridge is secured to a platform of wooden planks that ring around a thick tree. The network of bridges continues from there. Alexa and Hope are significantly far behind them, barely halfway across. Phoenix and Cass make it look easy—Finnley, too: it's like they're running on clouds with winged shoes.

Hope and Alexa aren't so deft. They are so slow, so painfully careful, knuckles white and gripping the fibers. The longer they stay in one place, the more they sink, sink, sink. They sink so low I fear the fibers will give out and they'll fall to the ground, only to be showered—in their instantaneous deaths—by a snowstorm of cocoon-bridge remnants.

It seems the proper strategy is to simply *go fast*.

"It doesn't make sense for all of them to go before us," I say, now that they're far enough out of earshot for me to challenge Lonan. He made this call without anyone else's—without *my*—input, just like he did with the ledge. The silent eye daggers I shot him weren't enough to get him to abort. "What if there's another trigger? What if one of them cuts the bridge while we're on it? We'd never survive the fall." The fishing-line dagger shifting in the tree was an accident, I'm almost certain, but now that I've had a little time to process it, paranoia has grown roots.

"That's why I put Phoenix at the front," Lonan says. "He can handle them."

This makes me laugh. "Didn't handle them too well back there in the cave." It doesn't sound as lighthearted once the words are out of my head. I guess I didn't really mean for them to be lighthearted.

Lonan bristles. "He's prepared now."

"So are we."

It is a staring contest, neither of us backing down.

"Look," I say, the first to break. "I'm not disagreeing with you because it's *fun*—this could be our life or our death."

"Good, we're on the same page." He is all pirate-ship captain right now, all bravado and I-know-better-than-you. But then he softens, probably because of the look on my face, and sighs. "I want us at the back so we can keep an eye on them. They could just as easily slash the bridge from *behind* us, right?"

He has a point. One I don't acknowledge just yet.

"Phoenix is strong, Eden. Have a little faith."

I see in his eyes: it isn't Phoenix he's asking me to trust.

It surprises me how raw it feels to lose this, a wisdom battle. "Fine, fine. You win this one." Not like we have a choice who goes first now, anyway. The others are already at the far side of this first bridge, waiting for us on the platform. "Sorry," I say. "It's been just me looking out for myself for so long . . ."

"I get it."

He does. It's been the same for him, for just as long. Longer, if we're getting technical about who was orphaned first.

We really should get going, but I have more questions, so many questions, and we seem to have this unspoken under-standing to only *talk*-talk when we end up in pockets away from the others. As confident as he sounded about drawing out our enemy, back when we were on top of the world, he's been notice-ably quiet around Cass and Finnley.

"So, this lab you're hoping to find—it's, uh, in the trees?" I ask. "That would certainly explain why we haven't encountered a single soul, other than you guys, since we set foot here. Also why the temple was deserted."

"Wait—you found a temple?" He looks genuinely surprised at this, like it's the first time he's ever heard about it. Guess their map didn't spell out everything.

Heat rises in my cheeks. "A deserted one, yeah—"

"And you waited this long to mention it?"

"You shot down my Sanctuary theories, and haven't seemed all that interested in hearing about what we've already found." *Touché*, his face says. "And it was deserted, like I said, and not the most pleasant. It didn't sound like the lab you're looking for."

"Still, you could have mentioned it."

I shrug. "I'm not the one with the map." *Or the upper hand*, I add silently.

"Lo!" Phoenix yells, but it's muted from the distance. "Everything okay over there?"

"Coming," Lonan fires back. And then, just to me: "No more keeping important intel from each other, okay?" He pinches the bridge of his nose, like he's trying to pluck the perfect words from his brain. "And I'll try to be better about asking your thoughts on things."

I nod. "Yeah. Yeah, that sounds good."

"Sorry," he says. "Old habits and all that. I'm not used to people questioning me. It's kind of refreshing, actually." He smiles, dips his head toward the bridge. "We'll hit the temple next if these bridges turn out to be a dead end. You can do this, Eden, just don't look down."

Heights have never been my favorite, and that's an understatement, but I never realized I had such paralyzing issues with them until I experienced this island. Then again, I've been mostly on land or sea my entire life—never this close to the clouds. The human capacity for fear is fascinating, how it grows and stretches to hold innumerable *what-ifs*, as often as you think of them.

"Ready?" He takes my hand, gives it the tiniest pulse before letting go.

I am electricity itself. It's a wonder the entire jungle doesn't burst into light.

The first step of faith is the hardest, and the next aren't any easier, but soon I'm far enough out that my fear is overshadowed by sheer determination. I focus on the tree platform, concentrate on keeping my feet moving so they no more than skim the surface of the bridge.

We make it to the platform, and though the wooden boards are a little too warped and uneven for my taste, I've never been so happy to hug a tree.

It's only just the beginning. From the vantage point of the platform, the network of bridges comes more fully into view. There are a *lot* of them. Several trees along the way are nexus hubs for two or more offshoot bridges—it's like a Mensa-level maze with no ending in sight. Phoenix leads the others toward the next platform once it's obvious we're making quick progress behind them.

"Was the map explicit about which bridges to take?" I ask, when we steal another lonely moment.

"Nope," he says. "Not explicit at all. Phoenix is on the lookout for significant markings, things they might have left as reminders for themselves. The bridge system isn't exactly the most obvious means of exploring the place, so we're banking on the hope that they've underestimated our ability to find it."

"Sounds logical enough."

Even if a lost jungle wanderer dared to look up into the tree canopy, it'd be extremely difficult to trace the bridge network back to its starting place, given all its offshoots. Factor in that we had to conquer an obstacle course to find the cave in the first place, and it's plausible enough that they didn't have outsiders in mind when constructing it.

He gestures to the bridge at our feet as if to say *after you*, and we run.

The next tree we encounter has multiple cocoon-bridge off-shoots and a larger, more substantial platform than the others. Phoenix and Cass crouch, examining the wood for any telling carvings. It's hard to see from where I stand, at the back of the group—but then I have an idea, and it is so obvious: we just *came* from a place that seems significant, so it makes sense that if there are trail-marking symbols at all, there might be one attached to the bridge we just crossed.

I kneel, and Lonan shifts to give me room. There are no telling marks carved into the wood, nothing painted anywhere that I can see. But then—and I know I'm right as soon as I see it—there's a knot pattern where the cottony-white fibers are tied to the wood.

It's like an upside-down V, an arrow of knots pointing in the direction we just came from. There's an entire section in Dad's field guide about symbols used to mark trails—stones, pebbles, knots tied into tall grass—and this looks exactly like the pebble marking for *straight ahead*.

I bolt upright, nearly knocking into Lonan's jaw—I hadn't noticed he'd crouched so close behind me. "Phoenix, check the bridge netting for knot patterns—anything there?"

Hope, Alexa, and Finnley back against the tree so I can get a closer look at our options. Sure enough, one is marked with the upside-down V, one is marked with an arrow pointing left, and a third simply has a straight row of knots. *Do not go this way*, in scout translation. I open the field guide to the trail-marking chart, pass it around for everyone to see.

"Looks like we're going this way, then," Cass says, pointing to the bridge marked *straight ahead*.

"Seems pretty obvious, don't you think?" Alexa says. "Eden, do you not remember the moss? The beetles?" She leaves out the part where she had hallucinations of Cass, understandably. "You *really* think anything on this island is that straightforward?"

It does seems a bit too obvious, but then, you would have to know to look for the knot pattern to figure it out. And, like Lonan said, it doesn't seem like this was ever meant for outsiders to find, so why would it be a trap?

Still, though.

Phoenix is eyeing the *do not go this way* bridge, and I know this look: a degree of determination I've seen only once. I saw this same look—all it took to sear into my memory—on a girl who'd been a varsity cheerleader at our rival high school, as she watched ice cream melt over its cone and down a Wolf's too-smooth hand. Her sparkling eyes were eager, determined. Alive. She reached out and stole the cone right out of the Wolf's hands, took a face-smearingly huge bite out of it. Crumbled the cone, feasted on all the broken pieces.

This Wolf was not as kind as the one who'd thrown his cone in the trash for me earlier that day. Her bright red, razor-sharp nails blended perfectly with the cheerleader's blood. I heard rumors that the cheerleader survived, but I never saw her again.

Nothing good comes from a look like that. Maybe Before, but not now. Eager, alive determination is about as *do not go this way* as it gets these days.

But Hope pushes her way through and takes the first step past that straight row of knots—the caution-warning-stay-far-from-here knots—and Phoenix follows. Then Cass, then Finnley. Alexa.

Lonan, who continues to pick up the rear in these processionals, raises his eyebrows at me.

"This doesn't feel right," I say. "Shouldn't it *feel* right?"

Oh, though: I should know by now that you can't always trust feelings—which is especially problematic when you can't even trust the things that masquerade as facts.

Hindsight; that's the only thing worth trusting these days.

Two roads diverge in a wood, and I—I take the one less traveled by.

FORTY-NINE

WE FLY OVER the bridges, one after another. The humidity is so thick it soaks through our layers and down to our skin. We are swift, we are silent. Even Alexa.

Not a single thing seems out of place, or foreboding. Not at first.

Some of the platforms are narrow, not much wider than our feet. Others are so large we could stretch out and take naps. We don't. Yet another platform we encounter is covered in inches-deep sap, which saturates our shoes and clings to the cottony bridge: thick tufts rip out every time our shoes make contact. We tear so many layers from the bridge that Hope's foot plunges straight through—it nearly gives me a heart attack, even though I'm not the one halfway on her way to falling. Lonan's heel pierces another hole as we move to pull Hope back up. He barely avoids falling all the way through.

After that, we go barefoot.

We run, on and on, because nothing screams *we're there*, and because nothing screams that we aren't. Hope falls behind, especially as the humidity thickens. Lonan forces his pace to match hers.

The humidity should have been our first clue, as breathing turned into a process more akin to drinking a lukewarm soup that fights on its way down. But we dismiss the thick air as an unfortunate side effect of this unfamiliar ecosystem. At least, none of us acknowledges it out loud.

The bone shards do not go unnoticed.

It's a collective experience: Phoenix falls first, with an odd flinch as his bare foot recoils from the bridge. He falls with grace, contorting so he lands squarely on the bridge instead of falling over its edge. Cass is right behind, and the rest go down like birds with clipped wings.

I see every second of it, and yet I can't avoid it.

The cloud-soft bridge is suddenly a breeding ground for razor-sharp teeth, shards of bone woven into the cocoon fibers. It's white on white, except for where blood spills from our feet, our ankles, anywhere else we make contact.

Laughter.

Laughter, from Phoenix, from Cass—uncontrollable and giddy, like kids who've never had a sled or snow on Christmas, but suddenly have both. Like patients at a mental institution whose invisible friend has thrown all the pills away and unlocked every exit.

I'm about to ask—

Bats.

A thousand, thousand, thousand bats are flying at me, around me, hairy and black, and the *smell*, the smell is like death and dying and failure and loneliness all woven into their tiny skeletal frames. I still feel the bone shards, the way they slice me and sting me and spill me open, but instead of lying on the net I am at the mouth of a cave with people I don't recognize. I am tall, I am cold. My hands are not my own.

Behind the bats: a blade.

And even though it is not my heart the dagger slices into but someone else's, the too-cool metal tears into me. Skin versus stab; I feel every frozen-hot second. I feel the soul slip out as the body slumps.

I blink, and finally I see the bridge again, not a bat in sight, my heart and soul intact despite whatever it was I just experienced.

Which was *what*, exactly?

The others are in various stages of delirium, anguish, absence. Some flail, some sink deep into the white woven fibers. Finnley is too close to the edge—one sharp shift could end her. Only Lonan and Hope managed to stop themselves in time to avoid it.

Lonan reaches out his strong, lean arms and helps me back to the platform. "Here," he says. "Who's carrying your shoes? Maybe the sap has dried by now."

"Phoenix—has them—in his pack." I can't get a deep breath in this soupy air.

Also, I just experienced death. Someone else's death. I think.

Hope's eyes go wide, and I turn to look. The bridge is stained red where Finnley's cheek rests on it, and she's shifted so far to the edge now that her entire right arm dangles. She waves in the breeze like a vine.

I shout at Alexa, try to get her attention—she's closest to Finnley—but she's as gone as the rest of them.

Do not go this way, the knots told us.

It would be nice if there were symbols for follow-up messages, like, *because your blood might drip from the bridge like rain. Or because free-falling to the ground will be the last thing you ever feel.*

Or *because you might not die, but you'll taste death. And what's the difference, really?*

Hope's fingers curl around my elbow. Her nails dig so deeply I can practically feel the dirt beneath them embedding in my skin.

"It's okay," I tell her. "We'll get her through this." Finnley is a threat, but it's not like she asked to be. I should have spoken up when I heard the first twig snap that night.

I pry myself away from Hope. *This is going to hurt*, is all I can think.

I should probably be thinking about other things. But Finnley is about to fall, so I run.

Delicate, careful: I am neither. Nor am I brave, because fear taints bravery and I am most definitely fueled by fear. The bridge is at once the sharpest and the softest, innocence-stained, and it takes so much control to keep it from defeating me. Every step, every shard, brings a flash of pain, lasting only as long as I am in contact. Black, charred flesh—teal-blue breathlessness—red-hot, poison-boiled veins—a tight noose of yellow snakeskin.

It is a rainbow of death.

The net is laced with more and more shards, the farther out I go. I grit my teeth against the pain, try to push through, but it's hard to separate truth from vision. I burn, and drown, and suffocate, and lastly—

I fall.

FIFTY

THE RAINBOW FADES as soon as I'm over the edge. No more borrowed pain—I have my own now. The bridge is as wild as a dragon flying out of ashes toward heaven, and then there's me, clinging to its tail. Finnley has not fallen over yet, and it is only, miraculously, because I'm now pulling the bridge down in the opposite direction.

Pain, fear, and impossible choices—these are all I have left.

Choose, Eden: death by plummeting to the jungle floor, or death by strained shoulder sockets, ripped clean apart by my dangling weight.

Choose, Eden: clamber up to safety—become Finnley's sure death rather than her savior, because she will surely fall when balance is restored—or spend sixty more seconds of life feeling noble.

Choose, Eden: choose, choose.

Humanity is not wired to choose death.

Not our own deaths, anyway.

So I choose life. And the irony is, it doesn't feel any different.

FIFTY-ONE

LONAN AND HOPE are wearing shoes.

Hope is screaming. "Help," she says. Over and over, "Lonan—help me! Finn's going to fall!"

But Lonan helps *me*.

FIFTY-TWO

WE ARE BLOOD and tears, but there is no time to drown in them.

Lonan digs in Phoenix's pack, retrieves my shoes. The cotton and sap have hardened into a stiff plaster, not nearly as sticky as before. The soles of my feet are mangled and swollen, but I force them inside, where bits of sand lodge themselves inside the wounds. It stings, grates. And yet it is better than the alternative.

We work together, Lonan and I, to pull Phoenix up from the net and back into consciousness. Hope is blank, empty, as she wipes blood from Alexa's feet and slips them into shoes. She does the same for Cass.

We leave Finnley's sneakers as they are, laces knotted to the handle of Phoenix's pack.

"Turn back, or keep going?" I am fragmented. We all are. "Do you honestly believe there's more to all this"—I gesture widely at the bridge—"than just death traps and blood?"

Phoenix drapes an arm across Lonan's shoulders. They continue to the far platform, and I have my answer: they want to press on.

"Do you honestly believe they'd go to so much effort to make a trap," Lonan says, breathing hard under Phoenix's weight, "if there wasn't something they were trying to hide?"

I only hope we find what we're looking for on the far end of this blood-drenched day. The cure to defuse the Wolves' spies, the Atlas Project science that could crack the foundations of this war—we desperately need both if we plan to purchase peace and freedom, sand and sunsets. I wish I knew, for certain, that these bridges were the best approach.

It's a gamble, it's a mind game. We are either the stupidest people alive for hurtling headfirst into *do not go this way*, or the most brilliant. We are either the blindest people alive for continuing, or the most strategic.

Hope and I work together to pull Alexa up. She blinks, eyes glazed over, her skin paler than I've ever seen it. Lonan goes back for Cass after he's delivered Phoenix to the platform.

None of our gashes are deep, life-threatening—it is more like we've been attacked by a flock of origami cranes, paper-thin slices that crisscross over our feet and ankles and all the other bits of exposed skin that came into contact with the shards. We will heal.

All of us but Finnley.

I risk a look over the edge, my first in some time now. I'm not looking for her broken body, or for height-induced terror. I look for closure.

I find none of the above.

We are so high up there are treetops below us, a tier of leaves so dense it's impossible to see what's beneath it. The leaves are thick, so thick—but not thick enough to catch her. Dizziness hits me like a cannonball. I dig my fingers into Hope's shoulders.

Steady, Eden. Steady.

"That bridge was insane," Cass says. He sits on the platform, back against bark, legs splayed out. His head lolls to one side.

> in·sane | in-'sān | adj.—in a state of mind that prevents normal perception, behavior, or social interaction

"Insane," I say. "Adjective. In a state of mind that prevents normal perception, behavior, or social interaction." The trees turn from green green green to black and white. "Yes."

Lonan shoves a bottle of water in my face. "Eden. You're losing it." He opens my mouth, pours water in, a little at a time. It trickles out of the corners of my mouth, and I cough. "Swallow," he tells me.

> swal·low | 'swä-lō | noun—a bird. A bird who sings, and feeds on insects as it flies. A bird whose wings break as it falls through the trees to the jungle floor below.

"I broke her wings," I say. "I broke her wings and she fell through the trees."

Lonan presses his thumb into my wrist. We are alive, my pulse says. We are alive and Finnley is not.

We are alive because Finnley is not.

"Look at me." Lonan has eyes I want to swim in. "And listen to me. Are you listening, Eden?"

E·den | ˈē-dᵊn | noun—a place or state of great happiness; an unspoiled paradise

"I'm not happy, I can't ever be happy," I tell him. "I've spoiled everything."

His eyes are an ocean, and he won't let me dry off. "You can be, and you will be. This is not your fault."

Not. Your fault.

Hope's eyes say it's my fault. Lonan's fault.

Or maybe Hope's eyes are just looking for someone to blame.

Maybe I'm looking for someone to blame.

Lonan is still talking at me. "You didn't build this bridge," he says. "You were trying to *save* her," he says. "This is not your fault," he says. "You nearly *died* trying to save her," he says.

Maybe it's that that has me in fragments.

My rainbow of death, my impossibly gray choices.

White stars prick at my vision, and then black black black floods them out.

FIFTY-THREE

WHEN I OPEN my eyes again,
> I have a raging headache,
> the world's colors have evened out,
> and I am alone with Lonan on the platform.

The planks' edges dig through my thin T-shirt and into my back, through my hair and into my skull. My shoes are off again—the soles have been picked over, scrubbed clean. It must have taken a lot of effort. Lonan's rubbing something into the tiny slices on the soles of my feet, and already, they're stronger. Not tender like before.

"What is that?"

"Raw honey and witch hazel," he says. "Speeds up the healing process."

"You had this before, when you told Hope to stay behind because of her leg?"

He gives me a small smile, a shrug. "I save the good stuff for people I'm certain I can trust." He pulls something from his pocket—the last remaining piece of what looks like a silk tech medicine card. "Let it dissolve under your tongue."

I take it from him. "Pain meds?" It's light blue, meaning it's nothing too loaded.

"Strong enough," he says, "and you won't have any side effects."

I close my eyes, cover them with my palms. Dig my fingertips into their corners where it throbs. "This isn't the last of your supply, I hope?"

Another shrug. "Just take it, Eden." He gives me a small grin. "For every piece I've used, there are another ten times I've just gritted my teeth instead. I'll be fine."

This headache is killing me, so I place the med tab under my tongue and let the saliva do its work. The relief is immediate. "Thanks for that," I say. "Really."

"I'd do it again," he says, his eyes on mine in a way that makes me blush.

"So . . . um." I look away, clear my throat. "How long have I been out? Where are the others?"

"Do you want the good news first?"

"I was out long enough for there to be news?" It takes effort to push myself up to a sitting position. I brush the hair out of my face. Open my eyes because I can't close them forever.

He hands me a bottle of water, and I guzzle it. "This is the end of the network," he says. "No more bridges, anyway."

"And that's good news?"

"There's a ladder carved into the side of this tree—Alexa and Hope found it."

"I don't see how that's good news."

"That's not all," he says. "They found another cave."

"Caves have not, in our history thus far, been good to us."

"They found another cave *with a net attached to it.* A big, wide net with no trace of anything that might slice a person up," he continues. "Right underneath our death bridge."

This: this is good news.

"Is Finnley—did she—"

His grin turns grim. "We don't know. What we *do* know is that she isn't on the net."

"Do you think, for sure, that it would have caught her?"

"It's as big as an Olympic-sized pool, Eden."

I take in his words, struggle to wrap my head around what he's saying. Because the last time I checked, girls don't fall ten, twenty, thirty feet and then just walk away without a word. They scream, they call for help, or they are dead.

And the dead don't walk away at all.

"You sure have a twisted version of the term *good news.*" I pull one shoe from where it rests near Lonan, shake out the excess sand. Repeat. Slip them on, press into the soles where most of my wounds are—good enough.

Finnley's disappearance: it's a carrot, dangling from a string, and we are hungry white rabbits.

Our treasure hunt expands with every hour.

Phoenix, Cass, Alexa. Hope, Lonan, me. We are an army of six: six wounded, six grieving, six compromised. Six determined.

Six against too many, and too many unknowns.

I'm convinced now that Lonan's right—that whoever's here on this island wouldn't have gone to all this trouble unless they had something major to hide. We've come too far to give up, too far to turn back. We *will* find the lab. We will find *answers.*

On the platform outside this new cave, Cass submits himself to having one arm bound up into a sling made from braided reeds—he is, in fact, the one who suggests it. "I fell hard on it," he tells Hope and Alexa. "Felt something pop."

But Phoenix already has the sling braided and ready to go, as if he and Cass discussed it privately before mentioning it to the group. Lonan leans discreetly toward me and says, in a low voice, "He doesn't trust himself."

"Because the cave may be another trigger?"

Lonan nods. "Because *anything* could be another trigger."

I take one last, long look at the net. It is too bright, too clean. Too empty. "Am I a horrible person," I say, testing the words in my head before I let them escape, "if I admit I'm the tiniest bit relieved that she isn't with us right now?"

I am a contradiction. Because how can you grieve someone and at the same time feel relief at their absence? How can you feel relief at your own shot at survival when it's at the expense of someone else's?

His eyes are cool and calm as they search me. "All I see in you is empathy."

"Yeah?"

"Yes." He offers me his hand. "Ready to go? They're waiting on us."

I hesitate.

It doesn't mean anything, I tell myself. It doesn't mean I don't care about Birch—just that Lonan's trying to be there for me. That I'm trying, after all this time, to trust enough to let someone in. Right? What am I afraid of?

Finally, I put my hand in his. His skin is warm, yet it sends shivers coursing through me as he pulls me to my feet. We find ourselves, once again, at the back of the group.

I should pull my hand away, I tell myself. I should loosen my grip, at the very least. But the message doesn't make it to my fingers, which shift and curl until they've woven between his. We're locked, linked.

He doesn't pull away, either.

The cave is black inside, where no one can see the flush of my cheeks. I hardly know Lonan at all—what business do I have holding on to him this tightly? He held me earlier, on the roof of the cave, but that was different. That was one human holding another one together. It was wax pressed into the veins of a cracked clay jar in order to keep it from bleeding itself dry.

This is different. This is a choice, one we continue to make every second we don't let go. Despite everything I don't know about him, and everything I do, I choose this present comfort. I trust him just enough.

A more highly evolved version of the boys' beach lantern blooms to light, the same torch used to illuminate our first cave.

Twigs and sticks and the remains of a match burn in the basin of a glass jar, which Phoenix holds by its twisted-wire handle. His hair looks especially red in the glow of the fire, his cheekbones especially sharp where there are shadows.

This cave is nothing like the other. Its roof is so low I could touch it without standing on my toes, and the tunnel is narrow and sloping steeply downward. Further confirmation that we are Alice's white rabbit, on a mission.

Memories strike without warning: my collection of glass apothecary bottles, all shapes and colors and sizes, inspired by the DRINK ME scene in *Alice's Adventures in Wonderland*. I wonder how much dust they've collected on my bathroom shelf. I wonder, too, about the tea set we used at my sixth birthday party, and about the blue-and-white dress my mother sewed for the occasion. And the book itself—what I wouldn't give to hold it again. The thought alone brings back the smell of my mother's shampoo, of nail polish remover, of honey and warm milk: her bedtime routine and mine for so many months, that year before the accident.

Lonan tightens his hand in mine, pulls me out of myself. "You okay? You slowed down." He's close at my back, so close I fear he might be able to feel my heart slamming in its cage.

I shake my head. "I'm good. Sorry."

He must know I'm lying—or trying to talk myself into a truth, at least—because his hand stays just as it is. "We can talk later, if you'd like."

I just nod, like some brainless bobblehead on a dashboard.

Because what is there to say? Everyone has lost someone. Everyone is homeless. No one can rewind time and go back to the days where our biggest problems amounted to spilled nail polish and broken teacups. Dwelling on it won't help anything, especially not today.

FIFTY-FOUR

BIRCH AND I were fourteen when he first held my hand.

It was three years to the day after my bee-sting birthday party. The parents had just finished forcing us, and Emma, to pose for pictures until their smartphones ran out of memory; our hair was sweaty and matted from being stuck under graduation caps for too long inside the stuffy gymnasium. I remember thinking it was stupid to celebrate something as unremarkable as completing the eighth grade. At the time, I expected I'd have a normal graduation from high school to look forward to. Everyone did.

The rain snuck up on us. Silver-gray clouds rolled in and poured buckets of water on everyone's repurposed Easter dresses and fancy shoes. All the parents tucked their picture-loaded phones away and darted off to retrieve their luxury SUVs, while all of my classmates huddled together under the not-quite-sufficient awning outside the school.

Birch gave me his jacket. Then he gave me his hand. And even though we eventually had to let go, for practical purposes—we did live in separate homes, after all—it felt like nothing could ever come between us.

That feeling never did go away. Not even when he died.

No one is more surprised than I am that my hand fits so well in someone else's.

FIFTY-FIVE

WE MAKE A sharp right turn, and the sloping ground of the cave levels out. A patch of white light spills across the dirt at the very far end, where Phoenix's lantern won't reach for a while. Lonan and I trail behind the rest of the group. They've been mostly quiet until now, save for the brush of shoes on stone, but up ahead, one of the boys mutters something. It's hard to make out whose voice it is.

"Well, you don't have to be an *ass* about it," Alexa says.

"I've told you three times now not to walk so close." Cass. Loud and clear, definitely Cass. "We're not together anymore, Alexa. You don't get to act like we are."

"And why exactly *aren't* we together, Cass?" She flings his name at him like it's covered in acid. "What happened to forever? What happened to escape?"

I want to tell her, want to shout *He didn't leave on purpose!*

To unspool the full truth of why he left, though, would be to unravel all their secrets. I hate seeing Alexa like this, but I can't jeopardize Lonan's trust in me. Not after all we've been through.

"This isn't the time, Lex." Cass's voice is steady, intense. It slices like a knife.

"When would be a better time? You've hardly bothered to say two words to me since you showed up on our beach. What are you *doing* here, anyway? *How?*" The pitch of her voice rises, shakes. It's the most honest thing I've heard out of her yet. "This was your plan all along, wasn't it—to escape without me! To leave me behind!"

Hope's quiet voice pokes a hole in the tension. "This really doesn't seem like the best time, Alexa." We are all at a standstill now, a volatile collection of humanity in this claustrophobic tunnel.

"It isn't like that," Cass says. He's losing his grip on even, emotionless speech. "I didn't leave you behind, but thanks for the accusation."

"You should stop," Phoenix says under his breath.

But Cass doesn't hear him, or doesn't listen. "Since you're begging for the truth, though, how's this: I haven't trusted you since the day you tied that rope around my neck. You're gorgeous, Lex, but you're unpredictable and you're selfish."

He yanks the lantern out of Phoenix's grip. Shadows and light dance on the cave walls, following him as he makes his way, alone, toward the white patch of sun at the very end.

"That was too far and you know it, Cass." Lonan's voice bounces from the tunnel walls; our footsteps chase after it. This is the first time we've been the leaders of the pack. And we do lead, but not by much—Alexa steps on my heels more than once, trying to get to Cass, but Lonan and I are careful to keep her behind us. There's been enough bloodshed today.

"Last I heard, honesty was a virtue," Cass replies, his voice cutting through the darkness.

"Last *I* heard, so was kindness."

Phoenix snorts. "You're one to talk, Lo."

"Name one unkind thing I've done today," Lonan says. And maybe I've been wearing kindness-colored glasses all day, but I can't think of anything. Sure, there was our disagreement just after the cliff ledge, and earlier, the knife he held at his throat. But the sum of those was kindness, greater than its parts.

"You ate the last of my venison jerky," Phoenix says.

"That was yesterday. Try again."

But he doesn't try again—none of us do—because now we are bathed in late afternoon daylight and the dimming embers of the glass-jar lantern, having finally reached Cass and the far end of the tunnel. More than that, we are stunned silent, stunned still.

There's a lodge.

A multitiered, grass-roofed, warm-glow-in-the-windows lodge is nestled no more than fifty yards away, amid a thick hedge of foliage. Glassy, onyx-black water curves around the foliage wall, snaking all the way back around to the mouth of our tunnel. A rickety plank walkway hugs the entire length of the canal, and closer to the lodge, a series of roughly hewn canoes bobs idly in the water. I'm guessing those aren't meant for us.

So who are they meant for?

"The lights are on," Hope whispers. "The *lights* are on."

Electricity.

Humanity.

We are not alone.

But we've known that for a while now.

"Water, walkway, or back to the nets," Lonan says. "Those are our options."

A half laugh escapes me. "You say that as if we *have* options."

"I like to be thorough."

"Do you think that's where they took Finnley?" Hope says, pushing her way through the group. "It looks . . . cozier than I imagined."

"Looks can be deceiving," Cass says, giving Alexa a pointed look.

"Leave it alone," Lonan says.

Alexa doesn't respond, but I've been around her long enough to pick up on her stubborn way of expressing gratitude. She gives Lonan this look now: a subtle narrowing of both eyes, with the sentiment of a wink and the focused intent of telepathy. I've never seen the expression on any other person. It makes me wonder what else is left to discover of humanity.

"So I think we can rule out going back to the nets," I say, eager to get on with this. Finding Finnley, dead or alive—finding the lab—finding *answers*. "The water doesn't really seem all that viable. At the very least, the walkway to the lodge seems like the most obvious option."

Something doesn't sit right about taking the walkway, though, and not because of its rickety planks. In the most basic of ways, the Wolves have won, and it sickens me: they've created in me a petri dish of suspicion. Nothing can ever be simple again, I fear.

"Do what you want," Hope says. "I'm going to find her." She stretches one long, thin leg out from the cave. Once she's firmly on the wood, she shoves her hands in her pockets and walks away from us without a backward glance.

It's a very un-Hope thing to say, a very un-Hope thing to do.

Losing the people we care about can do that, I guess. Change us. Make us desperate enough to head straight into enemy territory with nothing but our demands to keep us company.

Cass runs his free hand through his hair. "You shouldn't go alone," he calls after her, glancing from Phoenix to Lonan. He's twitchy, exasperated.

"Then come with me," she says. She doesn't slow down in the slightest.

Lonan doesn't want to, I feel it in his hand—it's just as warm as before, and just as soft, but somehow there are more angles.

But Alexa steps out after her, jumps to the walkway with the grace of a cat. She lifts her chin to Cass, like, *See? I'm not the selfish person you think I am.* His expression doesn't change, so it's hard to discern exactly why he steps out next—for Alexa? For Hope? For his own conscience? Who knows.

What I do know is this: it takes only one follower to start a movement, and another follower after that to give it momentum. It is the momentum that compels Lonan and me across the walkway, and Phoenix, too, most likely. I try to find comfort in Lonan's words, back at the cave—that seeking out enemy territory for the sake of finding the cure, and the Atlas Project science, has been part of the plan all along. That it's necessary.

I try to find comfort, but it doesn't want to be found.

Best way to find what you're looking for, Lonan said, *is to draw out the enemy and force them to lead you straight to it.*

But is that really what's happening here?

Perhaps we are the ones who are being drawn out, and not the other way around.

FIFTY-SIX

THE COMPLICATIONS BEGIN at the end of the plank walkway.

It is a total dead end, and doesn't lead anywhere significant—just to more foliage, and behind that, rock. The water, with its strange glassy-black surface, curves around to the far side of the lodge. Unless we go in blind with canoes or attempt to climb up and through the thick barrier of foliage, we won't be able to get any closer.

Phoenix and Lonan have an entire conversation with their eyes. Finally, Phoenix says, "You want lead, or should I take it?"

"Go ahead," Lonan says. He glances my way, which I take as an invitation to voice any objections. I decide to stay out of it, for now, unless Phoenix says something that makes absolutely no sense.

Phoenix nods, tightens the straps on his backpack. "Alexa, Cass—you're with me. Eden and Hope will go with Lonan."

Alexa, Cass, and Hope all start to protest, and I'm on the verge of joining in—it seems like a better idea to leave Cass behind altogether, given his HoloWolf complications—but

Lonan's voice overtakes them: "This is the best split, so please try to get over yourselves. A lot more than our own comfort is at stake here. We have a better shot at finding Finnley if we're looking in more than one place."

He conveniently leaves out the part about looking for the cure, as the girls don't know about it, and he definitely doesn't mention his secret mission for the Allied Forces.

We all have our secrets. Like the dread and hope fluttering within me, twin butterflies that chase each other in circles: Did the people here know my father? Are they the ones who sent me the vial, the book? Are they the ones who pried the ring from his cold, dead finger?

Are they the reason he's gone?

"We good?" Phoenix says, glancing cautiously from Cass to Alexa, then to me.

If these people did take my father from me, there's nothing I'd love more than to take something back in return. I have so many questions, though— What does the cure look like? How do we administer it? How will we know if it worked? Where is the science kept, and how do we plan to steal it, let alone lock the Wolves out of it?—but I'm guessing Lonan has exactly zero answers. At least I know what Envirotech's old blueprints looked like. That's a start.

"Yeah," I say, finally. "We're good."

"Okay, then," Phoenix goes on. "Lonan's group will take the canoes. Everyone with me, get ready to force your way through the foliage."

"Cass," Hope says, "how's your arm? Is your sling going to get in the way?"

The guys have another wordless exchange. Lonan appears to be the hesitant one of the group, but Phoenix speaks up: "It's been a little while since you hurt it— Was it okay while we were in that last cave?"

I'm guessing this must be code for *Well, you haven't tried to kill anyone in a while, so maybe we're past the trigger points.*

Cass looks a little reluctant, but one glance at the foliage-heavy barrier says he thinks he'll be useless without both arms. He certainly wouldn't be much use in a canoe.

"Yeah," he says. "I think I can manage without the sling."

"Be sure and help him if it starts to hurt again, Phoenix," Lonan says. More code, I assume.

"Anything else before we split?" I ask. I'm on board with their strategy, I decide. It's obvious they're not going at this thoughtlessly—Lonan would have considered leaving Cass behind, I'm sure of it. He must think we'll be stronger this way, even with the added risk. "Are we planning to meet up after we're finished here? How will we know everyone made it out okay?"

Phoenix fishes around in his backpack, then pulls out a pair of thin black devices. He keeps one and tosses the other to Lonan. "Two-way radios, so we can reconnect," he explains. "Solar charged. Also, Hope, if you could please take off that blasted sweater, we'll have a better shot at blending in."

My cardigan is tattered and stained, hardly the bright yellow it once was, but it's still an unnatural color amid all this green. Hope leaves it in a crumpled heap on the cave floor. It's all I can do not to pick it up—but carrying a bright yellow cardigan isn't all that different from wearing one, when it comes to blending in. If only Phoenix's pack weren't so full.

Lonan clips the small, sleek radio to his pants, just above his right hip. "Okay, everyone," he says. "Do your best to stay out of sight, but be prepared to defend yourselves. And if all goes to hell, we're aiming to accomplish two things: get what we're looking for, and try not to die."

Neither task will be without its challenges.

Hope, Lonan, and I choose our canoe arbitrarily. It's an exact replica of the other four that bob idly against our dead-end walkway, except for a faded red stripe down its nose. I pray the red is paint, and not the dried remnants of someone else's life.

I steal an extra pair of paddles from one of the other boats, and then all three of us pile into the same canoe. Even if we don't use them, they may come in handy as weapons.

"You have experience with tandem paddling?" he asks.

"Only five summers' worth at sleepaway camp." Not that I *asked* for so much experience—it was a mandatory part of every camper's schedule. "I'm good in either position. You?"

"Same."

Just because I'm experienced in canoeing, it doesn't mean I've ever enjoyed it. I had nightmares, all throughout my childhood, of snakes in dark water. So very many nights, Dad would check under my bed to reassure me that none were waiting to sink their fangs into me. He must have spent a fortune on flashlight bulbs.

The fiercest nightmare, the recurring one, was of water moccasins: at first, in the dream, there is only one. It slithers past my calf, coils itself around my ankle. And then the others come, a pair from each direction on the surface of the water, more than I can count underneath. They never strike, but instead kill me by squeezing all the air from my lungs.

I wake up every time with my heart pounding in my chest, trying to jump-start my lungs back into action and remind them to breathe.

Oceans full of sharks don't scare me, and neither do clear-to-the-bottom streams.

It's murky, stagnant water that's hard. And being surrounded by it on all sides.

"Breathe, Eden." Lonan has nearly perfected the art of calling me back to myself. I wish he hadn't had so many chances to work on this art. "Your mind is stronger than your circumstances. Remember that."

I nod. He's had plenty of opportunities to perfect his strong mind, too, I remind myself. Cleaning his parents' blood from their kitchen tile was likely a harsh way to begin.

"Thank you," I say. "You're right." Because what are imagined threats compared with the venom that's stolen my family, my Birch, my life? This should be nothing.

We dip our paddles into the water. Lonan's at the bow, for

optimal rowing power, while I sit stern, in the steering position. Hope is between us, our lookout. Every slice of our paddles pulls us farther from the relative safety of our plank walkway, and closer to whatever waits for us around the bend. Water surrounds our canoe on all sides now, with trees and leaves and every shade of green spilling over the banks. This canal isn't the widest I've ever seen—it's two canoe lengths across, at most—but still, it is oppressive. Mind over fear, I remind myself. My mind is stronger than my circumstances. There are no snakes.

The foliage is so thick and steep between our canal and the lodge that from this angle it's hard to see much of the lodge at all. Only the top tier is completely visible, warm yellow lights glowing through the windows underneath the thatched roof. Soon, the sun will set, and we'll see even less.

We paddle, on and on until we've made almost a half circle from where we started, but we don't find the obvious entrance we hope for. The canal bends slightly away from the lodge and into a stony, moss-covered cave; the roof is so low we will barely be able to sit straight up, let alone stand. I have a sudden flashback to the Pirates of the Caribbean ride at Disney World—the panic attack I had, at age seven, when I saw we'd stood in line forever just to ride boats in dark water that went to places I couldn't see.

A faint, high-pitched beep comes in over Lonan's two-way radio. He stops paddling, and so do I, just outside the cave.

He pries the radio from his waistband, and I get a flash of skin just before his T-shirt falls again. A blue light turns on when he speaks. "Lonan here. Find something?"

The radio crackles. "Yeah," the voice comes through. I'm pretty sure it's Phoenix. "We're past the foliage barrier and we can see the entrance, but it's impossible to get there from here." Between the crackling and the way he's borderline whispering, it's a wonder his message makes it through as clearly as it does. "I think you may have a shot, though. Looks like your water goes straight to the door of this huge main room, but both the bottom level of the room and the canal are partially underground, somehow. Does that line up with what you see there?"

Panic attacks begin the same way at age seventeen as they do at age seven, it turns out. We're going to have to go in this cave. There's no way around it. Breathe, Eden.

"Yes," Lonan affirms, apparently not fazed at all by the idea of canoeing to our murky doom. "We'll check it out. Keep your guard up, though—just because you can't get in from where you are doesn't mean they're not prepared to keep you from trying. They've got eyes everywhere—remind Cass."

Lonan glances at me over his shoulder as he says the last line, and I am certain it's another bit of their codespeak. Either it's not encrypted enough or I've become fluent, because I can easily translate it to mean *Remember, they know exactly where you are, because Cass is with you and they can spy through him.*

"Will do," Phoenix says.

Lonan clips the radio back in place and picks his paddle up. "Ready?"

"Ready for anything, if it gets us closer to Finnley," Hope says.

I open my mouth, but words don't come out like they should.

Lonan turns all the way around to face me. "Eden? Ready?" He looks like he's on the verge of losing patience. He doesn't understand—and why should he? I conquered my fear of heights today, numerous times, and I've been fine in the caves. And he already gave me his easy-fix mind-over-matter advice. My mind may be strong, but my body doesn't want to hear about it.

"I . . ." They're both staring at me now. "I don't do well with this kind of water. Especially in dark caves. Especially if there might be, uh . . . water moccasins." It sounds so stupid to say it out loud. I am a five-year-old in a seventeen-year-old's body. "And it's really dark in there."

Lonan's jaw twitches. "Hate to break it to you, but it's only going to get darker the longer we wait."

"Seriously? *That* makes me feel better, thanks."

"Well, what do you suggest we do? I thought you were stronger than this, Eden. I *know* you are stronger than this."

Such a compliment has never made my blood boil so furiously. "You don't know me. You're wrong."

All strong people break, eventually.

Hope averts her eyes, studies her hands. Sorry, Hope. You are stuck in a canoe with the perfect example of humanity when it's pushed to its fracture point.

"I've been wrong about a lot of things in my life, but this is not one of them," he says. No one has ever pressed me this hard, and it ties up my ability to fight back. "You *can* do this. I refuse to watch someone with such strength utterly crater in the face of fear."

"You're kind of diminishing my fear by acting like it's the easiest thing in the world—like I should be able to just get over it."

"No," he says. "The more difficult something is, the stronger you prove yourself when you overcome it. I absolutely believe this is terrifying you—you're white as the moon; you're not breathing right. I don't think it will be easy for you, but I do believe you're strong enough to conquer it."

Again, the image of him scrubbing bloodstains from his kitchen floor shames me. He doesn't bring it up—he doesn't have to. It's written all over his face, the memories he sees every time he has to summon his own strength. Every time he summons mine.

Something clicks: he's not trying to hurt me with his words, I know this, but I assumed he was trying to tell me I should just pretend the fear away when things get rough. Pretend nothing is ever painful, nothing is ever misery.

Now I'm certain that's not it—those things don't have to work against me, I realize.

He's trying to show me how to *thrive* on them.

I collect myself, all the parts of me that are trying to escape this boat and the responsibility that comes with it. "Okay," I say. And again: "Okay."

We dip our paddles into the black, black water.

FIFTY-SEVEN

WE ARE FLYING through clouds, we are sliding down rainbows.

These are the things I tell myself as my world turns black and breathless.

It helps enough, in that I am still paddling. Still alive, still moving forward.

Our breaths echo. The dips of our paddles, the drips of the water: they echo, too. *This is the sound of fear being killed*, I tell myself. I carve my paddle hard into the water. I breathe.

Lonan's radio beeps, the sound amplified by the hardness of this space. It is so dark in here the blue light looks like a neon sign. It stays firmly at his hip.

"You going to answer that?" I ask.

"I'm otherwise occupied right now," he says.

"It might be urgent."

"I won't be able to do anything about it. And for your sake, I want you to know I'm prepared in case things become urgent here."

His admission that this cave likely poses a threat to us is both comforting and unnerving.

A hint of bluish green glows on the water up ahead. "Whoa," I breathe when we get closer, and find that the cave curves around sharply to the right. It is like someone has scattered stardust all over the ceiling, a constellation of fireflies. As dark as the cave was before the bend, it is now bathed in a dim, ethereal turquoise glow. A droplet of something sticky lands on my forearm, followed by another on my knee. If I listen closely, I can hear the droplets as they fall into the water. Hope's eyes are wide as she takes everything in, as wide as my own.

Lonan's radio beeps again, and again after that.

"It's okay," I say. "They might be trying to warn us of something."

His radio light rises, and a loud crackle echoes through the chamber. "Phoenix?" Our canoe slows down now that Lonan's not paddling. I let my paddle hover above the water. "Everything good up there?"

No answer.

Another crackle—not from Phoenix's end. "Cass? Alexa?"

Nothing.

Lonan mutters a curse. "If you can hear me, and if you're in trouble, don't worry about us. Do what you need to survive. We'll find you later." One last crackle fills the cave.

But the blue radio light never makes it back to Lonan's waist. Our boat dips sharply to one side as Hope springs from her bench like a black widow has just landed in her lap, and then the radio is airborne. And then waterlogged. The light glows blue for about half a second before it dies.

"Holy—"

Lonan's voice is the last thing I hear before I am overtaken. Hope is fast, fierce: her thin frame has some force to it; her fingers are vises. I choke on her hair in my face as she forces me overboard and follows me into the water.

I kick, I thrash, I struggle against the urge to breathe underwater. Stars prick at my vision, reminding me I'm not dead yet. I break the surface, gasp for air, but she plunges me right back under. There are no water moccasins—there is nothing but Hope and hopelessness. Water moccasins would have been preferable, in a way. A quicker death without the pain of betrayal.

The turquoise glow isn't so dim anymore, at least. Every time Hope's forearms meet water, it amplifies the faintly glowing wolf on her skin until it is a shimmering and iridescent hologram. My death will have its very own spotlight.

I fight back, pry at her fingers, dig my nails into her skin until I'm sure she's bleeding. This buys me a little bit of air, a chance to get away. When was she compromised? How long has she been this way, how did we miss it? This starlit bend in the cave has to have been the trigger—the sticky droplets that fell on us, maybe?—but before that, she seemed so *with* us.

Lonan is in the water now, too. His arms show no trace of light, no trace of wolf. This is the most air I've taken in at once, likely because he's put himself in Hope's path. It's also the first time I notice how shallow the water is. When I'm completely stretched out, my toes graze the bottom.

"Sedate her!" he shouts. He succeeds at keeping Hope from me, but she is quick—I see the glow of her hologram as she slips from his grasp on her, as she darts to his unguarded side. He's quick, too. She doesn't get through, can't take him down.

"I can't," I say, breathless. "No syringe."

"In my pocket—left side."

I swim back toward him. Hope grabs my wrist and she yanks, hard, pulling me directly into Lonan's backside. My pulse races for all the wrong reasons as we collide—or all the right reasons, if you're looking at it from a *reasons to stay alive* perspective.

Focus, Eden.

Syringe. Syringe first, out of the water next. Lonan after that.

I work my hand into his pants pocket. It's a tight fit, not much room for anything but the syringe. I find it with little effort.

Lonan has finally forced Hope to hold still. I go to where the hologram glows brightest, run my hand up her arm until I'm sure it's her shoulder—she and Lonan are tangled together, shadow on shadow, and I don't want to accidentally sedate Lonan.

Hope is like a fragile bird, all bone-wings and feathery hair. I plunge the needle into the spot where she has the most muscle, and immediately, the wolf goes black. Lonan shifts to support her limp weight.

We are breathing hard, hard in this echo chamber of a cave. Everything spins like a time-lapse video of a clear night sky.

"Still afraid of snakes?"

Yes, I want to say. Phobias don't just go away because there are even greater things to fear.

FIFTY-EIGHT

"THEY MUST HAVE done something to her that night they took Finnley," I say as I guide our canoe to a shadowy strip of water that isn't so bright. Best to stay as hidden as possible, given that we've taken down one of their HoloWolves this close to the lodge.

"It makes sense, now that I think about it," I continue. "Of course they wouldn't let us wander the island without some means of keeping an eye on us. But why wouldn't they just take us all at once?" I struggle to climb back up into the canoe without tipping it over. It isn't easy to do in the dark, especially since Lonan has his arms full of Hope. One desperately awkward maneuver later, I finally land myself back inside. It was likely not the most flattering thing to watch, and for once, I find myself grateful for the dark.

"I can think of a few reasons they might not have taken you all at once." Lonan's voice is closer than I expected. "A little help here first?"

I feel around in the direction of his voice. My hands find his face, the stubble on his perfectly angular jaw. His lips.

I am still grateful for the dark.

"On three," he says as I move my hands south in an attempt to find Hope. "Grab under her arms and pull—I'll push from here."

The canoe dips slightly as I reach for her, but not so much as to cause disaster. With a bit of grace and a lot of effort, we settle Hope onto the floor of the canoe. An inch or two of the murky water has found its way into the boat; at least she is unconscious and won't notice it grunging up her hair.

Lonan climbs in so effortlessly I don't even realize he's out of the water until he speaks again. Since he lived on the ocean throughout the whole war, it's not surprising. Climbing in and out of boats is probably as second nature to him as it was for me to climb into my bed at barracks.

"Reasons they might not have taken you, number one," he begins. "If working as a Deliverer taught me anything about the Wolfpack, it's that they are purposefully illogical about things. In their eyes, it makes them more difficult to predict. In my eyes, too. Phoenix and I've intercepted, oh, twenty of their ships in the past few months alone. Some are manned with minimal crews of only one or two, others have ten aboard. Makes it harder for the Resistance to plan for attacks, if that makes sense, and it messes with our minds—intercepting a small crew causes us to let our guard down, and large crews are intimidating at best, devastating at worst."

We seem to have mutually decided to take a breath before hashing out the next steps of our plan. Hopefully we have *time* for a breath, because we definitely need a plan—especially with

Hope unconscious in our canoe.

"So, all that said, the one thing I've noticed they're consistently predictable about is that they send the compromised people back to the mainland in small batches."

"It makes it easier to slip them back in unnoticed," I say, knowing I'm right even before he affirms it. Which he does.

"Reason number two," he continues, "is that Alexa was with you. She still has the markings of a Wolf—perhaps they decided to watch her for a while before jumping to conclusions about her loyalty."

It is incredible how quickly the world can turn. How, given the choice between Alexa and Hope and Finnley, Alexa has become the most trustworthy.

"Reason number three is simple common sense."

He says it so plainly. As if he's communicating something as obvious as *water is necessary for survival*—but he's talking to someone for whom water nearly became the opposite of survival, in a world where seawater may become the death of humanity.

Nothing makes easy sense anymore.

"There's nowhere else for you to go," he says, "so there's no hurry for them to take you all at once. Leaving a spy in your group helps them study Alexa, for one, but maybe it was also an experiment—maybe they wanted to see if they're as well-hidden as they think they are. Maybe they wanted to see how close someone could get to their lodge without knowing where to look, or knowing it exists at all."

"Obviously, they know by now that we know about the

lodge—and that we've actively been searching for it."

"Obviously."

"But they haven't come after us, or tried to stop us." Even as I say it, I realize that isn't true. They're coming at us the lazy way: by using the people we trust to do their dirty work.

"Haven't they?" He gives a low, rueful laugh. "Between Cass and Finnley and Hope, not to mention all the island's . . ."

"Security features?"

"*Yeah.*" The word is half breath, half disbelief. "All of the above says they've done a hell of a job so far."

"What do you think happened to the others?"

Lonan is quiet for so long the silence folds in on itself, until my ears are acutely aware of the void where sound should be. There is not as much as a drip that rips through the silence of this cave.

Finally, he sighs. "Nothing good."

I can't come up with anything encouraging to offer. Their silence was a bad sign. The fact that they haven't come looking for us—despite our radio going dark, despite our less than quiet conflict with Hope—is *also* a bad sign.

A skittering, scuffling sound echoes from the mouth of our cave, back around the bend where we first entered. I freeze. Even if it's not human, it could be more beetles. Or something worse.

"We need a plan," I say, two shades from silence. "What's our plan?"

Now that I've thought of the beetles, I can't unthink them.

I imagine they are covering the low ceiling of this cave like a carpet, waiting for one of us to slice a finger or a shin, waiting to devour us. And then I try not to imagine it.

There is another noise now. Another paddle dipping in the water.

"Eden?" says the voice. "Is that you?"

Alexa.

"Get the syringe ready," Lonan says, his voice barely audible. "Just in case."

I used it all on Hope. I used it *all*.

Our canoe is in shadows, but only barely—most of this section of the cave is dotted with the turquoise glow of firefly starlight, with tiny ripples from all the dripping. If they managed to compromise Hope without any of us picking up on it, it's possible they got to Alexa, too.

"Yeah, it's me." My voice shakes. "What happened? Where are Phoenix and Cass?"

"Cass collapsed up there; he was barely breathing." She is frantic but not loud. "Phoenix and I ran to help him, and Phoenix was only a few feet ahead of me, but a tiny blow dart with blue feathers stuck him in the neck, and he collapsed, too"—she hardly pauses for a breath—"and I slipped back behind some thick trees before I could see who shot him, and before they could shoot me, and I came around here as fast as I could. What the *hell* is going on?"

The tip of her canoe edges around the corner. "This is going to sound pretty odd," Lonan says, "but I'm going to need you to put your arms in the water before you come any closer."

"Put my—what?"

"Your arms. In the water."

But she doesn't stop; she just keeps paddling until her boat is entirely bathed in turquoise light. Blood rushes in my head—the droplets, or even just the glow, could already have triggered her. Hope's hologram was faint against this light unless it was underwater.

Our canoe dips as Lonan reaches over the edge. There is a clunk of wood on wood: he's pulled Alexa's boat right next to ours. "What are you *doing*?" Alexa says, wildfire words. Her eyes are wide, wide. Just like Hope's were.

I wish I had another syringe.

Lonan is swift, strong, as he takes her hand and plunges it underwater. "It's a test to make sure"—drip, drip, drip, water from skin, darkness—"oh, good. You're not."

"We had a little . . . incident," I add. "With Hope."

Lonan gives her a brief, not very thorough explanation. Perhaps it is the urgent tone to his voice that keeps Alexa from asking questions.

"So now we need to get inside the lodge," he concludes.

"And when they shoot *you* with blow darts, what are we supposed to do?" Alexa is all bitterness, but it's not a bad question. "What are we going to do with Hope? And assuming we find Finnley, what if she's unconscious? Are we just going to lug them both around?"

Working out complicated plans while in a cave where I was

nearly drowned: this is not something I've always dreamed of doing. I am a split second away from suggesting we turn back, head for the beach, catch and cook a boatload of fish. But that leaves us worse off than before, an army of three against an enemy who'll continue to pick us off one by one. The stars will be pretty for one night, and the fish will take away the hunger pains I've gotten too good at ignoring—but then what?

This is our best chance at a better life, my best chance at answers. If they pick us off as soon as we emerge from this cave, at least we will have *tried*, rather than just accepting our fate. That would be like volunteering ourselves to be turned into spies for their horrid, greedy war. Like volunteering to become cadavers.

"We're going to split up." Lonan's voice is calm and clear.

"Bad things happen when we split up," I say.

"Worse things might if we don't," he counters. "I think this time will be different, though." He goes on with his plan: Alexa and I will paddle Hope all the way back out to the edge of the sloping, narrow tunnel that led us to the water, where we first glimpsed the lodge and the plank walkway and the canoes— where Hope still seemed like herself, where Cass said things to hurt Alexa.

Perhaps this accounts for her silence. Cass collapsed in front of her, and some of the last words he said to her were of the meant-to-wound variety. Perhaps Alexa is in shock.

"Eden, help Alexa get Hope out of the canoe and as far into that tunnel as you can. From there, Alexa, I need you to stay with her. Here"—our boat dips a little—"use this syringe on her if she's out of her mind when she wakes up. Eden, once they're settled, try to break your way into the lodge."

He says it like he's asking me to lie down in a field of wildflowers on a sunny summer afternoon. As if it should be the easiest thing in the world.

And of course he has more than one syringe. It must have been in his other pocket.

"What if they see us? What if they *shoot* us?" I ask. Blow darts could come from any direction—being out in the open canal seems like it'd make us easy targets.

"I'll make sure they don't."

"And how are you going to do that?"

He takes a loud, deep breath. "By turning myself in."

Earlier, when he said he meant to walk right in and ask for the things we hope to find, I thought his plan was of the knives-at-throats variety. That was bad enough—this is even worse.

No. No, no. "*No,*" I say. "They'll kill you."

"They won't, I told you before. They *should*, for all I've stolen from them—but they won't."

"And why's that?"

"I'm captain of the Deliverers, one of the commanding leaders of the Resistance. My people trust me." I see where he's going with this, and it gives me a sick, sick feeling. "I'm of excellent use to them alive. Use me as their spy and they'll have direct access to the entire Resistance, all the leaders who've hidden themselves so well. I know who they are; I know where

they are. I know how to get to them. If the Wolves were working through me, they'd easily be able to take down a good lot of
their opposition—maybe all of it."

A wave of rage roils in me. At him, for never mentioning
just how valuable he is to them. At me, for not putting things
together before now. "This . . . is, like, the *worst* plan."

"It's better than us all getting killed," he says.

"*Is* it?" I'm not so sure.

"It definitely is," he says. "We're going to capsize this whole
damn war, Eden. As long as you find it in time."

"*It* the Atlas Project science, or *it* the cure?" I glance briefly
at Alexa, worried we've said too much in front of her—but she is
still expressionless, lost in her own head. Hopefully she'll snap
out of it when it comes down to it. I can't pull off our half of the
plan on my own.

"Yes. Both, either." He runs his hands through his hair. "Find
the lab, go from there. They're both pretty crucial, and we'll
have some gaping vulnerabilities if we don't make it out with at
least one of those."

No pressure at all. "Any idea where to look for said lab?"
The lodge has at least two levels, maybe another hidden by
the thick trees—they could have tucked it deeply inside any of
them. And the cure, assuming Lonan's intel holds up and there
even *is* a cure, is likely buried even deeper. Not to mention how
deeply they must have buried the research and development
plans for the Atlas Project, information so secret Lonan hasn't
even told the guys about it.

"In the place that's hardest to get to, I'd guess," he says. "Your judgment is as good as mine."

It is both the most fortifying, and the most terrifying, thing he could say.

I hate him for putting himself in this position. I hate him for putting *me* in this position. There are so many ways this could go wrong. Either we succeed, or we are catastrophic failures.

I imagine the Wolves are sandcastles, easily crushed and easily washed away. I imagine there will be a day when they are nothing but a memory.

I imagine that day will start tonight. I *plan* for it to start tonight. Success is my only option. Because as much as I hate Lonan's plan, I have to admit it's a more strategic approach than going in all at once. If he can create a diversion, and if I time things right, I may be able to slip in under the radar, especially if I can find a different way in. There was stone behind the foliage—maybe there's a way to scale the wall.

"Won't they come looking for Hope and me once they see you're alone?" I say, my last holdout.

"I'll tell them you're dead. That Hope drowned you, and that I knocked Hope out and left her up in the trees where Phoenix and Cass were taken down. If they search there, it will buy us some time." And then he adds, "I'd be surprised if they don't have a way to monitor their spies' vitals—I can't tell them Hope is dead because they'll likely be able to verify that she's not."

"Do you want your knife back?"

"No, you should keep it," he says. "No way they'll buy

I'm turning myself in if I'm armed. I can defend myself the old-fashioned way if it comes down to it."

Fists and fury, I assume. He is so quick with this plan, so sharp. As a Deliverer, I realize, Lonan has had years of experience in strategic efforts against the Wolfpack. His plan sounds too risky to me, but he's managed to keep himself alive this long. It gives me a little more confidence.

I have no more arguments. Alexa, for her part, when we press her to finally come out of her fog, seems content to Hope-sit while Lonan and I are actively on the offensive.

"Okay, then," I say. "Let's do this."

Alexa will join me in our original canoe, we decide, while Lonan continues in the other one toward the entrance to the lodge. It's a risk—if they've paid close enough attention, they'll notice Lonan isn't in the red-tipped canoe anymore. But this way, we'll have to move Hope only once, after Alexa and I have paddled all the way back out to where the far end of the wooden walkway meets the stony, narrow opening of the tunnel-cave. It's worth the risk to conserve our strength. Lonan holds both canoes steady until Alexa has climbed all the way in.

"Don't forget, Eden"—Lonan's voice is close and quiet—"your mind is stronger than your circumstances."

And then his palms cup my face, his gentleness totally at odds with the lightning bolt he sends coursing through me. He slides his hands up until his fingers are in my hair. Our lips meet: I taste hope, desperation, bitter memories on his. I'm sure he tastes the same on me. Though I've had a hundred kisses before this one, I've never known one so layered. I'm surprised to find I want to keep peeling back the layers until I'm acquainted with everything that's underneath.

"Remember," he says when we pull away, "this is the last time you can trust me until you find the cure."

Because they're fast, he doesn't have to say. Because he'll be compromised as soon as he turns himself over.

It is the perfect benediction. The Wolfpack has stolen *everything* from us. Now that I know it's possible for me to trust another person again—now that I know there is another person alive who's worth trusting—I refuse to let them take that, too.

Lonan's been my defender today, the person who brought me back to myself every time I started to spiral. Now he's about to risk his life to turn the tides of an entire war.

It's time for me to return the favor.

FIFTY-NINE

OUR CANOE ZIPS along, now that the mass of one Lonan-sized person isn't there to anchor it down. Alexa and I paddle like our lives depend on it—that could also have something to do with our speed.

When the canal bends out of the cave and back into the open air, the night is alive. A river of stars fills the clearing above us, as if this black water has somehow managed to reflect a spar-kling, shimmering light on the canvas of the sky. The lodge's yellow glow makes it easier to navigate: we're not completely in the dark. Leaves and limbs toss and sway in the breeze.

I focus on carving my paddles into the water with every-thing I have. If anyone sees us, they'll shoot us. It won't change anything if we see them first—where is there to go? So we row, row, row with as much drive as we can muster.

Every snap, every swish, every shuffle sets me on edge. But no one comes for us. No one shoots.

We are slick with sweat by the time we reach the mouth of the tunnel-cave. Better sweat than blood, at least. Hope is still as death in the floor of our canoe, oblivious to our efforts to remain sensitive with her body as we heave it out and onto the cave floor.

"You good?" I ask. "Got the syringe?"

She nods. "Hopefully I won't need to use it."

"Just don't let her near the water. She was fine in this cave before, and I don't see anything obvious that might be a trigger, but I wasn't paying attention to her arm." I wouldn't have been able to see it even if I had been paying attention—Hope had still been wearing my cardigan back then. I reposition her thin, limp limbs so I can better look for her hologram. It seems impossible that these arms nearly managed to drown me. "I don't see anything, so you should be good—unless it only activates when she's conscious. That seems overcomplicated, though, so let's just hope for the best."

There's something unreadable in her face. It isn't fear, and it certainly isn't the narcissism that so often radiates out of her.

She catches me looking. "What?"

"You tell me." I fold Hope's arms across herself. She needs a hug as much as the rest of us.

But then Alexa doesn't answer, and *oh*. Oh, no. This is why I don't recognize the look: she is about to cry. "Do you—" she starts, her voice breaking. "Do you think Cass meant all those things he said about me?"

My body fights against itself. I don't have time for a counseling session right now, don't have *energy* for a counseling session. But it appears Alexa is in need of one, unfortunately. She'll be more alert if she can stop replaying the worst two minutes of today on a loop. An alert Alexa is an alive Alexa.

"Yes." I cringe as I say it, but it's the truth. "I do."

Two silent tears race down her cheeks. She doesn't meet my eyes. "Do you think he's right about me?"

I bite my lip, think about how much help she wasn't when we sailed here, or when we arrived at our beach. "I think people change." This is a delicate subject. "And I think Cass is having an extraordinarily bad day today. I haven't lived his life, or known you as long, so I can't say if he's right. But I know what I see," I say. "At times, you verge on self-absorbed"—this is true, but I didn't mean for it to actually come out; to my relief, she doesn't bat an eyelash—"but I've seen that less and less the longer we've been here."

I think back to the dark and hungry water as Hope tried to flood out my breath, how hard it struck me that Alexa's proven more trustworthy than either of the other two girls. Not that Hope or Finnley asked to be used against us—they will be angry and ashamed, no doubt, when they find out what they were forced to do. Hope will be, at least. It may be too late for Finnley.

"If you want to know the truth, Alexa, I'd trust you with my life. I mean it."

Finally, she meets my eyes. "Yeah?"

I nod. "Yeah." Hope looks so innocent between us. A broken angel, a princess in need of a good bath. "So do your best to stay alive, okay? I may need you." I attempt a smile, but it falls flat. "And on top of that, I kind of just want you to live."

SIXTY

A COMMOTION OUTSIDE pulls my guard back up in a heartbeat. I am taut as a bowstring, sinews and ligaments and determination all ready to snap.

I press up against the tunnel wall. Listen.

Voices collide, not weapons—and not as close as I thought. All of this is in my favor. I carefully slip out into the star-studded night, keeping myself tight against the wall in case I'm wrong about how close they are. I recognize Lonan's voice in the midst of it all, amplified and escaping through whatever opening allowed Alexa and the others to see the lodge's entrance earlier. The voices fly like crows from the far face of the lodge. One quick scan of the yellow-lit windows on this face: no silhouettes poised to kill me.

Time to go.

I dart out onto the boardwalk, run along it until it ends. I reach into the foliage until my hand meets rock, feel around. It is stony but smooth, not a crack or crevice anywhere I can find. Scaling this wall is not an option.

Back to the dark-water cave it is.

For as many canoes as there are lined up, I'm disappointed

to find that none of them have paddles. Was it like this before? I didn't pay attention—it's possible Lonan chose our canoe because it was the only one that came fully equipped. Well, one of *two* that came fully equipped. I shouldn't have taken those extra paddles earlier.

Two voices rise above the rest now, Lonan's and another man's. They are loud, but slightly more civil than before. I can't make out their words, only the tone. It is the first time I've ever wished for voices to be less than civil.

Civil means Lonan will be compromised soon. Civil means the diversion he's created could end at any second—that it won't be long before my time runs out.

I am just about to run back toward the tunnel where I left Alexa, so I can grab a paddle from our canoe, when I hear a fresh set of voices.

These are close. Just-above-me close, on the balcony.

I back up into the foliage, as far as I can go, careful not to rustle the leaves any more than necessary. If I haven't been noticed yet, it's only because they're looking in the wrong direction.

"No way she's still alive," one of them says. Male. "His grief is too raw."

Lonan's grief, I assume. About me.

"He's a liar and a thief." The new voice, female, is cold and confident, matter-of-fact. She does not sound like someone I want to meet. "He's staked his life on killing our efforts, and now he's turning himself in? No. He wouldn't."

This woman is smart. Logical, strategic. Who was she, prior

to this war, and what made her so eager for a life like this?

A bright white spotlight scans the water, back and forth twice before it goes dark again. "Canoe," the man says.

Canoe becomes the most terrifying word in the English language.

It takes only a split second to realize he's not talking about the canoes directly in front of me but the one I abandoned near the tunnel where Alexa waits with Hope. Stupid, stupid. I'd been focused on speed when I left it there—the decision to run the planks instead of paddling in open water, alone, had been an easy one.

But now I've practically left a neon arrow pointing to their hiding place, and there's no way to send warning. I am lightheaded. I am floating, bobbing like one of these miserable canoes. Breathe, Eden.

I can't save everyone. I maybe can't even save myself. And given the choice between going after Lonan or the girls, I have to choose Lonan—aside from the fact that it's too late to help Alexa and Hope, there's a lot more at stake on his side of the situation. *I'd trust you with my life*, I told Alexa.

I hate that she can't trust me to save hers.

A heavy, knotted rope ladder swings over the edge and nearly knocks into me. The foliage begins to shake out a plodding rhythm: someone is climbing down. I shift more completely out of the ladder's way and back up until I hit the solid rock wall, where I'm almost entirely shrouded in leaves. Darkness has become my best friend.

"Pull Pellegrin from the lab and have him roll the ladder up after us." The woman's voice is so close now, we could be sharing a double-strawed milkshake. "Don't want to risk her slipping past us."

I hold my breath, squeeze my eyes tight so not even their whites, or the flutter of my lashes, will draw attention to my presence. My hand is tight on the hilt of Lonan's dagger, but I can't bring myself to pull it out—there are two of them, only one of me. A single blow dart, or a syringe, that's all it would take to ruin everything. So I stand, as still and unbreaking as the wall at my back.

It is the woman who slips past me, not the other way around, and the man follows soon after. Their steps are practiced and silent on the boardwalk as they head away from me, toward the cave where I left Alexa and Hope.

Now is my chance. I'm tempted to just climb the ladder, but Pellegrin, whoever he is, will roll it up any second now. Even if I made it to the top, the fact that he's coming from a lab doesn't bode well for my survival. I need to end up there on *my* terms. And he may be essential to finding the cure, and the Atlas Project science, so knifing him isn't my best move, either. A knife at his throat could work—but I'm not about to do that without first seeing who I'm up against. He could be three times my size, he could crush me like a cockroach under a boot. This is all helpful information, at least. The lab is on the top floor, on the farthest side from the entrance. There is an escape ladder there. Other things I need are probably there, too.

I have only one option left.

A scream echoes from the tunnel-cave: Alexa. I hate that I have to leave her, but this is my best chance to do the most good. My heart beats in my stomach, turbulent and strong and sickening.

Your mind is stronger than your circumstances, Eden.

Darkness has indeed become my best friend. It won't be long now until the enemy comes back for me. It'd be good to have a head start.

I take a breath and slip, silently, into the onyx-black water. It is where all my fear lives, and where I will kill all my fear.

SIXTY-ONE

WHEN THE WOLVES stole our oceans, and our sand, and our freedom and comfort and loved ones, I took back my sunrises.

The sun was faithful, the sun was true, the sun shattered darkness into a billion invisible pieces with rays of yellow, orange, red, sometimes even pink and purple. I watched as many as possible, alone except for the early morning guards, from the boardwalk planks.

It is dark now—maybe the darkest night of my whole life.

I plan on seeing the sunrise tomorrow.

SIXTY-TWO

I SWIM AS far as I can without coming up for a breath. When I do, it is fast and full, and then I make myself disappear again.

Just because I've been in this water before does not mean I am any more comfortable in it. Without Hope's merciless hands plunging me under, I'm all the more aware of my surroundings.

Black water. *Warm* water, the sort of lukewarm that feels like I've been sitting in bathwater for too long, with the same mucky consistency.

My clothes, so tight and efficient during the day, slow me to a heavy crawl. I seriously contemplate removing them, but there are too many complications. Either I'd have to hold on to them while swimming—along with the poor soaked field guide that's been tucked at my back all day—or go nearly naked into the lodge. Not that going dripping-wet into the lodge is the best alternative, but it is a better one.

I compromise: shoes and pants off, in hand with the field guide, everything else on. It's cumbersome, but effective.

I'm faster already.

Now, though, I *feel* things—my bare legs brush against plant tendrils, or fish, or who knows what else. Every soft and slippery thing sets my body to full alert. My mouth goes dry; my breaths are more frantic.

Calm down, Eden. Calm. Down.

I tell myself there are no snakes. I tell myself that even if there *are* snakes, none have bitten me yet and none have squeezed the life out of me.

I try to listen to myself.

It works. But only just enough. Every second inside this water, I fight against the fear that it will become my grave. That I'll be bitten and dead before I even have the chance to scream for help. The fear never lets up, not even when I turn the corner and find myself bathed in the ethereal turquoise glow, under the firefly sky where we parted ways with Lonan. It's gorgeous in here, stunning. But I know better than to mistake those for safe.

Finally, yellow light spills out onto the water. It's still a little way up ahead, but it has to be the opening I'm looking for. I'm coming for you, Lonan—wherever you are. I hear no more voices, no more commotion, no more diversion. It will either be very easy or very complicated to get inside. I'm not betting on easy.

I come to a stop in the darkness just beyond where the yellow light illuminates the water. No one stands guard. Of course, that doesn't mean it isn't guarded. I think back to the laser system and the beetles at the deserted temple—I should be prepared for anything. More, probably. And *why* was there so much security at the deserted temple? The lodge is the heart of things, I feel it. Why would they go to such great lengths to keep us out over there?

Once I am as convinced as I can be, from where I stand, that there are no actual humans lying in wait to seize me, I tug my heavy pants up and slip into my beat-up shoes. The field guide is equally tattered, but hanging on; I tuck it in at my back. Time to get out of this water and *never* get in again. I will find my way up to that terrace and take the rope ladder exit to escape—or I will take Lonan's idly bobbing canoe, ten feet ahead of me and bathed in yellow light.

The roof of this cave is so low, all I see from this angle is water, along with a wide set of stony stairs emerging out of it. I swim farther out into the light, carefully, in case there are guards I haven't yet seen. I doubt it, though—I am more vulnerable in the water, and surely they would've heard me by now.

Just outside the cave, my perspective expands. I am greeted by a formidable grand entrance that rises from the top of the steep, stony stairs. A massive chandelier made of antlers hangs from a thick iron chain, its light glittering in the entrance's floor-to-ceiling windows. I risk ten seconds to look at my surroundings: foliage, everywhere. Phoenix and Cass skirted the opposite edge of the lodge's perimeter in search of an entry point—it's possible someone shot them down from this very clearing. And if not from here, somewhere close. Perhaps from the roof of the cave, which is also thick with green.

The stone staircase is nearly vertical, its steps barely wide enough to fit my foot when turned sideways. At least it isn't a high climb—it's five feet out of the water at most. I keep to the far side, hopeful that it'll be easier to slip in unnoticed before someone spots me through the entryway glass. Water drips from my pants, and from my hair, as I scramble up. Good riddance, dark water.

As soon as my palm meets the entry platform at the top of the stairs, sickness roils up in me.

It is no longer stone against my skin.

It is snake.

SIXTY-THREE

VIPERS. THE *ENTIRE platform* is a slithering mass of vipers.
Pink. Orange. Green. Teal.

All the vibrant colors in nature that remind me of sunsets
and wildflower fields, of life and of freedom: it's as if the snakes
have sucked the world dry of its beauty and kept it all for themselves.

If they suck me dry, too, will they turn a nice shade of Eden?

They slither and coil, over each other and under. Every flash
of their eyes sends a shock of dread coursing through me. It
takes massive self-control to stay balanced, sideways, on the
stairs. Only fear keeps me from going back in the water—if
there are this many snakes up here, who knows what's in there.

My sanity is held loosely together by the singular fact that
the vipers seem oblivious to me. Oblivious might be too strong:
uninterested in my blood is more accurate. When my hand
first landed on one—pink as saltwater taffy and eyes like yellow moons—they were like moths to a flame. When I pulled it
away, they spread out again as if I had never been there at all.
I'm still close, *too* close. But though they slither along the edge
of the platform, not one ventures down the stairs.

It reminds me of the beetles, the invisible wall that contained them just outside the temple ruins.

Could this be . . . a security feature? If I step from the stairs to the platform, where I first rested my hand, will they swarm around me again?

My mouth is dry, my mouth is cotton. I wouldn't be able to speak—or scream—if I tried. If this is an illusion, it is an incredibly realistic one. No visible projectors peek out from the building's crevices, or the foliage. Besides that, I felt every scale slide against my palm as if it were the true thing, and the hissing—the hissing will be in my head for days.

The beetles were quite capable of interacting with us physically; I'll never forget how they went for the blood on Hope's leg. I'm not bleeding anywhere, which is a relief in more ways than one. But what if these snakes feed on sweat—or fear?

I won't know until I *know*.

I will either make it inside this grand, beautiful entrance, or I will become snake food. Or some other in-between alternative that is more devastating than I can imagine, especially if the snakes are trained to torture and not kill.

I swallow my terror: it is sharp, double-edged, and settles at the pit of my stomach. *They're harmless*, I tell myself. *They are koi in a pond.*

My muscles are stiff after standing, petrified, for so long. I grip the stone ledge, bending my fingers in an unnatural way that makes my knuckles go white. I avoid touching the vipers until I absolutely must.

The way they slither toward me really does remind me of fish in a feeding frenzy. They climb over themselves to get to me—all this based on my scent alone. As soon as I cross the invisible barrier between us, it is my worst nightmare.

I have to make space in order to walk through them, plant my toes where there are no openings. Where I step, they part, but then take it as an invitation to climb me like vines on a trellis. Soon, the black fabric of my pants is completely obscured: my left leg is a lagoon, my right is a rainforest.

They are not gentle. And they don't stop climbing just because my legs end.

I gather my rapidly unspooling sanity. If they wanted to bite me, I'd be dead. If they wanted to suffocate me, I'd be unconscious. I repeat these things over and over until they stop sounding like the ramblings of delusion. I take one slow, heavy step after another.

Almost halfway.

A teal viper with yellow eyes springs, suddenly, from the far side of the platform and coils around my neck. Its scales pull at the hair that's fallen out of where I tied it back. It's not tight—yet. But even this minimal pressure pinches my windpipe like a garden hose.

This is the breaking point. Enough.

Another snake springs at me—lemon yellow—and wraps itself around my waist. I focus on the choker first, prying as hard as I can and digging my fingernails in until I am certain the dirt underneath has been replaced with this snake's cold blood. It writhes in my grip, fangs snapping too close to my ear, until it falls limp.

It is both the best and the worst move.

As soon as the snake dies, the other vipers hiss so loudly they're practically screaming—like my one act of defense has alerted their collective consciousness to turn against me. They rush at me even harder than before, vicious and unstable and seething. Those that already cling to my body squeeze tighter and tighter. My blood rushes, an ever-present reminder that I'm still alive . . . even if only for a little while longer.

But I can breathe again. And I am certain now that this is a security feature.

Though I'm sure this is all in my head, somehow, it doesn't make the pain—or the panic—any less real. *Mind over circumstances, Eden,* I imagine Lonan coaching me. *Throw them off.*

One by one, I peel them from my limbs, my torso. I grab just under their heads, squeeze as hard as I can, and throw them as far from me as I can manage. There is an invisible barrier at the edge of the platform: when I try to throw them in the water, they stop in midair and slide back to the stony ground.

I am three-quarters of the way across when they begin to strike.

Their fangs pierce deeply, and yet there are no holes and no blood.

Their venom is acid in my veins—*fire*—and yet my body has not seized up on me.

They kill me, over and over again. And yet I live.

I live, and I fight. There is an invisible barrier on the side closest to the grand entrance, too. When I cross it, I shed my snake skin: they fall in a heap behind me, and I collapse right after them. I am so close. I've lived my worst nightmare. But this has been the longest, longest day, and I am famished, and I cannot take a single step more without first catching my breath.

As I meet the cold white tile—a mosaic of tiny jagged pieces—I am vaguely aware of glass breaking. A maroon stain spreads around the two teeth that have clanked against the vial in my pocket for so many months now. I am always careful to keep it in the deepest, most secure part of my pocket, cushioned by a thin strip of leather I stole from my bunkmate at barracks. But the vial has slipped out of the leather, out of my pocket. Onto the unforgiving tile. The vipers must have shifted it.

The image of my father's teeth in a pool of his blood is more chilling than everything I've just experienced. And then I realize.

The floor isn't tile after all: it's teeth. *Human* teeth.

The grand glass door opens. I see a pair of black, polished boots.

"Hello, Eden," a deep voice says. It echoes from the glass. "I'm going to need you to come with me."

SIXTY-FOUR

A BLAST OF frigid air-conditioning hits me as soon as we're through the door, and it is like being transported to the past. Zero Day, when they sorted and branded us, was the last time I felt artificial air. We had only oscillating fans in barracks—during all six infernal months of Texas summer—and quilts in the winter. The ice-cold air makes me realize how much I've come to appreciate the natural fluctuations of the weather. What I associate with air-conditioning now are the things I used to have, and the people who took them away.

The man in black boots doesn't introduce himself. He is definitely the sort who could crush me with little effort. Luckily, he doesn't. But he does confiscate my knife—I'm surprised at how naked I feel without it.

He carries on a coded, one-sided conversation with someone in his ear who I can't hear. He guides me through the door, his grip tight on my upper arm. I don't resist, but only because getting inside has been part of my plan all along. After the viper pit, there's no way I'm turning down an invitation—even if it is the complicated, mandatory sort. Lonan is in here somewhere. Finnley, too, I assume. Cass and Phoenix? More than likely. I don't know how I'll slip away to find them, let alone get to the lab, but I will find a way. I have to.

For all its one-with-the-island exterior, the inside of the lodge is pure sophistication. The stained-concrete floors are the color of warm caramel, with a border made of dark fudge. Everything shines, everything is polished, everything is clean. Even the teeth just outside the front door.

A gleaming copper balcony hugs all three of the foyer's non-glass walls. There is a second balcony, but it is much smaller, stretching only partially along the wall to my left. Three floors, I note, not two like I previously assumed: the lab must be on the second floor, not the tiny tier at the top. Only the second floor spans the entire building—the third wasn't visible from the canal.

"This way," the man says. He pulls me hard to the right, toward an opaque, green-tinted glass door. A wolf-face emblem is etched into its center, the only feature that is completely transparent. The door slides open automatically as we approach it.

Everything I can think to ask, or say, seems too risky to let out. I don't know how much he knows about what I'm up to—I should probably assume he knows everything. But just in case he doesn't, I don't want to give anything away.

"Where are you taking me?" I finally manage. Anyone would ask that, given the circumstances.

"Below," he simply says. As if this sloping, claustrophobic hallway wasn't enough to clue me in that we're headed underground.

The pieces aren't lining up. The lab is upstairs. As are, I assume, all the ingredients necessary to create their HoloWolf spies. Assuming they want to turn me into a spy, too, wouldn't they take me upstairs, not underground?

Perhaps I am making too many assumptions.

This hallway is endless. Or maybe, by *below*, Black Shoes meant he was taking me to the center of the earth. Or the Underworld. The hallway doesn't turn, and there are no doors. The lighting is comfortable enough, in the way that a doctor's waiting room is comfortable enough. Unlike a doctor's office, however, there is no pretense of warmth. No stock-art prints of lilies in gilded frames, no faux plants in need of a good feather-dusting, no bowls full of mints or even handrails to hold on to. It is merely soft white light and cold gray concrete. And it never ends.

Black Shoes touches his tiny earpiece. "Aries, we're headed your way." His voice is incredibly deep, and it startles me every time he speaks.

Finally, we come to another sliding glass door, set flush into the right wall. It doesn't open automatically, and there is no keypad, or any other visible means of gaining access to the room behind it. The transparent image on the glass is not of a wolf this time, but of a ram with giant, spiraling horns.

"This is Gray, requesting entry," Black Shoes says, pressing at his ear again. Gray.

I hope I won't have to know his name for long.

We wait. Our hallway doesn't dead-end here, but it does level out, no end in sight for as far as I can see in either direction. And if *this* hallway exists, what's to say it's the only one? There could be an entire network of hallways.

They've been underneath us the whole time. It's no wonder Finnley vanished from our beach, and from the net—they probably have escape hatches all over the place. People-stealing hatches, rather.

Wherever I am, it does not look like a quick, under-the-radar escape back to the lab is in my future. I make a silent apology to Lonan.

Gray calls in a second, more urgent request. His deep voice is even but intimidating. A fault line waiting to rip.

The green door doesn't budge.

"Aries, I will not hesitate to shatter this door myself." His tone isn't so even now—it's the rumbling before an earthquake. "Comply at once, for your own good." He adds something in the same codespeak as before. The only word I understand is *kingpin.*

The word alone is enough to make my stomach roil. The kingpins are every jewel-colored viper combined; they are fang and venom and suffocation. They would devour their own Wolves if any ever turned against them.

Gray's finger hovers over his ear device, ready to rip the world in half.

The green door finally slides open. It is so neat, so clean, so seamless.

I am led inside by the tight vise of Gray's grip, which digs just above my elbow in spots still tender with the memory of snakebites. It would be easy to let the numbness take over, and not just on the outside. But I wear my pain like a badge of honor, a trophy of pride engraved with *I am still alive.*

The room is the cluttered mess of a maniac, an insomniac, a person with too much pressure and too little sleep. Screens and keyboards and strung-up twine and charts and maps and a grid of Post-its and full-to-the-brim corkboards and whiteboards covered in tiny black letters. And.

The handwriting. And.

The colored pencils. And.

The coffee mug I gave my father for his birthday ten years ago. It is at his lips.

SIXTY-FIVE

MY OLDEST MEMORY is not a nice one.

Two-year-olds, by nature, are fascinated with the bright and shiny, the colorful, and the bright, shiny, colorful pull of independence.

I stole my mother's phone.

I stole it to play with it, to push all its flashy squares and pull at all its moving screens. I vaguely remember her asking if I'd seen it and I vaguely remember answering no. *I need to message Daddy*, she said. *He's late.* I didn't know its purpose wasn't simply to entertain me—that my mother relied on it in emergencies.

That *others* relied on it in emergencies.

I thought the vibrations were part of a game for me to play, the red IGNORE button that popped up at the bottom the way to win it. The vibrations came, over and over again, every time I pushed the red button. And I pushed it a lot.

I pushed it until the police showed up at our door. My mother left our kitchen sink full of soapy water, full of the knives I knew I shouldn't touch, to answer it.

"Stay out of the kitchen, Eden," she called. She thought I was playing with crayons.

When she came back, two men with uniforms and badges at her side, she scooped me up in her arms. I remember burying my head in her neck so I wouldn't have to see her face anymore: it was the first time I'd ever seen either of my parents cry, the first time I'd ever seen either of them afraid of anything. When the phone fell out of my hands and into the sink, she didn't even scold me. Not that day. That day was for hugs and tears and hospital waiting rooms and animal crackers and a brand-new set of crayons.

"Never lie to me again, honey." She handed me another animal cracker. To this day, I associate zebras with the importance of being honest. "Lying is one of the worst things you can do."

My parents modeled this well. They never lied, not even about little things. They were meticulously exact in their speech.

And yet.

I've believed my father dead for nearly two years. I've been *alone*—I've suffered a war on my own—I've grieved everyone and everything I've ever had or known. I made a religion out of his field guide; I carried his blood and teeth like they could somehow bring him back. I wear *till death do us part* on the chain at my neck.

My field guide is wet and wilted. My vial is shattered and spilled. And it is the vows that have died, not my father. He

drinks coffee from the mug I gave him when we were both honest, before we found ourselves deep in the heart of Wolfpack
headquarters.

This is a betrayal on so many levels.

SIXTY-SIX

HIS WRIST IS dark with the classic Wolfpack tattoo.

It is not a hologram, but a black and bold display of his choice to join them.

His *choice.*

It's possible he was forced into this, but it isn't like he's in chains—he had the opportunity to go back and get the mug I gave him, it looks like, along with a number of other things I recognize from home. This doesn't exactly scream *taken against his will.*

All this time, he's been developing the Atlas habitat for the Wolves. All this time, he's let me believe he was *dead.*

Our eyes lock. "I kept your book." My lips, jaw, voice, confidence: all of me trembles. Not out of fear, for once. "I've read this"—I pull the still-drying field guide from where it sits at my back—"like the Bible, every day and night and midnight since you died." I fracture, I break. I spill through the cracks.

He sets his coffee mug on a messy stack of papers. His face shows none of the softness I remember from him, none of the remorse I expect.

What. *Happened?*

Gray's grip tightens on my arm. As if it weren't tight enough already. "What is your daughter doing here, Aries? What information did you leak?" He pries the field guide from me with his free hand, lays it open on the paper-covered island. Water marks bloom on the papers where water seeps from the book.

Aries is not my father's name. It is William.

William wears glasses; Aries does not.

William is young and happy; Aries is not.

William has a daughter. Aries has an underground lair.

"Search it." My father's voice is unchanged at least, brimming with soft-spoken authority. "There is nothing conclusive there—the plans are secure, bloodlocked. And if there is any question, check the records. I fought to keep it, but Zhornov insisted it be sent back to my daughter as proof of my death."

Zhornov. Of *course*. He knew Dad from Envirotech, knew exactly the guy he'd need to resurrect the project and see it through. No wonder they named him fifth kingpin: he pulled off the greatest heist in history, with the most exclusive payoff.

Gray gives a little grunt, flips another page. It is still so saturated with water, it tears as he turns it. And I am still so saturated with love for the book—for my father, despite all the things I see and cannot understand—that I tear, too.

Whatever information Gray thinks Dad put in the field guide doesn't matter anyway. The blue ink is so muddled now, it's nearly impossible to read. While the printed text and scattered colored pencil markings are undisturbed, the legibility of any given page corresponds directly to how much ink Dad put on it. This particular page, with the Morse code, is completely useless—most will be, I suspect. I can think of a few pages that will be easier to read, but only a few.

Gray doesn't have the patience to seek them out.

"Explain." His voice is a low rumble. "Explain how your daughter ends up with the captain and inside HQ. Explain, or your benefits will expire."

My father meets his glare with a look I've seen a hundred times: it is the look I'd receive whenever I pushed the limits just a little too hard. "I'm afraid that's a risk I'm willing to take." Not defensive, nothing to prove—this is the father I remember. "Especially since you don't have the authority to revoke my benefits, and since I'm under no contractual obligation to explain myself to you."

"She's *here*, Will!" Gray explodes, and it is as loud as I feared it would be and more. His fingers dig even tighter. This time I see stars. "Your actions have been more than questionable lately, and it is absolutely within my rights to demand an explanation."

Gray reaches for his earpiece again. "Backup at Aries," he says. "Bring a single dose from the lab." He lowers his finger, focusing all his energy on Dad—and my arm—again. "Pell's taking the zip, so he'll be here any minute. When he arrives, you will prove your loyalty to the program you've helped us build. Wolves before blood, remember the pledge?"

Dad's eyes meet mine for the briefest of seconds before he averts them. Everything shifts with this one look: he is still in there. His kindness, his warmth, his compassion, all of it. It's there, but he's hiding it for some reason.

He'll defend me. He's been sketchy with his answers because he has something else up his sleeve—there is nothing in the world he wouldn't do for his family. I've read it over and over on the respiratory physiology page of the field guide, his words to Mom: *I'd do anything for you.*

Gray pulls me to the far wall, where security feeds fill twenty, thirty high-def screens. He pushes an unmarked button on the control board beneath it; the green glass door slides open.

A short, thin, black man who wears tight white pants and a white V-neck—like Lonan's outfit of choice, but in reverse—strides in, a full syringe in one hand. It is terrifyingly familiar, but filled with bright purple liquid instead of amber. He opens his other hand and sets a tiny silver case on the table, shaped like the one Emma used when she wore contact lenses.

"Well, Aries?" the man says. Pell—short for Pellegrin? "You want this one, or should I do it?"

I truly, truly believe it is for my safety when my father nods, and takes the syringe, and picks up the silver case—that all of this is an act put on for the sake of keeping these things away from the people who want to hurt me.

I believe these things wholeheartedly.

I believe it right up until he plunges the needle into the hollow of my neck. The purple liquid disappears underneath my skin, and I melt with it.

"You can trust me," my father says.

He is not speaking to me.

SIXTY-SEVEN

THE ROOM IS a buzzy, fuzzy haze of varying shades of white. I'm warm down to the core, like my veins are oozing with the slippery, viscous hot oil treatment I tried on my hair when I was in seventh grade. It still stings at the base of my throat, where the needle pierced me. There is a crumpled paper towel on the table now, right next to Dad's coffee mug. The paper towel is smeared with the remains of purple they wiped from my skin. Also, my blood.

I am led to a chair that reminds me of the dentist. Gray finally, finally releases me and I sit. My skin sticks to its mint-green patent leather covering. Various tools rest on a nearby tray. None of them appear to be dental tools.

"What is happening?" I try to say. "What are you doing to me?" Even to my own ears, my words are an indecipherable slur.

"It's best if you hold still, Eden." This voice is not deep, and it's not my father's. Pellegrin appears at my right side. His dark fingers are soft and silky, a contrast in every way to Gray's. He is careful with my arm as he positions it forearm-side-up on the armrest, delicate with the straps as he buckles me into place. The oozing purple liquid suppresses my instinct to fight so much I'm surprised I feel it at all.

He picks up a pot of iridescent liquid from the tray of tools, pulls a cone-shaped metal stopper from its opening. *I am at a carnival*, I think. *I will be painted, and then I will stuff my mouth with cotton candy.*

The paintbrush holds all the fire of ten thousand wasps in its tiny pinprick tip.

My instinct to scream is coated in a thick layer of purple liquid, too. And I don't feel it, but I'm crying. I know this because my father appears at my left side with another paper towel. He is all tenderness as he blots my tears away. As if he doesn't have everything to do with creating them. I've come so very far, searching for answers, but I've found no closure, no clarity. All I have is more questions. What is he *thinking*?

Pellegrin is a quick artist. Or perhaps my sense of time is skewed. Either way: he turns on an ultraviolet light, and there it is.

I am officially compromised. One of the HoloWolves.

Eternally hollow, I amend. Never a Wolf.

The image is mesmerizing, shimmering with the illusion of depth. I stare and stare until someone—Pellegrin again—gently leans my head back against the chair. He swiftly parts my right eyelids, like he's done this a hundred times, a thought that is comforting and frightening in equal measure. My eyes struggle against him, fighting to close, but before he allows it he puts pressure directly on my pupil. He repeats the process on the left side.

I blink.

The world is clear again, clearer than ever. Which is strange, because my vision was already clear long before I was made to sit in this chair. The purple liquid made it hazy, for sure, but now it's *digitized*, almost, like I'm seeing everything through an enhanced filter. It's like they've fused some new form of silk tech to my eyes.

"Activate her," Gray directs.

My father moves toward the control panel on the far wall. He does not hesitate to turn his back on me.

"After he activates you, you won't remember any of this procedure," Pellegrin tells me. As if it should comfort me that they have the ability to cause pain in me and then wipe my memory clean.

I can't fathom a world in which the pain of my father's betrayal isn't a raw, gaping slice straight through my chest. But then, he probably isn't talking about that aspect of the procedure.

Pellegrin squeezes my shoulder. "This is it," he says, so low I'm sure I'm the only one to hear it, as Dad leans down toward the control panel. "Hold on tight."

But Dad doesn't push any of the buttons.

I've never seen him move so fast—a small, slender tube rests in the grooves of the control panel, but not for long. He grabs it, he puts it to his mouth, he blows.

A needle-thin dart lodges itself in Gray's chest, just above his heart. He slumps to the ground.

"Now," my father says, "we can talk."

SIXTY-EIGHT

MY EMOTIONS ARE whiplash; my head is confusion.

He injects me, but he blows a dart at Gray.

He stands by while Pellegrin marks me with the wolf, but he doesn't push the button to activate me.

He lets me feel pain, but he is apparently not against me.

He lets me think he is dead, and there is still no explanation.

"Gray won't remember who shot him," Pellegrin says. To me, I think. I'm vaguely aware of him affixing Lonan's sheathed dagger back at my hip. What is going on? "The darts have an amnesiac effect that dulls the details of the immediate before and after surrounding the time at which the consciousness blinks out." He laughs. The man who just put a hologram on my arm *laughs*. "We've been waiting to take that guy out for a while now."

His words are a string of licorice, long and sticky and strong. I'm listening. But I watch my father, who is frantic but focused, as he flips through the pages of his field guide. Many of them have dried and look stiff to the touch.

"Aren't you afraid they'll hear you on the cameras—that

they'll see what you've done?" I ask. "The other, uh, people who work here?"

Pellegrin gestures to the wall of security-feed screens. "Will, do you have a problem with anything I just said?"

Dad doesn't look up from the book. "Nope."

"See? Nope. Will's the only one on duty and he doesn't care. Non-crisis averted."

"Only one on duty *for now*," Dad says. He turns another page.

"When they ask—and they *will* ask—you just tell them you found the blow dart on Will's panels. Tell 'em you shot him in self-defense, and tell 'em we activated you, okay?"

My head spins. "Please slow down. You're making my head hurt."

The corner of Dad's mouth quirks up, but he merely flips another page, and another.

I sort through everything Pellegrin just said. "Did you just say you want *me* to take the fall for this? They hate me enough already—"

"Found it," Dad interrupts. "Pell, you're getting ahead of yourself. Eden, honey, come take a look at this, please." He looks up and sees me, really looks at me, for the first time. It is like a sunrise, the light in his eyes—like he's waking from a cold and sleepless night and only just now realizing he's survived. That *I've* survived.

It is relief.

He is at my side in a heartbeat. I am still strapped into this monstrosity of a chair. "Get her out of here, Pell!"

Pellegrin unclasps the buckles, apologizes. The shackles fall away, and I am free to move, but after everything I've been through today I barely have the energy. Dad pulls me up into an awkward embrace, like he wants to hug me but doesn't know if it's welcome. Like maybe he's forgotten how, or maybe we both have.

Or maybe we've simply grown scar tissue in the places where we were torn apart, the places we used to fit so well together.

When it ends, he steadies me until I'm firmly planted on a mint-green stool at his island.

"I could also use some food," I say, "if there is any."

"Yes, yes!" Dad says. "Of course. Yes." He shifts aside, pulls at one of the island's many drawers. Another sound I haven't heard in far too long: the sound of a refrigerator opening. Or, in this case, a refrigerated drawer. He puts together a plate of pear, Brie, and green grapes—he drizzles it with honey—he cracks some black pepper—he produces a hunk of French bread from another drawer nearby.

It is an aching reminder of everything I've lost. All the days at our kitchen island at home, after school with Birch or Emma or both, eating this very snack. I haven't had Brie in years. I haven't had *any* of these luxuries in years, save for the grapes I ate in the cave earlier today. And here, Dad has had access to them the entire time. I am heavy with all the *why?*

I eat like someone who has never before in her life experienced the sense of taste. Formless, gray slop has a particular talent for refining only one area of the tongue:

Bitterness.

The field guide is open to the page I know and love more than all the rest, the respiratory physiology page. The *I'd do anything for you* page.

It is a mess of ink now. At least the image of it is burned into my memory. At least I know the story by heart.

"I love this one," I say. He never shared the field guide with me Before—when they delivered it to me, it was like opening a treasure box filled with my father. A big fat tear plops onto my plate, right on top of some crumbs. I want, so badly, for this page to be true. But I can't, I just *can't*. I can't deal with the fact that he's alive. That he's been alive this whole time.

That *this* is the way I'm finding out.

It's better than him being dead. It is.

My bread crumbs will be soggy soon.

"Look closer, sweetheart," he says. "What do you see?"

I see a page full of dry formulas about respiratory physiology. I see blurred blue ink.

And then I see everything.

It is the jar full of colored pencils that calls my attention to it. A vague glow of light green subtly illuminates one word here, another word there, a third word farther down. And then, where the story about his date with Mom has been blurred away by the water, a fourth word appears, negative-space letters defined by the green glow of the pencil.

RESISTANCE IS OUR LIFE.

"I made a deal with the Wolves," he says. "What they don't know is that I'm a sheep in wolves' clothing. Pell and I both are."

SIXTY-NINE

RESISTANCE IS OUR LIFE.

My worldview zooms all the way out, until I am a moon rock peering down at earth and everything on it. How is it possible to have a world's worth of feeling inside me, when I am smaller than a speck that doesn't even register amid the blues and greens and swirling whites?

"What do you mean you made a deal?! What *kind* of deal?"

Dad is visibly stunned by my outburst. I'm sure he saw it coming—he let me think he was *dead*. We were never anything but close, Before. This raw, bleeding love is new territory for us both.

"I put a lot of thought into the way I laid out this book," he says, careful and steady and even. But there's effort in his voice. He tries so hard to keep his love and his pain separate, when the simple fact is they're like the illusion of a Möbius strip. "The story about your mother—did you ever read it? The cat, the amputation? The cabernet?"

"I already said I loved it."

"I didn't know if you were just saying that."

"I *loved* it, loved it. I have it memorized." It was all I had left.

He studies me. "Do you remember the last line?" His eyes are soft now, like I remember. It must have taken great effort to put so much hardness into them when Gray first brought me in. Hard eyes are unnatural on him.

"I'd do anything for you," I recite.

"I'd do anything for you, Eden," he repeats. *"Anything."*

I blink. Something about the context, the two of us here together at the very edge of *anything*, pulls all the pieces sharply into focus. "You'd pretend you were dead."

He nods, slowly. We break eye contact, because it is still too much.

"You'd work with the Wolves," I continue.

"They pulled me for this project because of my background," he says. "The old Envirotech project, not the refuge like I told you. They lied to me."

His background—*the* Envirotech engineer. A thorough, honest, trustworthy engineer who had sailing experience, navigational experience, and wilderness skills, the lead developer on the most coveted project on the planet. What irony: in order to pull off a war against professionals who made too much money, they had to use a professional who made too much money.

"I . . ." I look around the room at every scratch, every scribble, every formula and diagram and coffee-splattered sticky note. He knows how to handle everything, always has—of course they wanted him. I wanted him, too.

"It was either join them or die, sweetheart. *Really* die." He averts his eyes. "But I believed in the project, always have, and

Zhornov knew it. When I found out what was truly going on, I had to choose. I could refuse, and let the science die with me— or I could do my part to develop it, on their dime, with their blessing, and work like hell to figure out how to lock them out of it."

It is too much. Too much, all at once.

"It was the same for me," Pellegrin says. I'm so wrapped up in Dad I've forgotten we are not alone.

"Pell and I were pulled in together, same time, same way," Dad says. "He was the most cutting-edge scientist at MIT when the war broke out, and had been developing for Enviro-tech almost as long as I had."

"They wanted me for my first doctoral thesis, which focused on psychobiological security systems," Pellegrin adds, bubbling over with syllables. He looks so young, at least ten years younger than Dad. He must have been some sort of child prodigy. "I'd figured out how to make human skin cells react to nature in extremely specific ways, and how to individualize the psychological experiences attached to said reactions. I'm afraid my work here has proven quite the nuisance for you."

What a brazen understatement, that he'd refer to his work as a mere *nuisance*. I'd been half kidding before, when I'd referred to the beetles and the vipers as security systems, but it sounds like that's exactly what they were.

"So the snakes—the moss—"

Pellegrin cringes. "Yes, yes. Very sorry about all of that."

I think of the way I was strapped to the dentist's chair not five minutes ago. "And the—what do you even call it here? The human spy stuff." This is uncomfortable. "Whatever you did to me. Did you create that, too?"

"Unfortunately, yes. When your life's work is devoted to proving to the world just how many scientific barriers you've been able to break, people take it upon themselves to twist and push your research to unethical places."

"And you let them."

Finnley. Cass. Hope.

Me.

"The sensory modification wasn't always meant to be used like this," Pellegrin says. "I developed it for Envirotech initially, a foray into a new realm of silk tech exploration. The ink, the eyepieces—unlike the silk most people are familiar with, these do more than simply transmit digital data for us to observe. When combined with the smartserum, they have the capacity to interact with the human brain and nervous system on a variety of levels."

The ink. The eyepieces.

How many cocoon-cradled moths have I boiled to stillness in the vat? How many times have I had to talk myself into it— they'll be turned into medicine, they'll save lives.

My silk has saved no one but the Wolves.

My silk has saved no one *from* the Wolves.

"So," I say, reeling myself back in before I completely unravel, "*Envirotech* was planting spies?"

"Wouldn't surprise me," he says. "But to my knowledge, the

technology was primarily intended to be used on the Atlas habitat's test subjects before the Wolves repurposed it."

Test subjects. "Like . . . on rats?" Wishful thinking, I know.

One look confirms it: the test subjects were living, breathing, sentient. Very clearly *not* rats. At least Pellegrin looks sorry about it. "We needed to make sure humanity would actually be able to survive down there," he says. "Subsea conditions were unpredictable."

"And hostile," my father adds. "We had to test oxygen levels, ensure there were no water or air leaks in any of our chambers, figure out the generator situation, make certain the entire development was structurally sound against creature collisions and ocean currents. Along with a hundred thousand other things."

"Couldn't you have sent test subjects down there *after* you'd checked those out, though?" My stomach turns at the thought of sending people into such conditions, sense-altered or not. Who knew blueprints, ink on paper, could be so dangerous?

"Someone had to build it first," Dad says. "The sensory modification enables our construction team to work efficiently, without fearing for their lives."

"And it allows them to have a peaceful end, without suffering, whenever things don't go as planned," Pellegrin says. "All for a greater good, of course." Just like Lonan said.

Fire floods me. "A greater good? You're telling me all of these 'test subjects' are on board with risking their lives for this? Seriously?" Pellegrin opens his mouth, but I keep talking. "And never mind what all of this was originally meant for—it's doing tons of damage *now*. Hope nearly *drowned* me out there."

"Our hands were tied when it came to Hope and Finnley—we tried to make the best of it," Dad says, intervening between us. "We kept Hope with you for your own protection, so we could keep a close eye out—especially since you arrived here with a Wolf in your presence, a volatile one, and we didn't know if you'd be in danger. But what happened in the water was not supposed to happen, Eden, trust me! It was an oversight, a side effect of the science—"

"Oversights like that are kind of a big deal."

"Oversights like that are what happens when sociopaths push science past its natural limits," Pellegrin says. "We don't like it any more than you do."

"So why do it, then?" Somewhere, rationally, I know it's more complicated than this. The words come out anyway. "Pellegrin creates the drug—"

"*Formula*," they both correct at once.

"Drug, formula, whatever," I amend. "Pellegrin creates it, and what, Dad—you activate it? And where do your 'test subjects' come from? What, do you just pluck them out of the camps, one at a time so no one will notice?"

Shame mixed with guilt washes over his face. "The construction crew is largely composed of my old Envirotech team. We've only lost a handful of them to the project, good guys who did solid work. Every single one of them knew what they were getting into when we pulled them out to resume work on the project. I told Zhornov it was the only way I'd do it," he says.

"But the rest of all this—when I'm not on site at the habitat island, I'm stationed here at HQ—half of the Aries team." He gestures to the wall of display screens. "Aries is all about sowing lookouts into the sectors so Wolfpack can keep a close eye on the movement around camp."

"Spies," I say.

"Spies." He nods. "I mostly just monitor what we pick up through their feeds, alert them to anything that could pose a threat to the Wolves' authority—the silk lens film installed on your eyes is equipped to transmit digital information, like Pell said before, video as well as audio. And to be clear, your lens film isn't transmitting now, given that we never finalized your activation."

He's quiet now; they both are. We sit for a while in silence as I try to piece all of this new information together. It's hard to figure out where to even start.

"If you were just going to shoot Gray"—finally I am able to tear away at the layers of my raw confusion, finally able to sort it into words—"why would you put me through all of this?"

"It's complicated." He sighs. "You know me, sweetheart. You remember who I am, right?"

I search his eyes and find that I do. I remember everything—that's part of the problem.

"I'm still in here," he says. It's true, too. It's just a little hard to see through all of my shattered illusions. "I would rather die than allow the Wolves to win this war." There is a long pause. He glances at Pellegrin. "It's required more than a few excruciating sacrifices to land myself—and *keep* myself—in a position where I can actually do something about it."

"Where we can do *everything* about it," Pellegrin chimes in.

I want to know more about their plan, badly in fact, but I'm stuck on the notion of sacrifices. I understand them—I do. It's just hard when people focus on the so-called greater good without setting aside a piece of their hearts to grieve. I nearly became one of those greater-good sacrifices, despite the fact that neither of them can bring themselves to admit it.

But is that really what's happening here? Dad is not that cold: he loves life more than anyone I've ever, ever known. He loves for *others* to have life. He looked truly sorry when talking about the guys he's lost to the project.

Dad's coffee mug. His colored pencils. His refrigerator full of my favorite snack foods. It is starting to sink in that he's been grieving his losses every bit as much as I have. Maybe more, even. I know, *know*, he would not let me believe him dead for no reason—and I know it is true when he says he'd rather die than allow them to win. So if it is his choice to be here, he must have one hell of a reason.

"You still haven't told me what kind of deal you made," I say.

I've seen my father cry a handful of times. The day of his accident, when we visited him in the hospital, was the first time. The last was at barracks, on the day he told me goodbye. "Your life." It is barely a whisper. "They've agreed to let you live, in relative peace, if I work with them on all of this."

It isn't only the world he's been trying to save.

It's me.

I am small again, curled up in his lap as he reads to me. I am older, picking wildflowers from the backyard and bringing them to him in a vase. I am crying into his shoulder when Emma and I have our first big fight.

I am not the orphan I feared I was. Not even a little bit.

SEVENTY

THE HAZE CLEARS: If I take the fall for shooting Gray, I live. If it comes out that Dad turned against another Wolf, they'll kill me to punish him.

"So . . . at what point do you stop turning people into spies? When do we get to cure them?" I slide off the stool and check out the wall of surveillance screens. "Is Lonan—did you do the procedure on him, too?"

Neither of them says a word. When I turn back, they wear sheepish *I'm sorry to have to tell you this* looks. "What?"

I start to worry when they still don't answer. "What happened to Lonan? Is he okay?" I've taken too long, *so* long. It was unwise to get this comfortable—if you could even call it comfortable.

"Oh, no, sweetheart—he's in a recovery area, and he made it through the procedure just fine," Dad says. "Most people do."

Most.

"So, what, then?"

Pellegrin is the one to break the news. "Lonan has been our endgame all along," he says. "It's why we pulled Sky Cassowary from New Port Isabel, Eden—we knew it was the only way to draw Lonan out. He's quite the elusive pirate, if you weren't already aware."

"And I'm sorry to tell you," Dad chimes in, "but there is no cure. Pell has a formula, but the kingpins haven't sanctioned its testing or development yet. It was just a lie told by the crew on Cassowary's ship to draw Lonan in."

Well. This is quite the predicament. It's like a blow dart, a nuclear one, to our entire plan.

"But—I thought the Wolves wanted to use Lonan to take down the Resistance?"

"Oh, they most definitely do," Dad says. "We were pretty convincing on that point."

"Not that it took much convincing," Pellegrin adds.

The three of us stand for a minute, in sticky truths and awkward silence.

Dad takes a sip of cold coffee. He hasn't changed a bit on that front. "*Oh*," he says. Like his magic elixir of understanding was in the sludge at the bottom of his mug. "You're confused because you believe Pell and I plan to use Lonan, and all the spies we've created, to take down the *Resistance*. Which, yes, you're right. That doesn't make sense."

A grin spreads across Pellegrin's face. "We really are convincing, aren't we, Will?"

"Apparently," he says, but his grin is a shadow compared with Pellegrin's. "Eden, Lonan's influence will tip this war; that is one thing we can count on. The kingpins have been insistent that Lonan receive the procedure, ever since it got in their heads that we could use him against the Resistance—they're obsessed with him, want to admire their pet weapon as soon as possible. You know now what would have happened if we'd refused."

"So," I say, piecing things together, "if you're secretly anti-Wolf, that means you're going to use Lonan to *help* the Resistance in the war?"

Now my father smiles, and it is radiant. "We're going to use him to win it."

SEVENTY-ONE

DAD MOVES TO the wall of display screens, adjusts a few of the controls on the tech board just below it. "Lonan, you there?" he says quietly into a long, thin microphone.

A few of the screens spring to life in a blur: it's like waking up, disoriented, from three separate perspectives. Once the images steady out, different iterations of the same scene show Phoenix, Cass, and Lonan, all alert and together in the same bleak, poorly lit room. I see Alexa in the background, sleeping in the corner behind Cass. Only the guys have had their heads screwed with, apparently, or maybe they're the only ones my father wants to talk to right now. Pellegrin must have done the procedure on Phoenix and Lonan as soon as they were brought in, up in his lab.

Dad types some numbers on a keypad, and each of the three screens takes on a faint red tint. Virtual gauges and dials line the bottom of each display, along with heart rate and blood pressure monitors and a whole mess of numbers. "The fact that you're hearing me in your heads right now is completely normal," Dad says, into the microphone once again. "This happens every day, all the time. No need to question it. I am not your enemy." He flips a switch and the screens go back to their normal colors.

None of the guys react, or show even the slightest bit of recognition that Dad's said anything. It's a little frightening, how very normal they act. "Did you just—like—*brainwash* them?"

"That's the only time I'll do it, sweetheart, I promise," my father says. "It's just that the girls are in there now"—he gestures to Alexa, on-screen—"which means Ava and Stark aren't trying to pin them down anymore. We may not have a lot of time to work with, and I didn't want to waste it jumping through hoops."

I understand, and I trust him when he promises, but it does not sit comfortably. He and Pellegrin watch me, as if they're waiting on my permission—as if my permission means anything here. "Fine," I say. "I get it. Let's go."

Dad nods. "Lonan," he says, "I understand you've come to this island to pirate my science and lock the Wolves out of a project I've been developing for more than half a decade, yes?" Every gauge on Lonan's screen spikes. His perspective blips to stained gray concrete. The way Phoenix and Cass stare him down, I wouldn't want to meet eyes with them, either.

This is *not* where I expected Dad to start. "How did you—" I say, just as Lonan says, "What did Eden tell you?"

My father looks at me. "Eden doesn't share secrets," he says. I can't quite tell if he's impressed that I've known about Lonan's secret mission and haven't mentioned it, or vaguely distressed. "Stéphane Monroe has been in touch once a month, like clockwork, through Resistance channels, since the Allied Forces first formed." The name is vaguely familiar—I recognize it from Wolfpack propaganda, from a series of anti-Alliance graffiti art sprayed on a wall near barracks. Someone took great care in painting all the ways they hope this one man will die. "Always asking if I'm ready to give it up, my life's work. Always pressuring me to change my mind."

Lonan doesn't immediately respond—not to Dad, anyway. Cass and Phoenix are quiet but urgent, their questions tripping all over each other. They leave hardly any space for Lonan to explain. When things finally settle on their end, Lonan asks, "So what changed your mind? Why give it up now?"

"Giving the project over has never been a question," Dad says. "It's *who* Stéphane wants me to give it to that's been the issue. Also, the timing." He slides a stool over from his work island to the microphone, perches lightly on it. "The habitat isn't fully developed—even as recently as last week, we've been dealing with water leaks in one of our community chambers, and that's not the only issue. Stéphane is intent on getting my research into as many hands as possible; I'm sure he told you this, and I'm sure you bought into it like everyone else." Dad sighs. "No fault of yours; it's on him for not presenting all the angles."

Lonan's vitals spike again, not as drastically as before. "You don't believe in developing as many habitats as possible?" He sounds defensive for the first time, challenging. "You'd rather watch most of the world's population be flooded out from the vantage point of your safe little bubble?"

"Not at all," Dad says. "I don't believe in spreading research that isn't *fully developed*. He's rushing me on this, and believe me, it *will* lead to disaster if he tries to throw hundreds of copy-cat habitats together as fast as he possibly can. Half a million people could drown if we push this too quickly, if it isn't thoroughly tested, if it is anything less than perfect. I refuse to stand by and watch it happen."

Lonan is quiet on the other end, vitals evening out. "So what's the alternative? And again, why *now*, if it isn't ready to go?"

Dad motions for me to hand him his field guide, and I do. He flips to the title page, one I've never paid as much attention to, and gives it back to me. At a glance, it looks like Dad has sketched in a simple map of the world. Now, though, I see the continents aren't simply drawn with solid lines, but more Morse code. Three locations are marked with tiny pinpoint dots—one in Europe, one in New Zealand, one in South Africa—and each has a name beside it. These, I've noticed. I've known the names forever, colleagues from Dad's university days. An inscription, plain English in the middle of the page, reads: *For those who travel straight and narrow, for those who go steady and slow, for those who do good and do well.*

This book, I realize—it was not meant for me.

It was only supposed to *look* like it was meant for me.

That it isn't mine, mine alone, feels a little like the earth crumbling under my feet.

"There are exactly three engineers I trust to do right by my research, and Stéphane refuses to consider a single one of them," Dad says. "He wants to use *his* guys, and who can blame him? Everyone wants to go with someone he trusts. But this is *my* research, and I'm familiar enough with his guys to know they're not as careful as they should be. My people won't rush it, and it'd be a while before we could make it available to the public at large—but at least we could save a remnant if it came down to it. Noah's ark for humanity, that's how I think of it, as many cultures represented as possible. Scientists, too. Engineers."

Pellegrin clears his throat. "Ava's pinged me twice," he says, tapping the face of his sleek black wristband. "Just so you know."

My father nods. "When Eden showed up on our shores, I knew the only way she could have found the island was if she'd used the fail-safe I'd hidden with her, my old logbook," he says, "to answer *why now*." All my secrets, laid bare: Has Lonan made the connection yet that this man he's talking to is my father? More important, will he forgive that I've kept such a colossal detail from him? "The gulag Wolves wouldn't have had the first clue what any of my notes meant," my father goes on, "but here at HQ? They're smarter than that. If they'd found the book on her, and if they'd picked it apart like they do with every other thing, that would've been the end."

Of his plans, he doesn't have to say.

Of *him*.

"I risked some emergency correspondence," he continues.

"Through Eduardo, at your Resistance island, to my guys. To Zhornov."

My breath catches, and from the looks of their vitals, all three of the guys are equally affected by the name. My father has been in touch with Zhornov—on *purpose*?

"I'm sorry, did you say Zhornov?" Lonan says. "As in, one-fifth of kingpin power?"

"*I* am his power," Dad says, and every hair on my arms stands on end. "He only rose to his position because of his connection with me, and what my research and development means for the kingpins and their future survival. If Zhornov loses the science, he loses everything. They *all* lose everything."

And just like that, things would begin to fall apart.

Lonan's words earlier, about how the Alliance is aiming to destroy the Wolves from within: What better way to start the implosion than to cause strife among the kingpins themselves? Freedom is so close I can taste it. The end of the war—life, together, with my father—with Lonan and the others. Family, home. Peace.

"That's where you come in," Dad says. "We're going to take it all away from th—"

But he is abruptly interrupted by the shattering of glass.

And so it begins.

SEVENTY-TWO

THE TINTED-GREEN DOOR falls like hail from a summer sky, sudden and loud, into a heap on the floor. Dad's fingers fly over the control board. All at once, the entire wall of screens, dark ones included, fills with vibrant color. No more gray holding cells—it's like looking out windows into thirty different worlds. More HoloWolves' perspectives, no doubt.

A prim woman with her dark hair in a low, neat side bun near the nape of her neck steps over the shattered glass. She wears three-inch heels and, like Pellegrin, is dressed all in white. One corner of her starched collar has a navy-blue ram's head emblem embroidered in it—perhaps she is the other member of Team Aries.

Her eyes drift toward Gray, who hasn't so much as twitched since the blow dart tranquilized him. "Will, Pellegrin—is your situation contained? I've pinged you both, multiple times. What's going on here?"

The woman's voice. It is the same as the one from before, when I was nearly discovered out by the water: the woman who headed for Alexa and Hope in the cave. A still-bleeding gash on her arm stains her white clothes.

"She was a bit combative, as you can see by the blow dart," my father says, meaning me. "But we've completed the procedure."

I keep perfectly still, careful not to draw more attention to myself than is necessary. It's imperative this woman believes I'm the problem here, not Dad—both of our lives depend on it. For his part, Dad is all steel and ice, like he was when Gray first brought me in. How hard it must be for him to wear this heavy shell of a personality every day.

"And she's been activated?"

"We've worked together this long, Ava," Dad says. "Do you really think I would be so careless?"

Ava appraises me. Narrow eyes, I've learned, are seldom a good thing.

"I served as witness," Pellegrin says. "He activated her right in front of me."

This seems to ease her concerns. "Pell, Will—a word, please?" She sends a silent message with her eyes. I am the only other person in the room: What does she not want to say in front of me?

"Attentive," Dad says. It is so odd to hear such sharp, short communication on his lips.

Ava cocks her head. "In case I wasn't clear, there is highly sensitive information at stake. Would you like to alter her senses, or should I?"

"Since when do you ask permission?" The tone of Dad's voice as he moves back toward the control board is light enough that it comes off as friendly banter. Except I'm pretty sure they're not friends.

"It's your shift," she replies. "I'm simply following procedure."

Dad pokes and prods at various buttons and switches. It is a complicated piece of machinery, like the mixers used in recording studios before the war. I know Dad is actually adjusting the settings on it because various lights blink on wherever he presses his finger. If I'm supposed to be feeling any different, he hasn't pressed the right ones yet.

Perhaps the sense-altering—what a terrifying thing, if it is what it sounds like—only works on subjects who've been activated.

"There," he says. "I've set her sight to a two and put her memory on a loop."

Ava eyes Dad's work but doesn't comment.

I have no idea what that means, though I can guess. It would have been nice if he'd prepared me for how to behave in a situation like this. Do I stare into a void? Do I go about my business like a normal human being?

I must look like a deer in headlights, because Ava says, impatiently, "I'll give the directive."

"Still following procedure?" Pellegrin says under his breath, so quiet I barely hear it.

Ava doesn't seem to notice—she is too busy adjusting the control board's microphone. She depresses a button at its base, and a green light blinks on. "Go to sleep in the procedural chair, Number—"

"Seventy-Three," Dad supplies.

"Seventy-Three," Ava finishes. "Wake again in five minutes."

I suspect this is my cue. I go directly to the mint-green chair, curl up in it.

The display screens don't change simply because she's focusing on me, I notice. I pray she won't check, pray my blind obedience will be enough to convince her.

No sooner than my eyes close, Ava speaks. "We've got a situation." There's something new in her voice, undertones of frantic urgency. "Stark and I followed a lead a little while ago, into the Burrow. We found two of the girls there—Number Seventy, and the Wolf who was in a relationship with Sky Cassowary. I'm sorry to say we now have concrete confirmation that the Wolf has most definitely defected."

If the Wolf is Alexa, Seventy must be Hope.

"Were you able to bring her into custody?" Dad asks, as if we haven't already seen her in the cell with Lonan and the others.

There is a pause. "I'm afraid she was in possession of a sedative dosage." Another pause. "Stark and Seventy are still unconscious in the Burrow."

My breath catches. No wonder the guys' video feeds never showed Hope in the cell—she wasn't *in* there. And what have they done with Finnley? I focus on breathing, on breathing without shaking, on breathing without vomiting.

"What about the Wolf?" Pell asks. "Do I need to go up to the lab and prepare another procedure?"

Ava laughs. It is like honey on ice cream, enough sugar to

make someone sick. "For a defective Wolf? Come on, Pell—who's not following procedure now?"

She is every bit as sharp as I guessed. *All* meanings of the word sharp.

"Well, Gray's out at the moment, so we'll have to put the kill off at least until he wakes up," Dad says.

It takes everything I have not to react to the word *kill*.

"I was worried about that," Ava says. She genuinely does sound alarmed. "When he wasn't guarding the ground level entry, and when he didn't pick up my pings, I was afraid Seventy-Two had overtaken him somehow. But Seventy-Two and the others were in holding when I went to lock the Wolf in, so I thought it might be something even more serious."

Seventy-Two, I gather, can only be Lonan—he was the last of us to enter the lodge, and Dad called me number Seventy-Three. And that would make Seventy-One . . . Phoenix?

There is a long, drawn-out silence. "Well," Dad finally says, "what do you suggest we do? Zhornov wants Seventy-Two and his crew out on the yacht ASAP." A *yacht*? Dad mentioned earlier how he'd risked contact with Zhornov—and how eager the kingpins were to meet Lonan—but I never explicitly put the two together. What has he planned, if it isn't exactly what they expect? "You're the one who put the Wolf in holding with Cassowary, Ava. You've been monitoring her for as long as I have—she's not going to let us take him without a fight. Or any of the others, for that matter."

Ava clears her throat. "My shift here starts in two minutes," she says. "You and Pell can flip for who gets to kill the defective Wolf. Procedure, and all that."

There is the clinking of change, the slide of silver on silver, the slap of palm on palm.

"I call tails," Pellegrin says.

A second passes. "Tails it is," Dad says. "And, Pell—take Seventy-Three with you."

SEVENTY-THREE

WHEN MY FATHER said earlier that Pellegrin had taken the zip here, I imagined him driving a zippy sort of golf cart, or one of those rolling podiums tourists always used on city tours.

I did not expect the endless concrete hallway outside the Aries office to be equipped with a removable panel in its roof, or a steel ladder that plunges down like a death threat. We climb and climb—we were deeper underground than I realized.

When we come up for air, there are more things I did not expect.

Like, for example, that we are not in the lodge anymore.

And not only are we *not* in the lodge, we aren't outside, either. It's dark, so dark I can only see what's visible in the leftover light from the hallway far below. The smell is familiar, stale and dank. I look up: a dome of carved-stone windows lets starlight and moonbeams in whenever the leaves shift in the breeze.

We are in the temple. In the temple rotunda, to be exact, where Hope first noticed all the beetles. No wonder it is so heavily secured, with the Aries station directly below it.

"This way," Pellegrin says.

I follow him blindly, first because it is dark, but also because

I trust him just enough. I want to ask, *You aren't really planning to kill Alexa, are you?* and *Are Lonan and the others really going to board the yacht Zhornov wants them on?* and *Are Finnley and Hope going to be okay?* But I think better of it when I remember Ava is on security duty now. Who knows what she can see or hear. Even if I'm not officially activated and under the Wolves' control, I should act like I am—there are probably cameras all over the place. Pellegrin might even be monitored somehow, so it's unlikely he could give me a straight answer if he wanted to.

We wind through the temple—not through the narrow, serpentine hallway I took with the girls, but in the opposite direction. My eyes adjust to the darkness as we walk.

I do not hear a single scuttle of beetle feet.

Pellegrin pauses to press a button on the wall. A complicated web of blue lasers flickers in the darkness before blinking out of existence. The lasers remind me, again, of Hope: assuming she and Finnley were compromised at the same time, Hope would have been under the Wolves' control the day we found this place. How much of what happened was actually manipulated by Dad or Ava? Hope's accident with the lasers drew blood, the blood drew out the beetles, the beetles drove us away.

Perhaps it wasn't an accident at all.

She is also the only one of us who refused to sit on the poisonous moss.

She is the only one of us who didn't get assaulted by tentacle plants.

A deep and lingering chill spreads out from my spine and

into the rest of me. I wasn't even the one compromised—but I was the one who ended up suffering for it. The pain of the moss, the Birch hallucinations.

I can't start believing I'm safe just because Dad refused to complete their horrific procedure. Complacency is my enemy.

We dead-end at the base of a thick tree. Either the passageway was designed that way, or the tree grew up later and blocked the path. At any rate, the Wolves have found a way to use it to their advantage.

"Careful on this ladder," Pellegrin says. "Some of the footholds are narrower than others."

The rungs are carved directly into the tree, like the ones at the net where Finnley fell. Merely thinking of having to cross the cocoon-bridge maze again is exhausting—I don't have it in me right now. To my relief, when we get to the wooden platform, there are no bridges; instead, we will use a zip-line system, the sort that is functional in both directions.

"The harness is more solid than it looks," Pellegrin says.

If this is an attempt to reassure me, it isn't working—I can't clearly see the harness, thanks to the darkness. It doesn't feel frayed or like it's falling apart, but it is insubstantial, flimsy as the Spanx my mother used to wear under her party dresses. Pellegrin offers his harness for me to feel, too, and it is exactly like mine. If he trusts these, uses them every day, surely they will hold up.

He helps me slip inside, hooks the harness to the carabiners and the wire, and gives me a brief rundown of how to stop when we get to the end of the line. He goes first so he can be there to help me, just in case.

I take one last glance at the temple, all of which is below me at this point. A temple hidden in ferns, just like my father wrote in his field guide. I had such high hopes for it, such different expectations, the day we first found it—and found it abandoned.

Except it isn't really abandoned at all, now that I think about it. *Temples hiding among ferns, structures formed of stones and secrets. Monks who grant refugees immunity from both sides of the war by inducting them into their monastery. Hologram tattoos given to all who approach peacefully, without any hint of hostility.*

It is a good thing the ink on that page of my father's book became blurred beyond legibility.

Of all the times I've read that passage, I've read it only in the context of finding freedom—and I've only taken it at face value, not as a coded clue.

Hologram tattoos. Approach peacefully.

It was a warning meant to protect, should anyone ever find their way to his lab. It was a warning about the things he would have to do, the things it'd be best to go along with. His notes weren't a map to Sanctuary so much as they were a map to him, the monk inside it. It isn't the freedom I expected, but perhaps it is the freedom I need.

My father is alive. My father is *alive.*

I am alive.

I jump, I zip, I fly. The temple, the ferns, the stones, the secrets: they are nothing more than a blur of wind and wonder, for just a little while. And then my feet find solid ground again on a second temple—the lodge—hidden among more ferns, more stones, more secrets.

"Ready?" Pellegrin says. We are on top of the lodge, where Ava and the man—Stark, she'd called him—were talking while I hid below, by the canal. There's the rope ladder, I note, crumpled in a heap at the base of the barrier wall. Pellegrin's lab must be close. "You're going to have to trust me on a few things once we get inside holding."

How far will Pellegrin and Dad go to convince people of their loyalty? Not so far as killing Alexa, I hope. Surely not.

The night air is fresh but thick. I take a deep inhale and follow him inside.

SEVENTY-FOUR

PELLEGRIN WEARS AN earpiece just like Gray's. He touches it as soon as we're inside the lab, holds up the other hand in a universal *wait for a second* sign. Guess we're not going to holding just yet.

"Good on our end," he says, not to me. "You?"

We are inside his lab, which is a crisp contrast to where my father works. I always imagine labs as being perfectly white, but this one is softly lit and the color of a spring sky. There are three more dental chairs, also mint green, and three silver tables with identical sets of tools. The far wall is lined with a counter full of microscopes, test tubes, beakers full of colorful liquid, and various office supplies like masking tape and Sharpies. A corkboard covers almost the entire wall, with innumerable samples of fern and vine and palm and moss—amid who knows what else—pinned to it.

Sorry, Pellegrin mouths to me. "How long has she been out?"

My ears perk at this. I continue pacing the lab, try my best not to look like I'm hanging on his every word.

"I should go ahead and give it to Seventy-Three, then?"

It could be anything. I'm not sure I want any *it* Pellegrin might offer, especially if it comes from this lab.

Two of the walls are mostly windows, ones that overlook the canal. It's probably a beautiful view during daytime—how very nice for Pellegrin that he gets to operate on unsuspecting innocents while surrounded by such a peaceful atmosphere.

Pellegrin rummages around in a drawer near the microscopes, so I occupy myself by checking out the fourth wall. This one is full of screens—a grid of nine—but they don't look like they're for surveillance. A small silver keyboard sits, lonely, on the countertop below. The meticulous spotlessness of this lab is the most striking difference from the Aries office.

"I'll let her know," Pellegrin says. He pushes the drawer shut until it clicks. "Anything else?"

There's a three-dimensional rendering of the entire island on one of the screens, surrounded by ocean. A cluster of red dots glows from one area close to the far northeast shore: Perhaps each dot represents a person? Is this where we are? If so, we're much closer to the coast than I realized.

"That's the barrier projection." Pellegrin's voice is so startlingly close I practically jump out of my freshly hologrammed skin. "Sorry, didn't mean to scare you." He points to a gray line that circles most of the way around the island. "This is how we deflect unwanted visitors," he says. "We've anchored the line at eight hundred points so it stays in place, and the line projects filaments of light that stretch as tall as the Freedom Tower. If you look at it from the outside, it looks like the ocean goes on forever."

"That . . . is kind of amazing." It feels like so long ago that we were on our boat, when Hope and Finnley first spotted the island and Alexa couldn't see it. "What about this?" I point to a swath of blue at the bottom of the screen. "Most islands are attached to the bottom of the ocean, aren't they?" It looks as if the entire island has been scooped from a larger hunk of land and set adrift. Sky above, water below. If Alexa had ventured much farther out to sea that night when the guys arrived, she might very well have fallen off.

"Your dad ever talk about protocells when you were a kid?" he asks. "Artificial reefs, like they crafted to keep Venice from going under?"

I nod. "I remember a little bit. That's what this is?"

"This island was one of a few prototypes we built for Enviro-tech when we first started researching biosynthetics, materials that can heal themselves. We grew the foundation to be like limestone, but porous, so it makes a sturdy base without being in danger of sinking. And this layer"—he swipes a finger across the screen—"we built with ancient reed technology out of Peru. Everything on top of it, we cultivated on our own."

His finger moves to a thin green line underneath the island. "This is the tether—it holds us in place and automatically lets out length so our island can rise with the sea if needed. We're basically a living raft that never moves."

I'm speechless. My father is brilliant, but this man is an off-the-charts genius.

"Sorry for so many questions—but—this? What is it?" I say

finally, pointing to an enormous blue triangle. It spans much of the Gulf and stretches all the way out into the Caribbean.

"That's the magnetic barrier," he says, not fazed by my barrage of questions in the slightest. I guess it isn't often he gets the chance to talk about the things he's so passionately created. "Just one more way to maintain maritime control. Our ships are equipped with charts so they'll know when and how to adjust their compasses."

"And Lonan's people?" If they make their living out of intercepting Wolf ships full of spies, they're sailing the exact same water. "How do they know how to deal with it?"

But I already know the answer, as soon as I ask for it. *Knives at throats have an uncanny knack for producing information*, Lonan told me, when we were on top of the world.

"They . . . have their ways," he says.

It turns my stomach to think of Violent Lonan, so I stare harder at the map on Pellegrin's screen. "And you invented all of this?" No wonder the Wolves snatched him up for their cause. I don't want to know what they're holding over his head, what he gave up in order to help them.

He nods. "You sailed in through here." He points to a narrow opening on the west coast side. "And this is where you'll sail out. You'll need this," he says, placing a small silver case in my hand. It's like trying to hold ice, metal straight out of the borderline-too-cold refrigerator. "Open it."

Three syringes line one side, held in place by snug elastic. Two are full of amber liquid. "Sedatives?" I ask. "And where exactly am I sailing?"

"We'll get to that," he says. "And, yes, those two are the sedatives. Just in case Ava wakes up and overtakes the control board, you might have to fight off the others." I open my mouth to ask, and he adds, "Your friends."

For all his words, he's not the clearest communicator. I hold on to my logistical questions for now. "What happened to Ava?"

A sly smile spreads over his face. "Your father mentioned that unfortunately Ava has been detained by another stray blow dart."

I get an idea, possibly a brilliant one. "Can you do the procedure on her, the same thing you do to control the spies? And Gray, too? They're already knocked out—"

"Top-tier staff has been vaccinated against it," he says. "You have no idea the hell people went through when the kingpins directed me to create *that*. Rough couple of months. Ava told me every day how lucky I was that I was the scientist, not the test subject." He laughs, but it is brittle and broken.

"I thought my father said you didn't have a vaccine?"

"He said we can't *cure* it. Big difference. A vaccine won't reverse anything—it just prevents the procedure from taking effect in the first place. It's what I injected you with, actually."

Oh. *Oh.*

It's reassuring—it is. In a way. I can trust Pellegrin, I can trust Dad, I can trust myself. None of us can be compromised.

But I'm not there to take the blow-dart blame this time, is all I can think. "Won't they figure out who shot Ava?" Part of me wishes, and how horrible, that Dad would take her completely and permanently out of the picture. But like Dad's love and pain are flip sides, so are his mercy and his confidence. I know he won't become a direct agent of death unless he absolutely has to—even at his own expense. He would have killed for Mom, though. And definitely for me.

Pellegrin's deep-chocolate eyes are bitter melted with sweet. "More than likely, I'm sorry to say. He may have to resort to extreme measures to keep that information contained." His blunt bedside manner is so honest it hurts. "But this is everything we've worked for, and there's not going to be an easy way to do it. We're both well aware of the risks."

There are no pictures on his desk, no prized-possession mugs on his countertops. I wonder if it's because he doesn't have anyone to remember, or if it's simply too difficult to remember. "Do you . . . have a family?"

The sweetness has all but evaporated from his eyes. "Had one," he says. "Long time ago." He looks like he's on the edge of elaboration, but then he pulls back. "Will's my family now. And even though you've never met me before, he's told me everything about you. Feels like you're family, too."

That he lost his family, that he's heard all about me from Dad, that he feels like he knows me well enough to call me family—I don't know how to respond. To any of it.

Fortunately, Pellegrin clears his throat and changes the subject rather abruptly. "This one"—he points to the third syringe, the one filled with liquid the color of this sky-blue room—"be very careful with this one. Use it only if your life is explicitly threatened. Don't let anyone steal it; don't even take it out of the case until you're certain no one will overtake you and stab you with it."

A pit forms in my stomach. "Why even send it along, if it's that dangerous? Who's the target?"

"As much as I wish there were a target, and you didn't hear me say that, this is not a kill mission," he says. "But it is imperative for you to stay alive."

He moves to his counter full of equipment, to the test tubes and beakers, and presses his palm against a glass door just below. Piercing blue light scans his palm print, followed by a series of soft beeps as he cracks the door open. A fog of cold air is there, and then it's not: he's fast to reach in and retrieve whatever it is he needs.

"If anyone sees this, they *will* kill you."

You, he says. But it's clear *you* means more than just *me*.

"This is a bloodlock. Inside it is—"

"My . . . father's blood?"

Pellegrin's expression changes, as if I am an equation he hasn't yet worked out. It's only a matter of seconds, I'm sure, before he puts it all together.

The test tube in his hand: it is so exactly like the one I've carried for two years, so exactly like the one I just shattered outside this lodge.

Perhaps the field guide wasn't my father's only fail-safe.

He nods, once and finally. "A bloodlock is the most

comprehensive method of information transfer on the planet. Everything your father has felt, imagined, lived—all the knowledge he's acquired—specifically here, in regard to the Atlas Project—it is in this tube. We bloodlock at the end of every day, destroy the previous day's contents. We don't have a backup system, because the information is entirely too sensitive. This is *the* most recent, and it is the only."

The truth falls like a feather, but it holds the weight of worlds.

If anything happens to my father, this tube is the only thing left.

If anything happens to the tube, my father's lifelong work will be gone.

And if anyone finds out just how valuable this tube is, my father could be in an extremely vulnerable position. A tube of information would never betray the Wolves like its living human counterpart could—and said traitorous human counterpart wouldn't be of any value to them anymore.

I meet his eyes. "Why are you giving it to me?"

Pellegrin puts the tube in my hand, closes my fingers around it. "You're the only one he trusts."

SEVENTY-FIVE

THIS IS THE plan: in the middle of the ocean, not far from here, there is an island.

On this island lives the hope of our drowning world—the Atlas habitat—and one of its great terrors, Anton Zhornov. It is like an iceberg, the island, 90 percent of it hidden below the surface. Zhornov lives up top, above the water, the great privilege of the man who made it possible for the Wolves to pursue its completion at all. No one lives below. It isn't ready yet.

A man will meet us on this island, Dr. Reem Marieke of Cape Town, South Africa. He requires a demonstration of the habitat before he commits to work on it, Zhornov has been told. He offers expertise where my father is lacking, on sustainable subsea waste management, Zhornov has been told. He is necessary for the completion of the project, the last piece. Zhornov has been told a lot of things.

What Zhornov doesn't know could fill another of my father's books.

Like, for example, that Dad has known Dr. Reem Marieke for more than half of his life. He's one of the colleagues from Dad's university days, one of the three names written in the front of the field guide. It is true, according to Pellegrin, that he has skills where Dad's are lacking. But the rest of it—that he's accepted this meeting with Zhornov as a first step toward partnering with the Wolves; that Lonan and I, and the others, will be present solely to perform as test subjects who'll go below the surface, in a demonstration of how safe and promising the habitat is—couldn't be further from what's actually going on.

In truth, he's accepted this meeting with Zhornov because it's the only way anyone on the outside would be allowed to breach this hemisphere. And it is necessary to make a connection with someone on the outside in order to transfer the bloodlock *away* from this hemisphere. Specifically, into the hands of one of Dad's only trusted colleagues, who will then go on to work with Stéphane Monroe and the Allied Forces.

It is my job to get it into his hands. And all of us share the responsibility of making the transfer as seamless as possible: everyone stays alive, Zhornov included. If the other kingpins get wind of any of this, the Alliance will lose its advantage— and who knows what would happen to Dad, and Pellegrin, and all of us.

They'll find out soon enough, after Dad locks them out and they can't find the island again. That will be a sweeter misery than death, he says, for them to watch and wonder and weep.

I can't say I disagree.

SEVENTY-SIX

WHEN WE LEAVE the lab, we become tech and procedural patient to anyone who might see us. There is no warmth
between us, nothing to betray our secrets. The vial of blood
rests securely in my pocket, padded by a slim neoprene sleeve,
and the silver case full of syringes has replaced the field guide
at my lower back: a sharper and more deadly way to protect
myself.

"Stay with Lonan on the yacht," he says. He leads me along
the balcony in the grand entrance to a narrow, gilded staircase.
We make our way up to the abbreviated third floor, en route to
the holding cell. "As long as Ava is out, your father will be able
to give directives to him, and the others—what to do, how to
act."

Something about this pokes uncomfortably at my conscience.
"So he'll still be controlling them?"

"Not exactly." Though Pellegrin keeps his voice low, these
hallways must not be as closely monitored as I thought. Or, if
they are, it's likely Dad who's doing the monitoring now. "It
needs to *look* like he's controlling them, for when Gray and
Ava wake up. But he's planning to set your friends' senses to

autonomous, which means they'll have the freedom to act, think, feel, and process their surroundings on their own."

We arrive at the first non-glass door I've seen in this entire lodge—this door is a solid sheet of iron. It's like the Wolves want to look like they live in glass houses and don't throw stones, when really, they rule with iron fists.

Pellegrin presses three fingertips to the door and a circuit of blue lights blossoms into being—it reminds me of the map the boys activated back at the beach, on the enormous stone totem.

"Biosecurity," he says simply. He traces the lines with his finger—it looks like he's working a maze. "But back on the directives—it's basically a simple means of being able to communicate with you from afar. We have some eyes on Zhornov's island, so we'll be able to warn you of things that might get in your way."

"But I won't be able to hear any of it." I'm stating the obvious, but it's best to be clear before I'm aboard a yacht headed toward Zhornov's island with a bunch of HoloWolves, with so much at stake. *Eden and a vial full of blood, versus the war,* the history books will read.

I want them to have the right ending.

"Correct," he says. "That's the only downside to not activating you, but your father and I agree that the benefits of giving you the vaccine outweigh the risks of this particular handicap." The blue lights have gradually transitioned to green, and there is a subtle *click.* He pushes the door open—there is no handle. "Also, your father's been filling Lonan and the others in on the plan ever since Ava's unfortunate incident, so there's no need to discuss it out loud. In fact, I'd rather you didn't discuss it at all."

I am buzzing with nerves: there is so much that could go wrong, so much that hinges on everything working perfectly.

The other side of the door looks as bleak as it did on the screens in Dad's office. It is just a windowless, blank room full of everyone I trekked here with—except for Hope, who I assume is still unconscious in the tunnel, like Ava said. Ava was strong enough to bring only one of them back on her own, I guess. The guys stand, determination on their faces. Alexa glances at them, confused, and slowly rises to her feet.

As soon as we enter, I am at the side of a different Pellegrin. Of course: we are surrounded by human spies. Even if Ava isn't awake to see our live-action show, she will most definitely search the footage to make sure Pellegrin did his job.

And he does.

"What—"

Alexa falls to the ground, cut off by a swiftly drawn syringe to the skin just below her clavicle.

A trickle of sky-blue liquid drips down her chest.

SEVENTY-SEVEN

CASS IS THE first one on the ground, the first one to yell obscenities, the first to run his fingers through Alexa's hair and wipe the oozy blood and blue liquid from her skin. Lonan checks for a pulse; Phoenix adjusts her clothes—they shifted when she fell, and now they're not covering the things they should.

I am standing, shocked. Only I know how very dangerous the blue liquid is.

When Pellegrin turns and is facing just me, his mouth silently forms two words: *Trust me.*

And then he puts a finger to his earpiece. "Aries, activate the directive at once. Things are getting out of hand." I see a glimmer of silver in his hip pocket: it is a twin to the silver case he gave me in his lab.

Almost immediately, the boys stop fussing over Alexa and stand at attention. Only Cass's face betrays his hesitance to leave her side, and only for a split second—it is this that reassures me they are being informed, but not controlled.

This is all for show, I remind myself. It isn't real, can't be real.

It sure looks real. Alexa isn't moving at all, and her breathing is weak. I don't understand why Pellegrin would go out of his way to warn me about the blue-serum syringe, then turn around and inject my friend with it—*trust me*, he told me.

I try, do my very best to trust what I know, not what I see. I'm mostly convinced Pellegrin wouldn't go so far as to actually kill Alexa—if anything, his science reassures me he's the king of illusion. And if she's not dead, there's nothing to worry about. Right?

So I don't ask questions. If I start asking questions that show I know too much, it could bring down our entire mission if Ava replays the footage. She *is* the sort who will replay it, I can tell. She's too sharp to let anything slip.

"This way," Pellegrin says.

We file out of the room, little ducks in a row, all of us but Alexa. She is silk hair and soft skin, long lashes and short shorts, fire tamed to embers.

We leave her slumped and unmoving on the cold concrete floor.

SEVENTY-EIGHT

PELLEGRIN MAKES MORE calls than I can count as he leads us down the narrow staircase, along the balcony, and back into his lab. We don't stop there, but head straight through to the terrace where the zip line dropped us off.

"Burrow Canal," Pellegrin says. "Party of four, to be positioned on New Port Isabel." Clearly, he's not broadcasting the truth of our destination for everyone to hear. "West side," he adds.

The west side: it's where the red barracks are, where Hope and Finnley came from. It feels like so long ago that I saw their names in red ink for the first time, tattooed on their pinkies. The chaos Alexa caused at the beach didn't kill our camp entirely, it seems.

My stomach lurches. Finnley. Where is Finnley? I should have asked earlier—how could I have failed to ask? I've been more than a little distracted, sure. But that doesn't make it okay.

I am the first person behind Pellegrin in line. I can risk a question if I'm careful. He is the leader, and as long as he keeps facing forward, his face isn't in danger of being caught in the guys' spy vision—it's possible he could give me an answer without it being too obvious.

He bends down to untangle the rope ladder. The others gather nearby, at the ledge. I inch closer, close enough to be heard at a whisper. "Where is Finnley? The girl from the nets?"

His shoulders stiffen in his pristine white shirt. Other than that, there is no indication he's heard me.

"Did she—is she—"

He stands, so suddenly and close I have to take a step back, and throws the rope ladder over the edge. "Climb down," he says, addressing the entire group. "Wait on the boardwalk until the transport vessel arrives to take you to the yacht. They should be here any minute now." He doesn't look at me, makes a great effort not to. "Lonan, why don't you go first."

Lonan does meet my eyes, and it takes a good measure of self-control to stay rooted in place. It is the first time I've seen him in the light—really *looked* at him—since our kiss in the cave. And now that I'm looking, I'm having a hard time looking away. So is he.

"Aries, could you check the sense levels on Number Seventy-Two, please?" Pellegrin says, touching his earpiece. For once, though, the little light—the one that says he's actually connected to someone on the other end—is dark. "He seems a little slow."

Lonan gets the hint and starts over the ledge. Phoenix and Cass follow, until it's just Pellegrin and me up on the terrace.

"Brilliant," I say when I realize what he's done to separate us from the others.

He looks at me intensely, the whites of his eyes pure light against the deep darkness of his skin. This is the true Pellegrin again, not the shell he's worn since we left his lab. "We don't have much time," he says. "As soon as Cassowary reaches the boardwalk, you have to go or else Ava will pick up on it when she comes to."

I *knew* I was right about Ava, that she is sharp. "Where is Finnley? Why isn't she with them?"

Warmth and compassion and contrition flood his face, and I have my answer. "She was alive when she hit the net," he says, eyes shining. "But only barely."

"Is she still—"

He shakes his head. "Your father gave her the directive to turn on Stark, who was taking her down to Medical—he explained it away as a psychotic side effect of the bone-shard hallucination you'd all just experienced."

Cass is firmly on the ground now. I should start climbing, but I can't. Not until I *know*.

"I'm sorry, Eden," Pellegrin says. "Stark is impulsive, and his perception of right and wrong has become incredibly muddled over the years. He snapped her neck as soon as he saw her start to turn on him."

The world is a blur.

The rope ladder, the foliage, the transport vessel when it

arrives: all blurs of white, green, gray.

The faces around me: Lonan, Phoenix, Cass, Pellegrin—who will be joining us on the yacht, apparently—tan, freckled, pale, ebony.

I squeeze my eyes shut. Where there should be blackness, I see Finnley. It isn't only my fault, I know that, but all I can think of is the cocoon bridge. Her fall. How I am still here, how she is gone.

Right, wrong, purity, pollutant, joy, pain, grief, goodness: they distort, they intersect, they fuse. Life is full of double-edged swords. Life *itself* is a double-edged sword.

I open my eyes. Breathe. Try not to feel guilty that I *can* breathe: try to use it as fuel, as fire. Finnley did not deserve to die. All I can do now is to do well with the life I still have, for as long as I have it.

On the canal, our vessel veers left instead of right. It's odd: earlier, when we paddled our canoe into the cave, there was very clearly a barrier of jungle on our left.

Now there very clearly is not.

We aren't just *close* to the shore—we are on it. "Biosecurity again?" I murmur, and Pellegrin gives a discreet nod. Incredible. When I look back, there is no trace of the canal, the lodge, or the opening through which we came. It presents itself as an unbroken jungle that spills out over a low, rocky cliff—and our small transport vessel is out on open water. A large, white, extremely modern-looking yacht awaits us not fifty yards away, lit by spotlights and on-board lamplight.

I never aspired to this: that this yacht will take us to the man who dragged our world into war. That the war could crumble based on the mission I've been assigned—as long as I'm able to follow through. That the guilt I feel over Finnley is a drop in the ocean compared with what I'll feel if I let my father down.

If I fail. If I'm found out.

If they kill him for it.

I never asked for any of this.

SEVENTY-NINE

I'VE NEVER SEEN a boat quite like this one: it is one part luxury yacht, one part art display at the MoMA. Two of its sails hold a soft-sculpted form, with striated seams that make them each look like the underbelly of a giant whale. Its bow gracefully arcs into a long, sharp point—a masterful blend of form and function, no doubt—and looks like it could pierce straight through the cruelest waves. A pointed decorative sculpture mirrors it, jutting out directly above it to puncture the sky. It is as if the two pieces together are a vicious beak waiting to devour anything that gets in its way.

Pellegrin directs us onto an open-air deck on the middle level of the yacht, where windows have been carved out to make an unusual, sinuous pattern. It's impeccably designed, more window than wall, and meticulously executed. Once we're all on board—Phoenix, Cass, and Lonan, then Pellegrin and me—he pulls the door shut behind us. It is the most gorgeous yacht I've ever been inside: the interior a rich vanilla cream with walnut trim, narrow-boarded wooden floors tinted with a nutmeg stain.

"NPI, west side?" one of the yacht's men calls from the far end of the deck.

"Affirmative," Pellegrin replies.

"Y'all settle in," the man says. "It'll take most of the night, and tomorrow will be a long day."

I look to Pellegrin for clues—when exactly are we going to make our move toward changing course for the habitat island?—but his face betrays none of our secrets. Which is good for the secrets, not so good for my paranoia.

"Want to sit?" Lonan is beside me, while the others have claimed a pair of couches on the starboard side.

If I sit, I will sleep. If I sit next to Lonan, I may never want to get up again. This could be a problem.

But I am so. Very. Tired.

My answer must be plain on my face, because the next thing I know, he takes my hand and leads me aft, to a long, cushioned bench with nautical-themed throw pillows. The bench over-looks the water, and the island we've left behind, both of which would be a far more beautiful sight in daylight.

But darkness isn't so bad. There is starlight, and salt air, and ocean waves. And Lonan.

He sits first, holds his arm out as a welcome for me to sit close beside him. I sit, lean into him, and rest my head just below his clavicle, where the muscle is the best kind of firm-but-tender. He pulls his arm around me, tight, until we are as close as possible.

It is not close enough.

We are both exhausted—I feel it in the way he holds me, the way we melt into each other. I was right before. I never want to get up again.

The yacht picks up speed, bringing with it a blast of cool breeze. I wish I hadn't had to leave my cardigan crumpled on the floor of that tunnel. Lonan runs his hand over my arm, scorching the chills away.

"I'm glad to see you again," I say. There are so many other things I want to say, but this, I figure, is safe. I *hope* it is safe.

His smile is soft in the moonlight. "I'm glad to see you, too, Eden." His eyes drift down to my father's ring, where it hangs on its chain. He lifts it gently and runs his thumb over the smooth, curved metal. "I miss my family, too."

I go rigid—Lonan already told me about his parents, so why bring this up unless he's telling me something else? The *too* at the end confirms it: he knows.

He knows this is my father's ring. He knows it was my father's book.

The war would not exist without my father, but it doesn't mean he *caused* it—I know this, but I never talk about it, because if there's anything this war has taught me, it's that you can't assume other people see the world in black and white. Some people are intent on seeing red, no matter what. Especially if they've been hurt along the way.

Lonan knows, yet he moves closer, not farther away: this is *everything* to me.

He tips his head to mine, and we kiss. It is slow and careful, soft, not the urgent hunger of fear, or goodbye, or pure relief at surviving a near-death experience—no. We kiss because there is understanding between us, even if it's just the very start of it. Because our losses are deep, and grave, and complicated.

Because we are finally brave enough to risk loving someone again, knowing full well what it means to have to lose them.

I don't know how long it lasts.

All I know is that I am kissing him, and then drifting off, and then waking abruptly as my head clunks against the seat's hard bamboo trim.

Voices.

A commotion.

The sick, swirling feeling of waking from a deep sleep. The sick, swirling feeling of knowing, *knowing*, that nothing comes for free and that victory won't come easy.

And my dagger—*Lonan's* dagger—is missing.

Lonan is gone, too.

EIGHTY

THIS IS THE *last time you can trust me until you find the cure,*
Lonan said. His parting words, back in the cave.

But there is no cure.

So, what, am I never supposed to trust him again?

EIGHTY-ONE

LONAN'S VOICE CUTS through the all the others. He's not even on this deck anymore—I am all alone in luxury—and I still hear him clearly. I creep up the spiral staircase that leads to the top deck, a small room composed of tinted windows and bankers' lamps and navigational equipment. There are too many people inside it.

"You will sail to Zhornov's private island," Lonan is saying when I step inside. "Do you, or do you not, understand?"

It is incredible how context can change the way someone sounds. How soft seats and soft light and soft skin can smooth out all the sharp edges. How a knife blade at a yacht captain's throat can do exactly the opposite.

This is a side of Lonan I haven't seen. It's one I knew existed—one he *told* me existed—but one I've been able to pretend away. You can't expect a diamond not to have a good number of facets, I guess.

Cass has a knife at the throat of the first mate, whose more technical title should be *only* mate. This leaves Phoenix free to perform any navigational maneuvering that's out of the captain's reach. I suspect Pellegrin or my father arranged it this way on purpose, where we are more than double their number.

"I said, *do you understand?*" Lonan's face is as hard as it was the first night we met, before he decided he trusted me enough to let his guard down.

"I'm scheduled for an NPI-West run," the captain says, struggling to get the words out without having his throat sliced by Lonan's blade.

"Schedule change has been approved," Lonan says. "We have the authorized paperwork right there, signed by Will Andersen and Zhornov himself."

"Can't be—gotta be a forgery!" The yacht captain looks to Pellegrin for help. When he finds none, his eyes grow as wide as the spotlights outside the tinted windows. "They're going to have your heads for this, you know," he says. "You more than anyone, Pell." His biceps are covered in tattoos that remind me of samurai swords, and his voice is pure grit.

Pellegrin is unmoved. "It's no forgery, Rex, simply a rare exception, and one we've been instructed to keep tight lips about. If you want to test this order, be my guest, but you know Zhornov will end you immediately if you're found noncompliant." Not the best argument, in my opinion. Especially since Rex obviously thinks *our* orders would lead him to noncompliance. "If you *refuse* to help us, I promise to do my best to drag out your death for as long as possible." Pellegrin cocks his head, gives a little *checkmate* smile that likely makes Rex want to rip his face apart. "Which would you prefer?"

As risky an argument as it is, Rex is visibly about to crack. But then he says, "I don't want any part of it. Show me what you've got." He glares at Pellegrin, though it's still Lonan who holds the knife.

"No!"

Everyone turns to look at me.

My cheeks are flaming. I don't have a better suggestion—I just can't bear to watch. I can't bear to watch Pellegrin or Lonan, or even Cass or Phoenix, intentionally torture someone. I don't want to believe they have it in themselves to do so.

"Just—look at his pictures," I say.

There are two small photographs, not in frames but tucked haphazardly into the bamboo trim on the wall. I recognize Spaceship Earth, the iconic geodesic sphere at Epcot Center, in the background of one: Rex stands with a petite brunette, holding a little girl in a princess costume. The other picture is of a newborn, facedown on a scale, so freshly acquainted with the world its skin hasn't yet been wiped clean.

I gather my courage. "Even if we don't understand why, he's standing up for what he thinks is right—isn't that the very thing we're fighting for? He may not want to help us, but he definitely doesn't want to die, even if he says he's willing to." My voice shakes, but I steady it. They're all still listening for now, and I might not get another chance to speak. "He's trying to live with integrity here. I think we should at least let him keep that."

Rex's face is unreadable. You'd think that after a stranger went out of her way to speak up on a person's behalf, said person would at least acknowledge it.

He doesn't.

But Lonan does. He doesn't move his blade from Rex's throat, but there are pinpricks of compassion in his eyes when they meet mine.

"I'm going to give you one last chance to answer," Lonan says. "If you refuse to help us, we will not kill you, but we will leave you to starve until someone discovers you've been locked on the lowest deck. I have extensive navigational experience—all I'm asking for are the coordinates, and any pertinent information regarding security." His eyes are still locked on mine. "If you do help us—and if all goes as planned—we'll do all we can to keep you alive. We will also do our best to reunite you with your family. What is your answer, Captain?"

Tears are the last thing I expect to see on a man with samurai-sword biceps, but today is a day where expectations are as worthless as the bank accounts in our fallen economy.

"Bring me the nautical charts," he says. "I'll do it."

Lonan and Cass stay with the captain and his first mate. No more, and no less, than the four of them at all times—these are the terms we all agree to.

This leaves Phoenix, Pellegrin, and me alone on the main deck. We stretch out on the thick-cushioned benches and sleep, we raid the refrigerator for its bottled water, we eat our fill of precut mango and pineapple, we drop crumbs from all the crackers we eat.

We also take turns freshening up in the bathroom—it is the first private bathroom I've been inside since before the war. I scrub layers of salt and sand and dirt from my skin, tame my hair into a tight fishtail braid like Emma always wore.

The mirror holds me hostage: not for the scrapes, or the bruises, or the way my shoulders are bonier than before, but for my mother, who stares back at me. I look more like her than I ever knew. I stare into my features—*her* features—for so long Pellegrin comes to check on me. Like if I stare hard enough for long enough, I can bring her back. Have a whole family again, at the end of this war. Go back to Before.

Her ghost, my memories: they aren't enough.

But it isn't like they ever were.

I collect myself, leave the mirror behind.

Phoenix sleeps, deeply, on one of the main deck's cushioned benches. I head for the back of the boat, where Pellegrin sits alone, on the same sectional where I slept on Lonan's shoulder.

"I've been wondering," I say, sinking onto the cushion beside him. "You and my father have been so careful about all of this . . . but that, upstairs, was the opposite of careful."

Dawn will break soon. The sky is light enough now to see the plume of white trailing behind us as our yacht slices across the water. Pellegrin stares at it.

"We can't keep our secrets forever," he says. "Ava and Gray have been awake for hours now, for sure. Your father and I intentionally waited until his next shift began before putting pressure on the crew about our navigational intent."

"But won't Ava see what happened up there when she goes back over the footage? That you lied to Rex?"

"Her next shift won't begin for another few hours," he says. "And actually, that was no lie. Zhornov is expecting us, but for security reasons, he rarely allows anyone but the construction team and his own personal staff to set foot on the island."

"But why wouldn't the captain know about it? It doesn't make sense to keep it from him."

"Makes sense when you consider how easily captains can be bought," he says. "You saw it with your own eyes—he's only out for himself, doesn't want to suffer. If even he doesn't know when he's scheduled for an island run, he can't spill intel to people who try to slice it out of him. It's for his own good, really."

I don't say what I'm thinking: that the most ruthless may slice anyway, unconvinced that he truly has nothing to spill.

"So, Ava and Gray," I say, in an attempt to focus on things less bloody. "They know about all of this?"

Pellegrin exhales, long and loud. "Your father told Ava the truth—not the whole truth, but the version Zhornov knows—because she's the sort who makes everything her business even if it isn't, and often jumps to wrong conclusions. But officially, she's not supposed to be in the loop." He looks away, looks like he wants to say something else but then thinks better of it.

"What?" I ask. "If there's something I need to know, just say it."

He bites his lower lip, but still doesn't speak. "Ava," he finally says—then pauses—"is loyal to a fault, and one of the sharpest people I've ever met. She's suspected for a while that we are up to something, and she's right, which is why your father was as open as was wise with her. But he suspects Ava knows she hasn't been told the full truth—and that's a potential problem." Because the full truth reveals Dad as a disloyal, defective Wolf, he doesn't have to add.

"Dad can't tell her the full truth," I say, working it out, "without everything falling apart."

He nods. "And Ava won't go to Zhornov with her suspicions, because she wasn't granted clearance to know about the meeting in the first place," he says. "Which means she will most definitely take matters into her own hands if she thinks she has reason to."

"Like . . . what, though? What does she *think* we're going to do?"

But even as I say the words, I know. It's what all of us wish we could do, what we most certainly *would* do if it would make any real and lasting effect on the war besides simply reducing the kingpins from five to four.

A tiny sliver of fire bursts through the horizon to our left.

It is the most unadorned sunrise I've ever seen, no clouds, no birds, no pageantry of any sort. The sun simply climbs the sky and settles into place, silently devouring all lingering darkness.

"Something a lot darker than what we've actually planned" is all he says, and my stomach twists.

This is how it will be when we turn the war: we will be like the sun.

EIGHTY-TWO

PHOENIX WAKES WITH a start and cradles his head in his hands.

"Make it *stop*," he groans. His wavy red hair is tied in a knot at his neck, except where the shorter pieces have fallen out to frame his face. "Her voice is too loud. Make. It. *Stop*."

Pellegrin is asleep, has been for about twenty minutes now. He slept only for short stretches at a time, off and on, all night. I'd rather not wake him if I don't have to.

I'm not quite sure what to do.

"Phoenix? Everything okay?"

He doesn't answer, just keeps pressing his fingers to his temples and squeezing his eyes shut. I go over to him slowly—he hasn't seen me yet—and put a hand on his shoulder.

He startles anyway.

"Hey," I say. "What's happening?"

"I can hardly hear you," he says. "Alexa—*Alexa*. If you can hear me, I need you to stop talking."

"It's Eden," I say. If he thinks I'm Alexa, he's further gone than I thought.

He looks at me like *I'm* the crazy one. "In my head," he says.

"Alexa. She's saying all sorts of crazy things and I cannot get her to slow down. Something about your dad."

I spiral from break-of-dawn optimism to end-of-the-world panic in two seconds flat. "What? What happened?" Phoenix's eyes are closed again. "Look at me, Phoenix—Alexa, can you see me? Am I on the screen?"

Finally, the chaos evaporates from him. "She's quiet." He waits, listens. "She sees you."

"Okay," I say. "Alexa—can you slow down and tell Phoenix what's going on?"

Phoenix keeps his eyes open but stares into space as he listens. I've never seen a face tell such a complicated story.

"What?" I hope he will remember everything. "What's that look?"

"Your dad communicated with Hope in her head, like this, when she woke up in . . . a cave?" he says. "Told her where to find Alexa and walked her through some complicated maze to unlock the door." He pauses. "Whatever paralyzed Alexa was only temporary, she says. It wore off and she feels fine."

That, at least, is a relief. But if she's fine, why is she so frantic?

And more than that . . . if she's talking to Phoenix in his head, that means my dad isn't around to do it himself. Neither is Ava—but that brings its own set of concerns.

"Oh—oh." Phoenix's eyes shine in the morning sunlight that streams through the carved windows. Their twisty design leaves an interesting shadow on his face. "Yeah. Just a second."

"What?" I am a broken record, breaking into more and more pieces the longer I wait.

He blinks several times in rapid succession. "There are a lot of things," he says. "Alexa says she and Hope heard an argument on their way to your dad's office—they tried to wait in the hall until it was over, but it just kept getting worse. They heard a woman confronting your dad about how she'd seen you on the footage, but had no footage from your perspective." His eyebrows knit together, like he's trying to keep everything straight. "And then she said something about a yacht being off course."

Oh, no.

This is all very, very bad news. It seems overly optimistic now that any of us ever thought Ava wouldn't figure out that I hadn't been activated. We were meticulously careful about so many other things, but in the end, only one mistake mattered.

"So, what? Is she sending someone after us?"

He pauses, shifts his eyes. I'm starting to recognize this as his listening-intently expression. "I'm not putting it off, she just asked—fine." He looks directly at me. "Eden, the woman shot your father. I'm not sure with what, and I'm not sure how critical it is. Alexa says that whatever the woman used didn't make a noise. She and Hope went to check it out when the argument ended so abruptly, and found your father in a pool of blood."

I blink.

Phoenix is the one with all the tears. I don't have any.

I should have tears.

"Alexa also says she's not sure what the woman was up to when they arrived—she was poking around with her back to them, talking into the microphone they're using now."

His words are just noise, but they are nothing compared with the noise in my own head. My own head is the loudest freight train, full of frantically screaming livestock, in an EF5 tornado. My own head is so loud it becomes a black hole, void of everything other than its own black hole–ness.

Phoenix touches my wrist. He doesn't have the warmth Lonan has, but it works to call me back to myself nonetheless. "Your father isn't dead yet, Eden. Hope tracked down someone who took him to the medical ward."

Not dead yet.

He isn't dead—and he never was.

"You don't have to worry about the woman, either," he says. "Alexa panicked when she saw what happened to your dad."

"Ava's dead?" I ask.

"Two blow darts at the same time are lethal, apparently. Alexa says she only meant to knock her out." I think of how readily Dad reached for the blow dart to take out Gray earlier—he must have kept a stash of them at his disposal, scattered all over the room for easy access. Ava herself probably still had blow-dart poison left over in her system from earlier. That couldn't have helped. "The woman stopped breathing soon after the guy from Medical left with your dad, though. Alexa's freaking out about it."

Phoenix's eyes are green as jade, sparkling in the sun. I get on my knees so he doesn't have to squint up at me anymore, look directly into the camera lenses I know he's been fitted with.

"Alexa," I say, with more conviction than I've ever expressed toward anything in my life, *"thank you."*

EIGHTY-THREE

CASS FLIES DOWN the spiral staircase, but only halfway. "There's land on the horizon, and it's close," he says, leaning over the railing. "Get ready." He disappears back into the navigation deck without another word.

There is no acknowledgment of my conversation with Phoenix: I take this to mean Alexa was on a private call. But she said Ava was up to something on the microphone when she arrived—why would Ava have made a private call just to Phoenix? He seems like the least threatening of the three. Unless she called all the others individually before Alexa got to her, and Phoenix was simply the last.

Pellegrin is quick to wake, and the stairs are his first mission. It occurs to me that Pellegrin has no idea what happened with Ava, or my father. I fill him in. He mutters an obscenity.

"Is it going to affect us a lot, that my father isn't there to give directives in the moment?" I ask. Earlier, when Pellegrin told me the plan, he mentioned Dad would be coaching the guys so their behavior would appear convincingly sense-altered. Also, with a close eye on all the monitors in his office, he'd be watching through the guys' perspectives for subtleties of our meeting with Dr. Marieke and Zhornov—his intel could make or break my attempt at transferring the bloodlock, as far as perfectly timing it goes.

Pellegrin shakes his head. He's a little bit frantic, and it sets my nerves on edge. "No, no, that won't work now." I see him running equations in his brain, which—no doubt—runs extremely complicated equations far more efficiently than mine ever worked basic ones. "It isn't going to ruin us," he finally says. "But it will make your job more difficult. Lonan won't be able to give you the all-clear signal anymore, so you'll need to pay extremely close attention—in a subtle way, though. They will be under the impression that you're sense-altered, so you can't look too alert, or appear to be assessing the room by your own volition."

The news just keeps getting better and better.

The island is clearly visible out of the port-side windows now. It is unusually long and narrow, all sandy white beach and no visible sign of the enormous habitat structure I know lies just beneath it. A menacing wall of jagged black rocks juts out, a barrier that sits forty or fifty yards out from the shore. At the very tip, there's a break in the barrier where an odd structure bobs in the water.

"What is that?" I ask.

"Geodesic sphere," Pellegrin replies. "It's a giant cage used for trapping fish. Fish swim in through the small triangular openings, then hook themselves on the baited barbs attached to a couple of poles inside."

The bulk of it is under the surface, I gather, like an iceberg of steel—like the habitat itself. Zhornov's monthly catch is probably enough fish to feed an entire sector, and yet we lived on cold oats and whatever leftover moldy scraps the Wolves tossed our way. How many dead fish go to waste, and how many prisoners starve, simply because a few men have such an appetite for power?

Unlike the island we sailed from, this one is almost completely devoid of trees. It is almost as if the kingpins had it commissioned for themselves: enough sand, dumped into a pile in the middle of the ocean, and they've created their own sandcastle empire.

The more I think about it, the more convinced I am that that's not far from what actually happened here. It's definitely man-made, but in a different way—and for a different purpose—from the one we just came from. I know from Dad's blueprints that the island surface was meant as a vacation home for those who'll eventually live, full-time, underneath it. Bonus points that it looks like a regular island, at a glance, making it much more difficult for the uninvited to find. It would never show up on any of the prewar nautical maps—it is the perfect place for a kingpin to live as if he is actual royalty.

Two rows of perfectly spaced palm trees mirror each other down the entire length of the island, starting at the tip near the geodesic sphere and dead-ending at a sprawling mansion made of glass. Even from here, I can tell the lawn is perfectly manicured, the pillows on their outdoor furniture perfectly plump.

It must be nice, killing the world in order to live in this sort of oasis, and not having an ounce of remorse over it.

I am struck by this: I would take the ability to feel remorse over the bliss of having my own private oasis. In a heartbeat, I would take it.

"We'll dock here, where Zhornov and Dr. Marieke will receive us," Pellegrin says. In the time I've been dwelling on sociopaths and their dream homes, he has drawn out an elaborate map on a party napkin. It isn't a bird's-eye view, but as if the entire Atlas iceberg has been sliced top to bottom.

"Most likely, we'll be escorted through here when we enter." He draws the tiniest, most perfect asterisk I've ever seen, on one end of the mansion, close to where we are to dock. "The entrance to the habitat is quite grand, and extremely safe"— another tiny asterisk—"so I assume Zhornov and Marieke will accompany you at least that far before splitting from you."

That they'll be splitting from us does not come as a surprise. The whole reason we're present at this meeting—as far as Zhornov's concerned, anyway—is to give a virtual demonstration for Dr. Marieke of how secure the habitat is. My father must have been extremely convincing, if the kingpins are willing to treat Dr. Marieke as if he has a choice in the matter. Whether he actually *has* a choice in the matter is less clear. Surely they know an eager and willing scientist is far more valuable than one who is simply trying not to die? At any rate, this meeting is being held under the pretense that Dr. Marieke must be convinced to join Dad's team, which implies he can decline.

I glance over my shoulder, make sure we're truly alone down here. Even with Ava dead, we can't be too careful. If Stark or Gray overheard, it would ruin everything. "Dr. Marieke knows I have the—he knows about the transfer?" My fingers settle over the vial in my pocket, an instinct.

"Dr. Marieke knows *everything*," Pellegrin affirms. "You'll need to be extremely alert, and fast—look for an opening and give him the bloodlock the first chance you get. He's prepared, ready for it at any time. Don't try to get his attention first, and don't expect him to acknowledge you after it's done." He sighs, like the whole weight of the world is falling off his shoulders, only it isn't going far—now it rests on mine.

"Trust him, Eden. Your father does." A patch of brilliant sunlight sets his eyes on fire. "He's well aware of what's at stake here."

He: I'm pretty sure Pellegrin means Dr. Marieke, not my father, and yet I can't hear it any other way. My father is well aware of what's at stake here.

Of how drastically this vial full of blood—and so much more than blood—has the power to heal the world.

Of how he will die, and I will die, and probably all of us will die, if we are discovered as the traitors we are.

But even in this drowning, desperate world, where power triumphs at the expense of love, where throats bleed and Wolves run wild, I want to *live*.

So I cannot be found out, and I will not fail.

EIGHTY-FOUR

I AM SURROUNDED by war faces: Lonan, his ice-blue eyes cool and hard. Cass, whose intensity radiates from his skin like summer heat on asphalt. Even laid-back Phoenix wears grave focus as an armor, his usual nonchalance buried deep inside so nothing vulnerable peeks through the cracks. Pellegrin looks more or less the same—which is not to say he isn't intimidating.

Our yacht settles into place at the end of a long pier. One hundred slats of weathered wood, give or take, separate us from the men who will turn the future.

Zhornov's face is easily recognizable, though they must have done something in all the kingpin propaganda to make him look taller and sleeker. He looks happy, and why shouldn't he? He is a king in a castle, welcoming more peasants who will prolong his wonderful life. Only a paper cut–thin line of dried blood on his face betrays this image. I imagine one of his various attendants letting a straight-edge razor get a little too dull, cut a little too deep. Deep enough to remind this man he is still human, not deep enough for it to look like anything more than an accident.

The other man has hardly aged a day since his college graduation. Dad never kept many pictures, not until I came along, which is why I can remember the few he had in vivid detail. I remember this man more than all the others, with his wavy blond hair and light blue eyes and long, pointy nose—his creamy tan skin that seems so at odds with the rest of the genes that fought their way through. He has a distinct combination of features that are unlike any I've ever seen. *Reem is Dutch-Lebanese*, Dad told me, when I first noticed the picture. *Born and raised in South Africa.*

However long it took Dr. Marieke to travel all the way from Cape Town, he looks perfectly well-rested. Sunlight catches all the subtle shades of his hair, shows no wrinkles on his face or in his crisp, pale pink button-down.

They are silent and staring, as if our single-file processional down the pier is more formal than it is. Which, I don't know. Maybe it is more formal than I realize. We walk like the mind-numbed HoloWolves we are supposed to be, heads held high, eyes seeing but not perceiving, silent amid the sound of waves as they lap at the pier. Pellegrin leads the way, the only one among us who is meant to still have a mind.

"Right on time!" Zhornov's face looks strange with a smile on it—it is a real smile, too, one that lights his eyes. His gaze rests just past me, at the end of our line: Lonan. *They're obsessed with him*, Dad said, back in his office. *They want to admire their pet weapon as soon as possible.* Just before we lined up to walk this pier, Lonan laced his fingers between mine, only for as long as it took to whisper *be strong* in my ear.

I should have done the same for him.

"Anton," Pellegrin says, nodding. "Nice to see you again."

Zhornov cracks out a burst of laughter that ends in a phlegmy cough. "I'm sure, I'm sure." He extends a hand, helps Pellegrin from the pier. As if Pellegrin *needs* help from the pier. It is a gesture that brings bile to my throat, this single small thing that will help Zhornov rest easy in his bed tonight, something to convince himself he's a good guy.

He turns away without introducing Dr. Marieke and Pellegrin to each other, curling two fingers in the air as if to say *follow me*.

But the doctor doesn't turn. "If I may," he says, with the same sort of gentle-but-assertive manner as my father. "Thank you all for coming."

Zhornov shifts, eyes him sidelong. Laughs like a wheeze. "You want an introduction?" Suspicion, a challenge. "You haven't needed an introduction for anyone else on the island."

Dr. Marieke is calm, doesn't miss a beat. "They've come all this way for my benefit. The least I can do is acknowledge them."

Perhaps this is his attempt to get our business out of the way early. A handshake, an exchange. My father should have given Pellegrin the bloodlock. *You're the only one he trusts*, Pellegrin told me. Unless that was only a half-truth, and he simply didn't want his own hands anywhere near something so risky.

No matter: Zhornov's introductions are perfunctory, limited to the doctor and Pellegrin, and he turns him away—claps a hand on Dr. Marieke's back, as if they are much more familiar than they are—before anything resembling a handshake can happen. Clearly, he's on guard. And this is a *friendly* meeting, one he eagerly agreed to, according to Pellegrin and my father.

This is going to be even more difficult than I imagined.

We take a pathway made of perfectly rectangular strips of slate. I count fifty-four before losing track. The pathway leads directly to the door Pellegrin indicated on his napkin, the entry point en route to our final destination. No doubt its simple-looking glass architecture is more structurally complex than it appears.

Zhornov waves a hand. The doors open automatically, perfectly obedient, patient enough that we pass through without increasing our pace even slightly.

Sparkling steel appliances line the long white interior wall, and there is an island countertop in the middle of the room. Persimmons and pomegranates loll on a curved bamboo platter, a red ceramic dish holds fresh eggs in a line, and I see an array of staff members wielding skillets and sharp knives. In the next room over, a bamboo table built for twelve is empty, save for a single seat at the far end. How incredibly *lonely*, is all I can think.

Zhornov leads us from the bright, naturally lit kitchen and into a maze of hallways, tightly wound as the gray matter inside the human brain. It would be easier than expected to hide in this glass house, if it came down to it.

For one, there are shadows in every place that isn't directly lit with daylight, like in the deep corners of these interior maze-halls. Dim purple light saves us from pitch-darkness, but they are by no means well lit. It's obvious this path is meant to be cumbersome for anyone who doesn't know it by heart.

For another, the walls are glass for a reason—what's on the outside is inherently more interesting to look at than what's on the inside.

Lastly, this particular glass house is nearly as empty as a mausoleum. It appears the ghosts who do roam the premises are all tied to specific spaces: the dining room, the laundry, the yard. They keep to their areas, and Zhornov keeps us to everywhere else. It would be the perfect place to perform the transfer, here in the shadows. But Zhornov keeps a tight arm around Dr. Marieke's shoulders, and any time Pellegrin comes closer than six feet away, he says *Space!*, like Pellegrin is a dog who performs tricks.

Glorious daylight floods us when we are finally led out of the depths of this place and into an enormous entry hall. The amount of space in this room could hold more than a hundred people, but is used for the enjoyment of one. The ceiling stretches all the way to the top of the estate, and the room is practically as wide as the island itself.

The panoramic view is incredible: I see all the way out to the jagged rock barriers on both sides of the island, surf and then sand, parallel rows of palm trees and tropical flowers that continue straight down the center of the island until there is only ocean at the end.

Everything here is modern and crisp and clean except for an

antique baby-grand piano sitting in the corner of the room. Its wood is worn and uneven in color; its keys are yellowed. There is not a speck of dust on it.

Zhornov drops his arm from around the doctor, finally. A band of sweat mars the otherwise perfect pink shirt. "Stay where you are." He directs his command to no one in particular, but we all stop dead in our tracks, even Dr. Marieke. Zhornov makes no move to correct him, or invite him any farther. He simply walks the rest of the distance, alone, to his piano.

His back has been turned away from us the entire time, and yet this is the first time I don't feel his eyes on me. My pulse quickens, my throat goes dry—but by the time I realize *this is my chance, this might be my* only *chance*, he's turned to face us again.

Six notes ring out from the piano as he plays, slow and clear and haunting, a melody that lodges itself in my blood as soon as I hear it. I will never *un*hear it. It sounds like a songbird making peace with its own death.

The final tone, the lowest of the six, is still ringing from the walls when the floor opens. Not the entire floor—just a gaping hole where there wasn't one before, with a wide staircase spilling deeper than I can see.

"Shall we?" Zhornov, for all his paranoia, could not look more genuinely thrilled. Of course he does. This meeting is one step closer to his future being secured, one step closer to earning the forever favor of the other four kingpins. "Lonan, take us under."

Lonan starts for the stairs, not a heartbeat after the command, and I'm next—I follow.

I follow as if I don't notice the glory in Zhornov's eyes. The prized captain of the Resistance is at his beck and call, the prized captain of the Resistance is *his* now, the prized captain of the Resistance is no longer working against him! I follow, because he needs to believe these things for as long as possible. It will be so sweet to strip his glory away—theirs, really. The kingpins will fall, and so will every other Wolf, if the pieces crumble as planned.

I just need to kick off the crumbling. But time is thin, and we are running out of it.

EIGHTY-FIVE

MY BREATH CATCHES on instinct once we're fully below: the ocean presses in on both sides of us for the entire length of this tunnel, kept at bay by walls so clear they're practically invisible. The space is at least as tall as the room we just came from, and—by my best guess—as long as the entire island. Except for the row of black-diamond chandeliers that dots the ceiling, it's as if we're in a reverse aquarium. I imagine all manner of sea life swimming up to study us, sharks and jellyfish and other stinging, biting things, content to be on the side of the wall that's safe from humanity.

Dr. Marieke cannot hide his awe. He breaks away from our group, places a palm against the glass. We aren't so far below the surface of the ocean that it's dark—between the sunlight from above and lights on the structure that stretches deep below us, the water outside these walls sparkles like a picture-perfect postcard.

"Impressive, no?" Zhornov barely spares a glance toward the school of bright yellow fish as it swims past. "If you decide to work with us, you'll be entitled to one of the upper-level living suites near the coral reef Will's team is cultivating. Now *that's* a sight to wake up to."

It takes all my focus to remain unflinching at the sound of my father's name. I can only hope he's faring well in the medical ward, hope he didn't lose too much blood where Ava shot him. The vial of his blood burns a hole in my pocket. All of this would be so much easier if I could just stab Zhornov with one of the sedative syringes Pellegrin gave me, but that's out of the question. This meeting needs to end with Zhornov at peak confidence—and nothing undermines trust like a needle to the neck.

"This way," he says, herding us like mindless, obedient sheep to the underside of the stairs we just descended. He is careful to never turn his back. "Take a good look, Doctor—we'll view the remainder of the demonstration from my sitting room."

We dead-end at a striking set of double doors. They are deceptively delicate, hand-forged gates with bars like iron ribbons. Turquoise-blue light streams through the cracks.

My pulse pounds all the way up in my throat. Dr. Marieke is only four feet away from me, so close it's almost laughable, the impossibility of all this. He'll be gone soon, Zhornov is about to whisk him away—this may be my only chance, and I cannot fail, I *can't*—

Zhornov turns. He has no choice, as there is a retina scanner on this entrance.

My fingers close around the bloodlock. I slip it out of my pocket, careful and quick. It's never or it's now: I reach toward Dr. Marieke, whose hands are at the ready behind his back. I start for the handoff—his fingers brush the neoprene sleeve—but Zhornov backs away from the scanner, moves like he's about to turn.

The vial slips from the sleeve as both of us flinch—*why* did I not orient it to where the sleeve's opening faced the ceiling? If it hits the stained-concrete floor, it's all over, and it's all over if I dive to save it. I've not been careful enough.

But reflex won't let me stay still. I swipe blindly and pray for silence.

It is *so* silent as I lay hold of the vial, all I hear is the rushing inside my own head. Better than shattered glass and bloodstain, is all I can think. Better than secrets spilled.

I shove the vial, sleeveless and smooth, back into my pocket with no time to spare. Dr. Marieke crumples the neoprene until it's invisible inside his fist, so smoothly even I doubt what I've seen. Zhornov turns just as the double doors open behind him. This isn't the end, this cannot be the end. Tears creep along the rims of my eyes; I do my best to will them away. The sense-altered don't cry.

"Hold them just inside these doors for the next four minutes," he says to Pellegrin. "We'll have the viewing screens ready to go by then."

"I haven't had the procedure—I'm not authorized to go as far down as they'll be going." Pellegrin was supposed to be in charge of the viewing screens, so he could control whose perspective is shown at any given time. Namely, not mine, as it isn't an option and its absence will raise suspicion.

"Whose authority overrides mine?" Zhornov smiles, all blunt yellow teeth as he claps a hand on Pellegrin's shoulder. "I want to send you down unaltered, *must* send you down—show the doctor just how far the project has come since we resurrected it."

Dr. Marieke clears his throat. "It's all right if that isn't an option," he says. "If it isn't ready, don't push things on my account. This is already an unprecedented feat of science—you're not going to have to do much convincing to pull me on board." He gives a calm, self-assured smile. I can see bits of my father in him, wonder who rubbed off on whom.

"Do let me try." Zhornov's eyes glitter like a gambler with a royal flush. It isn't a question, it is the end of the discussion, and everyone knows it.

This is it. This is where our best chance at a better world is escorted far away from us.

This is where things get complicated.

EIGHTY-SIX

ONCE UPON A time, the letter Z was my favorite.

It was peaceful sleep.

It was tigers and flamingos and butterfly exhibits.

It was lemon zest and sugar on the hottest summer days.

It was zebras in the Serengeti, and too many girls named Zoe because the Greeks said the word meant *life*.

Now, Z is the opposite of life.

It is zeal taken too far.

It is Zero Day, lives lost and lost liveliness.

It is Zhornov, and the other four kingpins who've forgotten they are flesh and blood, dust to dust.

What will it mean tomorrow?

EIGHTY-SEVEN

SENSE-ALTERED OR NOT, my father would not have sent us on a death mission. I'm not as concerned about Pellegrin—or myself, for that matter—going deep into the habitat as I am about being discovered as an unaltered through the video feed. A mistake like that would wreck what little chance we have at completing the transfer; hopefully they'll settle on Lonan's perspective and stay there.

Pellegrin checks his watch. "Three minutes to go. Sixty seconds max, then get back in formation."

Phoenix rests, arms folded over his knees and head on his arms, while Cass paces the narrow tube just inside the iron doors. We're all quiet, even though we don't have to be, not while we aren't being watched. It isn't until Lonan wraps both of his arms around me that I realize how tense I am. I am fire, frozen.

He tips my face up toward his, sending all the tears I've held back just enough out of balance. More than a few slip out. "You didn't do it?" His voice is barely louder than a whisper.

I shake my head, blink until the tears stop.

He pulls me in close and kisses the top of my head, tucks the forever-wayward pieces of hair behind my ears. "You will," he says. "This isn't over. You will."

I want to believe him. But I know more than anyone that hope and reality don't intersect just because you want them to.

Pellegrin's watch beeps. I should pull away, focus on looking unfocused—if they start watching now, through Lonan, all they'll see is my hair. It's so hard to let go, though. Our best chance at the transfer is behind us, and it makes the future feel entirely too thin.

Lonan is the first to break. Pellegrin's hand on his back makes me feel slightly better, that Lonan wanted to stay wrapped up in me as long as he could get away with it. But now we are back to bleak, back to standing at attention with even spaces between us. Back to this unfortunate reality.

"Here we go," Pellegrin says under his breath. "Follow the yellow stripes—green, red, blue, and violet are identical branches, but they aren't as finished as yellow. It's only a forty-minute demo, enough to see a sample dwelling environment, as well as the aquaponics and virtual world chambers. Even if you're not sure where to go, just walk confidently—Zhornov hasn't actually been down here yet, since he hasn't had the procedure. Whatever you show him, he'll spin it, but let's hope he doesn't have to."

Now would be an excellent time to have my father in his office, directing our every move. All my melted tension becomes brittle again as I think of Ava, of what she did to him, of how she ruined everything. It should have been simple: get in, get out, get back to Dr. Marieke.

Perhaps it should be reassuring that after years of all things complicated, hopeless skepticism doesn't yet rule me. Right now, I only feel unprepared.

Go.

It is more breath than spoken word, flame to a fuse. Lonan leads the way, with Cass and Phoenix after, Pellegrin and me at the rear. Our positions are strategic. If I am at the back, perhaps they will default to Phoenix or Cass for perspective if Lonan's isn't enough.

We pass from our holding tube into relative darkness, dim purple light against metal walls. This portion of the walkway is every bit as wide as the first, and yet it is stifling, claustrophobic without the illusion of space offered by ocean-view walls. Neon stripes, all the colors Pellegrin mentioned, line floor and ceiling in parallel. They lead us down and around a steep, sharp curve, until I'm certain we've done a one-eighty. When it levels out, we spill into a sort of vestibule, a circular chamber where the walls are clear again, and less imposing.

Five tunnels of varying steepness shoot off straight ahead—an upside-down V, with our yellow passageway at the apex. Violet and green must be the habitat's midlevel branches, blue and red the deepest layers of all. From this depth, I can make out various offshoots and tunnels in the water surrounding us.

Lonan walks straight yellow without any hesitation. The

gentle downward slope grows darker with every step, as we venture farther away from the shallow, sun-kissed water. I find myself holding every breath longer than I should, until I'm light-headed. It's instinct, for one, being underwater, but the air-quality levels could also use some attention.

Or maybe this is how my next anxiety attack begins.

Soon, the tunnel opens up into an enormous space, and I guzzle fresh air by the lungful. Everything is bright yellow, a honeycomb sphere with oversized hexagons lining the walls, surrounding an atrium of vegetation. Sparkling ocean water shimmers above the panel at the top of the dome. All of this—it's so much bigger than anything I expected to encounter down here. And there are *five* of these under the island? *Blueprints are so very one-dimensional,* is all I can think. My father's work is an absolute masterpiece.

"This is the largest and most advanced aquaponics project on the planet." Pellegrin says this loudly, as if it is for Dr. Marieke's benefit, and not the directional cue I suspect it is. Lonan takes the hint and veers toward the floor of plants. Kale, chard, an entire rainbow of produce—the vegetables are actually growing out of fish tanks, from at least a hundred individual aquariums. I'm extremely tempted to pluck a meal for myself.

We do a complete tour of the floor before Pellegrin announces we'll be making our way up to the honeycomb walls. "Once there are residents aboard, a three-step biosecurity system will grant access into their individual living spaces," he says. If Zhornov has a problem with Pellegrin playing tour guide, he hasn't silenced him yet. "For now, just use your imagination as the sensor authorizes us based simply on our presence at the door."

Again, Lonan takes the hint. This time, though, it isn't as clear where he should go—there are no obvious doors, just opaque, ten-foot hexagonal panels made of tempered glass. Bright yellow hexagons are embedded in the floor, one per panel. Lonan and Phoenix and Cass don't seem to notice them, or they've steered clear on purpose. I subtly step up and onto one, and *whoosh*: a portion of the panel slips down and away, glass so smooth and slick it appears seamless even as it recedes into the floor.

Phoenix starts toward me, but reverses as Pellegrin gives a nearly imperceptible signal for him to stop. Of course—no one was looking my way, so the doctor wouldn't have seen how the rooms open. Lonan realizes this at the same time I do, and steps forward to the hexagon nearest his feet. Another *whoosh*, and Lonan disappears inside.

We must be at least halfway done with the demonstration. Living quarters, and then one more place? Is that what Pellegrin said before? As amazing as it is to see what my father has created, I'm eager to get it over with. All the science, the blueprints, the research, the trial and error, the avoidable mistakes—all the details that could make the difference between life and afterlife—everything that can make these things available to the whole of the world, and not just Wolves, rests in the vial at my hip.

Every second we spend down here is necessary, I know, but it feels like we're jumping through hoops. I'm growing weary of it.

The living quarters, unlike the grand atrium itself, are quite small. It's like being inside one of the old Ikea showrooms, how pristine and efficient they were, except with great windows of ocean along the outside wall. Terraces of coral jut out from the building and into the water like a mermaid's dream balcony, pure eye candy.

The boys spread out through the rooms—two bedrooms, a kitchen-dining corner that's hardly separate from the living space, a bathroom—but my eye catches on a single detail, something only I would notice. It's like a love letter from my father.

I made it for him the summer after seventh grade, an abstract piece of line art. It is my favorite memory, blown up to a print that covers more than half the main wall: Mom, Dad, me when I was five—what's meant to be our silhouettes, anyway—the summer before we went from three to two. A pier, a seagull. Water, waves. A sunrise that would surely lead to a sunset, end-lessly, peacefully, as it always had.

The crisp lines blur. I cannot lose him, not after I just got him back from the dead. And I cannot bear the thought of Wolves living in these units, the shadows of my peace bringing beauty to their lives. They *killed* peace, mine and the whole world's.

A loud thud pulls me out of emotional paralysis.

I am alone in this room, and it's quiet. It's been quiet for most of the time we've been on the island—not that any of us preferred it that way—but this quiet isn't the same.

Something's wrong.

I stop myself from calling out, just in case my instincts are off, and dart toward the adjacent room. A shock of panic blooms and bursts in me, spine to extremities in half a second flat, when I see what's happened. "Cass—*no*, put him *down!*" Cass has Pellegrin by the throat, slammed so hard against the glass that a trickle of blood slides down it.

But he doesn't stop—where are the others?—and Pellegrin is fading, fast. I slip the silver case from where it sits at my lower back, fumble for a sedative syringe. I'm careful to pick the amber one, not the light blue, definitely *not* the light blue.

Careful works against me.

Cass sees me, sees my reflection in the window, just as I'm about to plunge the needle into his back. Pellegrin slumps from his grip, still with us but only barely—Cass turns and starts in on me. I dart away before his iron fists rip into me, kick the silver case away so that it's far out of reach for both of us. He pulls hard at my braid, so hard I'm afraid it will rip right off my head. Instead, he wraps it around my throat, tight. Stars dance in my vision.

I gather my strength and shove both elbows behind me, into his ribs, take in as much air as I can while I'm free and have the chance. Quickly, I jab the syringe into his thigh: he falls in a heap.

My breaths come sharp and jagged. "Lonan?" I call out. "Lonan!" What if Phoenix has him pinned in the other room?

I have to find him. Then again, what if *he* has *Phoenix* pinned? I should have considered this before calling out. Think clearly, Eden. Be smart.

Lonan pokes his head into the room, and relief: he is immediately, obviously affected by the sight of Pellegrin on the floor, by the blood still dripping down the window glass. He rushes to my side, takes my hand in his before I can stop him. It is warm, soft. It's comfort where I should be putting up walls.

Pellegrin wheezes, like he's trying to speak. Only a few words come out with any real conviction: *Formula. Cure. If I don't make it. In my lab.* Leaning in closer, I see there is more blood than I thought. "Ava," he says, more clearly this time. "Not dead"—deep breath—"no way."

No, no, no. So much no, all of this.

If Ava is alive, that's it. It's over. She must have lied to me through Phoenix, back on the yacht—used *Alexa* to lie—which means Alexa must be compromised. What else isn't as it should be? *She will most definitely take matters into her own hands if she thinks she has reason to,* Pellegrin predicted, and it looks like he was right. The implications of this—what it could mean for my father on the HQ island—what it already means, here. This is not good. At *all*.

And Pellegrin, he needs a doctor, not the scientist sort. His eyes flutter closed no matter how hard he keeps trying to open them. "Eden," he says, using what little strength he has to suddenly grip my arm. *"Run."*

But I have nowhere to go.

Lonan's hand tightens on mine, nearly cracks my bones. The look in his eyes tells me all I need to know.

Death starts like this: hope dies first.

EIGHTY-EIGHT

HIS EYES ARE blank; his voice isn't right as he says my name. He is empty, empty, empty.

Hollow.

I find what little weak spot he has, twist my arm out of his grip. The silver case isn't far, and it's still open, two syringes left, one amber and one light blue. Phoenix is here, too, now—he beats me to it, takes one syringe in each hand. Lonan pins my arms at the elbows, holding me firmly in place despite how hard I struggle.

I'm outnumbered. A pair of HoloWolves, a pair of needles, all against me. Ava must be more convinced than ever that we came here to assassinate Zhornov, especially now that the light blue syringe is out in the open. What better way to make sure he doesn't die than to use all the serum on someone else—and it looks like that someone is going to be me.

"Your father said to tell you goodbye," Phoenix says, turning the syringes over in his hand, "right before I put him out of his misery."

He is nothing but a messenger right now. A puppet-weapon.

It can't be true—I refuse to believe my father is dead unless I am shown definitive proof. Every word out of Ava's mouth has been a lie, so why should I start believing her now? The king-pins must have promised her the sky, and all the stars, too.

Strength sparks to flames inside me, more strength than I knew existed. I wrench out of Lonan's grip, lunge at Phoenix. Careful has done nothing but fail me today. I dive hard at his weaker hand, the one holding the amber-serum syringe, turn it on him until it plunges deep into his stomach. I pry the deadly blue syringe from his other hand, his grip still ferociously tight even as he collapses. If I have it, Lonan doesn't.

Which only makes him want it more. He backs me up into a corner, against the glass, slams me so hard I'm surprised nothing—skull, glass, the universe—shatters. It is a miracle the bloodlock hasn't broken, but it's only a matter of time, I'm sure. I am quick enough to slip away, over and over again. He is quick to force me back.

All his strength: it is against me.

All his fire: it ignites me.

All his vengeance: it is wrath upon me.

I keep the needle pointed as far from my skin, and his, as possible. I refuse to use it on him—this *isn't* him. I refuse to kill his shell when I know his soul is still inside it.

This line in the sand will be the death of me.

I know it as he pries the syringe from my grip.

I know it as we fall to the floor, and I jerk away just in time to keep from cracking my head open.

I know it as he looms over me, as he flicks the syringe to make the sky-blue liquid settle.

I kick, I plead, I search for something—*anything*—in his eyes that remains of the Lonan I so deeply trust. But he is not there. His empty smile is the last thing I will ever see, I think, as he plunges the needle down, down, down—

And into the flash of ebony skin that forces its way between us. Lonan throws Pellegrin like he's nothing, sends him crashing into the window, and it finally gives: a hairline crack spiderwebs from the impact. I twist away, momentarily freed by the sacrifice Pellegrin has made. How much strength did it take, in his condition, to do what he just did for me? I am still alive. I shouldn't be.

The effects of Lonan's syringe are immediate. I would not have thought Alexa dead before if I'd seen *this*: eyes glassy as marbles, lungs exhaling like the shriek of a miserable accordion, limbs as brittle as barren trees.

This syringe has become life to me, while Lonan may very well become my death.

Emergency waterlock activating in ten seconds, a voice says, entirely too calm. *For your safety, keep clear of the yellow line.*

Phoenix and Cass are on the safe side of the line, unconscious, but the waterlock will slice clean through me if I don't move—and Pellegrin's on the wrong side entirely.

It's too late to save him, though. It's too late.

Five, four, three, the voice counts. Beads of water seep through the spiderweb crack—the entire ocean presses for entrance, will overpower the window wall any second now. I make a break for the door, and Lonan follows. We barely make it out as the waterlock plunges down behind us, sealing Pellegrin and the bloodthirsty sea on the other side, forever.

EIGHTY-NINE

PELLEGRIN IS DEAD.

Pellegrin is *dead*.

I should be focusing on the transfer, mindlessly completing the demonstration, and yet I am running for my life because Lonan is still dead set on taking it.

I fly from the living quarters. I fly down onto the aquaponics platform. Leaves slap my face as I speed past, running as fast as I can, *out*. How tried and tested can that waterlock be, without ever suffering an incident like this? This entire chamber could flood in a matter of minutes if it fails.

Lonan chases me, and he is not far behind. I follow the yellow line back to the vestibule, up and around the steep curve, pray the iron doors open automatically and that I don't impale myself on their delicate but deadly design.

The doors open, not nearly fast enough, but with enough space that I am able to squeeze through as soon as I reach them. Lonan is forced to wait, the only downside to being broad-shouldered and muscular.

I pick up speed, taking the stairs two at a time until I'm in Zhornov's grand entry room. Only the piano greets me: of course the kingpin would keep himself and his esteemed guest as far removed from chaos as possible. I spin around, frantically looking for an easy way out, but there isn't one. There are no doors in this room, only the mouth of the deep, dark maze of hallways. I'll be dead in seconds if I attempt to navigate that on my own.

Lonan surfaces from the floor below, every bit as quick on the stairs as I was. Move, Eden—move or die. I scan the room for something to hide behind when I see it: a hexagon in the floor at the base of the enormous window wall that faces the long strip of island and the double row of palm trees. Pellegrin designed the security here—it makes sense that there wouldn't be an obvious way to enter this room, not with the habitat's entrance located right here.

If I fail, it will be a spectacular failure.

The hexagon gives me confidence. Three times now, I've seen Pellegrin's trademark security feature veil truth in illusion. A row of light illuminates the base of the window wall directly in front of me, so subtle it could be sunlight—if the sun were shining the right way, which it isn't. I hurtle headlong for the wall with so much force I will shatter it if I have to.

But I don't have to.

A burst of saltwater air, warm and humid, rushes in at me amid the faint hum of an automatic door sliding to the side. It looks no different than before, even as I pass straight through it.

Lonan is fast, but I am faster. Not by much. I never considered speed one of my strengths, but then, I have never been this motivated to stay alive. My chest hurts from all the breathing; my legs burn so fiercely they're practically numb. I run the perfectly paved strip that spans the length of this island, palm trees and sunset flowers blurring in both sides of my peripheral vision.

We come to the end of the paved path—it just *ends*, as if the island's cutoff point caught the path-builder off guard.

The sand slows me down. That, and the fact that I am exhaustion embodied. Lonan is more accustomed to running in the sand—a girl doesn't get much practice when her home beach is laced with explosives—and catches up to me easily.

I drop all my weight to the sand, make myself a flat and heavy burden to carry.

It is not difficult.

I am heavy for Birch. For Emma. For home.

For the years I spent as an orphan, blood and teeth and tattered pages the only family I had left.

For Pellegrin. For Pellegrin who *died* for me.

For Lonan. How much regret he will feel when this is all over, how much pain.

We have come too far for this to be the way it ends.

So I dig in and fight. He pries at my hips, I hug them to the ground. He pulls at my collarbone, I ram my elbow as hard as I can into his rib cage. I push with everything I have left, dig the balls of my feet into the sand and pull with my fingertips until I am certain I am ripping apart.

We run out of island.

He does not stop.

I swim out as far as I can, toward the partially submerged geodesic sphere, the fishing trap I saw from the yacht. If I can just get inside—if I can just keep him *out*—I can cling to the bars at the top while I catch my breath, hide deep underwater until he gives up, or until someone finally decides to help me. Hopefully one of those things will happen before the tide is so high I can't get above the surface anymore. It's worth a chance. It is my *only* chance.

Lonan's long arms narrow the gap between us—I've never swum so ferociously in my life. The cage is close, so close.

But the door is secured with a padlock the size of my heart.

I am so tired, and so out of options, but I fight to hang on. He grabs my elbows from behind, shoves me into the cage's unforgiving bars. I cling to the steel with all I have and climb it like a ladder, one painful rung at a time. I'm barely high enough to get a clear breath. He is heavy, weighing me down—and then he's not.

But I am not free.

He tears at the chain around my neck, pulls it tight tight tight from behind. My father's thick wedding band—it digs, it chokes. The force of it is strong enough to hold me underwater, for long enough to steal my breath.

Lonan pulls tighter still, but then the chain snaps: freedom. I come up for air, gasping.

It takes a second for Lonan—Ava inside Lonan—to recognize what's happened. I take a deep breath and head back for the shore, swimming even more furiously than before.

I'm just out of the too-deep water when my lead expires.

Salt water stings my eyes, bites at my throat. Lonan's hands hold me under much more easily than Hope's did. I connect my knee where I know it will buy me time—breath—*life*. He recoils from the pain.

I grab a fistful of hair with one hand, dig my other set of fingernails into his neck until a trickle of blood seeps out. "Why are you so intent on killing me?" I yell, staring deep into his eyes, where I know I will be seen. "What have I done, Ava? What has my *father* done—what could you *possibly* have to gain? You've destroyed Zhornov's business meeting! Do you really think that's going to earn his favor?"

He plunges me under again, holds me there for so long the glittering sunlight on the water turns to pinprick stars. I tear gashes in his wrists, let the salt sting him as the blood swirls around my head and into my hair.

"Stop, Lonan!" I shout, when I bob above and steal enough precious breath, though it is useless. "*Please*, for the love, stop!"

Water, glittering light, pinprick stars, blackness.

There is no *for the love*. There is no *stop*.

And then: a wonder.

One second his hands are an iron vise. The next, they are *his* again—I can tell this at once; there are all things tender and gentle in the way he moves them over my body. I am limp in his arms, hair floating on the water. I leave all my tears in the ocean. There are no more in me to cry.

"Eden, Eden! No—no!" He is panic, he is pain.

He is there. Behind his eyes, Lonan is *there*.

He pulls me to the beach, wraps me in his arms. "Stay with me," he says, pleads. His lips are soft as he kisses my neck, my temples, my wrists.

Or maybe he is only looking for a pulse.

"I'm sorry, I'm sorry—I'm so, so sorry!" He cries this into my hair, over and over.

But all the air I need to form words, all the air he forced from my body, is taking its sweet time coming back. No desire to be caged in a human, I guess, now that it's found freedom.

It flies away and so do I.

NINETY

I WAKE TO dim turquoise light, alone, in a room that looks exactly like the one where the chaos began, except everything is backward. An electric-purple jellyfish pulses just outside the wall, tentacles trailing from its bell as it sweeps over the coral terrace. Another of my line-drawing prints watches over me as if to say, *Tomorrow. Peace.* It's a hope, not a promise. Tomorrow doesn't guarantee peace, and peace doesn't guarantee a tomorrow.

But if I'm in this room—to recover?—we have still not been found out. Someone tucked a blanket over me; there is a Havenwater bottle and an untouched plate of food on the table. How long have I been in here? Where are the others? We've not been killed yet, and we're still on the island.

Perhaps I haven't failed my father after all.

My limbs are heavy with sleep—all of me is—but my fingers find the vial in my pocket miraculously intact. I guess it shouldn't be so surprising. I carried the first vial around for two years before it shattered outside the lodge; no doubt the bloodlock's glass is stronger and more advanced than even that was.

Blood and glass: memories come flooding in.

No indication the waterlock failed in the chaos room—it must have done its job; we are not flooded. No trace of blood stains this floor, but what about the other one? Or does Pellegrin remain only in my mind, images I'll never be able to erase? I fear I will never be free of all the images that play in my head.

I throw off the blanket. It is too hot; I am slick with sweat. When I finally slip back into darkness, the nightmares play all night long.

NINETY-ONE

WHEN I WAKE again, I am immediately on edge.

My eyes fly open at the sweep-slide sound of a door panel. No one rushes to my side, no one calls out to me. There are only footsteps in the main room, soft and steady. And then a face I don't know, one it takes a moment to place. This woman, two-thirds my size in every way, but still with a *presence*, is one of Zhornov's kitchen staff. I saw her slicing fruit as we passed through the kitchen.

"Your presence is required upstairs," she says. S-A-B-A is tattooed on her pinky: she used to be one of us. I wonder if she, too, is a HoloWolf—I can't imagine Zhornov would allow anyone who hasn't undergone the procedure to live on his island. "The kingpin desires to speak with you."

My stomach flips. I need . . . more than food, really, but food is all I have right now. I pick a cracker from the fruit plate that's been sitting there for who knows how long. "Did you bring this down for me?"

She doesn't smile, but I can tell from her eyes she appreciates the acknowledgment. "You should have eaten it before now.

There's no time—follow me, please."

I pluck a handful of grapes from the stem, stuff as many pieces of sliced banana into my mouth as I can handle, and follow her out of the room. No use resisting. If she is a HoloWolf, I know all too well that she can be used against me if needed. Also, if there's even the slightest chance Dr. Marieke is still on the island, it would be good to get out of the habitat and back above the surface.

She doesn't initiate any conversation as we walk. I eat my fruit; she keeps her eyes straight ahead. Every step makes my heart ache over how *fast* I ran this exact same path last time. I wonder if Lonan was also called in to speak with Zhornov, if the others were, too. I hope they made it out.

"Saba?"

She flinches at the sound of her name. I guess she's not used to people using it here, either.

"What kind of meeting is this?" Zhornov knows, he must know about the vial—I haven't done anything wrong otherwise, nothing I can recall.

We wait for the iron doors to open, slip through into the grand reverse-aquarium room as soon as there's enough space. The water outside the walls is especially bright, sparkling with what I assume is morning light.

I start to repeat myself, but she cuts me off. "Whatever you do, don't look him in the eye unless he asks you a direct question. He's very particular about that."

And that's it. That's all she gives me. I could press her for more, but I don't. Better to save my energy, if this is going to be the sort of meeting that requires answers and answers and answers.

I have no answers. All I have are questions.

NINETY-TWO

SABA LEADS ME to an expansive room on the second floor, all white walls and ocean-view panorama. It is far too beautiful a room for a man who's had such a hand in breaking the world.

Far too spotless.

Far too transparent.

Far too few personal effects for one of the kingpins, one of the men who've stolen everything from everyone and could have anything they ever wanted. Not even a painting hangs above his simple white desk, when he could have the entire Sistine Chapel. The only remarkable object in this room is the enormous, low-hanging chandelier centerpiece—it is breathtaking, a geometric masterpiece made from thousands of black and white diamonds. They hang, innumerable rows of fringe, glittering in the sunlight that streams through the all-glass wall.

"No water for us?" Zhornov greets Saba. Clearly, his *us* means himself and Dr. Marieke, myself excluded. They sit on the wrong side of the desk, their backs to it, in form-over-function seats bearing more resemblance to modern-day thrones than chairs.

Saba positions me—physically places her hands on both of

my shoulders and leads me to a spot ten feet away from both men and with an unavoidably direct view of their faces—before disappearing out of the room. For water, I assume. She's quiet as a whisper, seamlessly slipping in and back out, as she delivers a pair of frosted-glass water tumblers, ice cold and full to the brim. Zhornov sips from his straw in lieu of a thank-you. At least the doctor smiles, nods.

Never in my life have I seen anyone look as uncomfortable in a chair as Dr. Marieke. It's a subtle sort of discomfort, the one-foot-constantly-tapping sort, nothing Zhornov will pick up on. My heart and his foot race to the same rhythm. At least I'm not the only one who doesn't want to be here.

"Eden."

My name on Zhornov's tongue is a shock: here is the man who could not be bothered with introductions when we arrived, the man who seems to address people by name only if they are Dutch-Lebanese doctors who have the power to construct an indestructible future for his own benefit.

And that wasn't a question—am I supposed to look in his eyes, or avoid them? His time of getting everything he wants is coming to a close. I don't really care what he prefers, I realize, and shift my eyes to meet his. He is steel and concrete, storm clouds with the thinnest hint of silver linings.

"I was at your mother's funeral, did you know that?" He is unbreaking, unblinking.

Wrecking ball approach, I see. Be strong, Eden, do not let him in.

"Brought your father some Scotch that day," he continues. "We've been in each other's lives for more than a decade now—he's one of the only people I've ever been able to trust without reservation."

My father never drank that bottle of Scotch. It sat on the top shelf of our kitchen pantry for years, collecting dust. It's probably *still* collecting dust on that shelf.

"Which is why," he says, even spaces between every word, "I need you to tell me the truth, Eden." He clenches the arm of his seat so tightly his knuckles turn the same shade of white. "I'm going to need you to answer a few questions."

This is no simple conversation.

This is a trial.

The bloodlock suddenly feels extremely obvious in my pocket, even though I know it isn't; I made sure of that. And Dr. Marieke—he *is* on Dad's side in this, isn't he? Surely he hasn't betrayed my father's plan just to get into kingpin graces?

"It has been brought to my attention that your father suffered an attack at the hand of one of his colleagues." Ava. Obviously Ava; he just doesn't know I have any idea who Ava is. "Which is distressing in itself, but after speaking to the colleague in question, she is convinced her actions were absolutely warranted."

Relief, twice over: if my father were dead, he would have worded it differently. *Your father's been killed*, not *your father suffered an attack*. And if this is about what Ava suspected, an assassination attempt, it has nothing to do with the bloodlock—which means Dr. Marieke hasn't broken Dad's trust. I'm not out of the woods just yet, but if I'm careful, I might escape with our secrets intact.

"You came to my island with a blue-serum syringe." His fierce eyes bore into me. "Why?"

I hold my head high, keep my eyes trained on his. "I was told I might need it for self-defense," I say. "Which, clearly, I did."

This answer seems to appease him, at least a little. "About that," he says. "I was told all of you had received the requisite procedure prior to your departure, and yet you—no small coincidence, being Will's daughter—arrived in your natural mind. Was it a lie when your father told me you'd undergone Pellegrin's procedure?"

"My father doesn't lie," I reply, though this is perhaps not as true as I once thought. Necessary secrets are better than self-serving lies—but secrets, by nature, are a few shades off from wholehearted truth. "Pellegrin gave me the procedure right in front of my father, but told me later he'd given me a vaccine instead. I have the hologram, proof he worked on me, if you need to see it."

"You're telling me your father had no knowledge of Pellegrin's decision to give you the vaccine?"

Careful, careful. "I'm sure there are a great many things my father knows, but I couldn't begin to tell you what happens in his head. I believed him dead until just before I was sent here, to your island—he doesn't tell me everything."

Zhornov is momentarily caught off guard by my tone, by my thinly veiled accusation. He attempts to cover it up with a hacking cough that lasts a little too long. *You attended my mother's funeral, and yet you effectively orphaned me*, I want to shout in his face.

But I don't shout. I let the past speak for itself.

Louder than the dig I just made, I hope he hears: *Will abandoned his daughter in barracks, Will let her think him dead, Will built me a paradise. Will is worthy of my trust, and would not send his daughter to assassinate me.*

He stirs his melting ice with the straw, narrows his eyes at me. He studies me like I used to study my father's field guide, for eternity and forever, looking between every crack for anything that might be hiding.

But like me with my father's field guide, he sees only what he wants to see.

His stony face softens into comfort, relief, all yellow teeth and wheezing laughter. "Good for us all that you didn't get killed down there! Quite a weapon, those young men, quite a weapon indeed."

Good for us all, yes, I agree. Though I'm sure by *us all* he mostly means himself, and the partnership he would have lost with my father if I hadn't survived.

"I'm impressed with you, young lady," he says, pointing his straw at me. For what? For not backing down from him, for having the audacity to *challenge* him? For staying alive, when I'm still not sure what caused Lonan to stop ripping me apart? "I need a replacement immediately, back on HQ. Ava has already been dealt with for all the damage and disruption she's caused—*you* are my new Ava."

His words are polish and shine, but I hear all the things he doesn't say: I know entirely too much to be sent back to barracks, and because I've had the vaccine, they can't use me as a HoloWolf. Whether he's truly impressed or this is simply an enemies-closest situation, I'm not about to fight it. Especially since it will land me on the same island as my father.

Zhornov stands first; the doctor follows. This is it, this could be *it*. I will myself steady, though I am a bundle of fluttering nerves. Zhornov turns his back for just long enough to put his water glass on the desk, only a few ice cubes remaining.

I slip the vial from my pocket, keeping it carefully in line with my wrist—and Dr. Marieke sees me do it. He moves forward first, coming in for a handshake, just as Zhornov turns back around.

The doctor smiles at me. "Thank you for your service here"— our hands meet, bloodlock discreetly hidden between—"and for all you've suffered on my behalf, for this demonstration." He pulls away, tucks the vial in his pocket so swiftly it is like it never happened. "Anyone Will trusts, I trust. I'd be glad to come on board the project."

I recognize his words for what they are—a promise of solidarity to *us*, not the kingpins, though obviously it's meant to sound loyal to the Wolves. I am all sunbeams on the inside, and it's difficult to contain, this hope. Hope, back from the brink.

Zhornov is oblivious to everything but his own hope. He calls for Saba, he calls for Scotch on the rocks. He is so relieved no one is out to kill him, he can't feel the foundation shifting under his own feet. It's not his death he should be concerned about—it's the rest of his life that's about to become miserable.

I'm almost tempted to be sad for him. Almost.

But then I remember Pellegrin.

Finnley.

Birch.

So many, many more lives that ended miserably—all the rest who wither in the gulags—all the Wolves who've become predators simply to avoid being prey. The kingpins have had their happiness, enough for lifetimes, at the expense of lifetimes.

Zhornov raises his glass, glorying in the moment. "To life!" he says, and guzzles his Scotch.

To life.

NINETY-THREE

THE WHITE YACHT with whale-belly sails waits for me at the end of the pier.

Lonan, Cass, and Phoenix are already on board—they boarded late last night, Saba tells me as we walk, so the yacht would be set to sail as soon as my interrogation ended. I was the only one brought in for questioning: I was the only one aware and autonomous during the chaos, thus the only one pressed with suspicion.

"Here is where I leave you," Saba says, when the slate path gives way to the pier's worn wood. Her subtle accent is like a lullaby. "Good luck." She's been much more open with me now that the meeting is over. Perhaps it's because I was allowed to leave it in one piece.

I nod, the best I can do at *thank you* right now. If I open my mouth, I will give myself away. Better to keep secrets under lock and key until I am absolutely sure it's safe to let them out. I may not get to use the key for a while, or ever.

The pier is long and lonely. I walk with ghosts, when it should be Pellegrin beside me. It is the oddest combination of feelings, this hope—this hope at a *cost*. Nothing comes for free, especially not freedom. More than anything, I'm just tired. I could sleep for years.

Captain Rex welcomes me aboard. Cass and Phoenix are sprawled over the long benches on the main deck, not stirred in the slightest by the enthusiasm of his greeting. The captain offers me fruit and fish and a host of other things he never offered on our first trip. He must have heard what happened.

"That one's been asking about you constantly," the captain says, pointing an apple wedge toward the far end of the yacht.

I turn to look, and there's Lonan, staring at me as if *I* am the ghost among us.

"Go on. I'll leave the plate for whenever you're ready." He devours the apple wedge in a single bite, talks through it. "Someone's got to sail this ship, anyway." His words fade as he disappears up the stairs onto the top deck.

And then it's just me with Lonan. *Real* Lonan.

"I won't blame you if you don't want to come any closer." There's a rawness to his voice, one I know well. I get it, too, after too many emotions have run their course. "Ava's gone, your father told me. He told me everything, everything that happened. I won't . . . I'm not going to . . ." He cuts himself off, swallows.

Not going to hurt me. Not going to kill me.

"Don't do that," I say, taking a step toward him. "You are not allowed to push me away."

I admit: it is not easy to unravel my nightmares from where they tangle with the truth—his hands on my throat, his empty eyes—but I refuse to let the nightmares win. We will get past this; we just need to drown those images out with new ones. True ones.

I make my way toward him, take a seat on the back bench. He doesn't sit until I invite him, until it is more than clear that I want him to. We watch the island shrink to nothing as we leave it behind.

"I cannot even begin to tell you how sorry I am, Eden." He searches for my eyes, I feel it, until I tear them from the empty ocean.

"It wasn't you who did those things," I say. "You would never."

"I did."

"*Ava* did."

His face is all grief, all guilt. "I should have been strong enough to stop it," he says. "I should have had more control."

"You couldn't help it."

"If it weren't for Hope, and your dad—" His voice catches. "I'm so, so sorry. I hate this." His words make tears spring into my eyes. His, too.

He tells me how Hope heard my screaming over the surveillance cameras, how she ran for help, how Gray shot Ava with a blow dart when he saw what was happening on-screen with Pellegrin. Gray couldn't nullify any of the directives she'd given, though, not without the Aries passcode. When he pinged my father, he discovered him locked in the holding cell where Alexa should have been.

He tells me how my father was never dead, never injured, never even close. So very many lies, spread so very convincingly. When very-much-alive Alexa was heard yelling for help from her holding cell, Ava tricked Dad into retrieving her—then locked him inside as soon his back was turned. Back in the lab, she altered Alexa all on her own and used her to deceive me through Phoenix. No one can figure out why she waited so long to turn the guys on Pellegrin and me—why she didn't just take us out before the yacht ever arrived at the island—and we'll never know for sure. Turns out *Ava's been dealt with* was a nice way of saying she'll never be a problem again, here or otherwise.

He tells me how his own sense-altering levels had been sky high—that Dad had to reset them all, one by one, until he came back to himself. Ava's efforts were so thorough, he almost didn't finish in time to save me.

"None of what you did matters to me," I say. Because it doesn't. It wasn't him.

Finally, he accepts this. Doesn't try to fight me on it. "I'm still sorry for what you went through. You nearly died—you have bruises on your neck, were dehydrated—you were out for more than a day. I hate it, Eden, I *hate* that I did this to you. You are the only good thing to ever come out of this war, and I almost *killed* you." He sinks deeper and deeper inside himself. So this is what it looks like from the other side.

"Hey," I say. He seems too far away, in every sense that a person can be. "*Hey.*"

He looks up, blue eyes bright.

"Do you trust me?" I ask.

He does, I can see it. "Since the moment I saw you run into the ocean after Alexa," he says. "And every minute since."

"Then trust me when I say I trust *you*, Lonan," I say. "We made it through this; we can make it through anything. This isn't your fault—it wasn't you."

There are fewer than three feet separating us, but suddenly, it feels like the entire ocean. I want to be closer, closer than I've ever been with anyone—closer, even, than with Birch. It feels almost wrong, with the nightmares of his death always tugging at the edge of my consciousness. But like the new lines on my father's face, the war has carved itself into me, too. I'm not the same person I was when I knew Birch. In a way, his death was what catapulted me into a place where I'd never be the same Eden again.

Lonan has scars like I do. We've been cut and carved, chiseled and broken, torn apart and held together by faith, by hope.

I am falling, sliding over the edge of a slippery hill, finally allowing myself to move on to where I've already been for some time now.

I pat the empty space between us. "Want to come closer?"

He is slow, careful. I can tell he wants to be a safe place for me.

"More than anything," he says.

NINETY-FOUR

DAWN IS JUST beginning to break—the sky is bleeding pink and orange and gold out over the endless, fathomless sea behind us. Ahead of us: pristine white sand, waves breaking against it.

Four people wait to greet us, standing in a row on the beach. I lean as far around the railing as I can for a better look.

Gray.

Alexa, Hope. Hope wears my yellow cardigan and carries a small urn, one I assume is filled with Finnley's ashes.

Dad.

"Is that—" Lonan asks, joining me at the railing.

"Yes," I say.

Yes is too small. It is too thin—bright, but not bright enough.

Knowing my father is alive and seeing him alive feel like two entirely different things. I was afraid to believe it, on some level, until I'd seen him with my own eyes. A smile more blinding than sunlight breaks on his face, and I know I'm the one who's put it there. He sees me.

We become a tangle of limbs and tears once we've docked. Dad, me. Alexa, who buries herself in Cass. He runs his hand through her hair, holds her tight. Life back from the dead: it has the power to create a blank slate like nothing else. They remain that way even after everyone else has begun the trek back to the lodge, where we'll stay until further notice.

There is still so much work to do, my father says to Lonan and to me when we are back in his office. Dr. Marieke will break the bloodlock as soon as he's settled in Cape Town—Dad's colleague from New Zealand, another of his trusted three, was one of the primary developers of bloodlock technology, and has created a complex database that will help them sort through and prioritize all the information.

Stéphane Monroe has agreed to let Dr. Marieke lead the Atlas Project for the Allied Forces, and development will begin immediately on eighteen new habitat sites. It won't be enough to shelter the entire world, not at first, but it should be enough to make a difference in the war.

Things should start to crumble immediately. Dad cut off access to the HoloWolf live feeds—for *all* of the kingpins, not just Zhornov—as soon as Dr. Marieke set foot onto his helicopter. And the Alliance doesn't plan to waste any time hijacking Wolfpack propaganda systems, where they'll offer free habitat housing to the first thousand Wolves to defect.

Best of all, the kingpins will be forever locked out of their own island. Rex is the only yachtsman with the coordinates, and no one will ever buy him for a higher price than my father has: he's tracked down Rex's family, and has already begun the process of reuniting them.

There are so many individual pieces, an overwhelming number of details that don't sound like big things, but my father insists they are. *Think of it like grains of sand,* he told me. *They add up to a lot.*

My father has his work cut out for him—we all do—but it will be *his* work. Ours. What we believe in, and what is right. We'll unlock the cages when kingpin castles fall, and let all the birds fly, fly, fly.

When the war began, I thought I'd lost everything.

I thought my scars were meant to kill me.

I thought I was without a home, without a family.

Without. Forever, without.

This is the beginning of the end.

ACKNOWLEDGMENTS

TO THE BEST literary agents a girl could hope for, Holly Root and Taylor Haggerty: thank you for your belief in me, as well as your patience, kindness, intuition, and wisdom. I can't speak highly enough about you, and I'm grateful to have such amazing agents in my corner. To Mary Pender at UTA, thank you for your fierce championing of my project in the film world. To everyone at Paramount and Appian Way—especially Nathaniel Posey, Jennifer Davisson, and Leonardo DiCaprio— thank you for all you've done in support of this project. To Heather Baror-Shapiro, thank you so much for the amazing work you've done to bring this book to so many other countries. And to my wonderful publishers in those countries, I'm grateful for each of you.

To Emilia Rhodes and my excellent team at Harper: thank you for saying yes to this book, and for all you've poured into it. Huge thanks, too, to you who worked behind the scenes, especially Alice Jerman, Jon Howard, Sarah Kaufman, Alison Klapthor, Gina Rizzo, and Bess Braswell.

To my incredible critique partners: Jasmine Warga, thank you for always being willing and eager to read, even on short notice. Amanda Olivieri, thank you for enthusiastically reading every single draft, and for all the brainstorming sessions. Alison

Cherry, thank you for your spot-on input and for the incredible amount of support you've given me throughout the years.

To the early cheerleaders whose enthusiasm fueled my fire— Salima Alikhan, Corey Wright, Jade Timms, Lola Sharp, Liza Kane, China DeSpain, Lodge of Death retreat friends—thank you. I'm also grateful for my debut-year friends who are walking this road beside me, especially: Kristen Orlando, Stephanie Garber, Lana Popović, Emily Bain Murphy, Anna Priemaza, Jilly Gagnon, Chelsea Sedoti, Heather Kaczynski, Carlie Sorosiak, and Kristen Ciccarelli. To Brent Bowen, who may not remember his words that changed my life: *You should think about writing a book.* Scarlett and Douglas at Austin Java, thank you for celebrating with me when I finished this book; Kelly Liggio, thank you for working ten thousand knots out of my neck over the years.

To my parents and grandparents, for always believing I could do whatever I set my mind toward, and for encouraging my dreams; and to my sister, the reader whose opinion matters most to me.

To Andrew—thank you for being endlessly patient and supportive, flexible, wonderful. I'm grateful for your support, and that you believed my time spent at the desk was worthwhile, whether my words were published or not. You are the best husband a girl could dream of. And James, I am grateful every day that God chose me to be your mom. I have more love for you both than my heart can hold. Finally, to Jesus Christ, my hope and my peace: in flood or famine or solitude, I trust I will never be *without, forever without.* All I need is You. | Romans 8:38–39